# THE CARNATION MURDER

## TAM MAY

**Tam May**

Published by Dreambook Press.



Click or visit:
https://www.tammayauthor.com

Cover Design © 2022 by Aries/100 Covers

ISBN: 9780998338545 (Print)
ISBN: 9780998338552 (ebook)

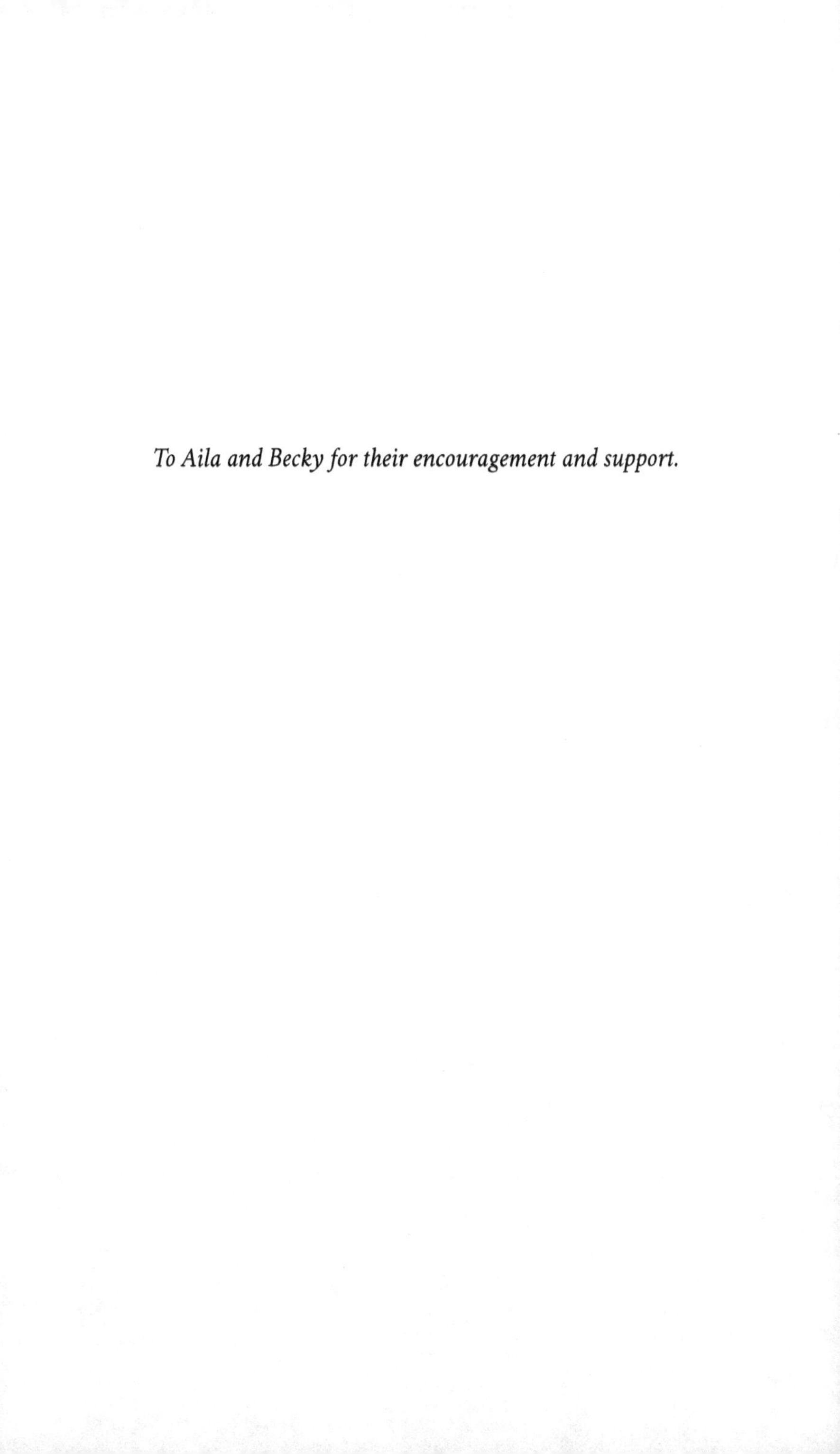

*To Aila and Becky for their encouragement and support.*

# CHAPTER 1

**If you're interested in reading more early 20th century mysteries, my free offer at the end of this book is for you! So don't forget to check that out when you get to the end. Happy reading!**

On a Saturday afternoon in July, Bridge Street, the main commercial district of Arrojo, was as busy as any avenue in San Francisco. Sales girls showed ladies their wares with an overenthusiastic smile, while their managers sat hunched in their offices calculating the weekly take in anticipation of closing time.

It was then they heard the automobile. The faint rumble sounded far away at first. People came out of the shops, staring down the street.

A covered wagon appeared. The man sitting next to the Mexican driver was tall and clean-shaven, well-fitted inside a dark suit with the collar folded up perfectly around his neck. Furniture peeked out of the back as the wagon bobbed along the rocky road. The man seemed anxious, looking over his shoulder as if aware one loose stone could send an heirloom mirror or a Chinese vase flying into the street. The agreeable-looking driver guided the horses with a clear sense of purpose and expertise. Despite that the well-dressed man's hands were elevated over each knee as if preparing to grab the reins at any moment.

Ladies turned to catch a glimpse of the young man, and he, in return, tipped his hat to them. Rugged and gentle features combined to form a charming countenance not lost on the younger women. They huddled closer to their mothers, giggling and lowering their eyes.

At that moment, the car appeared. The driver was a woman veiled in a chiffon scarf, her parasol bouncing on the passenger's side as if ready to fall from the anxious automobile at any moment. She stopped right in the middle of the street and descended from the car, pulling back the scarf, letting tendrils of chestnut hair tumble out. Her tweed jacket fit perfectly over her starched blouse and one of the newfangled corsets gave her the look of a proud pigeon.

She glanced around with a satisfied smile, oblivious to the stares. The fishmonger and his wife stood before her, and their gaping mouths matched the salmon sitting in an ice bed in the window. She smiled, but before she could speak, they disappeared into their shop, closing the door behind them with a thud. In the wagon a few feet away, the young man's face reddened.

The woman seemed unruffled but somewhat surprised. She advanced toward the ladies standing not far away. Two middle-aged women sniffed, two young ladies beside them giggled, and an elderly lady leaned on a cane, her prune face barely visible under her bonnet.

"Adele Gossling." The woman held out her hand to the elderly lady. Her voice was decided but courteous.

The woman turned her back and hobbled down the street. One of the middle-aged ladies hunched forward as if afraid the brazen young lady would address her next. The other spoke in an icy tone. "May I help you?"

Adele did not draw her hand away, confident someone would eventually show a sign of hospitality. "Well, ma'am, I was hoping I could help *you*."

The woman glanced at the automobile. "We prefer those newfangled machines be parked out of the main shopping district."

"I'll be residing here, so I'll make note of it," said Adele.

"Residing?"

"Yes, ma'am," she said "I just bought the Rosemont house."

"You mean you're going to *live* here?" one of the young women asked while the other let out a nervous giggle.

"You're from San Francisco, I take it?" The icy woman asked. Adele nodded. "Well." She contemplated this. "It seems the Rosemonts were less discriminating than we thought."

"If you'll direct me to the old Shoe Shine Shop, ma'am, I won't take up any more of your time." Adele's tone was no less exuberant but more tolerant.

"Shine closed down some time ago." The second middle-aged woman stared at her.

"I know that, ma'am," said Adele. "I'm to set up my shop there."

"Indeed?" The icy woman raised a pince-nez to her eyes, making them look smaller than they already were. Adele felt she were being examined by a very staunch raccoon. "You bought the house and the shop?"

"Yes, ma'am." Adele bowed.

"You must be very rich," said the young girl who had first spoken and her friend let out another giggle. The icy woman, whom Adele guessed was her mother, pinched her elbow.

"If I were, I wouldn't be opening a stationery shop," said Adele with a laugh.

"I beg your pardon!" The girl flushed. The two middle-aged women exchanged a look.

"I'm no pauper though," she added.

"One would scarcely go in for one of *those* contraptions if one were a pauper." The icy woman sniffed at the car.

"You don't you approve of them, ma'am?" Adele asked.

"I do not!" The woman glared. "They frighten the horses with their unbearable noise. You could cause a very nasty accident if you're not careful."

"I'm always careful," Adele assured her.

"Nevertheless," she said. "We hope not to see that contraption on Bridge Street in the future."

"I'll leave the car at home, ma'am," Adele promised. "I hope to see more of all of you, though."

"Indeed?" The woman eyed her.

"I invite you to come and visit my shop when I open," Adele said. "I'm sure you won't be disappointed by my wares or my manners."

"*We* order our stationery from Harley & Sons in San Francisco." The icy woman turned toward the milliner's down the street.

"They're terribly overpriced, if you want to know the truth, ma'am," said Adele. "I promise you the same quality for half."

A horse snorted, and she glanced down the street. The young man in the wagon touched the rim of his hat as if trying to send some sort of signal.

"Do you know him?" the second woman asked.

"I ought to." Adele smiled. "He's my brother."

"Will he be living with you in the Rosemont house?"

"Unfortunately not," said Adele. "He's only here to help me with my things. He'll be returning to San Francisco shortly." She added, "The grand opening for Adele's Stationery is next Friday. I invite you to come."

"Really, young lady." The blood drained from the woman's

cheeks. "That is most forward of you. One does not invite people to a grand opening."

"You mean a woman shouldn't try to drum up business for herself?" Adele asked dryly. "This is a new century, ma'am. Women have a right to make their living as much as a man." Her gaze swept across the four women in front of her.

"We don't take to that sort of progressive talk here, Miss —Miss —"

"Gossling," Adele reminded her. "And your name, ma'am?"

"We have certain expectations in Arrojo," the woman continued.

"And your name, ma'am?" she persisted.

She regarded Adele with a self-righteous gaze. "Mrs. Faderman."

"Well, Mrs. Faderman," Adele said, "I have a few expectations of my own."

"Oh, you're engaged!" The woman's face lifted with a sign of hope.

Adele looked at her with unmistakable horror. "Heaven forbid!"

Mrs. Faderman's expression turned icy again. "I don't think you should make light of it, Miss Gossling."

"I assure you, I'm not," Adele said.

"I was interested because it's been my experience ladies who are engaged do not stay in business long. Their time is soon occupied by other things." She coughed delicately.

"You mean more important things like a house, a husband, and children," Adele guessed.

"I didn't say so."

"Well, I plan on being in your midst for a very long time," Adele said with a smile.

"Unengaged?" asked her daughter.

"Unengaged," Adele answered.

"You may rest assured, Miss Gossling, we have the means to

take care of *that!*" Mrs. Faderman grabbed her daughter's hand. "New Woman or no New Woman," she added.

Adele burst out laughing as she watched the others follow her lead. They reminded her of ducklings toddling after their mother as the four ladies marched down the street in the direction of the milliner's.

When they had disappeared, she climbed into her automobile, adjusted the scarf and gloves, and, with more determination, shot down the dusty road, the wheels pounding the gravel behind her.

# CHAPTER 2

"I'm sure we'll find plenty of nasty creatures here." Jackson leaned against his walking stick as he surveyed the Rosemont house. The hallway formed a straight line through to the back door and was padded with dirt, leaves, and even tufts of tumbleweed.

"I should have expected it," Adele said. "I should have put the scrub brush and the broom in the back of the Beaton instead of burying them in the wagon."

"You can never foresee these things." He scraped the dirt from underneath his shoes on the ragged door mat.

"Tomas!" The driver of the wagon bobbed his head. "Have you a wife and children?"

"Yes, señorita." He held up eight fingers to indicate the blessed size of his family.

"I'd like you to take my car and bring your wife and the eldest daughter here immediately to help clean my house," she said. "Make that the two eldest."

"Really, Del," Jackson muttered.

"Why in heavens not?" she asked.

"You don't know what kind of people they are."

"My wife cleans well, señor," the man insisted. "My children too."

"Of course they do," Adele said. "You bring them all here, Tomas."

The man looked at the car as if it were a creature just emerged from the bottom of the San Francisco Bay.

"Oh, very well, take the horses," said Adele. "Tell them, if they come, I'll give you and your wife one dollar each, and fifty cents to each of your children. If you make haste, I'll give each of them a dollar and a half, and you and your wife two dollars."

The man grinned, unhitched the horses from the wagon, and with a quick shake of the reins, was gone.

Jackson bowed, acknowledging defeat as was usually the case when he tried to wrestle with his sister's determination.

"I thought you would approve." She eyed him. "Eventually."

"He told me he hasn't had much luck finding work this year," he said. "Not a promising future for a family of eight."

"I may just move the entire brood here," said Adele. "He and his wife can take care of the place for me. There must be plenty of room out back for them to build a house, and I'm sure it would suit them more than any work they might find in the city." She swung around, the hem of her skirt just missing a patch of mud on the porch. Her movements were slightly indiscreet for a woman. "I've a feeling I'll incur plenty of dust through these window cracks."

"If you wanted to avoid dust, you should have stayed in the city," Jackson remarked.

"This house may be dirty, Jack, but it has no memories." Adele removed the scarf, and tentacles of hair whipped in the wind.

"I thought you wanted to get out of the city because of John Bellows, not because of memories."

"Both," she said shortly. "I told you that before."

"We could have moved to another city where there are no memories," he said in a soft voice, looking down at the clumps of nettle bushes below the porch. "Like Los Angeles or Santa Barbara near Aunt Belle."

She put her hand on his shoulder. "This place has plenty of room for both of us. It would be delightful if you stayed."

"And help you fight off the nasty creatures?" He grinned.

"Help me fight off the lady crusaders," she said. "I have a feeling they'll try to get me engaged to some local fellow before long."

He laughed. "Heaven help them, and heaven help him!"

Her face grew serious. "I only want peace now, Jack." She grabbed his hand. "Come, let's see the rest of it."

"You mean show me the rest of it," he said.

"I bought the place sight unseen." She lifted her skirt as she descended the porch steps.

Wrinkles appeared around his eyes. "You mean you bought a house without knowing what it looked like?"

"Miss Lake said it was very pretty."

"Pretty!" He snorted. "I suppose pretty is what's important in the eyes of a woman estate agent."

She glared at him. "That was unworthy of you, Jack."

"No more unworthy of me than buying a house half-cocked was unworthy of *you*," he retorted.

"Sometimes you have to trust people." She took his arm.

Oak trees made the patchy yellow grass around the house look less desolate, and red and green shrubs gave the wilderness a lovely autumn palette. The dust was almost toe-deep, and even Adele had to lift her skirt all the way up to her ankles so as not to redden the hem.

To the left, a field of frazzled poppies pointed their orange petals toward the sky. To the right deep hairs of grass and weeds made a prickly fortress around the house. Further away, another house, larger and more ornate than Adele's, stood majestically against the background of hills far away.

"I wonder who lives there." She shielded her eyes from the sun.

"An eminent citizen, perhaps a property owner," said Jackson.

"How do you know?"

"You can see from here how the house is well built," he said. "A man who has money to spend on aesthetics."

"You really should have done more detective work, Jack," she said. "You have a marvelous eye."

"A cursed eye," he grumbled. "It's better I left the Anspach Agency when I did."

"Of course it's better," said Adele as they walked to the rear of the house. "The Anspaches have no pity. No shame either. They're worse than the Pinkertons."

He looked at the grass for a moment as they stood at the back porch. His handsome face glazed like a marble shield of lingering regrets. She hadn't yet found out what it was he regretted.

"What are those trees?" she asked.

"Maples, I believe."

"Jack, there's a gazebo!"

The white and lemon gazebo had not the slightest sign of wear. Its octagon sides were symmetric among the wild grasses and flowers, and the egg-shaped roof had a lightening effect. The inside, however, was more revealing of its condition. They found the anticipated creatures nesting in one corner. Jackson chased them out with his cane.

"It looked so untouched," she mused. "I have a feeling looks deceive in just about every corner of this place."

A young woman appeared in the garden of the big house as if she could not wait to take in the bright morning. She was dressed in white from her hair to her waist. She ran to a bush with hanging red flowers and threw out her arms as if ready to embrace it. Her simple delight almost made Adele forget the way the women had snubbed her on Bridge Street.

"Whistle to her, Jack." Her brother stared at her as if she had told him to jump off a bridge. "It won't be indiscreet. I'm sure handsome young men are a scarcity in a town like this."

"Certainly not!"

"Oh, for goodness sake." Adele tried to whistle but it came out like a shriek. She called and waved.

The young woman noticed and, with a laugh, called and waved back.

"You'll make her think you belong locked in an attic." Her brother led her into the house.

"You needn't worry about my not making any friends," she said. "I expect even the matchmaking hens will get used to me in time."

"You've never the better part of discretion, Del." Jackson frowned.

"Is it indiscreet to wave hello to a new neighbor?" she asked. "We aren't in the city with our windows nose to nose, perhaps, but we can still be cordial."

"Those are not the kind of people who are likely to converse with a neighbor over a fence," he said with a marked irony. "Not a neighbor like you, that is."

Adele stiffened. "Papa was one of the best lawyers in the city. I'll thank you to remember that, Jack."

"He was also a criminal lawyer," her brother reminded her.

"He wasn't perhaps in the same clubs as Mr. Hopkins or Mr. Stanford, but we had a social presence. In a place like this, I'm sure we would be considered well off."

"And you're going to be a shopkeeper," he said quietly.

"That's more for purpose than money and you know it," she snapped.

Horse's hooves saved him from answering. Tomas had returned, bringing his entire family with him.

# CHAPTER 3

*A* few days later, Adele left Tomas' wife Ruth and her eldest daughter to sweep out the cobwebs of the house as she hunted up the small building at 625 Bridge Street. It had fewer nasty creatures than the Rosemont house but the grime reached every corner.

"This red dust is rather like a parasite, isn't it?" she remarked to the woman standing in the doorway of the shop next to hers.

The woman didn't answer but only stared at her with cat-like eyes. She seemed petrified in some maniacal fairytale. She wore no hat, and her hair looked as if it hadn't seen a pin in years. Free-flowing and coal black, the waves swung past her shoulders. Her clothes were as loose as her hair with only the vaguest outline of a corset underneath. Her features showed a natural grace and her intense eyes made her beauty so spellbinding every child and man passing by could not keep from glancing at her. The wild woman met the children's eyes without smiling and pointedly ignored the men.

Adele wiped her hands on a clean rag and approached her. "Adele Gossling."

Unlike the hens, the woman accepted the greeting. Her grasp was fierce, as if trying to squeeze the truth out of it.

"And your name?"

The woman did not answer She dropped her hand and retreated back to the door, her eyes never leaving Adele's face.

Adele couldn't resist peering through the window of the woman's shop. "Charming," she murmured. Exotic scents floated out from the open doorway, reminding her of the mysterious stalls she had passed by in Chinatown.

The woman moved quickly in front of the window.

"I don't mean to be nosy," Adele said. "I only wanted to see so I can send my clients your way. You can send me yours, and we can help one another."

The woman turned her head away as if the idea of business was crude to her.

"Mine is a stationery store," she continued.

A smile appeared on the woman's lips. It was an odd little smile, not quite inviting and even a little teasing. The smile annoyed Adele.

"I'm quite serious about making my shop a success, " she insisted, "as I'm sure you are in making yours."

The woman seemed ready to answer, but a voice called for Adele from behind. It was the boy bringing the merchandise she had ordered. Behind them, a man who looked to be in his forties greeted her with cautious kindness. "Welcome, miss."

"The Arrojo welcoming committee at last?" she asked with a smile. "My brother should have been here to see it."

He removed his hat. "My name is Lowell Tanning. At your service, miss."

"I'm happy to see at least one person in this town doesn't regard me as an outcast."

He laughed. "You mustn't take the cold shoulder you received too much to heart. Arrojo was founded by the most excellent of men who, I'm afraid, believed they created the California landscape alongside the Almighty. I ought to know. My grandfather was one of them."

"I'm quite impressed with it," said Adele. "I expected a tiny town when I found the little dot on the map. But this is more like a small city."

"Indeed," said Mr. Tanning. "My ancestors and, I suspect, those of many others here, were a sight more forthcoming with their vision of commerce than those of us living here would care to admit."

Adele took his arm. "Would you like a cup of tea or coffee?"

"Tea would be ideal, miss," he said with a bow.

"Will you join us for tea, Miss —" But the woman had retreated into her shop and shut the door.

"An interesting wood nymph," Adele remarked.

Mr. Tanning followed her into the shop. "Most people around here think Miss Branch is some kind of witch or a sorceress. They find her more diabolical than interesting."

"You can't be serious." She stared at him.

He bowed his head. "I'm afraid I am."

She put her hand on her hip. "Do you believe she's a witch or a sorceress, Mr. Tanning?"

"I'm a much more plain-thinking man," he said. "I've heard Miss Branch has special powers — clairvoyance, I think they call it. Just as her mother did."

"I see," she said. "Perhaps you shall be plain-speaking as well, Mr. Tanning, and tell me just what savage wilderness I've stumbled into?"

He laughed as she put the kettle on a small gas stove. "I assure you we're as civilized as anyone living in Sacramento and even your San Francisco. Though much less hurried, I imagine."

"I'll tell my brother," she said. "He'll be relieved to know."

"The gentleman we saw in the wagon?" Adele nodded. "He's not staying with you?"

"I tried to persuade him."

"I can understand how he feels," he said. "Not much here for a man unless he's willing to resign himself to small town pleasures and reticence."

"Is it reticent?" Adele delivered the teacup into his waiting hands.

The man considered this. "I suppose one may call a small town reticent as compared to the city. And yet, people stay on because, well, we feel safer with the devil we know than the devil we don't know."

Adele nodded. "I sensed that the moment I arrived. Is there no hope for one like me in a place like Arrojo?"

The man fitted the cup inside the saucer. "I'm not sure I know what you mean, Miss Gossling."

"I'm neither a great lady nor an imbecile," she said. "I would very much like to live among you in peace."

"I don't suppose you'll have much trouble unless you're a criminal or a rebel." He grimaced.

"My brother thinks I'm a little bit of both," she remarked.

He laughed. "And what do you think?"

"We've entered a new century, Mr. Tanning," she said. "We have much to discover. We can't afford to tread in the waters of the past."

"I'm afraid you won't find many embracing that view in Arrojo."

"I'm not here to march in the streets with banners, sir," she declared. "I'm only after peace and small pleasures."

"That's a rather odd thing to hear from a young woman in the prime of life," he remarked.

She fiddled with the handle of her teacup. "My father died recently, Mr. Tanning."

He set the cup down on the dusty counter. "You and he were very close, I take it."

"Yes, we were." She opened her bag and took out a handkerchief, turning away to wipe her eyes.

"So close that you're using his handkerchief," he said in a quiet voice.

She stared down at it. The embroidered *O.G.* shone in the sun.

Mr. Tanning put on his hat. "Miss Gossling, you may not be approved by all, but you will not be disliked as long as there is kindness in your heart."

She felt at once grateful to this man who had obviously stepped away from decorum out of sympathy for the aloofness she had experienced her first day in town. "I assure you, Mr. Tanning, I will bear no one malice should they choose to disapprove of or even dislike me."

"I feel certain you'll find the peace you're looking for," he said. "I shall ask my wife to invite you and your brother to dinner one Sunday. Will he be coming down to see you often?'

"I'm afraid not as often as I would wish," she sighed.

"Ah, you miss him," he said.

"He insists on living in the city."

"But you needed to escape the memories," he guessed. "You needed your small pleasures and peace."

She felt the tears begin again and clutched her handkerchief.

"Please let me know when he's in town," he said. "I promise you a good dinner and good company."

"Thank you, Mr. Tanning," she said with a curtsy. "For everything."

The compliment seemed to embarrass the man, and he hurried down the street, nearly knocking over the boy delivering her merchandise.

## CHAPTER 4

A few days later, the door to Adele's Stationery stood ajar for a grand reception and found only dust and air. A few heads turned as people passed the shop, but no one stopped, and eyes did not linger past the GRAND OPENING banner. Children peered through the window bright with displays of yellow, pink, and blue letter paper, their mouths gaping as if they had never seen such fine colors in their lives. She bought a bag of lemon drops at Hyde's Confectionery and gave them to the children. They smiled at her, reassuring her Arrojo was not a wholly unsympathetic place.

In the afternoon, she made herself a cup of coffee and sat behind the counter. Her head ached from watching the door. Not a single person had entered or even peered inside with the least curiosity, save the children. She tried not to be disheartened but it was difficult to keep the tears back. She could see her father's face, a twinkle in the green eyes that were so much like Jackson's. She knew what he would say: *Be patient, be determined, and don't let them beat you.*

A young woman appeared in the doorway. The folds of her dress fluttered with ribbons, and the brilliant peach shade made the colored paper in the window pale in comparison. Her arms were filled with packages wrapped in brown paper. "Is that coffee?" She stared at the cup in Adele's hand. "Is it strong? Very strong?"

Adele smiled. The girl's loveliness came not only from her youth but the untroubled mind that belonged to a belle. "I'll make you a cup and let you decide. I'm Adele Gossling."

"Oh, we know that." The girl lurched forward. Her step was quick rather than careful.

"We?"

"I mean, my father told us," she said.

"Is your father Mr. Tanning?"

The girl's lovely face gathered with perplexity. Then a glint appeared in her eye. "Mr. Tanning is not my father. Perhaps the future will bring surprises."

Adele poured the girl a cup of coffee, not questioning the vague response.

"My father is Michael Blackstone," the girl continued. "He's the most elegant and respected gentlemen in Arrojo."

Now it was Adele's turn to show amusement. "You say that with a little too much pride."

"Do I?" The girl dropped into a chair, leaning her parasol across the counter. "I suppose I do have a little too much pride, but I never thought about it. I'm more capricious and headstrong. At least that's what my father says." She peered at Adele. "Should I be ashamed of that?"

"One may be anything when one hasn't the burden of years on one's soul," Adele studied Miss Blackstone's features. "I believe you're my neighbor."

The girl laughed. "I knew you were sharp the moment I saw you in your gazebo the other day. Unlike some of those girls I went to school with." The last was added with a sniff.

"You're Miss Blackstone?"

"Lucy Blackstone," she said. "You must call me Lucy, of

course. And I shall call you Adele, since we're to be friends." She grabbed her hand but did not shake it. Instead, she seemed to want to feel the strength of it.

"How kind of you to come into my shop to introduce yourself." Adele tried not to make her desperation obvious.

"I did not come to introduce myself." The girl fingered the pencils. "Not just that, anyway. I came to make a purchase." She eyed the empty store. "This is your first time owning a shop, isn't it?"

"How did you know?"

Lucy's eyes glowed. "Father knows everything. Sometimes before he has a right to know it."

"I see." Adele smiled. "Yes, this is my first shop."

Lucy cocked her head. "Why stationery?"

"I've always had a fondness for the epistolary," Adele admitted. "There's something rather elegant and utilitarian about writing paper and envelopes and ink."

Lucy laughed in a way that did not resemble the goose giggle of the young ladies in the society Adele left behind in San Francisco. "You clearly haven't had many love letters. They're anything but utilitarian."

"I've had my share," Adele said. "Have you really come to buy?"

"You didn't think I would leave you to your own devices. In Arrojo?" The girl snorted. "No one will set foot in your shop unless someone else buys first. It is an old-fashioned and terribly unjust custom here."

"I had no idea."

"Nor should you." Lucy's skirt swept dangerously close to a stack of envelopes. "I'm sure such antiquated ideas are not the providence of an exciting city like San Francisco. How I wish I lived there!"

"Perhaps you would change your mind if you did," Adele said dryly.

"Oh, it's a rogue's village, I know," said Lucy. "My mother often tells me. She was a Nob Hill debutante until she married Father and he brought her to this anthill." Adele could not help laughing. "Well, it's the truth. I wonder you ever wanted to come."

"San Francisco is the anthill," said Adele. "All the well-dressed ants scurrying from one corner to another. Most of them have forgotten wherefore and why."

"Perhaps they never knew." Lucy examined a sheath of writing paper.

"That's quite a philosophical suggestion," Adele remarked. "I see you've been educated."

"Oh, I've read Shakespeare and listened to Mozart." She shrugged.

"And what shall you do with your education, Lucy?"

The girl stiffened. "I want you to order me a special kind of writing paper."

"Certainly," said Adele.

"Lavender paper," added Lucy. "A very pale shade of lavender."

"I'll try my best," Adele mumbled.

"And can you get me this design?" The girl reached for a pencil and paper lying on the counter and scratched at it. She then handed it to Adele.

The design was so exquisite, Adele felt sure the girl had also studied drawing with less ennui than she had literature and music. The carnation wreaths with their claw-like leaves and flapping petals looked as if they belonged there. Adele could almost smell their spicy scent.

"You're a talented artist," she remarked.

"I only take from nature what she gives," Lucy said, flushing. "You couldn't see my garden from where you and that handsome man were looking."

"My brother, you mean," said Adele. "I don't think we noticed it."

"You must come and see it, then." She grabbed Adele's hand. "My talent lies not in drawing but in cultivating carnations."

"A rather conventional interest for an unconventional young lady," Adele said, amused.

"Heavens, am I unconventional?" asked the girl. "I hadn't thought about it."

"I would call a lady of your standing who comes into the shop of the town outcast and buys from her unconventional," Adele said. "I'm most appreciative."

Lucy took both her hands. "I intend to see you become one of us. I shall insist upon it."

"You always get what you want, don't you?" Adele eyed her. "Might I make a suggestion regarding your design?"

The girl bowed her head in an exaggerated way, which did not entirely convince Adele she was ready to accept advice. Listen to it, perhaps, but that was a very different thing.

She took up the pencil, and with a few swipes, two of the flowers opened their petals, their glory spilling into the corner of the page.

The girl snatched it from her. "I despise flowers in bloom!"

"Why is that?"

Lucy did not answer. With a stroke of her hands, she opened the parasol over her head and leaned against the doorway. "I'll expect you for lunch next Sunday afternoon. With or without your brother?"

"Without, I'm afraid."

"Oh, but he'll come soon, won't he?"

"If I have anything to say about it," Adele said with a smile. "I'll be sure to bring him around to meet you when he does."

The girl nodded. "When will the letter paper be ready?"

"By the end of next week, I think. I can bring it with me to when I come, if you like," said Adele.

"Splendid! I've a very special use for it, you see, and I'd like it as soon as possible." Her gloved hand went to her cheek. "Oh, but that's between you and me. We'll have many secrets between us, won't we?"

"My father once said a young woman apt to keep secrets is a young woman not to be trusted," Adele remarked.

"Oh, my father told me the very same thing." Lucy swept her skirt up from the dusty sidewalk. "I don't always believe every-thing he says, though I make him think I do." She waved as she crossed the street.

"I believed everything mine said." The words came softly, blowing like a warm wind inside the shop, now perfumed and airy in the wake of the young woman's departure.

ucy's prediction proved correct. As if everyone on Bridge Street saw her waving at Adele and bouncing out of her shop, they started tentatively coming in, and some even bought. Adele opened for half a day on Saturday and sold several more packets of writing paper, some stamps, and a few fountain pens, including one special order for Mrs. Cricket, one of the fussier ladies in town. The orders were small, but people's eyes wandered around the shop as if examining not only the merchandise but also the quality of its owner. Adele realized when Arrojo citizens became used to her presence, she could rely on a steady flow of customers.

She was eager to show her gratitude toward Lucy Blackstone and promptly arrived at the house on Sunday. It looked much larger up close, and the twisted pillars rivaled the surrounding tall trees. A rather obliging butler led her to the parlor, their steps echoing in the hollow hallway. The exquisite paintings on the walls and the statue of a shielded Venus made Adele almost wish she had asked Jackson to accompany her.

Lucy was staring out the open French doorways. Her mother and father sat as if for a portrait, the woman with her skirts spread over her ankles as she lounged on the couch, the man standing over her with his hand on her shoulder. A small boy who looked about seven years old sat on the floor pushing a tin toy car around.

Lucy gave her a peck on one cheek and then the other.

"Before I forget." Adele reached into her large purse. "I brought the paper."

The girl pressed her hand and whispered, "Not now. Later." Then, in a lighter tone, "Come meet my parents. Mother, this is Adele, our new neighbor. I told you about her."

Lucy's mother smiled, her face so perfectly pale, it might have been the model for the stone Venus. "I believe it's customary to call a woman who owns a shop by her last name, dear."

"Adele is my friend." Lucy's brow creased. "Her shop is a diversion, Mother. Adele is a woman of independent means."

"You mean she's rich like us?" The little boy pushed the car around Adele's feet.

"I'm not exactly rich." Adele smiled. "And who might you be?"

"Michael Blackstone Jr.," the little boy announced. "People call me Mickey."

"You're rich enough for our blood," Lucy said. "Isn't she, Father?"

Her father bowed. "Forgive my daughter, Miss Gossling. She's apt to forget her manners."

"I know what I'm about," Lucy insisted. "More than most people."

He threw her a sharp look, but almost immediately, his countenance changed. "I'm sorry if she offended you, Miss Gossling."

"I'm not in the least offended," Adele said. "In fact, I'm honored to be here."

"Oh?"

"I know the Blackstones are one of the oldest and most respected families in Arrojo."

He looked pleased. "We welcome you to our home, don't we, Marissa?" He looked expectedly at his wife.

"Indeed we do."

Adele smiled and held out her hand to the woman. Mrs. Blackstone raised hers but let it fall as if she hadn't the strength, laying a lace handkerchief like a pillow on her lap.

"I'm afraid I'm intruding," Adele said.

"Lucy didn't tell us you were coming until this morning," Mr. Blackstone admitted. "We usually prefer to keep Sundays between the family."

"I see what you mean by your daughter being impetuous." Adele glanced at the girl. Lucy looked as unconcerned as one who always got her own way.

"The family Sunday is a thing of the past, Father," she said. "Sundays are for company and leisure now."

"It's no matter," said Mrs. Blackstone. "We like having guests, don't we, Michael?" She glanced at her husband.

"That is true, my dear."

"I don't see why *I* can't invite my own guests." Lucy's voice was like steel. "This is my house too."

"I never said it wasn't, my dear," said her father. "We merely like to know these things ahead of time."

"You always have to know everything," Adele heard Lucy say under her breath.

Mickey made a noise like a motor as he steered the toy car. Mrs. Blackstone said with a recovering smile, "You're not intruding in the least, Miss Gossling. We're happy to entertain you."

"I imagine you don't usually entertain shopkeepers," Adele said in a light voice.

"We are always happy to welcome any newcomer to Arrojo," Mr. Blackstone insisted. "Especially our neighbors."

Adele felt a pull on her hand and smiled down at Mickey. "I'll be a great landlord someday, just like Papa," he said.

She laughed. "Do you know what a landlord is?"

"What has that to do with it?" The boy's tone was serious rather than indignant. Without waiting for the answer, he rolled the car around the couch.

"You'll find out when it's time, my boy," his father assured him. "I believe James just rang the bell for lunch, my dear."

The Blackstones warmed to her over the roast and potatoes. Even Mickey insisted on showing her his car, expertly pointing to the different parts as if he had built the thing himself.

"What brought you to Arrojo, Miss Gossling?" Mr. Blackstone pushed the wine further away from him, consequently putting it out of both Adele and Lucy's reach. It was clear he disapproved of more than one glass of wine for young ladies.

She thought of her conversation with Mr. Tanning. "I'm looking for small pleasures and peace."

"That sounds rather cryptic."

"Father prefers women to be straightforward." Lucy leaned over and plucked the wine bottle from the table, pouring a glass for both of them.

"Your father prefers everyone to be straightforward, dear," said Mrs. Blackstone.

"I shall speak plainly, then," said Adele. "My father died, and I wanted to get away from the city."

"I can understand that." Mr. Blackstone said. "But that's not the only reason, is it?"

Adele smiled. "You're right, of course. My, shall we say, marriage prospects were none too bright in the city, and there was a certain young man who was determined to change that."

"How utterly fascinating!" Lucy's eyes were shining. "You must tell me about it some time."

"I'm sure the young man you speak of meant no harm," said her father. "I'm sure he was only trying to do what was best for you."

Adele grasped her napkin under the table. "I'm sure you will appreciate young ladies these days would rather decide for themselves what is best for them, Mr. Blackstone."

"I realize that, Miss Gosling," he said in a firm voice, "Though I can't say I always agree with it. It depends upon the young lady." Although he did not look at his daughter, Adele had the feeling the speech was meant for her.

"Have you lived in San Francisco all your life?" Lucy asked. Adele nodded. "How splendid!" The girl sighed.

"It's not as splendid as you seem to think," Adele said gently.

"I don't think, I know," said Lucy.

"I've told Lucy many stories about the city," said Mrs. Blackstone. "I was born there, you see."

"Perhaps you exaggerated a little, my dear." Mr. Blackstone refused the green beans the footman put in front of him.

"Perhaps I did," Mrs. Blackstone agreed. "One is apt to romanticize one's youth."

"Father has lived here all his life," said Lucy. "He believes provinciality is God's intention for men. He won't see small towns like this offer nothing for young people."

The hard glance between father and daughter told Adele the argument was well worn in the house.

"Your daughter told me you were the belle of Nob Hill at one time." Adele turned to Mrs. Blackstone. "I'm sure you weren't exaggerating about its splendor."

"I don't regret one day I've lived in Arrojo," said the woman. "I imagine twenty years from now, neither will Lucy. Don't you agree, dear?"

Adele thought at first she was directing the question at her daughter, but she soon realized she meant her husband.

He turned to Adele. "And there's no chance this young man would leave San Francisco and come here?"

"No, indeed, sir." The odd glare in his eyes prompted her to add, "He's a partner in a law firm there and quite grounded in city life."

"No matter," said Mr. Blackstone. "I'm sure you'll find your-self with plenty of opportunities. A woman of your breeding always has opportunities."

Lucy shot her father a look. "You make her sound like a dog, Father."

"You know your father is always interested in your friends, dear," said Mrs. Blackstone.

"Yes, I know." Adele did not miss the irony in her voice.

"I suppose it was rather indiscreet of me," the man admitted.

"I don't mind." Adele grasped her napkin again. "I've nothing to hide."

Lucy picked up her wine glass. "You know, Father, some women prefer to marry later in life, and some prefer to marry right away. It all depends on when they fall in love."

"Poppycock," Mr. Blackstone snapped. "Marriage is much more than just a matter of love."

"Father believes in taking one's assets into account in every-thing," said Lucy in a sharp voice. "Even marriage."

"I imagine the ladies in this town will try to bring you to the mercy of the maypole," said the man with a smile.

"There isn't much chance they will succeed," Adele insisted. "Not for a while, anyway."

He rose and took Mickey's hand. "It's time for your nap, my boy."

Mickey leaned his curly head against his father's shoulder "You promised me pistachio fudge!"

His father nodded at the nanny who had just entered the room. "Miss Cummings, make sure Mickey gets a piece of fudge before you put him down. A small piece, mind you."

Mickey seemed satisfied, and as he was led out of the dining room waved at Adele and his sister.

They all retired to the parlor for coffee, and Adele couldn't help but remark to Mrs. Blackstone, "Your house is very lovely."

Mrs. Blackstone looked pleased. "Michael chose most of the furnishings. He has such good taste."

Her husband lit the cigar. "My father rebuilt this house three times. Most people add on, but he insisted if one is to change one's house, he must do so from the ground up. He did the same for the houses of his tenant farmers."

"My brother guessed you were a landowner," said Adele. "He said your house was so well kept, it could only belong to one who knew about such things."

"How very observant of him," said Mr. Blackstone.

"He thinks it's a curse," said Adele with a laugh. "He's a detective."

"Your brother doesn't live with you?" he asked.

"He insisted on staying in the city."

"Isn't that highly irregular?" Mrs. Blackstone ventured. "You're not married and–"

"He knows no harm will come to me in a town like this," said Adele. "Mr. Tanning reassured me of that the other day. Do you know Mr. Tanning?"

A sudden shadow of clouds appeared through the French doors, turning the dome of sunlight gray.

"He's an old enemy of Father's," Lucy said.

"Lucy!"

"Adele is bound to hear about it from the town gossips, Mother."

Mr. Blackstone coughed. "We have a business dispute, it's true."

"Business dispute?" Lucy eyed her father. "I believe it's more complicated than that, Father." She turned to Adele. "A piece of land Father thinks is dangerous so he wants to shut it down."

"And Mr. Tanning doesn't want it shut down?" Adele guessed.

Mr. Blackstone said in a forceful voice, "He won't have a choice. It's swampland and pestilent. I've sent the governor a letter, just as I said I would."

"Father, you have no right," Lucy insisted. "It's Tanning property."

"The town council agreed with me, my dear," he said. "It's infested with disease and dangerous. You wouldn't want your brother or his friends going there to play, would you?"

"Mr. Tanning offered to have it cleaned and put up a fence," said his daughter.

"He offered!" the man growled. "Offering and doing are two very different things."

"Lucy, stop." Mrs. Blackstone's voice was strong for the first time that evening, almost matching her daughter's vitality. "Leave your father to handle these things."

"I forgot I'm not allowed to have an opinion on anything," Lucy mumbled.

"Of course you are, my dear." Mr. Blackstone chucked her under the chin. "But your only duty now is to be beautiful and enjoy yourself."

"What about my duty to find a husband?" She eyed him.

"Find a husband, certainly." He gazed out the French windows. "When it's time."

"When it's time," Lucy scoffed in a low voice.

A tight silence filled the room again. Adele cleared her throat. "I would think you would have a lot of help in that area."

Lucy gave a hearty laugh. "You mean with the ladies in town? Have they started on you already?"

"I'm afraid so." Adele smiled as she accepted a slice of orange cake from Mrs. Blackstone's fragile hands.

"They might just have their opportunity." The sparkle appeared in Lucy's eyes. "I intend to give you a welcoming party."

A clatter sounded behind her. Turning around, she saw Mr. Blackstone pick up the empty cup he had dropped on the table.

"It will be a grand party," Lucy continued in a decisive voice. "Music and dancing, of course. They'll all come."

"You should have told us this before, Lucy." Mr. Blackstone's tone was a little sharp.

"I'm telling you now," she said.

"And when is this grand party to take place?"

"Friday, I think." Lucy blinked. "Yes, Friday."

"That's only a week away!" Mr. Blackstone growled. "You really ought to have been more considerate, my dear."

Lucy took Adele's arm. "Come, Adele. You *must* see my garden."

"By all means, do show Adele your garden." Mrs. Blackstone's voice was a little faint. "The carnations are so lovely just now."

Mr. Blackstone waved them away and settled in a chair, reaching for the Sunday newspaper.

The garden looked like a canopy of rainbow and velvet. The closeness of flowers brushed against her face and hands. At one point, she lost sight of her hostess, making her way through the mass of blooms on her own, feeling thorns and sharp leaves hook into her skirt.

"Careful!" she heard Lucy's voice somewhere at the other end of the garden.

At last she saw refuge in a small wooden bench, an octagon wrapping around what could only be the prize collection of violet and white carnations.

Lucy smiled and held out her hand. She noticed the young lady's delicate skirt was pricked and stained with green.

"I told you they're my life," said the girl.

"And your joy?" Adele laid her handbag on the bench.

"And my joy." In a softer voice, she said, "I envy you."

"I should think many young ladies envy *you*," Adele smiled. "A beautiful house, a beautiful garden."

"It's not my house," Lucy said. "And it's really not my garden. When I have a house of my own the garden will be much larger than this, and the flowers won't be so crowded. I had to crowd them because this is the only space I could get."

The hurt in her voice made Adele take her hand. "You shall have a house of your own and a large garden. Perhaps not too far into the future."

"No, not too far," said the young lady. She sat up. "You can give me the stationery now."

The moment Adele took out the package, Lucy snatched it from her and tore through the brown wrapping. The letter paper spilled over her stiff skirt, the carnations accentuated in raised purple.

"Thank you!" She threw her arms around Adele.

"I'm only fulfilling my duty as a stationer, Lucy." Adele couldn't help but laugh.

"You don't understand. I wish you could understand —" The furrow of her brow relaxed. "Sometimes a woman just needs her own private stationery." She looked at Adele with bright blue eyes. "Don't you agree, Adele?"

"Under certain circumstances, yes."

"Under certain circumstances," Lucy echoed.

Adele handed the girl a handkerchief.

"Oh!" Lucy stared at it with a jump.

Adele realized she had pulled out of her bag the heavy linen handkerchief with the initials *O.G.* rather than her own. "It was my father's."

"You keep it with you?"

"Perhaps I shouldn't." Adele felt her face grow warm. "Jack says I need to let go of the past."

"I think it's lovely." Lucy handed it back to her. "I wonder if I'll keep one of Father's handkerchiefs when he dies." Then, in a low tone, Adele heard her murmur, "No, I don't think I will."

Adele cleared her throat. "I'm glad the paper suits you. You might tell some of your friends so they're not afraid to come into my shop."

Lucy smiled and pressed her hand. "I shall. I think a woman

doesn't really come into her own until she has her own letter paper and can write – and can write to whomever she chooses."

"A woman usually doesn't do that until she's a wife," said Adele in a gentle tone.

"That's exactly what my father said!"

The remark was pointed, making Adele jump back. Lucy gathered the pages in a neat pile in her lap. "I shall make it known to all the nasty crows in this town that you fulfill your promises. You'll have more orders than you can handle within the week." She rose. "Shall we go inside?"

"One moment," Adele broached. "Your parents had no idea you intended to give me a welcome party, did they?"

"Oh, I probably told Mother, but she's so absent-minded," said Lucy. "She's not well, you see, so Father runs the house. That just leaves her to languish even more."

"All the same," said Adele. "*I don't wish to be a burden on anyone.*"

"Oh, nonsense!" The girl was genuinely annoyed. "Mother loves parties. And it's Father's chance to parade around like a peacock, showing off his fine home. Don't be fooled for a moment by their disapproval."

"It's a large undertaking," Adele pointed out.

Lucy patted her hand. "Expect the invitation within the next few days. I always get what I want, you see."

"In that case, since it's my party, I assume I may invite whomever I wish?" Adele eyed her.

"Naturally."

"I'd like to invite the Tannings." Her voice was firm. "Mr. Tanning made me feel welcome when no one else would, and I'd like to return the favor."

"Yes, he's a very nice man," said the girl quickly.

Adele looked down. "He reminded me of my father a little."

"Oh, I see." Lucy took her hand. "Yes, he's a very paternal sort, isn't he? Perhaps it's no wonder he and Father don't get on."

A gust of wind blew in, making a few of the tall carnations lean toward them. Lucy rose and cupped one in her hand. "They have a language all their own, you know. White for purity. Yellow is disappointment, and pink is gratitude. And the reds stand for affection or deep love, depending on the shade."

"How fascinating," Adele said.

"As for the striped ones," Lucy continued, "one must be careful. Striped is a gentle 'no' but a 'no' just the same. One may take a 'no' any way one wishes, whether it's lightly or violently."

Adele plucked a violet carnation that looked ready to leap to the ground. "And this one?"

"My favorite!" Lucy was delighted. "It suits me so well. Purple for capriciousness!"

Adele laughed. Then, in a more serious tone, she added, "You said you liked closed flowers. May I ask why?"

Lucy let out a laugh. "You're not afraid to ask probing questions, are you, Adele? Father would say it was unbecoming to a young lady."

"And what do you say?" She eyed her.

"What do *you* say?" The girl eyed her back.

"I don't deny it," Adele admitted. "But I give my trust to those who answer in return."

"You should be more cautious, then." Lucy looked down at the stationery sitting on the bench.

"I ought to be," Adele agreed. "I lived all my life in the city and saw things that would make even the strongest of men shiver."

Lucy smiled. "There's secrecy in a closed flower bud. When it opens, the mystery is gone."

"You sound as if you're quoting someone else," said Adele.

Lucy was about to respond, but the rustling leaves behind them indicated someone was coming. She grabbed the paper bundle and shoved it between the overgrown shrubs opposite the carnations. "Don't say a word about the stationery!"

Just then, Mr. Blackstone appeared, holding Mickey's hand. "We were rather worried about you."

"No need to be, Father." Lucy took Adele's arm. "We were just about to come back inside."

Mickey ran toward the carnations, burying his face into their blooms. His father pulled him back. "How do you like my daughter's flowers, Miss Gossling?"

"Very pretty," Adele said.

"And very exaggerated," he remarked. "I never understood why you had to plant so many in one place, Lucy."

"I like them." There was a stubbornness in her voice.

"You like the purple ones!" Mickey declared.

"They suit your sister," Adele said with a smile.

"We'll be in presently, Father," said Lucy.

"Well, don't be too long, my dear." He and Micky disappeared between the rose bushes closer to the house.

"He knows I don't like anyone in this part of the garden." Lucy's voice was tight. "He did that deliberately!"

"Perhaps he was just taking your brother for a walk," Adele suggested.

"No, he knew we were talking of secrets," Lucy insisted. "He was trying to listen in. He's always trying to listen in!"

"There was nothing for him to listen in to," Adele assured her. "I need to get back, Lucy."

"Yes, of course." Her friend patted her hand.

As they started toward the house, Adele ventured, "I have one more guest I'd like to invite to the party."

"Your brother?" Lucy smiled. "That goes without saying."

"No, a woman," said Adele. "I believe you know her. Miss Branch."

Lucy stared at her. "Anita Branch?"

"Is that her name?" asked Adele.

"Well, it's rather awkward." Lucy fidgeted with the edge of her sash.

"Because she's the town witch and sorceress?"

Rather than answer her, Lucy asked, "Why do you want to invite her to the party?"

"I think she's rather lonely," said Adele. "Lone women must stick together, you know."

"I suppose it can be done," she murmured. "She *is* of noble birth, after all. Yes, why not?" This resolve lent a sparkle to her smile as she led Adele into the house.

Mr. and Mrs. Blackstone were sitting on the couch. "Your father and I have been discussing this party of yours, Lucy, dear," Mrs. Blackstone began. "I don't see how we could arrange it so soon."

"We've organized parties in much less time, Mother," said the girl. "You know that."

"I don't want to be a burden on anyone," Adele murmured.

"You aren't, Adele," Lucy assured her. "I'll arrange everything."

"I'm sure Miss Gossling can take care of her own affairs," Mr. Blackstone insisted. "She doesn't need you to be her social secretary."

"You're not being very neighborly, Father." Lucy's voice was sharp. "It's up to people like us to show this town that Adele is harmless."

"Harmless, yes," Adele said dryly. "As every forward-thinking lady is."

"The party will give those backward-thinking ladies the kick up the skirt they need," said Lucy with a laugh. "They've been needing it for some time. You've said so yourself often enough, Father."

Her mother gasped, but there came an unexpected laugh from her father. "Well, it might be worth giving a party to see that." He bowed to Adele. "I'm sorry if we seemed inhospitable. We would be honored if you would allow us to arrange it."

"I don't see how we possibly could." Mrs. Blackstone looked alarmingly at her husband.

"I'm sure you and Lucy could manage it, my dear," said the man. "We'll engage the servants to help, of course."

"The servants have their duties, Michael."

"Then we'll engage more of them." It was clear by his tone he had made up his mind.

"Come now, Mother, you love a big party." Lucy turned to Adele. "Tomorrow she'll be flinging out orders and making lists. Won't you, Mother?"

Mrs. Blackstone, seeing her daughter and husband's resolve, smiled wanly at Adele. "Lucy's quite right. Don't mind me. I'm a little tired right now." She held out her hands. Adele took them, feeling their warmth. "You must promise to bring your brother so we can meet him properly."

"I'll get him to Arrojo if I have to horse-whip him," Adele promised.

# CHAPTER 6

*A*dele had no need to carry out her promise to Mrs. Blackstone, as Jackson readily agreed to come down on Friday for the party. He arrived in the afternoon just as a heavy rain cleared the dust from the front porch. At first, he coaxed Tomas into acting as his valet, but eventually shut him out of the second-floor room Adele gave him to do his own preening.

The late hour did nothing to lighten Adele's mood. She could do little more than wait in the parlor in a silver and blue dress her brother insisted was the only proper thing she had to wear. The crumpled silk and lace were so delicate, she couldn't sit down without creasing it so she strolled, tugging at her gloves.

When Jackson appeared at last, she had to admit the wait was worth it. His suit was pressed to perfection. The waves of his hair shone like wax, and his skin glowed with pride. Even his top hat framed his face just right. He looked like one of the illustrations in the Sears Roebuck catalogue.

"Perhaps you'll save me tonight after all." Adele took his arm.

"Save you?"

"From the ladies in town," she said. "They've been swarming

around the shop since they received their invitations. Not to buy, of course, but to scrutinize my marriage potential."

He laughed. "It might do you good." They stepped outside. "At least the rain has stopped."

"Isn't it heavenly in the country?" Adele took a deep breath. "None of that rancid city smoke."

"If you're trying to persuade me to move out here, you're wasting your time." He lowered his hat over his forehead. "I've none of your love for the backwoods, Del."

"Arrojo is hardly the backwoods," she insisted. "They're very civilized here. Let's walk!" She turned toward the Blackstone house. "It's a waste to take the car on a heavenly night like this."

"It's a beastly night," he complained. "One step in that mud and your dress will be ruined."

"Papa once said a woman of immaculate appearance was little better than a wax doll," she shot out.

"I know very well what he said," said Jackson shortly. "We're not talking about a little dust. We're talking about mud."

She lifted the train of her dress over one wrist. "I'll be careful."

He held on tightly to her arm. "Del, don't you want to make a good impression with these people?"

She stiffened. "Of course I do. But I want to be *me* too."

"You've a business now," he reminded her. "It wouldn't do to alienate one of the most prominent citizens in this town who is giving a party just to introduce you to society, would it?"

She looked at his face under the pale moonlight. "Perhaps you're right," she admitted. "We'll take the Beaton."

"We will not," he snarled. "We'll take the wagon. I don't think you'll make a very good impression roaring up to the house in that monstrosity."

She gritted her teeth at him but followed him to the street like an obedient child.

The Blackstone house illuminated with tear-shaped lights twisted around the porch and through the gate in a wave reaching all the way to the road. As they climbed out of the wagon, her heels scraped against fibers on top of the hard ground.

"Good heavens!" she said. "I believe it's a carpet."

"A red carpet for the guest of honor." The swell of violins from the orchestra playing over his reply.

It was indeed a rug, though a silver one rather than red. The flashing color nearly blinded her under the pale lights. Corkscrew lanterns strung all around the veranda twirled in the wind. Windows were flung open as if it were cleaning day, and even the front door was pulled back. She had not expected such a welcome.

The same butler with a collar as stiff as his posture approached them, holding out his hand. She whispered to her brother, "The card, the card."

Jackson dug into his pocket for the invitation Lucy had sent. The butler's croaking voice read, "Mr. and Mrs. Gossling?"

"*Miss* Gossling," Adele corrected.

Lucy swept toward them. Lavender pearls flew from the neck, and her dress was cream silk and a pale shade of violet. A large violet and white striped carnation was pinned to the center of her bodice. "At last!" She kissed Adele on either cheek. "The guest of honor."

"Had I anticipated such a spectacle, I never would have agreed to it," Adele murmured. Jackson pinched her elbow.

"It's quite gaudy, isn't it?" Lucy agreed. She lowered her voice. "I tried telling Mother, but she insisted if we were to host a party for a newcomer, it must be as lavish as possible." She regarded Jackson with approval. "Good evening, Mr. Gossling."

"Call me Jackson, please." He bowed. Adele felt proud of him with his tall demeanor and charming smile.

"I feel I must warn you. Once the ladies here catch sight of you, they'll get ideas before the night is over," she said with a laugh. "You see, most of the best men in Arrojo are already taken or about to be."

"I'm here as my sister's escort only," he said, a little stiffly.

"I'm sure you'll enjoy yourself," she said. "We have the most divine cook in the county. The canapés are nearly gone, but I'm sure we can arrange for more."

"I'm anxious to meet everyone," said Adele.

"I'm rather curious myself." Jackson handed his hat and coat to the butler.

"Jack considers himself my watchdog," said Adele. "Rather a nuisance, but most brothers are, aren't they?" She winked at Lucy.

"Only under the age of ten." Her friend laughed.

"Lucy has a brother named Mickey who is going to be a great landlord someday," said Adele. "He's well under the age of ten."

"Eight and a half, to be exact," Lucy corrected, taking her hand.

As she did so, Adele heard a ring of chimes. "What a splendid idea for a bracelet!"

The bracelet in question was a gold band about a quarter of an inch thick with rings hanging all around it like charms.

"I have awkward fingers," Lucy explained. "I can't wear rings, but I love them so. So I wear them like this."

"May I see it?" Adele asked.

Lucy seemed almost reluctant, but she held up her wrist. The rings were all gold with modest designs, and some of them had stones. One in particular caught Adele's eye. Its band was thicker than the others and held a stone as fleshy violet as Lucy's dress.

"A lilac diamond, isn't it?" Jack looked over her shoulder.

Lucy nodded. "They're quite rare, I'm told."

"A lovely thing," murmured Adele.

"It looks almost like an engagement ring," Jackson remarked.

A clash sounded near a rosewood table with cocktail glasses. A footman scrambled to pick up the pieces of a broken plate, while Mr. Blackstone stood nearby, adjusting his coat in the mirror.

"It is an engagement ring, as a matter of fact," Lucy said. "My great-grandmother was especially attracted to diamonds and Great-Grandfather bought it for her. He was always very generous."

"Your great-grandmother shared your love of the color violet," Adele guessed.

Lucy burst out laughing and touched the pearls around her neck. They were elegantly arranged in strands close to her neck, showing off her décolleté.

"A present from your father?" Adele guessed.

Mr. Blackstone came up behind her. "How did you guess?"

"My father told me once it's a father's privilege to give his daughter her first string of pearls."

"Father was very accommodating in your case," said Jack. "The fact that the pearls sit in your jewelry box gathering dust is no fault of his."

"I confess, it's true," said Adele as laughter erupted around her. "I haven't much use for jewelry."

"I always wear these pearls at parties." Lucy put her arm through her father's. "It pleases Father so."

"I should have worn mine, then," Adele said. "It would have pleased my father too." For a moment, a wave of sadness entered her heart.

"Lucy, your guests," her father reminded her in a low voice.

"The Gosslings are my guests too," she insisted. "Why don't you both slip into a quiet corner while I go find the rest of the canapés? It will give you a moment to breathe before the sight-seers descend upon you."

"Sightseers?" Jackson asked.

"They gawk at newcomers in Arrojo." Lucy closed her fan. "We don't always mind our manners here. I'll be back!" She disappeared among the colored skirts and black trousers.

"You must excuse me," said Mr. Blackstone with a low bow.

"She seems a spirited sort," Jackson said when he was gone. "Perhaps a little too frivolous."

"She's young, Jack," Adele said. "Though I do think a young girl flashing an engagement ring around like that might cause a misunderstanding."

"Perhaps that's her intent," Jackson said. "I've seen women hide their engagement rings when it suited them."

"Jack, sometimes you are wicked!"

The champagne sent a warm feeling in her throat. When it settled, she found herself looking into the eyes of the dark-haired woman who occupied the shop next to hers. Miss Branch looked as if she would rather be in a cave than the marbled room with its abominable lights. And yet, Adele was almost stunned by the striking beauty of her feline features, especially the eyes that stared at her with a wide-eyed wisdom. She a cherry red evening gown, the décolleté modest but alluring. Adele admired the simplicity of her appearance.

Before Adele could speak, the woman exclaimed, "You're Adele Gossling."

"Yes," she said. "I introduced myself to you about a week ago."

"I wasn't very cordial," the woman admitted. "I'm not very socially graceful. You'll forgive me?"

"There is nothing to forgive," said Adele, smiling.

"My name is Anita Branch," she said. "Friends call me Nin."

"My brother, Jackson." Adele turned to him.

Jackson, clearly taken by the woman's beauty, stared at her for a few moments. Then, he collected himself and gave her his usual gracious greeting. Nin raised an eye without really looking at him. "*Friends* call me Nin."

Jackson cleared his throat and looked away, embarrassed.

"If you'll pardon my being so bold," said Adele, "you look as if you're bored or lost or both."

She expected the woman to give her the unmovable eye she

had given Jackson. Instead, she smiled, a lovely smile that deepened her beauty. "And *you* look as if you want to throw kerosine over the lot of them."

"Not now, maybe, but I think I will very soon." Adele glanced at the knot of matron ladies who had begun gathering in a corner.

"Delightful!" The woman's smile deepened. "That's just how I feel about it."

Her playful wickedness made Adele laugh.

"Then permit me to ask why you came," Jackson said with a slight cough.

Nin gave him a look. "Miss Gossling was kind enough to ask me, and I would never have refused. I'm not as ill-bred as that, Mr. Gossling."

"I'm sure," the young man murmured.

"We're friends, remember?" said Adele. "Call me Adele."

"Adele." The woman looked anxious. "I want to ask you what they've been saying about me?"

"They?" asked Jackson.

She ignored him, grasping Adele's hand. "Whatever they told you about me, it isn't true!"

Jackson gave her a peculiar glance, but Adele understood what the woman was trying to say. More than once she had come up against scornful looks from people who thought her work with the settlement houses and her suffragist meetings were inappropriate at best, dangerous at worst. At first she had been hurt by their snickering but later, she realized people talked about her because of her unconditional refusal to be what they thought a woman of her standing ought to be – lightly education, married, and putting her time and energies into society rather than social reforms.

"I never listen to what other people say without forming my own opinion first," she said softly. "Certainly not about someone who makes a very favorable impression on me."

Nin pressed Adele's hand, her strong fingers digging into her gloves. She turned to Jackson and said, "Mr. Gossling, you may call me Miss Branch." She disappeared into the crowd, and Adele could not see her among the dresses and sashes.

She handed Jackson a fresh glass of champagne. "You look as if you just escaped from a large pair of hands around your throat."

"I'm not sure I haven't." He stared ruefully into the crowd.

"Don't take it personally, Jack," she said. "Some women simply aren't impressed by a gentleman."

He had no time to respond, as in an instant, they were surrounded by people. Eyes peered, and spectacles adjusted as if to get a closer look. Adele felt her dress tighten against her back, and her bag grew heavy around her wrist. Jackson touched the collar of his white shirt as a sign of his discomfort.

Adele took a deep breath. "Thank you all for coming to this party Lucy was so generous to give for me," she said. "I hope to see all of you in my shop. I – I'm sure I can accommodate you in any way you like."

The circle was silent, the swaying skirts frozen. Someone stepped forward, and Adele realized she was Mrs. Faderman, the same woman who had spoken to her the first day she arrived at Arrojo.

"The Arrojo Ladies Auxiliary welcomes you." Her voice was as grated and steady as it had been at their first meeting. "My husband, Mr. Faderman." A seamless-looking man with a balding head and paunch bowed. "My daughter, Vanessa. Vanessa!" One of the giggling young ladies Adele had seen on the street stepped forward in robin's egg blue, nearly tripping over her train. She curtseyed and retreated back into the fold. "My son, Percy."

A flustered, heavy-set young man with a red face fluttered to Adele's side. "Indeed, indeed! So happy to —"

"That will do, Percy."

He, too, retreated into the crowd.

"And who are you, young man?" Mrs. Faderman looked up at Jackson expectedly.

"My brother, Jackson, ma'am." Adele tried to sound braver than she felt. "He's only visiting."

"Oh, what a shame." The woman turned to her with a heavy look. "Miss Gossling, I feel I must tell you – I must *warn* you – we pride ourselves here on our excellent traditions and values."

"I'm sure my brother is pleased to hear it, ma'am," Adele said. "I fancy he was afraid I would become as wild as the landscape."

"Del!" he hissed.

Mrs. Faderman looked at him with a reptilian expression, as if trying to decide whether to be irked by the implication that Arrojo could be considered "wild," or pleased she had found a like-minded person. The nod she gave him did not clarify the matter.

"Perhaps you will understand, then," she continued. "We do not look kindly upon progressives and reformers."

"One may be progressive without carrying banners and shouting in the street." Adele stiffened.

"Oh, I wish you would!"

The outburst came from a pert little woman who had scurried through the circle and burst into its center. Her auburn hair flung in coils around her face, the twist half undone. Unlike the others, she was dressed in a light cotton suit and high-necked shirt and carried a pencil and notepad.

She held out her hand. "I'm Missy Grace, Miss Gossling. I own the *Arrojo Courier*. I am also its editor, reporter, and distributor."

"Only by default, dear," said Mrs. Faderman. "Miss Grace's brothers owned the paper, but they saw fit to leave us for the corrupted coin of the city."

Missy's face colored. She continued, "I'd like to do a story on your shop, Miss Gossling. May I stop by sometime?"

"I'd be delighted," said Adele.

Mrs. Faderman cleared her throat. "As I was saying, we do not welcome progressives here. I'm relieved to hear you have no plans to pursue any ideas in that direction."

Adele tried to keep her voice calm. "My purpose is to live a peaceful life. I hope that meets with your approval."

This seemed to satisfy the woman. She took charge, introducing people as if she were the party's hostess.

When the crowd dispersed, three tall, sandy-haired men and a straw-haired woman remained.

"Good evening, Mr. Tanning!" She had not seen the man since that day in her shop.

"I see you received your welcoming committee." He smiled and bowed. "I told you they're harmless."

"Jack, this is Mr. Tanning," Adele said. "He doesn't share the general opinion I've come to bring ruin to the city of Arrojo with my 'progressive ideas.' He shared a tea pot with me my first week here."

"I was only too glad to welcome your sister, sir." The man shook Jackson's hand. He introduced them to his wife, Frances, the straw-haired woman with a sweet but tired-looking face.

"My son, Richard." A handsome young man with a hearty manner nodded. His collar was already damp with perspiration.

The fourth member of the family grabbed Adele's elbow. "Do you like oranges? Oranges, oranges!" His eyes, though like Richard's, were much brighter, like the eyes of a child.

"Doesn't everybody?" She smiled.

"Papa doesn't," he said. "Papa likes lemons." He frowned. "Sour, sour lemons."

"Miss Gossling," Mr. Tanning said. "This is my elder son, Daniel. You must forgive his forthrightness. He's not used to so many people." He carefully unhooked his son's long fingers from Adele's arm.

"Cucumbers, I like cucumbers too," said Daniel. "They put 'em in bread here. Hate thin bread."

"You mustn't be afraid of him." Mrs. Tanning sounded as if she had said this so many times.

"Why would I be afraid?" said Adele. "Daniel, you know, you could take the cucumber out of the thin bread and eat it all by itself." Behind her, she felt Jackson's hand on her back.

"Fat bread, I like fat bread," he said. He clicked his heels together. "Cor-pu-lence!"

Adele burst out laughing. "You know some very big words, don't you?"

Lucy appeared out of nowhere, her spicy perfume filling the air around them. "I'm glad you could come. It's good to see you home, Richard."

"My son has been away at college for the last four years," Mr. Tanning explained.

"Reading, writing, and arithmetic," Daniel chanted.

Lucy took his hand. "Danny, how about some cucumbers?" There was a gentle tone in her voice. "Mrs. Brown went to the market today especially for them. She made a maple cake too."

"Mrs. Brown, always a frown and stamping her foot to the ground," Daniel sang.

"Mickey is waiting for you." Lucy began to lead him away. "He wants to show you his new toy." Their voices faded away.

"He's a sweet boy, really," Mrs. Tanning began.

"Tanning!"

Mr. Blackstone strolled up to them, his wife trailing behind, her pink dress lending a bright air to the circle. Mr. Blackstone now had a red carnation in the lapel of his dark suit. Mr. and Mrs. Tanning's faces tightened, and Richard clasped his hands behind his back.

"What are you doing here?" Mr. Blackstone demanded.

"I invited the Tannings, Father." Lucy returned to the circle. "I wanted Adele to meet everyone in town."

"I see." This came out in a low growl.

"It was at my request, Mr. Blackstone," Adele said.

Mr. Tanning said in a low voice, "We're not here to make trouble, Blackstone. We want to enjoy the party as much as you do." With a nod toward his family, they wandered away. Adele noticed Mrs. Blackstone's eyes followed them.

Mr. Blackstone turned to Jackson and said in a strained tone, "Your sister has caused quite a flutter, Mr. Gossling."

"She had no intention of doing so, sir." Jackson's expression became fierce and protective, though his tone was even.

"I'm sorry if it upsets you, Mr. Blackstone," said Adele. "But it is, perhaps, as Lucy said, the kick up the skirt some of the people here needed."

Mr. Blackstone laughed. "Your father must have had quite a time with you as a child, Miss Gossling."

"Why do you say that?" Adele asked.

"Oh, a mere observation."

"Father is thinking of me," said Lucy. "You see, he always speaks of how impossible it is to tame a woman once she gets ideas into her head."

"I don't know anyone should be tamed, man or woman," said Jackson. "We're not animals, after all."

The man shrugged. "Perhaps I'm simply not used to the way things are in the new century."

"And how are things, Father?" Lucy looked pointedly at him.

"I don't believe anyone has illusions about that," said Mr. Blackstone. "Chaotic, an explosions of sorts. Not with dynamite, but with deeds."

"With dynamite also," said Jackson. "I suppose you've heard about the riots in the coal mines."

"Not here, not in California," Mr. Blackstone insisted. "Certainly not in Arrojo."

"Arrojo is a peaceful town." His wife stroked her feathered fan.

"Sometimes, ma'am, even peaceful towns contain violent influences," Jackson mumbled.

"That's true." Richard approached with his father behind him.

"Jack used to work for the Anspach Detective Agency." Adele chose another glass of champagne even though she had no intention of drinking it. "He was often sent to so-called peaceful towns."

"Interesting work, I dare say," said Mr. Tanning.

"You can hardly compare, sir," Mr. Blackstone insisted. "Those towns in the Midwest aren't remotely related to what we have here. Your sister will surely tell you she could not find a better settlement."

"It wasn't only the Midwest, Mr. Blackstone," said Jackson. "My work took me to the narrowest pockets of the country. Sometimes I stayed in towns with no more than twenty settlers."

"The voices of devils lurk in the mouths of saints," Mr. Tanning murmured.

"Rather prophetic, Tanning," Mr. Blackstone snapped.

"As you well know, Blackstone," Mr. Tanning replied, his voice as calm as the other's was agitated. "Cloaks of respectability can't shield everything."

"Please!" Lucy clutched her glove. "We're here to enjoy ourselves."

"Forgive me, my dear." Mr. Blackstone took his daughter's hand. "May I have this dance?"

"I believe this is my dance, sir." Richard led her to the dance floor. Adele realized Lucy's hand looked as if it had been tucked under his elbow for some time.

"Dance, Del?" Jackson offered.

From the bouncing way her brother danced, she knew he regretted his invitation. Jackson was much more a waltz man, though she observed he always held his partner away from him as if her dress were on fire.

"You ought to be master of the dance floor, Jack," she said with a wink.

"I don't see why I should be."

"Every bachelor should be," she said over the orchestra. "You were always much too serious."

His pace slowed. "I'm not as carefree as Richard Tanning, if that's what you mean. We're about the same age, I think."

Adele glanced at the center of the floor Lucy was no longer dancing with him, but with her father. Their dance moved with deliberate steps while those around them swung around as if determined to leave their footsteps behind.

Richard stood in a darkened corner, sipping punch as if it were an elixir, his eyes on the dancers, but she felt they were really on one particular person. The tinkling bells from the orchestra made his intent eyes sparkle like glass.

"I don't think he is carefree," she observed.

"Why do you say that?"

"He looks like a young man weighed down by some trouble."

"He has his fortune to make, just like any other young man," said Jackson. "That can be rather taxing on the mind."

She glanced at him with a keen eye. "You made your decision about your fortune rather resolutely." The floor turned into a swarm of perfume and laughter, hurting her ears and eyes. "Can we stop, dear?"

They retreated to the rim of the circle formed around the dancers. She saw Nin lingering against the wall. "Don't you think Miss Branch is the loveliest woman in the room?"

"You don't give much credit to your hostess."

"Unlike you, Jack, I don't follow the dictates of property that demand flattering the hostess even if she doesn't merit it." Her voice softened. "Nin is an outcast in Arrojo. I'm sure others would warm toward her if you asked her to dance. You've made such a good impression."

"Her conduct toward me was not exactly inviting, Del," he grumbled.

"Nonetheless," she said. "As a gentleman —"

He sighed and approached Miss Branch as a hunter

circling a panther, bowed and extended the invitation. Adele expected Nin to rebuff him, but, to her surprise, her new friend allowed him to lead her to the dance floor. Despite the dragging skirt, Nin proved to be an accomplished dancer. She had such grace Adele felt almost like a duck in comparison.

She looked around the crowded ballroom. Richard was still in the dark corner, holding a slip of paper in his hand. As she neared him, he crumpled it up, shoving it in his pocket.

The young man retreated as Nin joined her.

"You waltz beautifully," Adele complimented.

"I learned with reluctance," Nin replied. Her face grew serious. "I'm sure Miss Blackstone thought it would be a lark to see me stumbling all over myself."

"Nonsense." Adele took her arm. "You were invited because I wanted you here."

"She couldn't very well refuse," the woman said shyly. "My mother's family established themselves as the monarchs of this valley just as much as the Blackstones."

Adele eyed her. "You speak as if you resent belonging to the monarchs of the valley."

"I don't belong with them!" Nin's voice rose above the strain of violins, and a group of young people near them glared. Lowering her voice, she added, "I resent anyone who moves against the cosmical forces."

"Cosmical forces?" Adele asked. "Surely, you don't believe–"

The woman's dark eyes were like hot coals. "I have a gift, you see."

"Oh?"

"I get feelings." Nin looked uncomfortable. "Vibrations, really."

"What sort of vibrations?"

"Oh, any sort," she said. "The world is always moving."

"I see," said Adele softly.

"I'm not evil!" The striking face gathered with fear. "You don't think I'm evil, do you?"

"I should say not," said Adele. "A little extraordinary, perhaps."

"I have my gifts as others have theirs," the woman insisted. "Perhaps I will pay for my gifts someday." She scurried away, and Adele caught sight of her against the wall, pressing her hands behind her and watching with her dark eyes.

She found Jackson, accepting the paper fan and glass of water he handed her.

"What a strange woman Nin is," she murmured.

"Quite strange," Jackson agreed as he found them two chairs. "I'd just as soon stay away from her, and you should too, Del."

"You're being uncharacteristically boorish," she growled.

"I've met similar women," he insisted.

"And just where and how you met them isn't fit for polite conversation," Adele said.

"Don't be vulgar!"

"For your information, dear brother," she said, "she's had as exclusive an upbringing as Lucy."

"I suppose you'll tell me next she knows what knife to use with the fish and when to leave her calling card."

"Better than either of us," Adele retorted. "We weren't exactly on the Nob Hill swells' invitation lists." She added quickly, "Not that Papa was ever lacking in social propriety."

"No, he made certain of that," her brother growled.

She looked away. It was not a night she could stand hearing Jackson's critical observations about their father.

At ten o'clock, she noticed some of the matrons taking up their wraps. Their offspring stayed, trying to coax Lucy into bringing out the punch bowl. Lucy shrugged them off while her parents watched on with approval.

The room was beginning to get stifling, the ladies' perfume mingling with cigar smoke. Adele and Jackson strolled into the hallway, where a breeze was coming through an open French door. Mr. Tanning saw them and nodded before going out to the porch.

"I think I'm going to like living in a small town," Adele announced. "Everybody knowing everybody else."

"And thus being ripe for gossip." Jackson took her hand. "Promise me you won't give them a reason, Del."

His authoritative tone enraged Adele. She slipped her hand out of his. "Why do you assume you must take on the role of my watcher since Papa died?"

"Because you need looking after."

"Hogwash!" She drew her shawl closer to her shoulders, as the wind was beginning to get chilly.

Mrs. Tanning rushed at them. "Have you seen my husband?" Her voice rose above the orchestra music.

"He went out that door a few minutes ago." Jackson nodded toward the veranda.

She smiled her thanks and hurried away.

"Perhaps your suffragist friends neglected to tell you," he continued in a tight voice. "Women may see themselves as independent, but this view isn't always shared by those who prey on them."

"I don't see much chance of being anyone's prey here," Adele said. "Not in a dangerous way, that is. Unless one considers the well-meaning intentions of society matrons as dangerous."

Jackson laughed. "I can't help but wonder if they aren't!"

As they wandered back to the ballroom, Adele caught a glimpse of Richard, as he wrapped in a dark coat, as he slipped outside the French doors.

"The Tannings must be feeling dangerous intentions," she said as they took a place beside Nin, the only spot the cigar smoke had not reached.

"What do you mean?" Jackson asked.

"They all seem anxious to get out of the house," Adele said.

"With the cold relations between them and the Blackstones, I shouldn't wonder they would want to leave," Jackson remarked.

"I don't think Richard left," Adele said. "A party like this is probably one of the few amusements young people have in a town like this."

"They find their own diversions," Nin said. "I try to take as little notice of them as they take of me."

"You're above reproach, Miss Branch," Jackson said. "Of that I'm sure."

"I've had my share of scandal, Mr. Gossling." She eyed him. "A woman, unlike a man, must be careful. People are ready to believe anything of her."

"You underestimate the sense of duty and honor of my sex," he said. Adele could feel his arm stiffen in hers.

"Duty and honor can be misplaced at times," the woman retorted. "Even in the best of us, man or woman."

He bowed and remained silent.

The clock above their heads let out a tired bong.

"Midnight already." She put the empty glass she had been holding on a table.

"We must be getting along," Jackson agreed.

"Nin, will you come with us or stay?"

"I've nothing to stay for." She shrugged and took her arm.

Even with the matrons and their husbands nearly gone, the room seemed more rather than less crowded, and it took them a while to find their hosts. They finally located Mrs. Blackstone, still the generous hostess, but retreated to a chair in the corner.

"Lucy does like bringing in the younger people." She fanned herself. "They simply adore her."

"Where *is* Lucy?" Adele asked. "I'd like to thank her personally for this party."

"We don't know." Creases appeared on her face. "We've been looking for her for some time."

"I expect she's around somewhere," Jackson assured her.

"I don't think so," said Mrs. Blackstone. "I haven't seen her. I just sent Michael out to the veranda to look for her."

Just then, noise erupted over the orchestra's stringy waltz. The violins ceased, and two men's voices rose over the smoke.

"This wouldn't be the first time, would it?" The voice belonged to Michael Blackstone.

"I could say likewise, but I'm too much of a gentleman to speak of a lady's–"

"A lady's what? A lady's what?!"

"Indiscretions."

Standing at the center of the room were Mr. Blackstone and Lowell Tanning. Mr. Blackstone had grabbed Mr. Tanning's wrist and was holding up his arm as if he meant to strike. "You will apologize, sir!" his voice roared through the crowd.

"I will," replied the man, "when you apologize for your insinuation my son could have behaved in such an unflattering fashion."

"I do not make insinuations, Tanning," he said. "I go by facts."

"My son is an honorable man," Mr. Tanning growled. "Perhaps you and I have different opinions as to what constitutes honor."

"Jack–" Adele nudged her brother.

With the stroll of a man who was always on the right side of the law, Jackson reached the two men. "Gentlemen, if you don't want to ruin the party, I suggest you cease."

"I had no intention of ruining anything," said Mr. Tanning. "But when someone makes accusations about my son —"

"Perhaps you'll agree to mutual apologies," Jackson said. "We can discuss this in a more private setting."

Mr. Blackstone looked as if he were about to transfer the strike he had planned from Mr. Tanning to Jackson. But his voice eased, and he said, "Perhaps you're right, Mr. Gossling." He let go of Mr. Tanning's wrist and nodded at the orchestra. The room filled with waltz music, and the dancers resumed.

Neither man seemed interested any longer in pursuing the

argument. Mr. Tanning led his wife and eldest son out the door. Mr. Blackstone sat at the foot of the stairs, wiping his face with a handkerchief. "You can expect nothing less from a man whose grandfather bullied his way into this territory," he growled. "I can only imagine how many women his son has led astray during those four years in college."

"You don't think–" Mrs. Blackstone's voice shook.

He put his hands on her shoulders, kissing her cheek. "Lucy is much too sensible, my dear."

"Of course she is." The woman sank back into the chair.

"If you'll tell us what that was about, perhaps we could help," said Jackson.

"It seems both my daughter and Richard are missing," said Mr. Blackstone.

"And you thought Mr. Tanning's son may have taken Lucy away somewhere." Jackson nodded. "You might have been more discreet about your inquiries, Mr. Blackstone."

"Perhaps I should have been," the man admitted.

"Mr. Blackstone, why do you think Richard led young ladies astray during his college years?" Adele asked.

"One hears things, Miss Gossling."

"But you said you go by facts, not rumors," she pointed out.

He took a carafe of water and poured a glass, which he pushed into his wife's hands. "In this case, it is of no consequence," he said. "I shouldn't be surprised if —"

"If what?"

"He does a respectable young lady harm one day."

Mrs. Blackstone let out a small scream, covering her mouth with her fan. In a gentler tone, he added, "I'm sure Lucy's upstairs, my dear, probably already asleep. She was telling me earlier how tired she was and would probably end up going to bed before the party was over."

"You might send someone to go and look," Jackson suggested. "Adele could look in."

"I shall do so myself if you think it wise." His wife dabbed at her eyes with a handkerchief. "Really, my dear, you worry far too much about her."

"We were just leaving, but we won't disturb her." Jackson took Adele's arm in one of his and tried taking Nin's in the other, but she pulled away.

"I'll thank her tomorrow," Adele promised, pulling her wrap over her shoulders.

"Not before noon," the man called out as he headed toward the stairs.

# CHAPTER 7

The night was clear as they stepped outside. The black sky showed stars as bright as the party lights.

"You can't say it's not beautiful here, Jack," Adele insisted.

"Beautiful, yes, but far too quiet for my taste." He pulled his hat closer over his ears. "Can we give you a ride home, Miss Branch?"

"I would rather walk," she insisted.

"Where exactly do you live, if I may ask?"

"I've a humble abode above my store, Mr. Gossling," she said. "I don't live in finery as you do."

"I wasn't trying to criticize, Miss Branch," he grumbled. "I merely asked.

This seemed to change her attitude and her face softened. "I changed my mind. I should be delighted for a ride home." She climbed into the wagon. "You prefer noise and chaos to quiet, Mr. Gossling?"

"He's used to big city crowds," Adele explained, settling beside her. "San Francisco and Chicago mostly."

"You'll get used to the sounds here," said Nin. "The birds and other animals. Flowers and trees speak too if you know how to listen."

"Are you perhaps part of the back-to-nature movement, Miss Branch?" Jackson asked.

"Must one be a part of anything to believe in it?" She asked.

"It sometimes helps to find like-minded people," Adele said gently.

"I am not an intellectual," she sniffed. "My education was erratic at best and even that is being too generous."

"I'm sure you have many fine qualities, Miss Branch," said Jackson.

"Of a different sort than yours, I'm sure, Mr. Gossling," she said. "Adele told me you used to be a policeman."

He stiffened. "I worked for the Anspach Detective Agency."

"You speak as if you're ashamed to admit it," Nin said. "Perhaps you ought to be."

"Don't believe everything you read in the papers about the Anspaches, Miss Branch."

"I seldom read papers," she snapped.

"I think Nin is right, Jack," said Adele. "You're different kinds of observers. Your gifts are logical while Nin's lie more in the spiritual."

"Oh?" He glanced at her, ducking from a hanging tree as he steered the horses. "Are you what they call a mesmerizing healer, Miss Branch?"

Adele could feel her friend's rage rising in the heat of the summer night. "Don't call me that! Don't ever call me that!"

Jackson shook the reins, and one of the horses let out a neigh. "I apologize if I've offended you." In a lighter tone, he added, "We ought to have gotten Tomas to drive us. He knows the waywardness of these country roads better than I do."

"At this time of night?" Adele asked. "I would sooner have woken up our hostess to bid her goodnight than tamper with the sleep of a man with five children under the age of fifteen."

"You're very gracious, Adele," Nin said in a soft voice.

They reached Bridge Street, and Jackson slowed the horses to a stop near Adele's shop. "Naturally we'll see you to your door."

"Naturally, you will not," Nin's voice rang in the empty night. "I've seen myself home many times."

"All the same, I insist." He laid the reins aside.

She jumped down from the wagon and looked squarely at him. "I've had the misfortune to come across gentlemen like you who try to feel superior in front of what they deem a 'fragile woman.' I'm not the least bit fragile, and, I suspect, neither is your sister. Perhaps you'll do us both the honor of allowing us to decide when we need your help." She pulled her wrap, a flimsy velvet thing without beads or ruffles, around her head like a scarf. "Goodnight, Adele. I shall see you tomorrow." She scurried into the building.

Adele burst out laughing at Jackson's startled face. Her laughter rang through the hollows of the empty street. She was sure Nin heard, as the woman glanced back. Had the lamps been closer together, she knew she would have seen her smiling.

As she and Jackson rode back, she took pity on him and suggested he stay the night. "You can't ride all the way back to San Francisco at this late hour," she insisted. "Think of the highwaymen and thieves. And the roads must be like a riverbed after that rain. Suppose the wheels got caught in the mud?"

"You haven't much faith in my driving," he remarked. "I won plenty of wagon races when I was a youngster."

"Exactly," she said. "When you were a youngster."

"You speak as if I am already an old man," he grumbled as they rounded Caliber Lane.

"Jack." Her voice lowered. "I'm not at all sure I like sleeping alone in such a big house."

He took her arm. "You'll get used to it, Del. You've only been here a short time."

"I'd like your company," she said. "Please stay."

He remained silent for a moment. "Is it because of what Mrs. Blackstone said about Lucy disappearing? Her father said she went to bed."

"It just seems odd." They entered the gate. "Lucy spent days planning the party. She must have come into my shop a dozen times, asking about everything from the finger sandwiches to the color of the napkins."

"A very accommodating hostess," he said with a nod.

"So why would such an accommodating hostess retire early from a party she planned so carefully?"

"Del, both of us have been to parties where the hostess retired early and left people to their own devices, relying on the servants to ensure no china would be broken or windows cracked."

"That was in the city." Adele stopped under a tree with large, sweeping leaves. "And what about Richard Tanning?"

"What about Richard Tanning?"

"Did you notice when the Tannings left, he wasn't with them?"

"Perhaps he left before they did," said Jackson. "God knows there were times when I wished I could do the same."

"But you never did, did you?" Adele pointed out.

"I was taught to endure every kind of annoyance," he said, "one of Father's most insistent lessons, if you recall."

"You were taught to be a gentleman," Adele said. "According to Lowell Tanning, so was his son."

The door flew open, and Tomas and his wife Ruth stood blocking the light. Tomas clasped his hands together, mumbling in Spanish. Ruth, much calmer, smiled and held out a knitted shawl, which Jackson put around Adele's shoulders.

"We were worried, señor and señorita," Tomas exclaimed.

"*He* was worried," Ruth corrected. They both spoke English well with only a small trace of an accent.

"Ruth, can you make up a bed in the room next to mine?"

Adele asked. "I've convinced my brother to stay the night rather than risk the road back to San Francisco."

"Very good, señorita." The woman nodded.

"Very good, very good." Tomas bowed. "Bad weather to ride tonight."

"I could make it, but I'm trying to be accommodating." Jackson smiled. "I've no clothes or anything of that sort."

"Not to worry, señor," Tomas assured him as he led him upstairs.

Once she was safely tucked in bed, Adele watched as the moon made patterns of light through the lace curtains. She realized the same moon had eluded the lace curtains on the French doors in the Blackstone house.

She woke early, seeing the sun make the same patterns through the curtains the moon had courted the night before. The air was a little chilly, and she threw on the knitted shawl Ruth had given her before she poured icy water in the basin and washed her face. She dressed quickly and put a dash of powder on her face, foregoing her usual dab of rouge, as Jackson hated seeing her too fresh-faced in the morning.

She peered inside the kitchen. Its stove already burned, and the coffee pot was sending up curls of steam. She smiled at Ruth scrutinizing a spot on a china plate while her eldest daughter, Maria, separated slices from the bacon with a knife.

"Is the coffee ready yet, Ruth?"

"Yes, señorita," said the woman. "I bring it to you."

"Jack likes his coffee very strong." Adele reached for the floral pot on the shelf. "He won't eat a bite without it. Very continental of him, don't you think?"

Before the woman could answer, the back door flew open, and Tomas rushed in. He seemed abandoned of all reason, words coming through in English and Spanish, none of it making sense. He was so pale, Ruth made him sit down, and Maria splashed a handful of cold water on his face.

"Señorita — lying on the ground — señorita — no move —"

"Calm yourself, Tomas," Adele ordered.

Between the ramblings and gesticulating hands, she managed to get the story out of him. He had gone outside early to sweep the porch and found a girl lying on the ground, and, though he was no expert in such things, he believed her to be "very dead."

Adele woke Jackson, who slept with the uncommon affection for the morning sun, and shoved a cup of strong coffee in his hands. When she told him what Tomas had found, they both were silent, neither looking out the window of his room, which looked out to the back part of the house.

Even though the girl was lying face down, they both knew it was Lucy. Adele almost screamed when she saw the gray blouse and red skirt caked with mud and torn at the hem.

"Jack what do we do?" she whispered.

Her brother was calm. "Tomas, run and get the sheriff."

"Sheriff, señor?" Tomas blinked.

"Oh, for God's sake!" The veins stood out on Jackson's neck. "The police, man, the police!"

"Where?"

"Ask around town!"

"Jack, there's no need to shout at the poor man," Adele said.

He took a breath. "I'm sorry. But this is very serious, Del."

"We realize that." She regained her composure.

Jackson pulled out his handkerchief. Adele expected him to wipe his damp face, but instead, he started folding something into it. Then he unfolded the handkerchief. "Mustn't touch anything," he mumbled.

"You know my friend Nin, Tomas?" Adele asked. The man nodded. "Her shop will be open now. Ask her to come and bring the sheriff with her." The man bowed and scurried away.

"We must tell the Blackstones." Adele leaned against the gazebo wall.

Jackson put his arm around her shoulders. "The police will do that, Del."

"I'm their neighbor!" Adele choked.

"All the more reason you have no right to interfere," he insisted.

"For God's sake, the girl is dead in my gazebo!" Her bones felt as if they were rattling. "They have a right to know."

Jackson blinked in the sunlight. He motioned toward Ruth lingering a few feet away, her hands clasped together, but altogether calmer than any of them. "Please go fetch Mr. Blackstone, Ruth, or send one of the older children. Don't tell him what happened. Say only that Mr. Gossling has asked him to come at once."

"Jack," said Adele, "did you ever accompany them to the crime scene?" The words seemed to startle him. "That's what this is now, isn't it? A crime scene?"

"Now and then."

"The best time to find evidence is when a body is fresh, isn't it?"

He glanced at her. "And how would *you* know something as gruesome as that?"

"I don't know," she said. "I'm only guessing. Don't you think you ought to look things over before the police get here?"

"Certainly not!"

"You're not some yellow journalist out for a morbid story," she pointed out. "You're a trained professional."

"And as a professional, I know enough to stay out of the way." He turned toward the house. "The police will be here soon, and then it will be in their hands."

Mr. Blackstone appeared wrapped in a silk robe and looking as if he had taken the time for a decent grooming. "What's this all about, Mr. Gossling?" He stopped, staring down at Lucy's sprawled body. He let out a howl and sank to his knees.

"Mr. Blackstone, I'm so sorry," Adele whispered.

"Please, sir." Jackson pressed his shoulders. "You mustn't disturb anything until the police get here."

"You are the police, aren't you?" Mr. Blackstone sprang up.

"I was a private detective," Jackson corrected.

"Well, then, do your duty!" He raised his voice.

"It isn't *my* duty, sir," said Jackson. "It's the duty of the police. I suggest you return to the house and wait for them."

"I have to know *something*." The man pleaded, "Please."

"You will when the police know enough to tell you."

The man's head snapped back. "Have you no compassion, man?"

"Mr. Blackstone." Jackson stood firm. "I really think you ought to go back home. Your family will be needing you."

The man's gray face set like ice. "Yes," Mr. Blackstone mumbled. "Yes, the family, must take care of them." He grabbed Jackson's hand. "You'll look around and come tell me what you found? Promise!"

"If you wish, sir," said Jackson with a gentle smile. "Maria, see Mr. Blackstone home."

The girl nodded and attempted to take Mr. Blackstone's arm, but, as if suddenly remembering his position, the man pushed him away and strode out to the road.

"Now are you convinced you must do something, Jack?" Adele asked. "That poor man, he's so broken up."

Jackson took out a handkerchief and knelt down, folding whatever it was he had dropped back in the handkerchief. Adele saw it was a striped carnation, tattered with dirt, its petals so opened, a few hung as if on hinges.

He inspected Lucy's shoes by gently probing at them with a stick. "Mud," he said. "Quite a lot of it."

"On her skirt too." Adele leaned over. "No leaves, though."

"But needles, yes." He lifted a handful of them clumped together with dry mud.

"Jack," said Adele, "those bushes you were talking about, remember?" He nodded. "These are the same."

"Lucy wasn't killed here, then," he said. "She was killed somewhere else and dragged here."

Adele felt dizzy again. Just as she dropped into a seat in the gazebo, a deep voice boomed, "Don't anyone touch anything!"

Coming toward them was someone twice the height and size of any man Adele knew. He was middle-aged with curly brown hair and exacting dark eyes. The rough redness of his skin was somewhat veiled by a short V-shaped mustache. The sturdiness of his figure did not come from corpulence but from buoyancy. He was dressed in a morning suit, but the silver star pinned to his lapel told of his position. Several young men trailed behind him, some of them looking hardly older than boys. Adele realized this was the Arrojo police – perhaps all of it.

Nin followed them, draped in one of her flowing dresses. She stood against a tree that hung over the gazebo, clutching it for support as she stared down at Lucy.

"I told you," Jackson whispered. He cleared his throat. "I assure you, Sheriff, nothing has been disturbed."

"Good man." He produced a roll of paper from his pocket. "Edison!" The boom echoed so loudly that a pair of birds, disturbed of their sleep, flew out of the tree where Nin stood.

A young man of no more than twenty sped forward. "Yes, sir?"

"Have some of the lads stand guard from here–" he indicated the beginning of the veranda, "— to here —" He pointed at the brush in the direction of the Blackstone house.

"Just a moment!" Adele stepped forward.

The man fumbled in his pocket and came up with a handkerchief, which he wiped his face. "Morning, miss. And you are?"

"And *you* are?" Adele gave him a square look.

He seemed undisturbed. "Sheriff Horatio Hatfield. I'm also the county coroner and, I suspect, a few other titles before the year is out."

Adele hid a smile. "I own this house, Sheriff. I'm Adele Gossling."

"Oh, yes," he said. "The new lady in town. I've been told quite a lot about you." He tipped his hat.

"I'm sure you have," she said dryly. "I'd like to know why you're ordering police on my property."

"Not your property, Miss Gossling," he said. "The crime scene. Always must watch for curiosity seekers and muckrakers."

"I'm glad to see you're progressive with police practices, Sheriff," Jackson said.

"We're not entirely in the backwoods, sir," said the man. "And you name? Edi-son!"

"Jackson Gossling." He held out his hand. "Miss Gossling is my sister."

"Jack has already discovered a few interesting things, Sheriff," said Adele.

The man's thick eyebrow flew up. "Has he?"

"You didn't expect us to wait when we had a professional in the house, did you?' Adele's face gleamed with pride. "Jack worked for the Anspaches."

"Their methods are different from the police's, miss," said the man. "Vigilante methods, as a matter of fact."

"I agree," said Jackson. "Which is why I left them."

"He's glad to be of any assistance to you and your men." A quick survey of the three boys mulling around the veranda, now fully equipped with coffee cups and thick slices of toast, showed they were hardly past manhood. "I dare say you look as if you need it."

She expected the sheriff to be offended, but the man threw back his head and let out a hearty laugh.

"Del, I'm sure the sheriff has no need of my help," her brother mumbled.

"We shall see, we shall see." The man stood with his hands on his hips. "So you've started already, Mr. Gossling. What have you found so far?"

"Miss Blackstone wasn't murdered here," he said. "That I'm fairly certain of. There's mud on her skirt and shoes." He showed him the clump of needles. "Her body was dragged from somewhere in the brush."

"Very keen observations. Edison!" The young man scurried forward with the twine twisted in his hands. "Get some of the lads to block off this section of the street too. The young woman lived next door, didn't she?" He indicated to the house nearby.

Adele nodded. "Lucy is — was — the daughter of Michael and Marissa Blackstone."

"Yes, I know." Sheriff Hatfield looked sad for a moment, then glared at Edison who was still lingering. "Well, go to it, lad!" The young man scurried away. "Anything else you want to tell me about, Mr. Gossling?"

"Just this." He handed him the handkerchief.

Sheriff Hatfield slipped on a pair of silk gloves and examined the carnation. "The girl was wearing it, I assume."

Jackson nodded. "It seems Lucy's carnations were infamous in these parts."

"I seem to recall my ma telling me something of the sort." He folded the flower inside the handkerchief as carefully as Jackson had wrapped it and handed it to one of the loitering young men. "You surprise me, Mr. Gossling. I've met many Anspach, and they always struck me more as men of action than observation."

"Perhaps that's another reason why I left." Jackson grimaced. "If you don't mind, I'd like to get my breakfast now. I think you should too, Del. And Miss Branch, of course, if she's had none." He started toward the house.

"I heard the Anspach never abandon their duty," said Hatfield.

Jackson spun around. "I beg your pardon?"

"I've met detectives who never reached such conclusions as

you have until days or even weeks into the investigation," said Hatfield. "That tells me something about your skills, sir."

"I gather that's a compliment," said Jackson. "But as I said, I'm no longer an Anspach."

"Nevertheless, once a detective, always a detective," the sheriff remarked.

"Not I, sir." Jackson stiffened. "I shouldn't even be here if it wasn't for my sister asking me to stay here last night."

"A lucky thing it was too," Adele chimed in.

"You don't want interference from an outsider, Sheriff," Jackson insisted.

The man continued, "A very great lawman taught me when one has the opportunity and the knowledge to fight for justice, one must do so." For a moment, there was a fading look in his eyes. "I shall be frank with you, sir. I'm dealing with lads." His hand swept toward the veranda where a few of the young men still dawdled. "Good boys, but lacking a little in quick wit and deduction, shall we say. I need all the help I can get."

Jackson remained silent. Everyone was watching, from Tomas to Nin, who was still leaning against the tree.

"Are you asking for my aid with the investigation, Sheriff?" he asked in a careful voice.

"Assuming you've nothing better to do with your time." He eyed him. "Am I right?"

Jackson gave a small smile. "You have good observations yourself, sir."

"Well, what do you say?"

Adele watched as her brother examined the ivy entwined with an angel carving on the gazebo wall. "Considering I knew the girl slightly, I suppose it's as you said — I have a duty now to help find her killer."

Sheriff Hatfield grinned. "Edison! Bring us all some breakfast."

"I'll get it," said Adele. As she passed by her brother, she squeezed his arm.

When she came back with the tray of coffee and toast, Jackson and the sheriff were crouched over Lucy.

"Strangled, poor girl," said Hatfield. "What do you make of these?" He pointed to Lucy's neck.

Adele set the tray on the gazebo bench and glanced at the dead girl's head. She had never been ashamed of the more violent parts of life, whether an amputated leg of a factory worker during one of her hospital rounds or a prostitute's mauled face in a settlement house.

She saw what the sheriff meant. There were marks on Lucy's neck, sunk deep into the skin. The tiny globes created a perforated line across her throat.

"The pearls!" Adele gasped. "Jack, the lilac pearls she was wearing at the party last night. My God, he strangled her with the pearls."

Hatfield balanced his hands on his bent knees. "I hope you don't take offense, Miss Gossling, but are you one of these women who aims rocks into the windows of politicians' houses and chains herself to their gate?"

"If you mean, Sheriff, am I a suffragist," Adele said, "the answer is yes. However, I have never thrown a rock nor chained myself to a gate in my life. I believe there are better, more peaceful ways for women to win their rights."

"I'm glad of that," said the man. "Now, will you explain to me what pearls and what party last night?"

As she spoke, Hatfield examined the gazebo floor, circling the body. "These are the pearls in question?" He opened his hand to reveal two violet globes shining in the sunlight. "Their size matches the grooves on Miss Blackstone's neck."

"It seems odd she would have worn the pearls without the party dress," Adele murmured.

"Perhaps my theory about her being murdered elsewhere is wrong," Jackson remarked.

"Not necessarily," said Hatfield. "If she had been murdered here, we would have found many more." He cupped the pearls in his gloved hand. "A few caught in that blouse she's wearing when the body was dragged."

"A crime of opportunity," Jackson suggested. "The murderer used what was on hand."

"We shall see. Edison!"

The young man appeared, slightly shaken, and Hatfield carefully wrapped the pearls in a piece of paper.

Adele joined Nin near the tree, comforted by the slight scent of mint surrounding her. "It's so distressing, isn't it?" she whispered.

Nin shrugged. "I don't really see, it but I feel it."

"Feel what?"

"The cold," said Nin. "She's been chilly all night."

"Well, it was a cold night," Adele pointed out. "And if she's been lying there that long —" She shivered.

"That has nothing to do with it," Nin insisted.

"Sheriff," Adele said. "Perhaps Lucy was in a hurry to go somewhere last night."

"You mean a *rendezvous*?" He glanced at her.

She blushed. "She wasn't that sort of young lady. A little flirtatious, maybe, but there was no harm in her."

A young man appeared at her side, making her jump. He looked like a caricature of an owl with large eyes beneath magnified eyeglasses and a moony face.

The sheriff greeted him. "Good morning, Mr. Sanders. We haven't interrupted your breakfast, I hope?" He introduced the young man as the medical examiner's assistant.

"That's more in the line of Doctor Rhodes' peculiarities, Sheriff, not mine," Mr. Sanders laughed.

"Where is the good doctor?" Hatfield sniffed.

"Having his breakfast, sir," said the young man in a sheepish tone.

The sheriff snorted. "I can't say I'm surprised. I shouldn't think Rhodes would interrupt his hotcakes for a possible murder case."

"Probable, sir, not possible," Jackson said. "It *is* murder."

"My first murder case," Mr. Sanders sighed.

"Don't look so wistful, lad," said Hatfield. "You may have many more."

The young man slipped off his jacket and rolled up his sleeves. "Dr. Rhodes has given me full authority as usual, Sheriff."

"I should think in such a case as this, the doctor would want to be here himself," Jackson observed as he moved out of the way.

"Mr. Sanders is as capable of his job as you are of yours, Mr. Gossling," said Sheriff Hatfield.

The young man set down his bag and bent over the body. "I've examined many dead bodies in my time, sir. I did two years with the leper colony down near the border."

"I didn't mean to imply there was any question of your skills, Mr. Sanders," Jackson said.

"If you'll kindly all step back." The young man opened his bag.

Ruth brought out more coffee and toast. Adele tried to coax Nin to eat something, but the young woman refused, holding on to the tree as if it were her only anchor. Her shoulders and arms pressed closer to her body as if preparing for a storm.

Mr. Sanders brushed away the ivy stuck to his trousers and closed his bag. "Death by strangulation."

"You're certain?" the sheriff asked.

He nodded. "It happened very quickly, so I don't think she suffered much."

"I'm sure her family will be relieved to hear that," Hatfield said.

"Oh, and I picked this up under the skirt." He handed him a sheet of pale violet paper.

"The time of death?"

"She's been dead probably about ten or eleven hours," said Mr. Sanders.

"That's rather vague, sir."

"I imagine that would put Lucy's death between ten and eleven o'clock last night," Jackson supplied.

Hatfield nodded. "I apologize for my impatience, Mr. Sanders, but no one comes out alive at sea if they tell the captain the gale will rise at some hour of the morning."

"Lucky we're not at sea, then," Mr. Sanders mumbled. To Jackson, he said in a low voice, "Sheriff Hatfield was the captain of the *Lordes* for ten years, and I shouldn't wonder if he sometimes forgets he's on dry land now." He tipped his hat to the ladies. "You'll have my report in a few hours."

"Well, it seems clear where our duty lies, Jackson," said Hatfield. "Now we must roll up our sleeves and get to work."

"What about the inquest, sir?" Jackson asked.

The sheriff chuckled. "You've just witnessed it. We do things rather informally here."

"You're not going to leave her here?" Adele shivered.

"I'll be back soon to take the body to the doctor's office," Mr. Sanders assured her.

"Were there signs of any struggle?" Jackson called out as they headed toward the road.

The medical examiner's assistant glanced back over his shoulder. "None that I could find."

"No struggle," Jackson lamented. "She knew the killer then."

"Him or her," Hatfield added. "I've met some charming women stranglers in my time." He cleared his throat. "Begging the ladies' pardon."

Nin's head leaned away from the tree as she stared intently at Lucy's immobile body.

"I think it's time we had her taken away," Hatfield said. "Edison! Get the lads to cover up the poor thing and get her out of here."

"Wait!" Nin came into the gazebo and knelt at Lucy's side. She stared into the deadened face.

"Don't touch a thing!" The sheriff rushed forward.

Adele grabbed his arm. "I don't think she intends to," she said in a low voice.

She closed her eyes and clasped her hands together under her chin as if in prayer. She was so motionless. Adele thought for a moment that she had stopped breathing. Suddenly, Nin opened her eyes and stared for what seemed like a long moment. Then, she rose. "Someone lost his grasp in love and anger."

Hatfield took off his hat and brushed the rim. "I've heard things about your being a mesmerizer of sorts, Miss Branch."

The word made Nin lunge at him. "I am *not* a mesmerizer!"

Adele grabbed her by the shoulders in time. "It's all right, dear." To the sheriff, she said, "Miss Branch is no charlatan, Sheriff. She's a clairvoyant."

A subtle but incredulous scoff rose from Jackson.

"I never thought she was," said the sheriff.

"I inherited from my mother a gift for reading vibrations," Nin ventured. "I suppose that sounds mad or evil to you."

"Not in the least," he said kindly. The woman's face relaxed.

"You said 'his,'" said Adele. "Does that mean the killer is a man?"

"Really, I don't think–" Jackson started but she glared at him.

"A man, yes," said Nin.

"Yes, well, I take every bit of information into consideration." The sheriff buttoned his coat. "I don't think there's much more we can do here. Miss Gossling, tell your people not to touch anything back here until the body has been removed."

"I must go home." Nin looked as if the spark of life had deflated from her face. Her skin was almost gray and her eyes heavy.

"Edison will accompany you." The sheriff raised his hand at the young man.

"Really, it isn't necessary," she insisted.

"You look as if you're about to faint, Miss Branch," he said. "I won't have that on my hands. Edison!"

The young man immediately came to order and seemed happy to lead Nin away, stealing glances at her rare beauty as they walked slowly down the street.

# CHAPTER 8

By Monday, Jackson had been to the city and back, bringing several suitcases with him and settling in the room across from hers. Adele was happy he had chosen to stay with her rather than the Arrojo Hotel even as she was saddened by the circumstances that brought him there.

Around noon the next day, her brother and Sheriff Hatfield entered her shop. Jackson looked grave but Hatfield was almost bouncing. "The official papers have been filed," the sheriff said. "Now we have license to see the family," he said. "I'd like you to come with us, Miss Gossling."

"I'm no law woman." She shrugged.

"No, but I've observed you have a certain sensitivity, and Mrs. Blackstone is likely to be more comfortable with a woman there."

"She may be indisposed, sir," Jackson pointed out.

"She may be," the sheriff agreed. "Nonetheless, duty is duty."

Adele got her hat and they set out for the Blackstones'. As they turned onto Caliber Street, the horizon was dotted with the dark suits of Hatfield's lads, along with a few dung-colored overalls.

"What are they searching for, Sheriff?" she asked.

"Anything and everything," he said. "If the body was dragged to your back yard, as we believe, something may have been left behind."

"A clue, you mean." She smiled. "I read detective stories occasionally."

"Speaking of clues —" Hatfield extracted the lavender sheet of paper the medical examiner had given him and examined it. "Looks to be an exclusive design and make."

"It is," said Adele. "I sold it to her."

Hatfield's eyebrows perked with interest. "When was this?"

"A week or so ago." She switched her parasol from her right hand to her left as it hit a tree, sending a sprinkle of dust onto her hat. "Lucy made the design herself."

"She had quite a liking for the color purple, I see." Jackson examined the stationery. "Why, it's blank!"

"A blank sheet of letter paper," said Hatfield. "On a dead body. Curious."

"Sheriff," said Adele. "I believe she kept the stationery a secret. She insisted I give it to her when we were alone, and I'm quite sure her parents didn't even know she had purchased it."

"Notes to a secret admirer," Jackson guessed. "Or a secret lover."

"It's not uncommon among young ladies of her standing to be melodramatic with their affections," Hatfield said with a nod.

"Perhaps it was more than melodrama," Adele murmured.

"Why do you say that, Miss Gossling?" the sheriff asked.

"I don't know." Adele shut her parasol as he opened the front gate of the Blackstone house. "It's more a feeling."

"Another clairvoyant in our midst." Jackson raised an eye at Hatfield.

"I don't want you to tease her, Jack," Adele said. "I like Nin."

"I said I take all information into consideration and I meant it," said Hatfield. He took Adele's arm as he led her over a pile of muddy leaves. "You and Miss Branch may say what you like, Miss Gossling."

She smiled. "For that, you may call me Adele."

The command in his stance left him for a moment, and he looked almost like a sheepish young boy.

The door opened to their knock and the Blackstone butler stood, looking grim in the dark suit. The family had wasted no time in preparing for mourning. A black wreath hung on the door, and the mirror and picture in the front hall were draped with black sheets.

Ignoring the sheriff, he bowed to the Gosslings. Hatfield seemed well versed in dealing with servile smugness. He removed his hat and gloves and said in an authoritative voice, "Please tell Mr. and Mrs. Blackstone Sheriff Horatio Hatfield would like to see them."

Mr. Blackstone strolled out to the hall. His face had regained its color, and the black suit looked as crisp as the one the butler wore. "Please keep your voices down. My wife is asleep."

"I must ask you to wake her, sir," Hatfield said. "We're now authorized to investigate your daughter's murder."

"I will not wake up my wife," he insisted. "The doctor has given her a sedative. Lucy was our only daughter, so you can well imagine how all this has been a shock to her."

"Yes, yes, of course." The sheriff's voice softened. "Forgive my impertinence. One becomes accustomed to speaking like a boor when one has dealt with insolent seamen and criminals."

Mr. Blackstone turned to the butler. "James, please bring coffee into the drawing room."

"Yes, sir." The man bowed.

"And, James," Sheriff Hatfield added, "please gather the servants and have them wait in the dining hall. I would like to speak with all of them."

James glanced at his employer, who nodded. "Yes, sir."

As they settled in the drawing room, Adele couldn't help but remember the first time she had come there and how keenly she felt the room's excessive sunlight under the scrutiny of the Blackstones. She saw Lucy's swirling skirt, her idealistic impressions of San Francisco, her insistence of the party. Tears gathered in her eyes, and she fished into her silk bag for a handkerchief.

"Here, dear." Jackson put his own handkerchief in her lap. Even as children, he had anticipated her moods, knowing when to deliver a calming touch, a handkerchief, or a listening ear.

Mr. Blackstone seemed to understand as well. "This was her favorite room," he said. "We preferred to read in the upstairs parlor, but Lucy was always down here or in her garden."

"Who will tend the garden now?" Adele asked.

"I will," he said.

A throat cleared and they looked at the sheriff, poised with a leather-cased pad and pencil. "I don't wish to upset you more than you already are, sir, but I must ask these questions."

"I understand, Sheriff." Mr. Blackstone lit a cigar.

"When did you and your wife last see your daughter?"

"My wife saw her at around eleven-thirty the night of the party," he said. "We were having a party. I'm sure the Gosslings told you."

"You say your wife saw her at that time," said the man. "And you?"

"I went up to Lucy's room at around midnight and looked in," he said. "I assumed she was asleep, so I didn't disturb her."

"You assumed?" Jackson leaned forward.

"I didn't actually enter the room," he admitted. "I opened the door a crack and glanced in. I thought I saw a figure in the bed. Lucy is – was – a very light sleeper, so anything more would have awakened her."

"When did the party end?" asked the sheriff.

"About an hour later."

"So your daughter left the party early?" the sheriff inquired.

"She was very tired," Mr. Blackstone insisted. "She said as much to a few of her friends."

"We'll need to speak to everyone who was at the party," said Hatfield.

Mr. Blackstone stiffened. "My reputation as a host would hardly be enhanced in this community if everyone who attended a party at my house was afraid of being questioned by the police."

"I can't help that, sir," Hatfield said with equal stiffness. "We're trying to find out who killed your daughter."

Mr. Blackstone's hands dropped to his sides.

The butler entered and set down the tray of coffee. "I'll serve, James," he said in a rough voice. As he lifted the coffee pot, it shook sideways, showing his composure was perhaps not as steady as Adele first thought. She caught his hand in time.

"Allow me, Mr. Blackstone," she said.

He stared at his knees as Adele spread the cups around. "I don't even know how she died," he mused.

"We needn't go into details," the sheriff said.

"Damn it, man, I have a right to know!" He grabbed Jackson's wrist. "I'm asking *you*. How?"

"She was strangled," Jackson said in a low voice.

"I can see you're not telling me the whole truth." The man's voice began to crack.

"Mr. Blackstone, please don't upset yourself," Adele said.

"Sir, was your daughter wearing a string of pearls at that party she gave for Miss Gossling?" the sheriff asked.

"Yes, she was," he said.

"We found evidence of the pearls, but she was wearing a gray shirt and red skirt when we found her," said Hatfield.

"I'm well aware of that," said Mr. Blackstone. "I did manage to see her before you came. The Gosslings were kind enough to notify me as soon as they found her."

"But you didn't know how she was killed?" Hatfield asked quietly. "The bruises on her neck were fairly clear."

"I wasn't looking at her neck!"

"No, of course not." Hatfield cleared his throat. "It seems clear she didn't go to bed as you thought that night."

"That's impossible." The man glared at him. "I tell you, I saw her asleep."

"When I was at sea, many a seaman used to fill his bed with pillows and go out on deck to smoke a pipe or play a game of cards," said Hatfield, leaning back. "The guard on duty never noticed."

Mr. Blackstone's face became hard. "What exactly are you implying?"

"It's possible your daughter told her friends she was tired so they would believe she had gone to bed."

The man leapt up, knocking over his coffee cup. "My daughter was not that sort of girl!"

Hatfield seemed unalarmed by the man's glaring eyes. "No one is implying she was, Mr. Blackstone," said Jackson. "But young women do sometimes keep things from their families."

"Not Lucy," said the man. "Not from me."

"Even the closest of father's daughters don't tell their fathers everything," Adele murmured. She felt her brother's eyes on her.

"Perhaps not, Miss Gossling, but Lucy was not that way." The man slowly sat down. "She told me everything. Everything."

"The sheriff is merely trying to establish some facts," Jackson said.

"These are not facts, sir, but insulting insinuations." All at once, he regained his equilibrium. "I don't deny, though, that Lucy could be, well, rather impulsive at times."

"Capricious," Adele murmured.

The man glanced at her. "She was easily swayed to adventure, but never indiscreetly." His voice broke.

"Naturally not," Adele said in a gentle voice. This seemed to calm the man.

"Mr. Blackstone," Hatfield continued, "this was found near your daughter." He unfolded the blank sheet of lavender stationery. "Have you ever seen this before?" The man shook his head. "Miss Gossling confirmed Lucy ordered this stationery from her store about two weeks ago. Lucy designed it herself."

Mr. Blackstone fingered the raised carnation buds. "Yes. It was her style."

"And you're sure you've never seen it before?" Jackson asked.

"Lucy could buy whatever she wished," he said. "She had a trust left to her by my wife's father when she was eighteen. It wasn't much but certainly enough to spend what she pleased." He reached into his pocket for his handkerchief but pulled it back quickly.

"Do you know if your wife has ever seen it?" asked the sheriff.

"I'm quite certain she hasn't." The man suddenly looked at him. "Why is this important?"

"Can you think of a reason, sir, why your daughter would purchase stationery without telling you?"

"I just told you, she often –" His face grew red. "I see what you mean. As I told you before, Sheriff –"

"Can you think of why a blank sheet of paper would be found on your daughter's person?" Hatfield interrupted.

Mr. Blackstone was silent, kneading one hand in the other.

"Mr. Blackstone?" Jackson touched the man's arm. "You *do* have an idea, don't you?"

"Once, when she was a little girl, my father told her she should believe nothing unless it was written down," he said. "You know how children can take what an adult will tell them and make a prophecy out of it. Lucy took it very seriously."

"But nothing's written on the page," Adele pointed out.

"That's precisely the point," he said. "Perhaps she meant to write something and never got the chance." He rose and stared out the French windows. From the gleam of the light, Adele could see tears roll down his cheeks.

"Have you any idea what she might have wanted to write down?" Hatfield asked.

"Hang it, if I knew, I would tell you!"

The sheriff adjusted the tails of his jacket. "I'm sorry to have distressed you, sir. I won't take up any more of your time for now, but I would like to see Mrs. Blackstone the moment the doctor allows it."

"I understand, Sheriff."

"And now, we would be most obliged if you would allow us to see your daughter's room."

The man's face grew white. "It's out of the question!"

"I'm sorry, sir, but we must insist." Hatfield was mild but firm.

"What earthly reason do you have for wanting to see her room?"

"We believe your daughter went out during the party," the sheriff said. "Perhaps something in her room could give us a clue as to where she went and why."

"We know where she went," Mr. Blackstone said. "To Miss Gossling's gazebo. She wanted a change of scenery, I presume." He looked at Adele.

"She was killed elsewhere," said Hatfield. "We've established that."

The man could hardly control his emotions. "None of this makes any sense, Sheriff."

"I promise you, sir, we'll make sense of everything," he assured him. "We'll find out who did this to your daughter and why."

Jackson cleared his throat. "Now if we may see Lucy's room."

Mr. Blackstone let the men file out of the room, but as Adele followed, he grabbed her hand. "Miss Gossling, a word." He lowered his voice. "I realize these are unusual circumstances but you won't let them disturb anything, will you? You'll see to it they're respectful."

"Of course, Mr. Blackstone."

"It's highly intrusive." His voice became agitated. "Strange men in my daughter's room. Most distressing."

"I'll see everything remains just as it was, Mr. Blackstone," Adele promised.

As they climbed the stairs, she couldn't help but think that, had it been her, her father wouldn't have given a damn whether police turned her room upside down as long as they found what they needed to catch her killer. But then, her father had known the workings of the law.

# CHAPTER 9

The room was as Adele would have expected of a young woman with indulgent parents and her own inheritance. Laces and frills permeated the four-poster bed, heavy wardrobe and chiffonier. A vanity table stood near the window piled with ribbons, bottles and jars. Jackson examined that while Sheriff Hatfield tackled the drawers and closets. She saw Mr. Blackstone need not have worried. The sheriff, though meticulous, was discreet and delicate, using gloves to go through the drawers.

Her brother removed the middle drawer of the vanity table, which revealed a hidden compartment. Behind it was the packet of letter paper she had sold Lucy.

Sheriff Hatfield peered across his shoulder. "Seems you were right, Adele. Miss Blackstone didn't want her parents to know about the stationery."

"She said she had a special use in mind for it," she murmured.

"So it seems," he said in a dry voice.

Adele fingered the grooming set fit for a princess encased in silver roses. A jewelry box sat majestically underneath the mirror. She examined the trinkets of gold and precious stones.

"Jack, the bracelet Lucy wore at the party is missing," she said.

The sheriff poked his head out of the closet.

"Lucy wore a charm bracelet," she explained. "It wasn't on her wrist when we found her either."

"Not that I remember." Jackson glanced at the sheriff.

"Was there anything particularly special about it?" asked Hatfield.

"She hung rings on it," said Adele. "She said she couldn't wear them on her fingers so she had to wear them that way."

"What funny ideas young ladies have," the sheriff lamented.

"I believe the word you're groping for is 'whims?'" Jackson asked dryly.

"Do you think *he* might have taken it?" Adele asked. "The murderer, that is?"

"He or she," Hatfield corrected. "It's possible." He brushed himself off as he emerged from the closet. "We'll check the evidence we have again when we get back to the station."

Just then, the door opened to admit Mickey.

Sheriff Hatfield removed his gloves. "Who is this little fellow?"

The boy ran to Adele and encircled her waist. "Is Lucy really not coming back?"

Pity rose in her chest. "No, Mickey. She's gone to a better place."

"But why?" He began to cry.

"These things happen, darling." She stroked his head.

"Papa says God sometimes takes people away because they're bad." He peered up at Adele. "Do you think Lucy was bad?"

"No, sweet." She kissed the top of his head. "Lucy was good."

"She said the good man would make her good." He buried his cheek in her skirt. "I heard her say so."

Jackson took the boy by the shoulders. "When did she say this, Mickey?"

"At the party," he said. "I was supposed to be asleep." He blinked. "You won't tell Papa?"

"We won't tell Papa anything," Hatfield said. "Mickey, what else did Lucy tell you?"

"She said she had to see the good man," he said. "She was going to see the good man and someday I would understand." He frowned. "Why do grown-ups always say I'll understand someday? What day is someday?"

"Mickey!" His father appeared at the doorway. "Your lunch is getting cold."

The boy looked at Adele a little longer before he took his father's hand.

"So Lucy was going to meet a man," Jackson said.

"Did you notice her paying special attention to anyone at the party?" Hatfield inquired. "Or anyone paying special attention to her?"

"Not particularly," said Adele. "You must remember she was the hostess. People are going to pay attention to the hostess whether they want to or not."

"Nobody stealing away from the party that you noticed?" he asked.

"We did see a few people, remember, Del?" said Jackson. "We saw Richard Tanning slip out the side door in the hallway and his father a little while later."

"Indeed?" The sheriff's heavy brows perked up.

"Now that I think of it, it did seem as if Lucy and Richard were dancing together a great deal," said Adele.

"Oh, I don't think we can jump to that conclusion," Jackson said. "Lucy was the belle of the ball. Every time I looked at her, she was dancing with someone."

"And every time *I* looked at her, she was dancing with Richard," Adele retorted.

"I've heard of the Tannings, of course," said Hatfield. "It's a devilish thing, not having a chance to meet people formally before being dragged into a murder investigation."

"You most likely wouldn't have met Richard," said Jackson. "He's been away at school and just came back."

"The family owns some property in the area," said Adele. "Mr. Blackstone calls it a swamp, but he may be exaggerating. It's quite clear he and Lowell Tanning didn't get along."

"Oh?" said the sheriff. "We shall have to find out more about that."

His heels were cracking down the stairs, thumping across the wooden boards. Mr. Blackstone looked clearly annoyed.

"My wife is still asleep, Sheriff," he growled. "If you've finished your business —"

"Not quite, I'm afraid," he said. "I'd like to see the ballroom where that party took place, Mr. Blackstone. And then, if you would be so kind as to remember, you gave me permission to speak to your servants."

"Do what you will," said the man in a stiff voice.

"No, sir," said Hatfield. "I'll do what I must."

It looked as if Mr. Blackstone finally reached his limit. His face blackened and the collar of his suit strained against his neck. In a cold voice, he said, "I will tell Jones he is to help you with anything you need. If you'll excuse me, I must attend to a wife devastated by the loss of her only daughter and a son who cannot understand why the sister with whom he was playing jacks only a few days ago is now in heaven!" He turned on his heels and strolled out, leaving a frosty air in his wake.

"Perhaps you were a little too abrupt with him, Sheriff," Adele suggested.

"I can't help that," Hatfield said. "We have a murderer to find."

"And every minute counts," Jackson added.

James showed them into the ballroom.

"I can't imagine what you think you'll find, Sheriff," Adele remarked. "The servants cleared every morsel of the party ages ago."

"One can never tell." He examined the floor. "We already

know the body was dragged from somewhere. It could have easily been from some hidden corner in this house."

"In a house this size, it's entirely possible," Jackson agreed.

"I beg your pardon, sir." James cleared his throat. "Mr. Blackstone was most particular about people straying too far from the ballroom. For young Mickey's sake."

"Young boys are always afraid of missing all the excitement," Jackson said ruefully.

"He particularly asked the servants to redirect anyone who wandered past the hallway," James continued.

"But Mr. and Miss Gossling said they saw some people going out the back door."

"Yes, sir," said the man. "It leads to the veranda. Mr. Blackstone had no objection to guests going out for a bit of fresh air."

"Can you show us?"

James led them to the hall and opened the back door. The lace curtains seemed limper than they had been a few nights before. Japanese paper lanterns were still strung up, though not lit.

"It must have been quite a spectacle out here," The sheriff remarked, eyeing them.

"We wouldn't know," said Jackson. "Neither Adele nor I ventured outside."

"Quite content to watch the intrigues going on inside, eh?" Hatfield eyed him.

"Quite." Jackson's voice was guarded. "If Lucy was killed out here and dragged, there would be a mark somewhere."

"I scarcely think it's possible that she was killed here, Sheriff," said Adele.

"And why is that?"

"The lights." She steadied a swinging lantern with her parasol. "They would have illuminated even the slightest movement. The curtains were drawn in the ballroom and as you can see, that room overlooks this part of the veranda."

"I see you and your brother both inherited strong powers of observation," said Hatfield with a gleam in his eye.

"Del's talent is pure nosiness," Jackson said. "Ever since she was a child, she slid in between shadows, watching and listening."

"I'd rather be a snake than a bunny like most of the young ladies you've courted," Adele retorted. The sheriff laughed.

Edison, cap tilted to one side and coat askew, bounded up the porch stairs.

"Be careful, man or you'll break a step," the sheriff growled.

"Sorry, sir," said the young man. "But — well — we've found something."

# CHAPTER 10

They followed him into the brush that led back toward Adele's house. As they neared the shrubbery, she saw a mass of matted grasses and swept bushes as if someone had gone through it with a plow. They reached a circle of wild flowers hidden among tall bushes.

Sheriff Hatfield gazed into the circle for a few moments. He turned to Jackson and said in a final voice, "Our crime scene."

Adele observed how the grasses were overturned, the brush torn, and deep lines formed in the mud.

"But the medical examiner said there were no signs of a struggle," Jackson pointed out.

"Adversary," the sheriff pronounced. His lips were thin and white. "Whoever killed Miss Blackstone did so with extreme violence."

"I can't believe anyone would do that to Lucy," Adele said.

"You only knew her for a short time, Del." Jackson took her hand. "You can't know what enemies she might have had."

"And look at this, Sheriff!" Edison grinned, one hand pointing to the mud.

"Footprints." Hatfield nodded.

"A man's footprints," Jackson said. "Heavy boots."

"They're going toward the house, not away from it," said Adele. "Odd."

Hatfield followed the footsteps in the direction of Adele's house. Between the gate and cypress tree, the footprints gave way to smooth ground.

"Ruth's already swept, hang it," Jackson grumbled. It was the first time Adele could remember him not minding his manners in front of her.

"I don't think there was anything to sweep," said the sheriff. "Edison!" The young man came running. "Get some twine around these hedges so no one can get through. It's part of our crime scene now. And get the man to make some plaster imprints of all the footprints you can find."

"Yes, sir."

"And don't for a moment think I won't know if you missed one," he barked.

As they walked back, he said, "We begin to get the picture now, eh?"

"Lucy has a *rendezvous* with someone the night of the party," said Jackson. "She tells everyone she's tired and goes up to her room on the pretense of going to bed. Then she sneaks out again and comes to the spot in the bush. Her killer was someone she knew, someone she was going to meet. The killer does the deed, then drags the body to the gazebo and leaves it there."

"Why not throw the body in Tanning's swamp?" asked Adele. "If it is indeed a swamp."

"Because it's too far away and someone might see him," Jackson argued.

"Or," said Hatfield, "it is a swamp of some depth and the killer knew we might never have found it. The killer wanted us to find Lucy. I'm certain of that."

"Why?"

"Ah, question marks, question marks," Hatfield sighed.

They entered the house again and James jumped to attention.

"Are the servants gathered, James?" asked the sheriff.

"In the kitchen, sir."

"Good," he said. "You don't think your cook could rustle us up some more coffee, do you? All this exercise has made me famished." He glanced back at the Gosslings as they followed the butler down the back stairs.

Adele leaned forward. "James, is there a gardener who takes care of the grounds?"

"No, miss," he said. "Mr. Blackstone sees to it himself. He rather likes natural surroundings."

Hatfield glanced back. "The answer to the riddle, then."

"I beg your pardon, sir?" The butler stopped

"We were wondering about the wild brush beyond the house," said Hatfield. "I imagine Mr. Blackstone hasn't the time or inclination to tend to them."

"Oh, it's not that, sir," said the man. "Mr. Blackstone insists on keeping that area untamed. He says it reminds him of the days when his father first settled here as a young man."

All the Blackstone servants were lined up in the pleasantly warm kitchen. Adele was surprised to see only five of them besides James – an elderly woman in a cook's uniform, two younger women in much-laundered aprons, and two young men.

"A smaller staff than one would expect in a house this size," she muttered.

"Mr. Blackstone, miss, does not believe in excessive help. I quite agree with him." The last was said with satisfaction and Adele imagined he found it much easier to lord over a small staff than a large one.

"Where is the servants' hall?" Hatfield asked.

James nodded toward the room separated by glass doors.

"Have coffee served to us there, if you will, and each one come in to speak to us when they're called."

A whimper escaped one of the young women with a tattered

apron and the elderly cook said in a soft voice, "Calm yourself, dear." Adele gave her a reassuring smile as they entered the servants' hall, trying to reassure the girl.

"James, you'll be so kind as to join us," Hatfield called over his shoulder.

He questioned the butler as they were served a lavish coffee. "You did not see Miss Blackstone go out the night of the party?"

"Hardly, sir," said James. "I was too busy directing the servants. Perhaps one of the footmen."

"I saw at least four footmen wandering about that night," said Jackson. "There were only two young men in the kitchen."

"That is correct, sir," said James. "Mr. Edwin Goodwin is Mr. Blackstone's valet. The other gentleman, Mr. Ralph Rawlings, is our only permanent footman. The other three were hired for the occasion."

"I will need their names," said the sheriff.

"*I* will need Mr. Blackstone's permission," the man sniffed.

"Very well." Hatfield dug into a slice of angel food cake. "Your cook is most extraordinary. Light as a feather."

"I will tell her, sir," said James, pleased.

"I prefer to tell her myself," said the sheriff.

"Would you like me to send her in, sir?" The man half rose.

"Not just yet," Jackson interrupted. James sat down again. "I have a few questions."

"Excellent. Give me a chance to enjoy this cake." The sheriff smiled.

"At any time during the evening, James, did you go out to the veranda?"

"Yes, sir," said the man. "Mr. Blackstone prefers I circulate as much as possible. I must be ever watchful, you know."

"I'm sure you do an excellent job," said Adele, making the man show something of a smile for the first time.

"I do my best, miss."

"Did you see anything unusual there?" Jackson continued.

"Why, no sir, not that I recall," said the man. "I did see Mr. Tanning and Mrs. Tanning —"

"Yes?" Jackson leaned forward.

The man cleared his throat. "They were exchanging words, sir."

"You mean arguing?" asked the sheriff. "A bit of a couple's spat, perhaps?"

"Not in that way, sir," said James. "They did not raise their voices, I mean."

"When was this?"

The man looked at the clock on the mantelpiece. "A little before ten-thirty, I should think."

Adele looked at her brother. "We saw Lowell go out at around ten, and his wife a little after that."

"Richard went out the back hall door just before ten," said Jackson with a nod.

The sheriff scribbled all this down in his leather notepad.

"Don't misunderstand my next question," Jackson continued, "but did you happen to hear what they were saying?"

"I'm afraid not, sir," said James. "The moment I realized they were exchanging words, I retreated back into the house."

As the man left, Hatfield observed, "Perhaps he does his job a little too well."

"Or not well enough and he's only covering," said Jackson with a grin.

"Covering who or what?" Hatfield asked. "His employer's daughter and her assignations, perhaps?"

"I wouldn't go so far as to call them that, sir." Jackson visibly blushed.

The cook came in next. She threw the sheriff a look of resentment when she saw him tucking into a plate of gingerbread. "I don't know nothing," she declared as she sat down. "And it ain't civil to go frightening young maids with police business, if you ask me."

Adele spoke before Hatfield could open his mouth. "Mrs. –"

"Brown," said the woman.

"Mrs. Brown, I'm here to make sure none of the ladies, yourself included, are frightened in any way." Adele shot the sheriff a glance. The man remained silent.

Mrs. Brown soften a little. "Thank you, miss. I remember you from Miss Blackstone's party."

"I suspect you had your hands full in the kitchen that night?" Adele asked.

The woman burst into tears. Adele slid by her side, putting her arm around her.

"I taught the little thing how to make meringue," Mrs. Brown sobbed. "Her mother never knew anything about domestic affairs, if you know what I mean, miss."

"I certainly do," said Adele. She glanced again at Hatfield, who seemed content to let her continue. "My mother never took to the kitchen either. I wish we'd had a great cook such as yourself to teach me how to make meringue."

She could feel Jackson's amused eyes on her. She knew he was thinking she would have thrown the egg whites in their cook's face, had she tried to teach her how to make anything.

"I made the pink meringues especially for her." The woman wiped her face with her apron. "Worked hard to get them the right shade, you know."

"And they were delicious," said Adele. "We all enjoyed them, including your kitchen guest."

"Guest, miss?"

"Mr. Daniel Tanning." Adele saw the sheriff's eyebrows rise.

"He's a nice young man, though an odd one," said the woman. "He likes to play jacks with Mickey."

"Was he playing jacks with Mickey in the servants' hall, Mrs. Brown?"

"He was indeed, miss, until his brother came down," said the woman. "He and Mickey played build-a-picture. You know –

somebody starts with a line, another one adds a line, and so on, until you got a picture." She gave a small smile and then, as if remembering herself, cleared her throat. "Not that I would have time for such nonsense."

"I'm sure," said Adele. "When did Richard come down?"

"I can't say for sure, miss," said Mrs. Brown. "Betty, the girl there, might know. Nice girl but eyes wander every chance she gets. Can't say I blame her. Not very interesting, scrubbing dishes."

"Did you notice when he left?" Jackson asked.

"Just before ten o'clock, sir," she said.

"How do you know that?" Sheriff Hatfield pushed aside his empty coffee cup.

"I looked at the clock as he was walking up the stairs thinking Mickey ought to be in bed. Little devil always tries to steal a half hour past his bedtime when he can. He succeeds more often than not."

"Did he succeed that night?"

Sharp edges stood out in her face. "He did indeed, until Mr. Blackstone came down and sent him to bed."

"When was that?" asked the sheriff.

"How should I know?" the woman snapped. "I was putting the roses on the cake just then."

Adele pressed her hand. "Was it well past Mickey's usual bedtime?"

"Far enough," she sniffed. "Don't approve of little boys and girls romping around the kitchen when the stars are out. My sister's girl, now – "

"When is Mickey's usual bedtime, Mrs. Brown?" Hatfield's voice rose over her chatter.

"Nine o'clock or thereabouts, sir," she said.

"All right, thank you, Mrs. Brown. Please send Betty to us."

"I'd like to sit in if that's all right with you, sir," she said. "The girl's got no mother, you see, so I've been taking her in hand."

"It would be better if we could speak to her alone," Jackson explained. "She might – well, tell us more if there were fewer people about. If we feel she would be more comfortable with someone else in the room, we won't hesitate to call you."

"Hrmph!" The woman stalked back to her kitchen.

"That was delicately phrased, Jackson," Hatfield said. "You might give Edison and the lads a lesson in police diplomacy one day."

Jackson gave a small smile, but Adele knew he was pleased at the compliment.

Betty was rigid at first, her hands clutching the edge of her apron, but she warmed up when she saw the sheriff kept silent while Adele asked her questions in a gentle, coaxing tone. But she had little more to say beyond confirming what the cook had told them about Richard Tanning's arrival and departure sometime later.

Rawlings, the footman, was called in, a rather spirited youth who could barely contain his excitement over what had happened, tapping one foot and then the other until Sheriff Hatfield regarded him with such a sharp eye he stopped moving altogether. He had only one thing to add to what had already been said by James: He had seen Lucy go upstairs at approximately ten-thirty and heard a door open and shut.

"What door?" asked Jackson.

"I assume to her bedroom, sir." The young man turned pink at the mere mention of a lady's boudoir.

"You don't know that for a fact, though?" Hatfield asked.

"No, sir," he said. "But I heard her telling Miss Regina Maise and Miss Gloria Banks how she slaved all week to put together this party and hadn't slept three full nights." He looked down at his lap. "Her words, sir, not mine."

The footman's exit brought in Eddie Goodwin, Michael Blackstone's valet. The moment he sat down, he shot out, "Who do you think did it, Sheriff?"

"Who do *you* think did it?" Hatfield shot back.

"Damned if I know." The man seemed oblivious to Adele's presence. "You're the police. That's your job, ain't it?"

"I'm sure you have some ideas, Mr. Goodwin," said the sheriff. "Otherwise you wouldn't have brought it up."

"I ain't got no one in mind so don't go accusing me —" The valet cleared his throat and continued in a more cultivated voice. "When do you think poor Miss Blackstone died?"

"I beg your pardon?" Jackson stared at him.

"The time," the man said.

"Why would that matter to you?" Hatfield eyed him.

"It don't — doesn't, sir," he said. "It might to the master."

Jackson started to open his mouth in retort, but the sheriff silenced him. "I'll answer your question, Mr. Goodwin. We think she died between ten and eleven on Friday night."

"Oh!" The man blinked. "And how did she die, if you don't mind my asking?"

"We do mind," Jackson snapped.

"Rather inquisitive, aren't you, Mr. Goodwin?" Adele remarked.

"No more than anyone would be under the circumstances, miss," the man mumbled. "Being a lady, I'm sure you can understand that."

"Sir, are you aware you're not only being impertinent but insensitive to your employer?" the sheriff growled.

"I only wish to know the facts so I can answer your questions, Sheriff." The man sniffed. "You'll agree I owe *that* to my employer."

Again, Jackson was ready with a retort but Hatfield signaled his silence. "She was strangled, Mr. Goodwin." A cry came from the kitchen and Adele knew it was the cook.

"How?" asked the man. "I mean, how was she strangled?"

"Look here –" Jackson jumped up, his tall figure menacing, but the sheriff held up his hand.

"Someone strangled her with the pearls she was wearing," he said.

This seemed to hush the man for a few moments. "I see."

"If you've no more questions, sir," Jackson snarled, "perhaps you'll allow us to ask you questions now."

The man was startled. "I told you I don't know anything."

"Being Mr. Blackstone's valet, you were with your master a good part of the time before and after the party, weren't you?"

"I would hardly be doing my job if I hadn't been," the man snapped.

"How long have you been Mr. Blackstone's valet?" Hatfield asked.

"Three years."

"And you get along well?"

"We tolerate each other," the man said. "Little more is needed in my position."

"Did Mr. Blackstone behave in any way unusual the night of the party?" asked Jackson.

"I hardly make note of my master's moods, sir," Mr. Goodwin answered.

"I find that hard to believe," said the sheriff. "You seem like a rather observant fellow, Mr. Goodwin."

"And as inquisitive as a woman," Adele said dryly.

"You're wrong there, Sheriff." The man rose. "As I can't tell you a thing, am I I free to leave?"

"One moment!" the sheriff's voice boomed as the man reached the doorway. "At what time did Mr. Blackstone go to bed?"

"I wouldn't know," said Mr. Goodwin. "He dismissed me for the remainder of the night the moment the guests began to arrive."

"Is that usual for him?" Jackson asked.

"At times," the man said. "Not always."

"Why do you think he dismissed you that night?"

Mr. Goodwin shrugged. "A man likes his privacy sometimes,

sir," he said. "I'm sure there were instances when you preferred your valet to be absent. Assuming you have a valet."

Jackson half rose, an enraged look on his face, but Adele pressed his arm.

"All right, you may go." The sheriff waved him away.

But the man lingered for a few moments. "It would take strong hands to strangle Miss Blackstone that way, wouldn't it?"

"You speak as if you've had experience." Jackson glared at him.

"In a manner of speaking," said Mr. Goodwin. "I grew up on a farm. We used to get a chicken on the table for Sunday dinner by breaking its neck." He smiled. "But a woman ain't a chicken, is she?"

"Nor is she always the busybody you seem to think, Mr. Goodwin," Adele said acidly.

"I meant no offense to you in particular, miss." The man bowed as he left.

"Mr. Goodwin seems to have definite opinions about the class he serves," Adele remarked.

"I met men like that in my Anspach days," said her brother. "But most of them knew how to behave with the police. This fellow was extremely rude."

"Rude and surly," the sheriff agreed. "And entirely too interested in the death of his employer's daughter."

"Inquisitive, like Del said," Jackson nodded.

"And perhaps not just out of nosiness," Adele said.

"Question marks, question marks," the sheriff lamented.

The last of the servants came in with a little apprehension and timidity not befitting her age or position. She was Gerda Jennings, Lucy's maid, a woman in her thirties with a sweet, ruddy face. But the ruddiness was now almost white as marble.

Adele felt a fierce protection. Gerda reminded her of those women she had seen in the settlement houses, their faces sagging with defeat as they tried to hide the bruises on their arms.

She guided the woman into a chair. The sheriff nodded at her.

"Gerda, can you tell us when Lucy went to bed the night of the party?"

"I don't know, miss." Her voice was too girlish for her matronly figure.

"You don't know?"

"She dismissed me for the night after I helped her dress."

"Isn't it rather odd she undressed and prepared for bed without your help?" Adele asked.

"You've no maid, I take it, miss." Her voice rose a little.

"No," Adele admitted. "I'm a rather independent type."

"So was Miss Lucy." She burst into tears.

"Gerda," the sheriff cut in, "you're not telling us the whole truth, are you?"

"I never –" The woman's face went from white to dove gray.

"It's all right, Gerda," Jackson said with a kind smile. "Your loyalty to your mistress is admirable."

The woman buried her head in her arms.

Adele patted the woman's shoulder. "You want to help us find who did this terrible thing, don't you?"

From inside the folded arms came her muffled voice, "Yes, miss."

"Then you must tell us all you know."

The woman wiped her face on her apron. "I don't want anybody saying she was a bad woman."

"We know she was good, Gerda," Sheriff Hatfield said kindly.

"Mr. James said Mr. Blackstone opened the door to Lucy's room just a pinch and saw her sleeping," she said. "But it wasn't Lucy, miss."

Jackson gave the sheriff a sharp look. "How do you know this if you retired before Miss Lucy went to bed?"

"I know her ways, sir."

"Oh?"

"Miss Lucy hinted she was going to use the dressmaker's dummy that night. She always confided in me about things like that because she knew she could trust me." She said the last with pride.

"The dressmaker's dummy," Adele repeated.

"She took the seamstress' dummy, dressed it like herself, with a wig and all, and put it in her bed so no one would know she weren't there." The woman grabbed Adele's hand. "She never meant no harm, miss!"

"I'm sure she didn't," Adele said. "Why do you think she used the dressmaker's dummy that night?"

"She was meeting someone and didn't want anybody to know."

The sheriff leaned back. "Who was she meeting, Gerda?"

"I don't know, sir," said the maid.

"Come, come," he said. "You attended your mistress very well, as your loyalty to her shows, and you told us she always confided in you."

"I don't want to–"

Adele could see the sheriff winding up, so she said, "Remember, Gerda, you want to help us."

"I don't know, miss." The woman shook her head, her face darkening with despair. "That is, not for certain. I know she was writing to someone because she sent me with the notes."

"What kind of notes?" Hatfield asked.

"I never read them!" The woman's head shook in her indignation.

"I mean what paper did she use, did she seal them up, things like that," said Hatfield a little impatiently.

"She wrote them on purple paper, sir," she said. "Pretty sort of paper." Tears filled her eyes. "Miss Lucy loved pretty things."

"It's all right, Gerda," said Adele. "She bought the writing paper at my shop."

"Then you know!"

"We don't know who received those notes," said Adele. "Can you tell us?"

"It was Mr. Tanning, miss."

"Which Mr. Tanning?" Jackson asked.

"Mr. Richard Tanning, of course, sir."

"Was she meeting Mr. Tanning that night, do you think?" Sheriff Hatfield asked.

Gerda did not answer at first. Then, looking down at her skirt, she mumbled, "I expect so, sir. I took him a note in the afternoon while everyone was having a rest."

"And do you know the nature of their relationship?" the sheriff asked.

The woman stared at him. "Whatever do you mean, sir?"

"He means, Gerda," said Adele in a kind but firm voice, "do you know if they were courting?"

"Certainly not, miss!" The answer came too quickly and indignantly.

Adele squeezed the woman's arm. "Thank you, Gerda. You've been a great help."

"You won't tell the master?" Her face darkened again. "But I suppose it doesn't matter now, does it?" She suddenly sprang up and ran out of the kitchen.

# CHAPTER 11

They found Mr. Blackstone finishing his breakfast in the dining room.

"Just a few more things and we'll be on our way, sir," said Sheriff Hatfield. "I was told there were four other servants hired for that party your daughter gave Miss Gossling."

"Yes, that's true." The man put down his coffee cup.

"I'll need the name of the employment agency where you got them," he said. "I'll also need a list of the guests at the party, as I told you before."

"Anything else?" the man grumbled.

"I'd like James — I'm assuming he'll be the one to provide us with the list? — to mark off any guests who left the party between ten and midnight."

Mr. Blackstone gave him a sharp look but called for his butler and dispatched the request. Adele couldn't help but admire the sheriff's decisive ways with a man who clearly felt himself more superior than the law.

"I appreciate your cooperation." Hatfield bowed.

"I want to find the person who killed my daughter, Sheriff," said the man.

"I never doubted that for a moment, sir," said the sheriff.

"We'll find him or her, Mr. Blackstone," Jackson assured him.

James returned with the lists, handing them to the sheriff.

"Is my man Edison still here?"

"I believe he's still rambling about," Mr. Blackstone said.

"Edison!"

Mr. Blackstone flinched. "Sheriff, my wife, please."

The young man appeared at the doorway. "See that everyone on these lists comes to the station for questioning."

"Yes, sir."

"And, Edison," he said, "ask each of the male guests to bring with him the shoes he wore to the Blackstone party." He turned to Mr. Blackstone. "We'll need yours, of course."

"Whatever for?"

"We found footprints outside," said Jackson. "The scoundrel who did this to your daughter may have left them."

"And you're certain they belonged to a man?"

"Very certain," said Hatfield. "In cases like these, we prefer to rule out more than we rule in, even the most obvious people."

"I see." The man's napkin slid to the floor. As he picked it up, Adele saw his hands were white.

"You've no objection to giving us your shoes, do you?" asked the sheriff.

"None whatever." He fiddled with the napkin. "Are you also looking to see what's on them?"

"Eh?"

"I only ask because you must appreciate most men would have had their shoes cleaned by now," Mr. Blackstone pointed out. "I know Eddie cleaned mine."

"We only need to see them, sir." The sheriff stood silent for a moment, looking out the French doors. "Mr. Blackstone, Lucy's maid told us your daughter may have been meeting Richard Tanning that night. They've been corresponding for some time."

"Good Lord!" The man choked, dropping the piece of toast on the tablecloth. "Lucy, Lucy, my darling girl!"

"I don't mean to upset you, sir, but it's an important fact if it's true," Hatfield said. "Of course, it's only a possibility."

"Well, I don't believe it!" he said. "The girl must be mistaken."

"She may have been," said Jackson.

"Mr. Blackstone." Adele leaned against her closed parasol. "Were you aware Lucy and Richard had been corresponding?"

"Certainly not, Miss Gossling."

She hesitated. "What have you against the young man?"

"Del," her brother cautioned.

"It's not just his father, is it?"

The question clearly rattled him. "I only wanted the best for my daughter."

"No one disputes that, sir," the sheriff said.

"I admit his father and I have had our difficulties," Mr. Blackstone said, "I really knew nothing about the boy."

"And yet you insinuated the same boy led your daughter astray," said the sheriff. The man stared at him. "Oh, yes, I know about that."

"You have no children, do you, Sheriff?"

"None so far," said the man.

Mr. Blackstone looked at him squarely. "When you do, come back to me with your accusations. Until then, I'll thank you to keep them to yourself."

Adele waited for the reaction she would expect from anyone at such impertinent words, but the sheriff only put on his hat. "We won't bother you anymore for now, sir," he said. "But I'd like to return later when your wife is awake. I'm afraid questioning her can't be avoided."

"We have our after-dinner coffee around eight," said Mr. Blackstone. "You may join us if you wish."

"We shall, sir," said the sheriff.

"But do try to be more discreet and considerate," he added. "I would prefer you not tell my wife about your suspicions regarding Richard and my daughter. It would upset her terribly."

"From what I've been told, you were the one with the objections." Hatfield strolled out of the dining room.

"The gall of the man!" Mr. Blackstone thundered. "I shall have a word with the city council. They should never have employed someone with such disregard for the basic codes of decency and courtesy."

"He's very determined to get at the truth," said Jackson quietly.

"I'm glad you're on the case." Mr. Blackstone picked up another piece of toast. "I don't mind telling you I put my faith more in you than him."

"Mr. Blackstone," Adele ventured, "would you mind terribly if I also came tonight and brought my friend Miss Branch with me? If the sheriff would permit it, that is."

"I was just about to ask you, Miss Gossling," he said. "I know my wife reveres you both and I think you would be a welcome sight to her amidst all this horror. Both of you come, the sheriff's permission be hanged."

As they left the house, Adele whispered to her brother, "Are they always so direct, Jack?"

"They?"

"The police," she said.

"They have to get at the facts, Del."

"The sheriff nearly lost his temper," she observed.

"I don't blame Hatfield," he said. "Mr. Blackstone was quite standoffish."

"He just lost his daughter in the most vicious way," Adele pointed out. "That would be enough to make any man testy."

Hatfield was waiting for them. "I sent Edison and the lads in the police wagon," he said. "The Tanning house is just on the other road, if I remember correctly. It's a fine afternoon for a walk."

"Then you do plan on seeing the Tannings?" asked Jackson.

"I plan on seeing anyone who can remove some of those question marks," said the man. He walked a little ahead of them the rest of the way with his military stride.

# CHAPTER 12

The Tanning house was less extravagant than the Blackstone house. Its mustard and green color gave in to a subdued pallor beneath the sunlight. And yet, Adele preferred it over the ornateness of her neighbor's mansion

Even the Tanning housekeeper was humble as she accepted their coats and hats. From the hallway, Adele heard angry voices.

"You led me to believe–"

"I never said a word, Father."

"You should have been more upfront with me, Richard."

"I never lied to you."

"You know Blackstone needs one reason, just one reason to–"

The housekeeper rushed ahead of them, and they could hear her speak in a hushed voice. Mrs. Tanning came out of the room, smoothing down her skirt and brushing her hand against her cheek. A forced smile formed on her lips.

"This is indeed a pleasure, Sheriff," she said. "I'm sorry we haven't had a chance to speak before. We heard you're like a bloodhound on the scent when it comes to your work."

"I prefer to think of myself as the fisherman on the scent of the fish, ma'am," he said in a hearty voice.

"Ah, yes, your time at sea." She led them into the parlor where her husband and son greeted the newcomers. "I'm sure it gave you as much experience as your work with Sheriff Nealy. He was a great man but he could be rather — domineering."

Hatfield chuckled. "That's the truth, ma'am, and I'll be the first to admit it. But he was a good lawman as well as a good friend."

"I've always wondered why you decided to leave the sea and settle on land," said Mrs. Tanning with her chin in her hand.

"That's hardly our business, dear," her husband said gently.

"I don't mean to pry." She blushed. "But you seemed to me so fitted for the wandering life."

"I was in my youth, ma'am," said the sheriff. "But my ma's not been well the past few years. Oh, she has plenty of vigor in her yet, but she isn't getting any younger."

"Who is, Sheriff, who is?" Mr. Tanning lamented.

Richard came into the light from a shadow near the window. Adele drew in her breath. The young man looked as if he had aged and thinned overnight. The bumbling youth expression she had found so appealing the night of the party was replaced by a deflated and drawn figure. Her heart went out to him as she approached him.

"What happened to Lucy, Miss Gossling?" he asked. "Tell me."

"We were hoping you could tell us, Mr. Tanning." The sheriff accepted the invitation to sit down in the largest chair in the room.

The young man glared. "I don't know what you mean."

"We just need to establish some facts," said Jackson.

Both Tanning men glanced at him.

Adele explained, "Sheriff Hatfield has asked my brother for his help because of his experience with the Anspaches."

"I thought the police were rather territorial about their work," Mr. Tanning said with a cough.

"Mr. Gossling's insights have been invaluable," said the sheriff. Jackson colored.

"We'll tell you anything we can, though I doubt that will amount to much," said Mr. Tanning. "We left the party early, as Mr. and Miss Gossling can attest."

"We looked for Lucy to say goodnight but we were told she had gone to bed," Mrs. Tanning added.

"Lucy's maid tells a slightly different story regarding your son," The sheriff said.

Richard sprang up. "I don't know what you mean!"

"We're here only to ask questions, not to make accusations." Jackson regarded him with a calming look that put Richard back in his chair, his legs twisted around each other.

"Exactly when did you leave?" Hatfield asked Mr. Tanning.

"My wife and I and our son Daniel left around midnight."

"You mention one son," said the sheriff. "And the other?" He glanced at Richard.

"Oh, Richard left too, of course," said the man.

Adele did not miss the worried glance Mrs. Tanning shot her husband as the housekeeper set the tea tray down in front of her.

"I'm sorry to contradict you, sir," said the sheriff. "But we know for a fact you and Mr. Blackstone argued about your son just a few moments before you left."

"What of it?" Mr. Tanning snapped.

"That argument was about both Lucy and your son missing from the party."

"Yes, but we met Richard outside," said the man.

"Papa," Richard spoke up, "I'm quite capable of giving the police my own story, if you don't mind."

"Then please do so," said Jackson.

"I didn't go home with my parents, as my father says," he explained. "I went home earlier and I was alone."

"How much earlier?" asked the sheriff.

"I don't recall."

"Were you home when your parents and brother arrived?" asked Jackson.

"I heard some noise from the hallway," he said. "I suppose it must have been them."

"How long after you arrived home did you hear this noise?"

The man blinked. "I see what you're getting at. A half hour, an hour, I suppose."

"You're quite vague about times, sir," said Hatfield. "Not that I blame you. Young men are often fickle about such things."

"Had I known I would need to have an excuse–"

"An excuse?" The sheriff's eyebrow went up.

"An alibi, then. That's what you're looking for, isn't it?" Richard leaned forward. "Why won't you tell us about Lucy?"

"It's not a pretty story," Hatfield said. "Mr. Tanning, you'll forgive my manner. I have a seaman's way of being jagged at times and not so very delicate. When I am trying to get at the truth, that is."

"I understand, Sheriff." The young man nodded.

"Then you'll forgive me for asking you outright, sir." He looked squarely at Richard. "Did you have a romantic encounter with Lucy that night?"

"Outrageous!" Mr. Tanning was on his feet.

"Mr. Tanning, we must explore every avenue," Jackson said.

The man sat down, still shaking, his light hair nearly white.

"We were told Lucy sent you notes regularly," the sheriff continued. "What was the nature of these notes?"

Adele watched the young man's face take on an even greater blackness as furrows appeared under his eyes. "It's not what you think, Sheriff. Lucy and I had been companions since we were children."

"Richard!" his mother let out a cry.

"I meant good friends, Mother. Good friends." He buried his face in his hands.

"How good?" the sheriff asked.

"Really, this is quite unfeeling." His father put his arm around his son's shoulders. "Can't you see how upset you're making him?"

"I'm all right, Papa." Richard grasped the arms of the chair. "The police have their job to do."

"I appreciate your acknowledgment, sir." Hatfield bowed.

"Lucy and I have been good friends since childhood, as I said," Richard continued. "We pretended to end that friendship when I went away to college mainly because we didn't wish to stir up trouble."

"Trouble?"

"From our fathers," he said. "No one seems concerned when children play together, but when the children grow up –"

"I see," said Jackson. "Go on."

"Since our friendship had to remain clandestine, we could only meet privately," Richard said. "Lucy sent me notes when she wanted to see me." Suddenly, he looked at his father, his face bundled with distress. "I swear we never did anything wrong, Papa. We'd go bicycle riding or for a picnic or a swim. It was all perfectly innocent."

"Of course it was." His father clasped his arm around him.

"You *were* going to meet her that night, then." The sheriff was less severe this time.

The young man gave a slow nod.

"When?"

"The note asked me to meet her at the spot crossing at ten o'clock."

"Spot crossing?" Jackson asked.

"That's what we call it," he said with a small smile. "Lucy and I used to play there as children. It's between Lucy's house and your house." He glanced at Adele. "But it's so hidden by brush no one ever goes there."

Jackson glanced at Hatfield. "That fits the description of where we found the footprints," he said in a low voice.

The sheriff nodded. "You have the note she sent you, Mr. Tanning?"

"I burned all Lucy's notes after I read them," he said.

"Pity," he murmured.

"But understandable," added Jackson. He spoke with the authority of one who had been in such situations before. Adele thought back again to the enclaves of the city where she had seen young men like her brother with top hats and capes steal into the alleyways with the streetwalkers. The thought of Jackson's face hidden under the rim of one of those hats nearly made her ill.

"More tea, my dear?" Mrs. Tanning pushed a cup in her direction.

"I'm all right," she murmured.

"What did the note say?" Hatfield asked. "Can you at least tell us that much?"

He shrugged. "She needed to see me, to ask my advice. That's all."

"Richard," Adele spoke up. "You and Lucy were such good friends. I'm sure you can guess what was on her mind. Something was on her mind, wasn't it?"

"Yes, I believe so," he sighed. "But I haven't the faintest idea what it was. That's the truth."

"A man, perhaps?" Jackson eyed him.

Richard's cup slipped out of its saucer and the maid rushed forward with a linen napkin. "How can you think–"

"You said Lucy wasn't involved with you," Jackson pointed out. "That doesn't mean she wasn't involved with someone else. Debutantes often go from one intrigue to another."

"Well!" Mrs. Tanning exclaimed.

Adele slipped to her brother's side. "Jack, this is most unfair of you," she hissed.

"We have to explore every possibility, Del," he hissed back.

"Lucy wasn't involved in an 'intrigue,' as you call it." Richard's voice broke through the strain of the overstuffed room. "Of that I'm certain."

"You said yourself that you suspected something was troubling her." Hatfield reminded him.

"But not a romance," he insisted.

"But you were clearly troubled about the note," Jackson said. "Am I right?"

The young man nodded. "That's why I was so anxious to slip away from the party to meet her. I believed she was going to tell me all about it." His body suddenly shook. "If only she had told me! I would have helped her."

"But she wasn't there," Adele guessed.

He stared at her. "How did you know that?"

"You just said you would have helped her if she would have told you all about it," she said. "But she didn't tell you. So that must mean she wasn't there."

"If it was someone giving her unwanted attentions –" Richard said savagely.

"We can't know they were unwanted," said Mr. Tanning.

"Papa, you can't mean that!" His son stared at him.

"You don't know the whole truth, Richard," he said. "You were away for four years. Lucy changed. There were rumors —"

"Oh, nonsense!" Richard exploded. "There are always rumors about everybody in Arrojo. Gossipy old hens who have nothing better to do."

"I only say she was much admired all over the county," said Mr. Tanning. "Much admired."

"Why shouldn't she be?" The young man's face was red. "She was a lovely, lively girl, and it's only natural young men should take to her."

"She went about like a bright little peacock," his father said. "A girl like that, one can only assume —"

"I don't believe that!" Adele burst out. Everyone turned to look at her. "I only wish to point out," she continued, "you mustn't judge a woman by her worship of womanly things. Lucy may have had an eye for bright colors, and she may have loved her flowers too much. But just because she was admired doesn't mean she admired back."

"Miss Gossling is right, dear," Mrs. Tanning said.

"Any woman who can hide a friendship so dear to her as yours was," Adele continued, glancing at him, "is not an idle-minded woman."

"Your point is well taken." The sheriff nodded. "It does no good to assault the character of the dead, at any rate."

"The dead." Richard let the words fall from his lips like crumpled petals. "Oh, God!" He grabbed his handkerchief and ran from the room.

Mr. Tanning rose. "As you can see, my son is quite upset."

"A few more questions for you and Mrs. Tanning before we go, if you don't mind," said the sheriff.

The man sat down again.

"Both you and your wife went out to the veranda during the party, is that correct?"

The man nodded. "Blackstone's house, for all its finery, always feels stifling to me. I went out back to get some fresh air."

"As did I," said Mrs. Tanning, a little too quickly.

"But you left at different times," said the sheriff.

"I don't see what that has to do with it," Mr. Tanning said.

"You don't, sir?" Hatfield eyed him. "No small detail goes unnoticed in a murder investigation. At least, not with me."

"I don't understand, Sheriff."

"The Gosslings said they saw you go out a little after ten," he said. "Can you confirm this?"

"I didn't look at the time, but that sounds about right."

"And your wife." Hatfield glanced at her. "I was told she came out some ten or fifteen minutes later in quite a panic."

"Really, Sheriff." Mrs. Tanning looked a little embarrassed.

"You did seem quite anxious to find your husband," Adele said gently.

"My wife is rather shy," Mr. Tanning said. "She feels uncomfortable when left alone at a social gathering."

"Your elder son was with you, wasn't he?" asked the sheriff.

"Danny was in the kitchen the entire night," said the woman.

The sheriff buttoned and unbuttoned his coat. "You'll forgive me if I say I don't quite believe you're telling me the whole truth."

Mr. Tanning glared at him. "What more could we say, sir?"

"I believe you noticed your son was gone," said Hatfield. "You went out looking for him. That's why you can confirm the time. Your son just told us."

"All right," said Mr. Tanning. "Yes, I did notice Richard wasn't in the ballroom. I went out to the veranda thinking he had gone for a cigar. I didn't find him."

"Obviously," said the sheriff. "If he was meeting Lucy."

"I really *do* get nervous at parties, Sheriff," added Mrs. Tanning. "Of that, I can assure you."

"You had no inkling your son was meeting a woman?" Jackson asked.

Adele was sure Mr. Tanning was going to lash out in anger, but instead, he looked blankly at Jackson's hands, remaining silent. "I don't pretend Richard doesn't have a few more wild oats to sow."

"I can understand, sir," said Jackson. "I can well understand."

"That doesn't make him a criminal!" Mrs. Tanning wailed. The maid, who had been standing in the corner, looked up from the spot on her apron she was trying to hide.

"Indeed not, ma'am." Hatfield brushed the last of the gingerbread crumbs from his lap. "An excellent refreshment."

Mr. Tanning rose. "I assume you've nothing else for us?"

"I would like to speak to your elder son," the sheriff said.

"He could tell you nothing," said the man. "As my wife said, Daniel was in the kitchen the entire night."

"So the Blackstone servants told us," he said. "I would like to speak to him, nonetheless."

Jackson whispered into the sheriff's ear. The man's face changed from official impassivity to embarrassment. "Perhaps another time, then." He cleared his throat.

As they came out into the fresh air, he regarded Jackson with a savage look. "I wish to the devil you would have told me about Daniel Tanning earlier!"

"It wasn't my place to tell you." Jackson adjusted his collar.

"I don't know as I agree a chat with him would not have yielded anything," said Hatfield. "Children are sometimes the keenest of observers because they don't always grasp the significance of what they observe."

"Daniel is not a child," Adele pointed out.

"He has a child's mind, your brother says."

"It's unnecessary," Jackson declared. "We have a solid suspect, don't we?"

"You mean Richard Tanning?" Adele leaned her parasol against her shoulder. "You can't be serious, Jack. Richard was a dear friend of Lucy's. Anyone with half an eye can see that."

"We have only his word for that." The sheriff snapped his hat onto his head. "It's time for us to make my appearance at the station, Jackson. Edison makes a strong cup of coffee, which is the main reason I keep him on." He grinned.

"I am at your disposal, Sheriff."

"I must get back to my shop," said Adele.

"Ah, yes," said Hatfield with a bow. "You'll have your share of business now. No one can resist being in the presence of someone who's been in the company of a dead body."

"Isn't that a bit grotesque?" Adele asked.

"I've never seen it fail," he mused.

They reached the L shape of Bridge Street. Jackson took both of her hands. "Come to the station at noon. We'll go to lunch, and you can tell me whether the sheriff was right."

She threw her arms around his neck. The somber interviews, the tears and weary faces made her think about the sadness she had left behind in the city, and she now felt the comfort of having her brother with her.

"If nothing else, sir, your presence here has made two people happy," the sheriff murmured.

She let go, knowing Jackson's display of affection had its limits.

As she approached her shop, Adele realized Sheriff Hatfield was right. A crowd of people, mostly women, were gathered around the door. They pecked around like hens, their hats swaying with the wind and their ribbons flapping at the back of their skirts.

Nin was sitting just inside the door of her place. She had clearly been watching the crowd for some time, and now she regarded Adele with what could only be described as a pitying look. Adele steeled herself as she approached the hens.

"Why, ladies, how nice!" She reached into her handbag for the key. "Forgive me for being late."

Mrs. Faderman regarded her with the same owl expression as the night of Lucy's party. "We know why you were delayed, Miss Gossling."

"Do you indeed?" Adele flung open the door.

"You needn't deny it." The woman stepped in, the hens filing in after her. "We know all about it." She studied her with the intensity of an inquisitor. "I hope you're not getting yourself involved in something sordid."

"It's my brother who's involved, Mrs. Faderman," Adele assured her.

"Nevertheless, a word after dinner here, a remark at breakfast there —"

"And one finds oneself tangled up in murder," Adele finished. She regarded the women with an exaggerated sigh. "And I was sure you all came to look at the new stamps I just received. The highest quality rubber."

"We came to discuss the latest tragedy," Mrs. Fourier blurted out.

"I could hardly do that, since Mrs. Faderman doesn't seem to approve," Adele said, her tone innocent.

"I never meant to imply you couldn't discuss it," the woman sniffed.

"As much as I would like to chat, I do have my living to earn," Adele said. "I'm sure you'll all excuse me."

"Oh, we came for the stamps too, didn't we?" Mrs. Abberton gave the others a look. The ribboned hats bobbed in agreement and soon dispersed around the small shop.

"I shall put on the coffee pot and call for some help," Adele said. "I wouldn't be much of a businesswoman if I let my customers wait to be served, would I?" She put the kettle on. "One of you will be good enough to watch this for me?" Without waiting for an answer, she rushed outside.

She found Nin and grabbed her hand. "How would you like me to treat you to lamb stew at Pringle's this evening?" Pringles was the only real elegant restaurant in town.

"That sounds like a bribe." Nin stepped out into the street.

"It is," said Adele. "I need help in my shop."

Nin shrank away. "With those chattering hens in there?"

"That's why I need help." The hand Adele touched clawed into hers. "Don't tell me you're afraid of them!"

Her friend stiffened. "I don't want them calling me names."

"No one will call you names while I'm there," Adele declared. "Don't worry, dear. I don't let people abuse my friends."

Nin's hand eased in hers, and she let herself be led out of her shop.

Adele whispered, "Don't let any of those hens walk out without at least an inkwell or a set of envelopes. They want gossip about Lucy Blackstone, and I mean to make them pay for the privilege."

Nin's eyes sparkled. "I promise every inquisitive tongue will pay heavily for it."

The women were put off at first to see Nin circulate among them with a sales book until Mrs. Lynn, whose husband volunteered with those who had searched the grounds near the Blackstone house informed them Nin had been in the presence of the corpse for just as long a time as Adele. Mrs. Jessel agreed Nin had as much knowledge of Lucy's death as anyone, and was just as good a source of information as Adele.

But when they inserted their questions about Lucy in between more offhand inquiries about stationery, Nin regarded them with an airy smile and placed whatever they had been looking at in a row on the counter to be tallied at the cash register, whether they said they would buy it or not.

Mrs. Faderman devoted herself exclusively to Adele, forbidding anyone else to intervene. She prodded Adele's arm with the sharp end of her parasol when Adele tried to turn her attention to someone else.

In her annoyance, Adele decided she would make the most of the woman's attentions. She led her to the corner with the most expensive writing paper she had in the shop. "I think, Mrs. Faderman, you'll find a complete change of your correspondence to your benefit."

"Yes, yes, certainly, dear," said the woman. "This is nasty business, isn't it?" She sipped the coffee Adele had given her.

"I assure you with my help reorganizing your correspondence, it need never be nasty business." Adele smiled.

"No, no, I meant this business about Lucy Blackstone." She sighed. "I wish we could say we've never had a murder in Arrojo, but, you know, in those wild days in the fifties –"

"Yes, I'm sure." Adele poised with her order book. "Cream or white paper?"

"We've never had a young woman murdered," said Mrs. Faderman with a click of her tongue. "Nothing as ghastly as this."

"I believe dove gray is all the rage right now," said Adele. "I rather prefer cream. Gray is a little too melancholy to meet one's eyes when one opens a letter, don't you think?"

"Yes, you're quite right, my dear." The woman leaned against a shelf. "Of course, Lucy's demise isn't as unexpected as it might seem to the apathetic eye. Mine is one of the keenest in these parts, you know."

"Your sense of decorum, Mrs. Faderman?" Adele mumbled.

"My eye for impending doom!"

"I have no doubt, ma'am." Adele scribbled in her order book.

"I've known Lucy was heading for tragedy for quite some time."

"Shall we go with cream, then, Mrs. Faderman?" she asked.

"If you think it best." Adele quickly put her down for two hundred sheets. "Young girls these days do what they like. Their equally young parents have nothing to say against it. I must say, I did expect Michael Blackstone to be a little more disciplined, but Lucy always had her father under her thumb."

"Do you like daisies, Mrs. Faderman?"

"I beg your pardon?" The woman peered through the pince-nez.

"I was just thinking the cream would look lovely with embroidered daisies on the edge in a powdered blue shade. I can show you what they would look like. Mrs. Jessel ordered something similar last week, and it just came in." She added, "Mrs. Jessel is in favor of woman-owned businesses, you know."

"Better make it orchids, then," said Mrs. Faderman. "I would never want to associate Mrs. Jessel's tastes with my own." She picked up an envelope dressed with lace edges in a carefully gloved hand. "Lucy was so well-behaved as a child."

"She ceased to be well-behaved when she grew into womanhood?" Adele thought of what Mr. Tanning had said.

"I don't like to speak ill of the dead," Mrs. Faderman sniffed, "but it's hardly a secret she broke nearly every young man's heart in this town and a few others in the county. You can't imagine what she did to my poor Percy. He's such a trusting boy."

"He's hardly a boy, Mrs. Faderman," Adele murmured. She guessed Percy Faderman to be at least twenty-five.

"I was speaking metaphorically." The woman glared.

Adele quickly swept up a packet of the lace-edged envelope. "A most excellent choice, Mrs. Faderman. These are the new style for this winter. Your friends will be most impressed."

"I'm sure," said the woman. "When Richard Tanning left for college, Lucy simply surrounded herself with male companions. You couldn't walk down the street without seeing her giggling behind her parasol and clutching some young man's arm. Most disturbing."

"We'll add orchid seals to the order." Adele jotted it down in her sales book, though her mind was on the words *Richard Tanning*.

"Yes, that would be delightful." The woman slung her bag over her shoulder.

"Why should Lucy encourage so many admirers?" Adele asked.

"To make him jealous, of course," Mrs. Faderman snorted. "Just as all young ladies do."

"Not all young ladies play such games, ma'am," Adele tried not to sound offended.

"Oh, I'm sure you're more sensible, Miss Gossling, but Lucy was that sort of young lady." Mrs. Faderman spoke in a lower tone of voice, "He used to write Vanessa every week, asking about this boy or that. I can't imagine how he heard about her conquests."

"Perhaps she wrote to him, if her aim was to make him jealous," Adele suggested.

"That's the way of frivolous young women these days." Mrs. Faderman let her pince-nez hang around her neck. "They seem so anxious to be like all you big city girls. Not my Vanessa, naturally."

"Naturally." Adele squeezed past Nin at the cash register. "Will you pay now or open an account, Mrs. Faderman?"

Nin glanced at her. "I've reminded the ladies you don't allow accounts to go unpaid for more than a week." She swept her hand across the crowd of hens, and Adele wanted to kiss her.

"Well, if you don't, you don't." Mrs. Faderman shrugged.

"Why make Richard jealous, I wonder?" Adele lamented. "Richard said they were only friends."

"Did he?" Mrs. Faderman looked up quickly.

Adele cleared her throat. "Will you be opening an account today, Mrs. Faderman?"

"I may as well," said the woman.

"Do you think Lucy liked Richard more than a friend?" Adele's mind wandered again.

"My but you're inquisitive, Miss Gossling." The woman glared at her over her pince-nez.

"No more inquisitive than you are about the same thing," Nin grumbled.

Adele pressed her arm under the counter. "I've been told that so often, I consider it a compliment."

"I wouldn't be so pleased about it if I were you," Mrs. Faderman remarked. "It's most unbecoming to a young lady."

"So you don't know why Lucy would want to make Richard

jealous?" Adele concentrated on the wrapping paper in front of her.

"Of course I know," Mrs. Faderman snapped. "They'd been seen together all the time."

"Well, naturally, they were friends since childhood."

"How in the world did you know that?" The woman stared at her.

"I hear things just as well as you do, Mrs. Faderman." Adele suspected it would be unwise to tell the woman she had accompanied the sheriff to the Tanning house that morning.

"Do friends lean on one another's shoulder or peck one another on the cheek?" Mrs. Faderman gave her a knowing look. "I must say, though, your innocence is rather refreshing and quite unexpected."

Two girls entered the shop, one blond and one a redhead. They both wore long white ribbons in their hair and dark blue dresses. "Good morning, Mrs. Faderman," they said in unison.

"Good morning, girls." The other ladies gathered around them, smiling and cooing. "Are you collecting today?"

"Yes, ma'am," said the blond girl. "Mrs. Wrigley's pointer broke, and we want to buy her a new one."

"Isn't that just too fine?" She turned to Adele. "The finest girl's school in this county, The Wrigley School."

"How very generous of you girls." Adele eyed them.

Nin came around the counter, her skirt billowing out so it touched the leg of the red-headed girl, who quickly backed away, her eyes a frightened green.

"This is my friend," said Adele. "She won't hurt you." The girl relaxed. "What's your name?"

"Beatrice, miss," she said.

"Do you always raise money for Mrs. Wrigley?"

"Always, miss," said the girl. "She gives us so much, and, well, charity begins in the home, doesn't it?"

"Indeed it does." Mrs. Faderman nodded with approval.

"Here's a nickel for Mrs. Wrigley's pointer, then." Adele rang open the cash register drawer.

"Thank you so much, miss." The girl curtsied.

"I'm afraid I haven't any coins with me," said Mrs. Faderman. "But you come around my house later this afternoon, and I'll give you something."

"Most kind, ma'am." Now the blond girl curtsied. As she and Beatrice left the shop, they hovered around the nickel as if it were a gold piece.

"Such polite and simple girls." Mrs. Faderman shook her head. "You don't find such manners in children these days."

"I have no children, so I'm afraid I can't say," said Adele.

"You will, dear, never fear." Mrs. Faderman smiled. "We'll find you a companion yet. Won't we, ladies?"

The hens nodded and filed out of the shop.

Nin snorted. "Generosity, my foot! Those girls are always giving syrupy compliments for nickels."

"I didn't think they were as concerned about their teacher as they pretended to be," Adele agreed.

"You shouldn't have given them anything," said her friend. "They'll buy candy with it."

"I expect they will. But I had my reasons for giving them the nickel." Adele fiddled with the cash register for a few minutes. "Have you ever read Sherlock Holmes?"

Nin looked down. "I told you, I haven't much education."

Adele chuckled. "Holmes can be very educational if you know how to read him right."

"What has he to do with anything?"

"He had ragamuffins to help him with his investigations." She peeled off the apron she had worn over her dress in anticipation of handling the inkwells and folded it in a corner. "Will you watch the shop for me for a little while?"

"Whatever for?" the dark girl asked.

"I must pay someone a visit," she said. "I've an idea."

She found the girls' school past Bridge Street, separated by a path crossing one part of the river. It was a tall, ornate house with points and arches. Adele felt as if she were stepping into the last century as she approached the stone entrance.

A woman with tightly pulled hair in a black dress with lace trimming greeted her, the robin-like figure thrusting forward. "Whom do you wish to see?"

"Mrs. Wrigley, if possible." Adele felt small.

"I'm Mrs. Wrigley."

Adele coughed. "I've a brother who has a little girl he wishes to receive a most delicate education."

"We can manage that very well." The woman became less severe. "We believe a solid education of the most refined graces prepares a girl to seek her fortune in a well-suited marriage."

"How appropriate," mumbled Adele.

"'A healthy spirit follows a healthy mind and body,'" quoted Mrs. Wrigley in a hearty voice. "That's our motto, you know."

"I'm sure you fulfill all of those promises, Mrs. Wrigley." Adele bit back a smile. "Especially the healthy spirit."

"How old is your niece?" the woman asked.

"My niece?" Adele clutched her gloves. "Oh! She's eleven."

"Perfect!" said Mrs. Wrigley. "I'm sure your brother will find our school a most suitable place for her. Would you care to make an appointment for him to come and see me?"

"I'd like to look around myself first, if you don't mind," said Adele.

"Please do." Mrs. Wrigley led Adele out the back door. The space opened into a large hallway and a spiral staircase leading up to a row of dark rooms. "I believe you'll find we offer an excellent education. I assure you, your little niece – what's her name?"

"Anita," Adele mumbled.

"Anita could find no better company than my girls," she sighed. "Such lovely creatures. Always eager to learn, and they do as much for God and their community as they do for themselves."

"I'm sure they do." Adele swept her skirt up as she approached the staircase. "There's no need for you to accompany me, Mrs. Wrigley. I like to explore on my own."

"I'd be happy to show you –"

"I'd like to get a feel for the place," said Adele. "I'm much more about feeling, you see. I simply can't get a feeling if someone is hanging over my shoulder. But once I have a feeling, my brother knows there is no doubting it. You understand me, Mrs. Wrigley?" She eyed her.

"Perfectly," said the woman. "Call me if you need anything." She swept back into a side room and shut the door behind her.

Adele found the two girls she had seen in town lounging with a third who looked slightly older inside a parlor-like room. Each had a stick of candy in her hand.

"I see you've put my nickel to better use than the new pointer for your teacher," she announced. The straps of Beatrice's pinafore slid down to her elbows, and the older girl shot her head up so quickly that the rubber band holding back her hair slipped down.

"You mustn't be messy." She carefully arranged the pinafore and tied the other girl's hair back. "I'm sure Mrs. Wrigley wouldn't like that. 'A healthy spirit follows a healthy mind and a healthy body,'"

The girls she had met earlier burst out laughing. The third sniffed. "Mrs. Wrigley is an old buzzard!"

"She didn't look very old to me," Adele said.

"I mean," the girl blushed, "only sometimes."

"Are you going to tell her?" Beatrice tossed back a sheet of her red hair. It really was a marvelous shade of strawberry blond.

"Why should I?" Adele sat down in one of the chairs. "Indulging in a stick of candy is no sin in my world."

All three girls smiled.

"This is Mary." Beatrice nodded at her blond companion. "And this is Rachel." The slightly older girl curtsied. She also had red hair, though not as brilliant as her friend's. Hers was more a dull copper color.

"I'm pleased to meet all of you." She slipped off her gloves. "Mrs. Faderman was telling me what cherubs you all are, and Mrs. Wrigley seems to agree with her."

The girls exchanged a sheepish look. "We really do try, miss!" said Mary.

"Call me Adele," she said. "You try, but you don't always succeed. Am I right?"

"We're only children, bum it," Beatrice declared.

"Hush, Bea," said Rachel. "Adele will think you're an ill-bred thing."

"I approve of a girl airing out her thoughts now and then," said Adele, unable to hide her smile. "I did myself when I was your age." She folded her hands in her lap. "Tell me, how many girls are there in this school?"

"Only twenty-four," said Rachel. "I think it's very pleasant not to have so many ill-mannered girls running around."

"Nobody here is ill-mannered, Rachel." Mary's stick of candy had disappeared, and her dress was smoothed down. "We're all nice girls, really we are."

"Does everyone in Arrojo think you're nice girls?"

"They must," said Beatrice. "We can get a penny or even a nickel whenever we want from just about anybody."

"Bea!"

"Well, we can." The redhead tossed her head. "We only go to those who can give it to us. Sometimes we give it to one of the children with the ragged feet."

"Yes, I've seen them," said Adele.

"I've never seen *you* give your nickel to any of them," Rachel retorted.

"That's a charitable thing to do, isn't it?" Beatrice demanded.

"Well, isn't it?"

"It certainly is," said Adele. "What if you could earn five cents instead of begging for it?"

"How?" Mary asked.

"People don't mind talking in front of children," said Adele. "Especially girls whom they think are very nice."

"Oh!" Beatrice leaned forward. "You mean spy on someone?"

"The idea!" Rachel said.

"I expect rumors are flying, and I want to catch as many of them as I can, whether they're true or not," Adele continued.

"Rumors about what?" Beatrice asked.

Adele hesitated before deciding to use the present tense. "Do you know Lucy Blackstone?"

But it seemed the girls already had their ears open wider than she realized.

"The poor woman who was killed?" A look of horror crossed Mary's face.

"Her head was chopped right off," said Beatrice with some authority.

Adele laughed. "Her head is just as straight as yours is."

"What about Miss Blackstone?" asked Rachel.

"People are saying things about her," said Adele. "They're saying she liked a young man in town."

"Did he kill her?" Beatrice's eyes were shining.

"Maybe," said Adele. "I'll give you each five cents if you find out all you can about Lucy and this man."

"What man?" asked Rachel.

"Mr. Richard Tanning." Adele searched the girls' faces for recognition, but they seemed too intent on the idea of pennies in their hands.

"Mary won't go. She's too afraid," said Beatrice. "But Carolyn will."

"How do you know?" Rachel glanced at her.

"Because *I'll* tell her to," Beatrice snarled.

"You must be very discreet," said Adele. "Do you know what discreet means?"

"Of course we know," said Rachel. "We know just how to listen and what to listen for." She now took on as much authority, if not more, than Beatrice.

Adele took out three pennies. "Here's one for each of you and one for Carolyn. I'll give you the rest when you come to my shop to give me what news you have. Mind Carolyn gets her penny." She eyed the fierce redhead.

The girl was instantly indignant. "Do you think I would cheat my best friend?"

"Naturally not, dear," said Adele.

All three girls suddenly rose and stood at attention, and Adele saw Rachel shove the stick of candy in her pocket. The headmistress was upon them.

"I was having a lovely chat with your girls, Mrs. Wrigley." Adele stood up. "You're quite right. They're very bright."

The woman beamed. "I'm so glad you think so. Back to your homework, girls," she continued with her stiff voice. The girls rushed down the hall, but not before Beatrice gave Adele a toothy grin to seal their bargain.

# CHAPTER 14

*P*ringle's was crowded that evening when Adele arrived with Jackson on her arm and Hatfield and Nin trailing behind. Heat from the fireplace made the room stifling and both ladies removed their wraps. Even Hatfield was willing to loosen his tie. Jackson remained fully dressed in his coat and vest. Adele marveled at how he could always remain so unaffected by heat or cold.

"I heard you had quite a day." Her brother poured her a glass of wine. When he tried to pour one for Nin, she gave him a withering look.

"The hens in this town wanted the gossip about Lucy Blackstone's murder," said Adele. "They knew enough to come to me to get it."

"And we made them pay for the privilege," Nin declared.

Jackson coughed over his soup.

"Just as I predicted." Hatfield's eyes were shining.

"You didn't predict I would get a lecture on the dangers of becoming too involved in such a sordid matter as crime," Adele said dryly.

"I gather that was before Mrs. Faderman started in on her interrogation." The sheriff laughed. "What did you tell her?"

"No more than what appeared in Miss Grace's paper this evening," Adele said.

"We have to be cautious." He examined the fish. "It wouldn't do to give too many details."

"Sheriff, my sister is no gossip," Jackson insisted. "She's worked in settlement houses and kept secrets of women hiding from lecherous husbands and fathers."

Hatfield now fluttered almost like a schoolgirl, his face red. "I never meant to imply I thought you wouldn't be discreet, Adele."

She smiled. "I may not know much about police procedure, but I know enough to keep my mouth shut about some things."

"So do I," her friend snapped.

"You believe us, don't you, Sheriff?" Adele peered at him.

"I'm not likely to doubt what you say, Adele," he said in a kind voice.

Nin stared at him with the same withered look.

"Henpecking can be rather beneficial at times," said Adele.

"Gossip is usually not worth the lips from which it falls." Hatfield started on the lamb stew.

"If you don't want to hear it —"

"Oh, I want to hear it," the sheriff mumbled, spearing a potato.

"When Richard went away to college, Lucy became more acquainted with the young men in the county," she said.

Hatfield chuckled. "Who told you this?"

"It came straight from the head hen's mouth." Adele said. "Mrs. Faderman."

The sheriff winced. "We had a charming visit from her at the station. I am to find who killed poor, unfortunate Lucy within the week, or my badge will be at the bottom of the river."

"Surely you didn't take her seriously?" Jackson stared.

"I don't know how many society ladies I've met who have

given me conditions," the sheriff chuckled. "I never let them bother me."

"Why would Lucy suddenly begin to accept the attentions of all those young men after Richard left?" Jackson asked.

"That was exactly the question I asked," Adele said.

"Mrs. Faderman thinks it was jealousy," Nin snorted.

"Oh, come now," said Hatfield. "The boy could hardly be jealous if he was away."

"According to Mrs. Faderman, he wrote letters to her daughter Vanessa asking about them," said Adele. "She suspects Lucy was writing of her conquests."

"A rather devious way to get a marriage proposal from a man," Jackson murmured.

"You think that's what it was, Jack?"

"I can almost guarantee it," he insisted.

"What were her parents doing all this time?" asked Hatfield. "I don't imagine Michael Blackstone would turn a blind eye to any hint of impropriety in his daughter."

"Lucy had him under control, according to Mrs. Faderman," Adele said.

"It certainly gives us a starting point, sir," Jackson pointed out. "Not that we weren't already starting there."

Hatfield dug into the pie the waiter put in front of him with relish. "You did well, Adele. And I don't mean just in the way of sales." His mustache twittered.

"I did one even better," she smiled.

Jackson looked up from his coffee. "More gossip?"

"Not yet," she said. "But I will have by tomorrow or the day after."

"You've put a listening device under Mrs. Faderman's skirt?" Nin asked. Both men dropped their spoons in their plates.

"In a manner of speaking." Adele enjoyed the masculine shock the idea had caused. "But not just under Mrs. Faderman's."

"Stop talking in riddles, Del." Jackson's voice was sharp. "This is not one of our playroom games."

"You once told me one of your Anspach ways was to cast a net of listeners," she said. "Saloon keepers, streetwalkers, petty criminals, all with their ears and eyes open."

"I think it hardly likely you'll find such a net of listeners in Arrojo," said the sheriff.

"Perhaps not among the adults," said Adele. "But children are a different story."

"Children!" Several heads turned. Jackson lowered his voice. "Don't tell me there's a band of street urchins running around this town."

She grinned. "School girls."

"What?" Now it was the sheriff's turn to make heads turn.

The waiter approached their table. "Anything wrong, sir?"

Hatfield shoved the coffee pot into his hands. "Our coffee is cold. Bring us a fresh pot, please."

Nin was leaning with her chin in her hands and her elbows on the table. Her eyes were almond-sharp. "It's those girls, isn't it?"

"What girls?" asked Jackson.

"The little liars," her friend snarled.

"Not liars, dear," said Adele. "Storytellers, harmless enough."

The sheriff stared. "Please explain, Adele."

"A few girls from the Wrigley School came into my shop," Adele said. "I knew right away they were hardly the little angels Mrs. Faderman and the other hens seem to think."

"You've made schoolgirls your spies?" Her brother gave her an incredulous look.

Adele stiffened. "Sherlock Holmes made street boys his spies."

Jackson's neck showed red with anger even while his face remained calm. "Of all the absurd notions—"

"Let's hear what she has to say," said Hatfield as the waiter arrived with the fresh coffee.

"I don't see why you should be so angry, Jack, dear," said Adele. "No one expects an angel to be an eavesdropper."

"What exactly did you ask them to do?" Hatfield picked up his dessert fork.

"Watch and listen for anything about Lucy and Richard," said Adele. "You've no idea how such girls devour romance." She chuckled a little as she poured another cup of coffee.

"Del, you didn't!"

She regarded her brother with a wary eye. He sometimes took his role as protector too seriously. "People don't think twice about talking in front of a child wearing a blue pinafore with a white ribbon in her hair."

"You realize if their parents knew, they might think you're corrupting young minds?" But Hatfield seemed more amused than abhorrent.

Adele gathered her gloves. "I was accused of as much by the poor mothers whose children helped keep their abominable husbands from finding them and beating them to death. Quite amazing how some people will insist on preserving childhood innocence even after life has already taken it away." She glanced at her brother.

"You ought to be proud of your sister instead of chiding her," Nin growled.

Jackson wiped his mouth with shaking fingers. "I know you had good intentions, Del, but you may put the entire investigation in danger."

"I don't see it could do much harm." Hatfield paid the bill. "As long as they keep their mouths closed just as they're keeping their eyes and ears open."

"They will," Adele assured him.

"They're being paid to," Nin said.

"I must say you're taking a rather offhand attitude about this, sheriff," Jackson mumbled.

"As I told you before, sir, I'm not one of those policemen who believe they can do the work all on their own."

"But school girls!" Jackson stood up, nearly knocking his chair over. Their waiter scrambled to catch it.

"Children naturally see the truth," said Hatfield. "And it's the truth we seek, is it not?" He rose. "We promised Mr. Blackstone to be there by eight, after all."

Nin grasped the back of a chair. "I don't know as I should come, Adele."

"Of course you should." Adele held out her arm to her friend.

"You don't know what they all think of me," said her friend. "What they thought of my mother. You don't know."

"I know you've been a great comfort to me so far," she said gently. "Mr. Blackstone himself said his wife liked us. She needs all the comfort we can give her."

The woman stared into the candlelight shining on the table. Her face lightened, and she accepted Adele's arm.

As they made their way to the Blackstones', Adele wandered near her brother and gently put her hand in his. "Jack, dear, these girls might help you catch a killer, just like Mr. Holmes' boys helped him."

"That was different."

"Because he's a man and I'm a woman?" she challenged. "Woman shouldn't be the helpers, not engage them, is that it?"

"Because Holmes is fiction," he snapped.

She looked at him. "Remember how Papa used to say you were worse than a swarm of buzzing bees over a jar of spilled honey when it came to something that didn't suit your idea of virtue?"

"I remember better than you do," he said. "Perhaps he should have been more of a bee too."

"You mean because he defended people who broke the law?" Adele asked. "That doesn't mean he had no virtue himself. His every breath and movement creaked of virtue."

"'Creaked' is the word for it, isn't it?" Jackson growled. "Like old bones ready to crumble."

"He let you do as you please," she retorted. "That's all you ever wanted."

She regretted her words. A few wrinkles appeared around his eyes, wrinkles of wariness and regret.

"All right, Del," he said in a tired voice. "If Hatfield doesn't object to your helpers, I certainly have no right to. I've no authority here, after all."

"Jack —"

"Sometimes you can see things the wrong way, Del," he said. "Remember that." He strolled ahead with his hands behind his back.

Nin took her hand, giving her a reassuring smile, and Adele wondered if she had heard their squabble, though she had wandered off. Hatfield glanced back at her with troubled eyes and then watched her brother, whistling a tune as if he were studying him.

Michael Blackstone looked less grim, though no less haggard. His handsome face stretched like parchment over a stone. Adele noted his eyes had dark circles as if he had been weeping. She realized Mrs. Faderman's observation about Lucy having her father completely under her thumb had been right.

In spite of his grief, his voice was strong and controlled as he greeted her and Nin. "I'm glad you decided to join the sheriff, ladies. My wife will be very pleased."

"You look as if you could use some soothing yourself," she said gently.

The man stiffened. "You needn't be concerned with me, Miss Gossling. My wife is the one with delicate health."

"Everyone must grieve when a loved one dies ," Nin said softly. "There's no shame in it."

Her words had a surprisingly calming effect on the man, and he bowed.

Marissa Blackstone was lying against a stack of pillows on the chaise, a blanket thrown over her and a handkerchief held over her eyes. Her lovely figure sagged under the cotton voile dress as if she had lost half her body weight within the last few days. Her hand shook as she tried to smile.

"I like people about me," she said. "It's a relief to know one isn't alone."

"If we disturb you, Mrs. Blackstone —" Adele began.

"Disturb?" The woman's eyes filled with tears. "I don't think I shall ever have any peace again." She began sobbing.

Nin suddenly sat on the floor near Mrs. Blackstone and took both her hands. Adele was touched to see the genuinely wretched look on her friend's face.

"Miss Branch, if you'll kindly sit here." Mr. Blackstone pointed to a chair.

"No, no!" Mrs. Blackstone emerged from beneath the handkerchief, her face composed. "Let her stay, Michael. I'm all right now."

"I'm glad you're feeling better, Mrs. Blackstone," said Jackson.

"As much as can be expected." Her husband reached for the cord on the wall. "I'll ring for coffee."

"We've just had some, thank you," said the sheriff. "A brandy will do just fine."

The man raised his eyebrow. "I should think you wouldn't drink while on duty, Sheriff."

"I'd like to see the men drinking brandy and the women drinking sherry, Michael," said Mrs. Blackstone. "A drink before bed always makes one sleep better, doesn't it?" She turned to Adele. "The doctor said sleep is the best thing right now."

"Of course, dear." He kissed her hand. "James, please bring the brandy and sherry."

"Mrs. Blackstone," the sheriff began, "we wouldn't be troubling you were it not vital to our finding who did this horrendous thing to your daughter."

"I understand," she said. "How can you catch whoever did it if you don't ask questions?"

"I thank you for your cooperation, ma'am," he said. "To begin, when was the last time you saw your daughter?"

"A little before ten the night of the party," said Mrs. Blackstone. "I knew we should have called the police when we couldn't find her."

"Mrs. Blackstone," said Jackson, "Lucy was killed between ten and eleven. There was little the police could have done."

"Yes, I realize that." But the thought seemed to offer her no reassurance.

"And you didn't go to her room to check if she was there?" Hatfield asked.

"I told you I did that," said Mr. Blackstone. "I do wish you would remember these things, Sheriff. It's most distressing to have to go through them again."

"I have quite an excellent memory but I do forget details the same as anyone else," said the sheriff. "That's why Mr. Gossling is here. Between two minds, you know." He sighed. "Was there anything unusual that happened in the days before the party?"

"Unusual?" Mrs. Blackstone stared at him.

"With Lucy's behavior or mood," he said. "Was she distressed or sad in any way?"

"Quite the opposite," said the woman. "She was happy planning the party. Don't you think, Michael?" She turned to her husband.

"You both were, my dear," he said. "Organizing social events has always been your forte."

"And before that?" asked Jackson.

"She had been quite elated for some days," said Mrs. Blackstone. "She fairly bounced around the house." Again, her eyes filled with tears. "Oh, my poor darling girl!"

"Dear, don't distress yourself." Her husband pressed her hands.

"You've no idea why she was elated?" asked the sheriff.

"She saw Adele as her new friend," she said. "She was always happy to make new friends."

"She was a friend to me even if for a short time." Adele patted her wrist.

"Mrs. Blackstone," Hatfield continued. "Are you aware your daughter ordered custom-made stationery from Miss Gossling?"

Mrs. Blackstone crumpled her handkerchief. "Is there any reason I should have been?"

"Daughters often confide in their mothers about such things when they involve — affairs of the heart." He coughed.

"Sheriff, please." Mr. Blackstone shot him a warning look.

"I want to hear it, Michael," his wife insisted.

"Very well." Her husband sank down in his chair.

"What do you mean by 'affairs of the heart'?" asked the woman. "It must be important for you to ask about something as trivial as Lucy's letter paper."

"We believe she ordered that paper to write notes to Richard Tanning."

This information seemed to puzzle Mrs. Blackstone more than distress her. "That might explain –" She stopped.

Jackson leaned forward. "Is there something you wish to tell us, Mrs. Blackstone?"

"I heard her arguing with somebody one night. Not long before the night of the party, as a matter of fact."

Nin's cat-like eyes were glazed as she stared at the china pug sitting on the table behind her.

"Are you sure, dear?" Mr. Blackstone asked.

"Quite sure." She settled the blanket closer around her feet.

"Was it a woman or a man?" Her husband was on his feet.

"I think it was a man's voice." She did not look at him.

"A man's voice!" He was on his feet. "That young scoundrel came to my house."

"You mean Richard Tanning, don't you?" Adele asked.

"Of course I mean him!"

"Mr. Blackstone, please," Jackson said. "Where did you hear this argument, ma'am?"

"Outside somewhere." She gave an embarrassed laugh. "My mind is rather muddled, you see."

"Thank God!" Her husband sank back into his chair.

"No – wait!" Mrs. Blackstone sat up. "It was in her room. Yes, her room."

"The young swine!" Her husband's hands crushed together.

"Michael!" his wife cried out. "They used to play together."

Mr. Blackstone was silent for a moment. "Yes, I suppose you're right, my dear. He's been in her room many times as a boy and a man."

"Mr. Blackstone, I hate to remind you, but it's a little late to be playing the outraged father," said the sheriff quietly. "We have a murder to solve."

"Yes, of course," the man said. "But if this ever got out –"

"There's no reason it should." Jackson shifted his walking stick so the butler could take the brandy tray away. "What were they saying, Mrs. Blackstone. Can you tell us?"

"I couldn't hear their words," she said. "I could only hear the anger in their voices."

"Because they had the door closed?" Her husband jumped.

"Naturally they had the door closed," his wife said with impatience.

"Did Lucy say anything about it to you?" asked Hatfield.

"No. And I didn't ask," Mrs. Blackstone added. "I know my children will tell me if something is wrong on their own without my having to pry it out of them. I was a bad mother, wasn't I?" The woman began to sob.

"Nonsense!" Nin's voice rose above the quiet sway of raindrops against the French windows. "You were not the painful connection in the house."

"I beg your pardon?"

"The painful feelings didn't come from you," Nin said.

"Oh, Lord," Jackson murmured.

"Who is the painful connection?" Hatfield was suddenly interested.

"I — I don't know."

Her hesitation made Adele feel she was not being entirely truthful. "What do you know?" she asked.

"Yes, yes, what do you know?" Mrs. Blackstone grabbed her hand. "Please tell me!"

"I forbid it!" Mr. Blackstone roared. "I won't have my wife accosted with the ravings of a cheap mesmerizer!"

"I am not a mesmerizer!"

"Please, Mr. Blackstone," Adele said.

Mrs. Blackstone's eyes glowed. "I want to know."

Nin's pitying look returned. "There are two who made a painful connection in this house. Now the connection is severed."

"What nonsense!" snarled Mr. Blackstone.

Mrs. Blackstone's neck was straining. "Why is it severed?"

"I can't say," said Nin. "I know only the feeling, not the reason."

The woman seemed to deflate to half her size. "Perhaps it's better not to know."

"Don't distress yourself, my dear." Mr. Blackstone was at her side. "It's all nonsense." He gave the sheriff a meaningful look.

Hatfield understood and rose. "We won't take up any more of your time, ma'am. Thank you for agreeing to see us."

"Miss Gossling." The woman grasped her hand as she passed. "Lucy's funeral is tomorrow. You will come?"

"Of course," she assured her.

"We'll all come," Sheriff Hatfield promised.

Mr. Blackstone insisted on seeing them to the door. His tone was low as he said, "I apologize for my behavior. This is all so deplorable."

"We understand, sir," said Jackson. "Mr. Blackstone, you

realize there's no evidence the man your wife heard in your daughter's room was Richard Tanning?"

"You surprise me, sir." The man stiffened. "First you and the sheriff insinuate he and my daughter were — involved. Now you sound as if you're trying to exonerate him."

"We're only trying to discover the facts, sir," the sheriff murmured.

The man lingered at the doorway with his hands in his pockets. "Perhaps it was the father and not the son."

"Mr. Tanning?" Adele's eyebrows rose.

"The man would stop at nothing to pull his son apart from my daughter," he said. "It's the one thing both of us agreed upon."

"You think he might have come to see Lucy to order her to have nothing more to do with your son?" Jackson asked.

"I wouldn't put it past him, sir."

"Thank you for your insights, Mr. Blackstone." Hatfield tipped his hat. "We shall certainly look into every possibility."

At the gate, Hatfield took leave of them, agreeing to meet them for the funeral the next morning. The moment he left, Jackson pounced on Nin. "That was most inconsiderate of you, Miss Branch."

"The woman wanted to know," she insisted.

"I've heard of spiritualists preying on a grieving woman, but that was insufferable!"

"Nin wasn't preying on anyone, Jack," Adele said. "She was using her gift to get at the truth."

"All the same, you might have shown more restraint."

"If you had any appreciation for the spirit life, Mr. Gossling, you would know one does not ignore the callings," Nin said.

"Oh, really!"

"I seek the truth," she said. "I don't try to impose my will upon it, unlike you and most men."

Under the pale street light, Adele could see her brother's

cheeks turn crimson. In a wooden voice, he said, "I'll go on ahead, Del."

"Poor Mrs. Blackstone," said the dark-haired woman with a sigh after he had gone. "It's a terrible thing when a woman is made to feel her mothering is flawed."

"How can you know that?"

She looked away. "Personal experience."

"Nin." Adele looked hard at her friend. "You do know who the painful connection was and why it was severed, don't you?"

The woman played with one of the rings on her fingers. It had an odd-shaped stone protruding from a silver casement. Adele wondered if the one accused of bad mothering had given it to her.

"It was severed because it had to do with Lucy, isn't that right?" Adele persisted.

"Yes," Nin said.

"And the connection?"

"A man, that's all I know. The vibrations wouldn't reveal more." Unwilling to say more, she drew the heavy shawl around her shoulders and scurried down the street.

# CHAPTER 15

*L*ucy's funeral was a communal affair. It seemed as if the entire population of Arrojo was there. Adele sidled up to the back of the crowd with her brother and Sheriff Hatfield. Nin appeared beside her and took her arm.

"Did they all know Lucy, I mean, really know her?" asked Adele as she watched people lingering behind the Blackstones, handkerchiefs in hand.

"Not even a dozen," said Nin. "Some of their offspring, perhaps. And only those who are at one with the moon. The moon is higher than the stars and the clouds, after all."

"I beg your pardon?" Jackson asked.

"The ones standing nearest to the gravesite," she said. "The well-to-do."

"I see. A riddle," he said. "This is hardly the time."

"I don't choose to go by a timetable, Mr. Gossling."

A few people glared at them. Jackson made amends in a soothing voice. Adele felt certain they would have all been sent away, Nin with her unbound skirt and hair, Hatfield with his over-starched suit clearly left to him by one who had been as uncomfortable in it as he looked now, had Mrs. Blackstone not held out her hand for Adele to come forward.

Adele caught sight of Mickey and his nanny. The boy dawdled near the trees outside of the graveyard. Adele's heart went out to him as she caught a glimpse of his bewildered face. She slipped away and held out her arms, folding Mickey into them.

"It's all right, sweet thing," she murmured.

"Lucy's in heaven," he said with a tearful sigh.

"Indeed she is, darling." Adele looked at the woman with the cap. "I don't believe we've met. I'm Adele Gossling, the Blackstones' neighbor."

"How d'you do, miss?" said the woman. "I'm Anna Cummings." She covered her face in her handkerchief. "Oh, it's awful!"

"A shocking thing to happen to such a fine family," Adele sighed. "I take it you weren't Lucy's nurse?" It was clear the woman was no more than thirty.

"No, miss," she said. "I didn't know Miss Lucy well, but Mickey loved her dearly."

"How is he getting on?"

"As well as can be expected," she said, "what with Miss Lucy's death – " she leaned in and whispered, "– not being from natural causes."

"Someone killed her!" Mickey's voice rang out.

"Don't you think about it." Adele pulled out an extra handkerchief and handed it to him.

The boy wandered into the small garden near the cemetery entrance. He bent over a row of daffodils.

"He's a brave little boy," she said.

"Oh, yes, indeed, miss," said the nanny. "But his father has forbidden any mention of what happened to Miss Lucy in the house, so he only talks to me about her. Poor mite." She sniffed into her handkerchief.

"I can understand that," said Adele. "This whole business is so dreadful."

She could make out the Blackstones standing near the grave, though their faces were heavily hidden. The Tannings stood near them, huddled together. Adele was touched at their genuine grief. She thought Mr. Blackstone was too, as he glanced in their direction once and his tight lip eased an inch.

"Richard's not here!" she murmured.

"I beg your pardon, miss?" The nanny had been preoccupied with Mickey, who had swiped a daisy and was trying to twist it into his buttonhole.

"The Tanning brothers aren't here," she repeated.

"Danny's like me, only bigger," said Mickey. "His dog ran away, and he cried and cried. *I* wouldn't have cried like that."

"It would hardly be likely," said Miss Cummings and finished off with a whisper of, "under the circumstances."

"But Richard and Lucy were very good friends."

"I wouldn't know anything about that," the woman shot out as she closed the top button of Mickey's coat. "It's time we returned home, young man. You shouldn't be here in the first place."

"I want to see them put Lucy in the hole." He peered up at Adele. "I promised."

She bent down to him. "What did you promise?"

"Lucy and I promised each other," he said. "The one who didn't die first was to make sure the one who did got put snug in the hole, or they would come back as ghosts!" His eyes opened wide.

"Really, if your father knew –"

"Don't you tell him!" Mickey twisted the edge of Miss Cummings' skirt in his fist. "Don't you dare tell him!"

"I'll make sure she gets put in the hole all snug," said Adele. "I promise."

"Well, that's all right, then." He straightened Miss Cummings' mashed skirt and dutifully took her hand as they retreated in the direction of the Blackstone carriage.

"Miss Cummings?"

The woman turned around.

"I believe you *do* know something about Richard and Lucy," Adele said. "Otherwise you wouldn't have denied it so quickly."

Miss Cummings' face grew red. "I saw him in the garden with her a few times. That's all I know."

"If you think of anything else," said Adele, "please tell me. My brother is helping with the investigation. You want to help us catch Lucy's killer, don't you?"

"Miss, please!" She glanced down at Mickey.

Adele reached Mrs. Blackstone's side just as the preacher closed his Bible and the men prepared to lower the coffin. A ravaged cry escaped the woman's lips and Adele put her arm around her shoulders. Mr. Blackstone went to the other side of the grave so she could no longer see his face. Another face peered like an owl behind his shoulder, intense and shifting. It wasn't until they retreated to the Blackstone house for the wake that she realized it was Eddie Goodwin she had seen.

She took her brother's hand. "Richard isn't here."

"I expect he won't be at the wake either," said Jackson.

"Perhaps he prefers to grieve alone," Hatfield suggested.

"But surely, for the sake of the family –"

"I gathered social propriety matters less to the Tannings than his rival." The sheriff glanced at Mr. Blackstone as he passed them with a dismissive bow.

The house was dark because of the drawn curtains and covered mirrors. The absolute silence unnerved Adele. People spoke in hushed voices when they felt compelled to speak at all.

"I must admit, I didn't think the entire community would feel the loss of Lucy Blackstone so acutely," she remarked to her brother.

"Arrojo is different from a big city like San Francisco," Jackson reminded her. "People knew her from a child."

"You don't have to like a person to grieve their death," Adele agreed. She couldn't help but glance at Mr. and Mrs. Tanning, noting their haggard look and gray faces. "Even the Blackstones' worst enemies look as if they just lost their own daughter."

Mr. Blackstone was clearly unhinged by Hatfield's presence. He sidled up to him, hissing, "I hope you don't intend to conduct your insidious inquiries here, Sheriff."

"I'm here to pay my respects like everyone else," Hatfield assured him.

Mr. Blackstone blinked as if he didn't believe him, then turned equally impertinent eyes on the Tannings. "I don't see how you dare show your face here, Tanning."

"We loved Lucy." Mrs. Tanning was firmer than Adele thought her capable of.

Mr. Blackstone drew away from them to receive more people entering the parlor door.

"I'm glad you said that, my dear," said Mr. Tanning. "Michael thinks he's the only one who loved Lucy."

"Poor, dear girl." Mrs. Tanning clutched her handkerchief, soaked through with tears.

"Ghastly business," her husband agreed. "Michael and I have our differences, but I wouldn't wish such a thing on him in a million years."

"Wouldn't wish it on your worst enemy, isn't that the phrase?" asked Hatfield.

He glanced at him. "I don't believe in worst enemies, Sheriff. There are only enemies. We all have them."

"Mr. Tanning," Jackson began, "we noticed neither of your sons were at the burial."

The man stiffened. "You've met my son Danny, sir. You can hardly expect him to be present on such a mournful occasion."

"We try to keep him away from such things," Mrs. Tanning

said. "He's like a child, you know. We see no reason to upset him about things he can't grasp."

"Understandable," Adele nodded. Nin glared at Jackson as if she dared him to interrogate further.

"And Richard?" Jackson persisted. "He and Lucy were friends from childhood. One would have thought –"

"It's precisely because they were friends from childhood that he chose not to attend," Mr. Tanning's voice rose. "He preferred to seek his own private solace rather than parade it in public."

The sheriff said nothing but put his hand on Jackson's shoulder in a heavy-handed way.

"I don't wish to upset you, sir," Jackson continued, "but we recently discovered —"

"Not now, Jackson," Hatfield said in a low tone.

"Why not now?" asked Mr. Tanning. "It seems to me we can best honor Lucy by finding the man who killed her."

"I'm glad you feel that way, sir," said Jackson. "I was going to say we recently discovered Lucy began seeing quite a few young men soon after Richard left for college. You hinted at as much yourself."

"What of it?" asked the man.

"It doesn't strike you as odd she abandoned all discretion after your son went away?"

"Mr. Gossling." The man faced him. "You're a man of the world. You can't tell me a girl of that age doesn't readily explore her options."

"I beg your pardon!" Nin snapped just as Adele said, "And why shouldn't she?"

Mr. Tanning bowed. "I mean no disrespect, ladies. I'm merely trying to make a point."

"So you believe it was simply coming of age?" said Jackson.

"Perhaps not," Mrs. Tanning said softly. "Considering her mother."

"Mrs. Blackstone is from San Francisco, isn't she?" Adele asked.

Mr. Tanning nodded as he accepted a sherry from Eddie Goodwin coming by with a tray. The scowling expression on the man's face showed he was none too pleased at his role as footman.

"She was a Parnell from Nob Hill," said Mrs. Tanning. "Have you any acquaintance with them?"

"I'm afraid our society was a little more modest than Nob Hill," said Jackson with a small smile.

"And yourself and Mr. Blackstone?" Adele turned to Mr. Tanning. "You're as good as Nob Hill in Arrojo, aren't you?"

Mr. Tanning smiled. "My father and Michael's, and others, were from a well-bred sector of the East. Their families had money and position, and the West was an adventure for them. They meant to establish a community of like-minded people, well-bred and conservative like themselves."

"It looks as if they succeeded." Hatfield glanced around.

The man nodded. "Even small towns have a way of absorbing all who enter their gates. Arrojo became known for its proximity to San Francisco and Sacramento while offering the so-called 'rusticity' many people sought in the last century."

"So now you have a mix of people like in the big cities." Jackson nodded.

"I prefer it that way," he said quickly. "So did my grandfather. Michael's grandfather had different ideas, and so does Michael." He glanced at Mr. Blackstone near the entrance to the parlor.

"I've heard the quality of any society lies in its breeding," said the sheriff. Something in his tone struck Adele as bitter, as if he were thinking of somewhere else.

"Let's say the idea of the upper and lower class is alive and well as much here as it is in San Francisco or New York or Boston," said Mr. Tanning. "My only consolation is we have none of the violent crime you find in the big city."

"None until a few days ago, that is." The sheriff coughed. "More sherry, ladies?"

Adele caught a glimpse of Mr. Blackstone leaving the parlor. The thundering look on his face was like a fire cracker exploding amidst the solemn air. She watched with interest as Mr. Goodwin set the half-filled tray of sherry glasses on the table and followed his master outside.

She held her hand to her forehead.

Her brother leaned forward. "Are you feeling ill, Del?"

"A little dizzy." She pressed his hand. "I must get some air."

She weaved her way through the parlor. People were milling around with grave faces, and servants stood pale and silent. The black chiffon dress she wore weighed on her shoulders. She stood in the hallway across from the open veranda doors as she had with her brother the night of the party. It was hard to believe the house, now so shadowed and dark, had been feted and decorated only a short while ago. She pictured Lucy whirling around in her lavender dress, her charm bracelet clanging to her lively dancing steps, the striped carnation bobbing at her breast.

"This is a damned fine time!"

Mr. Blackstone's roar startled her. She peered through the open French doors and saw the outline of his figure under the light. A man whose back was turned to her stood opposite him.

"You appreciate, sir, this is an urgent matter with me." The reedy voice belonged to Mr. Goodwin.

"For God's sake, man, I just buried my daughter!"

"Sad affair," said the man. "A pretty girl, full of life –"

"You blackguard!" Mr. Blackstone lowered his voice. "Eddie, there's a time and a place for everything."

The man turned around and sauntered back into the house. Adele pretended to be fiddling with her handkerchief. He bowed and strolled back into the parlor.

Mr. Blackstone came next. He attempted a smile. "Insolent man. Pestering me for his pay at my daughter's funeral."

"He didn't strike me as very sensitive when I met him," Adele said politely.

"He gets his work done." He took her arm and led her back to the parlor.

"I should think even the most insensitive servant would know better than to approach his master to ask for money on a day like this."

"Eddie worked on a ranch in Philadelphia before he become a valet," said the man. "He's not always aware of the inappropriateness of his actions." He faced Adele. "I'd like to thank you, Miss Gossling, for bringing my wife solace. It's been a very difficult time for her."

"I'm happy I can be of help," she said. "We *will* find who did this to your daughter, Mr. Blackstone."

"I have faith in your brother, naturally," he said. "I only hope the sheriff is as competent as he seems."

"He's very skilled, I assure you," said Adele. "Jack told me he worked for both the San Francisco and Sacramento police, and he was a Wells Fargo detective."

"All the same," he said. "I don't mind telling you I'd rather have a gentleman on my side looking for the scoundrel."

"We're all on your side, Mr. Blackstone," she assured him.

He bowed and returned to his wife standing at the French doors and looking out at Lucy's garden.

# CHAPTER 16

Things returned to normal on Bridge Street the next day. The crowd of women who mobbed Adele's shop for details about the murder withdrew, though Adele had had no shortage of customers. Although Raleigh's, the local general store, carried letter paper, envelopes, and writing materials, Adele's stock was of higher quality and it didn't take long for people in town to realize it. Her customers put in elaborate orders and paid the full price without question. Even Jackson was impressed by her business skills.

It grew windy after lunch but the breeze subsided in the late afternoon, leaving the air gauzy with dust. A wagonload of people came through town, obviously on their way to Sacramento, stopping at Pringle's for lunch and wandering down Bridge Street, peering through shop windows. Most took little interest in hers, but many went into Nin's.

She brought her friend tea, knowing she would be exhausted from having to deal with so many people at once. "You don't make much of a living from your store, do you?" she remarked, glancing at the chaos of knick-knacks inside.

"I don't need to," said Nin. "My mother left me a handsome inheritance."

"You're an heiress, then." Adele smiled. "I'm surprised the hens haven't tried to marry you off yet."

Nin glanced at her with a wary eye. "What makes you think they haven't?" She looked out into the street. "That was before they knew all about me, of course."

"I should think they would approve of you more than of me," Adele said. "You're Ancient Woman rather than New Woman."

Nin sniffed. "I don't follow anybody's rule book."

"So you told Jack," she said. "He means no harm. He's really a very sweet boy."

"He's a man, not a boy," said Nin. "Therein lies the first problem."

"And the second and third and fourth?" Adele asked.

"When I know you better, perhaps I'll tell you," Nin answered.

"How do you know I won't be offended?"

The woman regarded her with affection. "Because I knew from the first, you seek the truth just as I do. Whether painful or pleasant, you seek the truth."

"Jack calls it nosiness." Adele said. "My father warned me inquisitiveness might one day be my undoing."

"Men say that to keep women ignorant," Nin snarled.

"Perhaps he was right." Her mind wandered. "Nin, do you think one ought to listen in on private conversations?"

"One overhears things all the time," her friend pointed out.

"I don't mean that," she said. "I mean deliberately listen in."

"My mother taught me to open my ears to the voices," said Nin. "I expect she meant human as well as spirit."

"I'm not one to talk," Adele lamented. "After all, I did send three girls to listen in on grown-ups."

As if they had been summoned, her schoolgirl friends darted from across the street, surrounding her with bobbing hair ribbons and dust.

"Good afternoon." Adele smiled. "You must be Carolyn." She looked at a girl with mousy brown hair and eyes, clearly more timid than her friends.

"Pleased to meet you, madame." The girl put out her hand.

"It's Adele, no madame," Beatrice snapped. "Don't insult the lady."

"Pleased to meet you, Adele." The girl kept her hand out.

Beatrice slapped it down. "We've lots to tell, and Mrs. Wrigley already saw us leaving, so we must hurry."

"I'll tell her you were running an errand for me," said Adele. "It's not a lie, after all."

"But, oh, what an errand!" Rachel said in a breathless voice. All her previous horror at the devious nature of their task had disappeared.

"All right, young ladies, what can you tell me?" asked Adele. "Remember, there's four cents in it for each of you."

"A love affair!" Rachel sighed.

"Miss Blackstone and Mr. Tanning were seen together," Beatrice confirmed in a low voice.

"Where?"

"At the gazebo in the old Rosemont house."

Adele glanced at Nin.

"Imagine, right next door to Lucy's own home. How daring!" Carolyn said.

"Plain stupid, if you ask me," said Beatrice.

"Don't judge your elders, Bea," said Rachel.

"Lucy was hardly my elder." The girl stiffened. "And anyway, she's dead."

"All the more reason." Her friend reached into her pocket and took out a rosary. She began playing with it, her eyes half shut as if praying for forgiveness.

"Did they have many meetings?" asked Adele.

"Many, many meetings," said Beatrice.

"Many, many," echoed Carolyn.

Adele was silent for a moment. Nin set the teacup carefully inside the saucer.

"Well, don't you want to know what they were doing?" Beatrice asked.

"I believe my imagination can supply that," said Adele dryly. "More accurately than yours can."

"Oh, you might be grown up," said Rachel, "but *we* read. I'll lay anything we know more about it than you do."

"I think you ought to pay more attention to that rosary," said Nin, with a sharp glance.

The girl shrank back, cupping the beads in her hands.

"They were talking," said Beatrice. "Mostly talking, that is. They were also seen holding hands, and he –"

"Yes?"

"He kissed her! Several times."

"That's enough," said Nin. "We have the entire picture now."

"No you don't, you witch!" Beatrice screeched. "He gave her a ring too!"

Adele grasped the girl's shoulders. "What sort of a ring?"

"A diamond ring," Beatrice said. "It almost blinded the person who saw it."

"How utterly exquisite!" Rachel sighed.

"Not if it was an inexpensive diamond," said Beatrice. "The same person said she thought it was."

"Why is that?" asked Adele.

"It wasn't clear, she said." The girl fumbled with her hair ribbon. "My mother showed me a diamond necklace Grandmother gave her, and all the diamonds were clear like water."

"Who told you all this?" said Adele. "Who saw it, I mean?"

"Oh, we have our ways," said Beatrice in a knowing voice. "You can trust our sources are reliable."

"Not if they have as wild an imagination as you do," Nin snapped.

"At least we don't practice black magic on people!" The girl pushed Nin with both hands, sending the teacup flying.

"Ladies." Adele's tone was sharp. "If you're to work for me, I insist you show some respect for my friend. You may call her Miss Branch."

"You're such a beast, Bea," said Rachel. "I apologize for my friend, Miss Branch."

"Do we work for you?" Beatrice's eyes lit up.

"I may have further use for you," said Adele.

"Five cents each time?"

"We'll see." Adele stepped into her shop and came back a few minutes later with the pennies. "Mind you get back to school right away. And if Mrs. Wrigley says anything, send her to me."

The girls screeched with glory and scurried away, holding tightly to their coins.

"You don't really believe what they said, do you?" Nin asked. "Surely their imaginations got the better of them."

"The ring." Adele looked into the dust for a moment. "It wasn't clear like water. Maybe because it wasn't an ordinary diamond."

"I don't follow you," said her friend.

She held on to Nin's hand. "Come to my shop after closing time, and I'll explain."

"I would come anyway if only to give you back your teacup."

"I can take it now." She held out her hand.

"I must wash it first," said the woman. "I may be a witch, but I'm a clean witch."

"Oh, Nin, that was just girlish chatter," said Adele.

"Perhaps," said Nin. "But children mock their elders." There was a saddened look on her face, making her lovely features still like a painting. Adele realized for the first time how the town gossip affected her friend more than she admitted.

That evening, Nin brought her a sparkling clean teacup and a tiny sachem tied with a ribbon. "Chamomile," she said. "It soothes the nerves."

"Thank you." Adele tucked it in a desk drawer.

"You might do well to put it in your purse," Nin suggested. "Then you can open it and breath deeply when you need it."

Adele put it in her bag a gracious smile at her friend.

They walked arm in arm into the police station. The building was small but new painted and presentable. Two desks sat at near the entrance, both empty. Other desks filled the small room facing one another and a large desk with *Sheriff Horatio Hatfield* inscribed on a plaque. As they entered, the large chair behind the desk whirled around to reveal Edison, an unlit cigar dangling from his mouth. He was clearly embarrassed at being caught playing his better. As he jumped up, the cigar tumbled to the floor.

"It's all right, Assistant Deputy Edison." Adele tried to hide a smile. "We were just looking for my brother."

The young man swelled with pride at her using his official title. "He's having tea with Sheriff Hatfield, miss."

"Oh?"

The young man leaned forward. "At his home with the sheriff's mother."

"An odd time for tea, isn't it?" Nin eyed him.

"Well, miss, it's this way." The young man took the chair again, leaning back. "They went out of town to see Mr. Tanning's college professors —"

"I didn't know Mr. Tanning was in college." Adele couldn't resist goading him. "He seems rather old for that."

"I meant Mr. Richard Tanning, miss." Edison fumbled with the fountain pen on the table. "As I said, they went to see Mr. Tanning's professors and the sheriff called about an hour ago to say he and Mr. Gossling hadn't any lunch, and his mother absolutely *insisted* —"

"I think we understand," said Adele. "Could you tell us where we could find the sheriff's house?"

"Whatever for, miss?"

"None of your business," Nin snapped.

"We've some important news for them, Assistant Deputy," Adele said.

"New evidence on the Blackstone case?" He leaned like an eager fox. "I've heard you're taking an interest, miss."

"That's none of your business either," Nin said.

"In a way," said Adele. "We have information, but we must give it to them ourselves."

"I understand, miss." The boy looked rather like a startled chipmunk as he dipped the fountain pen in ink and wrote down the address.

"Thank you, Assistant Deputy Edison," she said. "You've been so helpful." She gave him the sweetest smile she could muster, and Nin snorted as they left the station, leaving Edison with a gaping mouth.

The Hatfield house looked like a charming villa she had once seen on some picture postcards of Sicily. The garden was especially beautiful, and Adele envied the brilliant purple, yellow, and orange colors radiant even under the fading sun. Honeysuckle greeted them as they thumped on the door knocker.

A middle-aged housekeeper answered and with a discreet nod, led them through the house where they found Jackson and Hatfield lounging in a garden as brilliant as the one in front. With them was one of the most imposing women Adele had ever seen. It was not in her height, for she sat in a chair on wheels and did not rise. Nor was it her age, which looked to be about seventy. But something in the dignified way she held herself up and her eyes regarding them without apology, made Adele feel humble. Even before they were introduced, Adele knew the woman could be no one else but Hatfield's mother. They had the same round face and booming voice.

"Welcome, my dears!" Her voice was deep and refined. "Won't you join us for tea?"

"You're very kind," she said.

"I know who you are," the woman continued, tapping the chair next to her with her cane. "Not that I got it out of your brother, of course. He's rather tight-lipped, isn't he?"

Jackson covered his face with his napkin, which Adele took for embarrassment.

"I can imagine where you heard of me," Adele remarked as she took the chair.

"The gossiping geese," said the woman. "I don't get out much, as you can see." She glanced down at her withered legs. "Rowena does the shopping and brings me back all their blessed little hearts care to tell." She cocked her head. "Don't you think Rowena is rather a grand name for a housekeeper? Horatio!" She vigorously slapped the side of Hatfield's shoe with her cane. "Your manners, dear. Introduce me."

The sheriff repositioned himself. "Miss Gossling and Miss Branch, may I introduce Lady Augusta Hatfield, my mother."

"Charmed." Adele took her hand. It had none of the frailty she had known from elderly women in the city. This one was smooth and agile.

"I'm sure you're wondering about the 'Lady' part," said the woman.

"I was more wondering about the 'Lord' part, or lack thereof, in your son's name," Adele admitted.

"I'm a full-blooded democratic American, Adele." There was something a little too insistent in the sheriff's voice as he said this.

"So am I, dear." His mother sat back, taking full pride in the inherent dignity she knew she possessed. "I was once married to one Lord Hatfield. I won't tell you about it, as this is America, and the best of us care nothing for such things."

"But you use the title nevertheless," Adele said.

She leaned in. "I suppose that makes me rather a hypocrite."

"Not in the least, Ma," Hatfield growled. "You're entitled to it."

His mother continued, "I use it because it has influence. Influence, in any country, is a valuable asset."

"Should I bow, then?" asked Adele.

"Don't be silly!" said the woman. "I meant I use it as influence with the gossiping geese here. To those who care nothing about it, I very gladly dispense with formalities. Don't I, dear?" She tapped her son's shoes.

"Indeed, Ma," he said.

"Tell me," The woman peered at her through glasses shaped like lozenges, "are you anxious to find a husband, as they seem to think in town?"

"Heaven help us if she were," Jackson mumbled.

Adele glared at him. "I'm content to be without prospects for now."

"Splendid!" the woman boomed. "You might accomplish something in this world, then. Early marriage very often ruins a woman's potential."

Hatfield cleared his throat. "Ma was married at the age of eighteen."

"I didn't mean *mine*, dear." She patted his arm. "Marriage is be-all, end-all for some women, I don't deny it. But these families nowadays, sending young girls to Europe to find a duke or a count. Their money would be better spent giving those girls a good education."

"Ma got her education before she got her lord." Hatfield shifted uncomfortably in his chair.

"The lord was pure coincidence, not deliberate on my part," said Lady Augusta. "Not like some of the title-crazy girls nowadays."

"I couldn't agree with you more," said Adele.

The noblewoman seemed satisfied and rolled her glasses further up her nose, looking over Adele's shoulder. "Who is this ravishing creature?"

Nin lingered behind near the wall. She came forward and stared at Lady Augusta with cloudy, vacant eyes.

"Oh, *God!*" Jackson murmured.

"You remember, Ma. I just introduced her as Miss Branch." The sheriff looked equally alarmed.

Lady Augusta looked at Nin with a bold gaze. "Yes, of course. Are you all right, dear? The sun can be mighty strong this time of day."

"You've had a sad life," Nin said in a breathy tone. "The lord was a good man, but his family were cruel to you."

Lady Augusta's face tightened for a moment. There was a clamor at the table as Hatfield dropped his spoon.

"Interesting woman," she murmured.

"Nin has a gift, Lady Augusta," Adele explained. "She feels things no one else does."

"Yes, so I see." The boom came back in her voice. "You must all come to dinner one night. Horatio!" She slapped the sheriff's shoe. "Make them promise to come once this dreadful affair is over."

Hatfield stood up and bowed. "You must all come to dinner once this dreadful affair is over."

"Which will be soon, I hope," said Adele. "We've had some news from my little helpers."

"Your schoolgirl cherubs have come through?" Jackson grabbed his hat and gloves.

"Official business, Ma." Hatfield bent down to give his mother a kiss. "I won't be long."

"Your garden is very beautiful, Lady Augusta," said Adele. "The violets are enthralling."

"Horatio, see Adele gets a bouquet of flowers on your way out." She held out her hand. "You'll come and see me now we've become acquainted. I'll serve you the best tea you ever had in this country. You too, my dear." She smiled at Nin.

Nin suddenly threw her arms around her shoulders,

embracing her like a favorite aunt. Lady Augusta's calm demeanor remained.

"I know who you are now," said the noblewoman. "I also know what they say about you, and I shall tell Rowena the next time she's in town to tell them to go to the devil."

Nin smiled. It was the first pure smile Adele had ever seen her give someone.

# CHAPTER 17

*O*nce they were at the police station, Sheriff Hatfield was businesslike. He sat back in the chair Edison had taken only a half hour before and listened as Adele told him what the Wrigley girls had discovered. "Miss Blackstone was wearing a lilac diamond the night of the party, you say?"

"Not wearing it exactly," said Jackson. "It was hanging like a charm on her bracelet."

"I complimented her on it," said Adele. "It's truly one of the most exquisite rings I've ever seen."

"And my sister has no awe of jewelry, Sheriff," said Jackson. "Most of hers sits at the bottom of a box gathering dust."

"And it wasn't a clear diamond," said Nin. "I saw it too."

"Maybe it was a family heirloom," Hatfield suggested.

"Miss Blackstone said it was," Jackson said.

"And yet, Mr. Blackstone was right there and didn't confirm it," Adele said. "He looked as if he didn't know what she was talking about."

Jackson sat at the edge of the sheriff's desk. "Perhaps it wasn't a family heirloom, then, and Richard proposed to her."

"Lucy must have accepted if she was wearing it on her

bracelet," said the sheriff. "Rather indiscreet of her if it was a secret engagement."

"Silly young girls don't hide such things," Nin said with a sniff. "Even if it's supposed to be a secret."

"Why not wear it on her finger, then?"

"She claimed she couldn't wear rings," said Adele. A large fly close to the lamp distracted her for a moment.

"That's not true!" Nin insisted. "There was a picture in the *Arrojo Courier* last year of Lucy at her debutante ball and she was wearing a sapphire ring."

"You have a good memory, Miss Branch." The young woman blushed.

"If it was a secret engagement, and it appears to be, or Richard Tanning would have told us, why would it be secret?" Jackson asked.

"Given the family feud between the Blackstones and the Tannings, I should think that was obvious," the sheriff said.

"Maybe she was wearing the ring the night of the party intending to give it back," Adele said.

Both men stared at her.

"There were no pockets on her dress, and she carried no handbag," she continued. "We know she was going to meet Richard later that night. Perhaps she put it on the bracelet to hold it for her until she could give it back to him."

"By God!" Hatfield sat up with a grin. "A woman would do such a thing, wouldn't she?"

"If she were practical, she would," Nin said. "If she were clever, she wouldn't have accepted the ring unless she was prepared to honor it in the first place."

"It would certainly give Richard Tanning a motive for killing her," Jackson said. "Men don't take a broken engagement lightly."

Edison clambered into the station. "You're back, sir."

"I said I would be, lad," said the sheriff.

"The boots are in the file room, sir, just as you said."

"And you have the lads checking them?"

"Yes, sir."

"Boots?" asked Adele.

Hatfield grinned, motioning them to follow him to another room. The cramped space contained a few wooden filing cabinets and two barred windows. The floor was covered with men's boots, all pointing toward the door. Two assistant deputies were bending over them.

"The lads had a time collecting them from the old goats," said Hatfield. "You know how the wealthy get their backs up when the police lay a hand on their things."

"I don't understand." Nin stared at them.

"It's quite simple, Miss Branch," said Hatfield. "I had a specialist go out to the place where the crime occurred and make a plaster impression of the footprints we found. Now the lads are checking them against the boots worn that night at the party to see if there's a match."

"But surely the footprints belong to Richard," said Adele. "He told us he went out to meet her that night."

"We must check every detail, Del," said Jackson. "That's the way it's done."

Hatfield patted the back of one young man. "Any luck so far?"

"No, Sheriff," he said in a throaty voice.

"Well, keep at it."

Jackson tapped his stick on the floor. "Sheriff, you note the footsteps disappeared as we came closer to the gate between Del's house and the Blackstones'. Why do you suppose that is?"

The man cocked his head. "Why do *you* suppose that is? Come, sir, you must have a theory."

"If you had just killed a woman," said Jackson, "and you wanted to move her body, how would you do it?"

"Why move it at all?" Adele leaned against the file cabinet.

"That's another question, Del," her brother said impatiently. "How would you move the body?"

"I'd carry it," said the sheriff. "If I were a strong enough man and the body was light enough."

"But what if you were dressed in your best clothes and wanted to return to a crowd of people?" asked Jackson. "Perhaps to establish an alibi."

"Richard didn't return to the party," Nin pointed out. "He went home."

"I'm aware of that, Miss Branch," Jackson snapped. Adele gave him a warning glare, and his tone lightened. "All right, say you wanted to avoid touching the body as much as possible so as not to leave incriminating evidence, like blood or mud."

"I see what you're getting at," Hatfield said. "Whoever killed Miss Blackstone carried her body part of the way and dragged it the rest."

"That's odd, isn't it?" Nin asked.

"Dragging makes noise, Miss Branch, especially if the ground isn't clear," said the sheriff. "The killer had to be sure he or she was out of earshot before they could drag the body."

"Why drag it at all?" Adele asked.

Hatfield grimaced. "Have you ever tried carrying a dead body, Adele?" She shivered. "Bones are like lead once a person has no more life, even the most delicate of figures. We know the killer chose to put the body in your gazebo, which is some distance away from where we found the footprints. He or she wouldn't have wanted to carry the body all that way."

"Easier also to hide what one is doing among the brush rather than what one is carrying over one's shoulders," Jackson added.

"Then it must have been a man," Nin said. "No woman could carry another woman across the brush."

"A very strong woman might," the sheriff pointed out. "We mustn't rule it out."

"So whether by design or accident, the killer erased his or her own footprints by dragging the body over them," said Adele.

"Exactly," said Jackson.

"Hardly the revelation of the ages," Nin remarked.

"But a start." Hatfield patted Jackson's shoulder. "Solving a murder is like clearing a forest. You start with one tree and then move on to another and another until there is nothing but stumps."

"Tomas and Ruth and the entire family were home," Adele said. "Why didn't they hear the killer dragging the body into the gazebo?"

"Their shack is at the back of the house, Del," said Jackson. "They wouldn't have heard a thing."

Adele nodded. "Have you Richard's boots here?"

The sheriff peered at the tags and found a pair of brown leather boots. He held them up to the lads. "Have you checked these yet?" They both shook their heads. He snatched the plaster cast from their hands and tried it against the right sole. It didn't fit, but the left one fit perfectly.

Jackson stared. "A match."

"Just about," Hatfield agreed. "All right, lads, you can return the others to their owners. And mind you go quickly!"

"We expected it," Adele pointed out as they left the room. "It doesn't prove a thing."

Hatfield wiped his hands on his handkerchief. "You like the Tannings, don't you?"

She stiffened. "They were very kind to me when I first came here."

"Be careful," he advised. "If there's one thing I learned in my years of police work, it's even the most amiable of men can be a killer."

Adele fiddled with her gloves and said nothing.

～

*T*hat evening Tomas and Ruth clucked like fussy hens. They coaxed Adele and her brother to eat generous portions of roast duck and then sent them to the front porch to "take in air" while they prepared the large bowls of custard for dessert. Adele had to admit the Arrojo night was far more pleasant than the city even with the moths dancing under the gas lamp. Jackson got out his pipe and took a long inhale of smoke.

"A chill wind might come at any moment." Adele settled next to him. He put an arm across the back of the swing in a lazy fashion. "It does kick up quicker here than in San Francisco. You wouldn't think so, what with the bay and all."

"I've noticed that too." His long legs swung them back and forth.

"What else have you noticed?" She leaned her head back.

"The good, the bad, or the downright illogical?" he joked.

"I'm trying to get you to admit it's not as bad in the country as you thought," she said. "So you might consider staying."

"I can't, Del."

"Good Lord, why not?" She sat up.

"Mind your language."

"I'll say what I like," she snapped. "Why not?"

"I've a life in the city," he insisted.

"A naughty life is a short life, as Papa used to say."

"He ought to have known," Jackson retorted.

They were both quiet as Ruth brought out the custard. When she had gone inside, he continued, "I haven't had a naughty life, at least not in years. You know that, Del."

"Then leave the fog behind and come live here with me in the country," she pleaded.

"And help the sheriff catch cow thieves and wayfarers who roll through town, I suppose?" He was amused. "And every twenty years or so, perhaps a murderer."

"I hardly think that represents the normal state of affairs here," she said.

He shrugged. "I'm no country gentleman."

"I hate to remind you of your responsibilities," she began, then quickly retreated. "No, I won't play the distressed damsel in need of a watcher."

He laughed. "You're more the devil in petticoats." He smoked on his pipe for a time. "I suppose you've a mind to abandon your young man for good."

"What young man?"

He gave her a comical look. "Young John Bellows."

"Surely, you can't be serious." She sniffed. "The man looks like a crane. He's about as insightful as one."

"He also has a house in Pacific Heights, a beach house in Monterey, and a yacht," said Jackson. "A rather impressive array of property for a young lawyer."

"Those things are unimportant to me."

"He's dependable," Jackson argued. "If you're in need of a watcher, he's your man."

"I find this conversation distasteful, Jack." She rose. "I'm going to bed, if you don't mind."

He dumped the dregs of the pipe into the dirt under Tomas' clicking tongue. "Yes, we've a busy day ahead of us tomorrow."

"Helping the lads return all those boots?" she asked with a twinkle in her eye.

"No, questioning Richard Tanning. We're bringing him into the station."

Adele glanced at him. "You're going to arrest him?"

"Question, not arrest." He was quiet for a moment. "I only mentioned it because Hatfield thinks you ought to be there."

"Isn't it official police business?"

"The sheriff in this town seems to have his own ideas about what is and isn't official," said Jackson in a wry tone. "I suppose small-town sheriffs have that privilege."

"I take it you don't want me there?"

"It's not a question of what I want," he argued.

"But you think I would interfere."

He played with the edge of his pipe. "The Tannings are fond of you, and Hatfield has a notion he'll be more open in your company."

She lingered on the staircase. "I don't know. I do have a business to run."

"You can't fool me, Del," he said. "You've needled me to death with questions about the Anspaches."

"I've already been accused of having a morbid curiosity for crime." She grinned.

"If the sheriff asked you to be there, I think you ought to," Jackson said slowly. "The sooner we get to the bottom of this affair, the sooner we can both get on with our lives."

"Maybe the slower you work, the more you'll come to like Arrojo," she said. "And you'll stay."

"Now you're using feminine wiles rather than being a damsel in distress." But he smiled and lit his pipe.

# CHAPTER 18

Hatfield arrived early at the Gosslings', taking advantage of the warm muffins and coffee Ruth set out on the table. "I'm glad you agreed to come along, Adele," he said. "I think Mrs. Tanning will be relieved to know you're there."

"Women don't comfort only women, Sheriff," Adele reminded him. "I've comforted many men in my work with the settlement houses."

"No doubt you miss that sort of work," Hatfield murmured.

"Comforting young men unduly suspected of murder is just as good." She looked steadily at him.

"Whether Richard is unduly suspected remains to be seen, Del," Jackson said.

The maid let them into the Tanning study. Papers were spewed all over the desk and floor. As they entered, a row of encyclopedias toppled down with Richard standing nearby. Jackson pushed the young man out of the way.

"Much obliged." Richard wiped dust from his forehead. "It's infuriating not to find the exact thing one wants at the moment one wants it."

"A little early for spring cleaning, isn't it, Mr. Tanning," asked the sheriff.

"I was going through my own things," said the young man. "I leave in a few days."

"Leave?" Adele sat down in a leather chair.

"It's time I made my way," he said. "I don't much care for that expression, but Papa is rather fond of it."

"You have your law degree now, of course," said Jackson. "Naturally you would want to use it."

"I have the degree but not the training." Richard rolled down his sleeves. "I hope to get an apprenticeship."

"Papa always preferred to work with apprentices directly rather than leave them to his partners," Adele said. "He loved seeing how a young man's knowledge of the law grew with each case."

"Your father was well thought of in San Francisco." Richard smiled. "I recall we studied some of his early cases."

"Thank you for saying so." Adele felt a sting in her eyes and dug into her bag for a handkerchief. Her brother remained silent.

"Will you be going to San Francisco?" Hatfield leaned against the desk.

"It seems the best thing." He dropped into a chair. "One can lose oneself in the city."

"One can also lose one's perspective," Jackson said in a tight voice. "Or one's moral standing."

The young man sighed. "Yes, I suppose that's true."

"We won't keep you long, sir," said the sheriff. "We'd like you to come down to the station with us."

"Oh?" The young man's eyes were immediately alert.

"We have a few more questions for you."

"Are you going to arrest me, Sheriff?"

"Not yet, sir," Hatfield mumbled.

"I've told you all I could." Richard leaned his head back and closed his eyes.

"No, sir," said the sheriff. "I don't think you have."

The man's eyes snapped open. He was more alarmed than angry. "I'm sorry you think so."

"It's true, isn't it, Richard?" Adele asked gently. "You haven't been lying to us, but you haven't told us the whole truth."

The young man wavered. "I'm not much good under fire. I would never make a good soldier."

"Or a good sailor, I dare say," said Hatfield under his breath.

Richard sat up. "I want to help. I do."

"You can help us by coming down to the station," said Jackson. "We won't keep you long."

"You can ask me questions here, can't you?"

"I prefer official surroundings," Hatfield said, his tone a little stiff.

"Very well." The young man rose.

"Perhaps you ought to tell your parents," Jackson said.

Richard shook his head. "It's best they don't know."

As they emerged from the house, a whistle came from across the garden. Adele looked to see a young man grinning at her.

"Danny, go back into the house," his brother ordered.

"Good morning, Daniel," Adele greeted him. "Do you know Sheriff Hatfield?" She made a gesture at the man.

Daniel looked carefully at him. "You're dead, dead!"

They all looked startled for a moment. Hatfield said in a kind voice, "I think you mean Sheriff Nealy, young man. I'm sheriff now."

"You remember my brother, Jack?" Adele continued.

Daniel grabbed Jackson's hat, gazing at it like a child. "I have a hat too."

Jackson gently pried it from the man's hands and put it back firmly on his head.

"Papa only lets me wear it at parties," he said.

Richard took his brother's arm. "It's chilly out here. You'd better go inside."

Daniel blinked at his brother. "Lucy is dead. Boom boom!"

The sheriff leaned in. "How do you know she's dead, Daniel?"

The man pointed to his ears. "Little pitchers have big ears." He laughed.

"Leave him alone, please," Richard murmured.

"She gave me candy," said Daniel. "Green candy." He produced a green stick with a white swirl going down.

"That was very nice of her," said Adele. "The next time I come, I'll bring you peppermint candy."

"My favorite!" The young man held up a mouse. "Present." He thrust it at her.

Adele heard her brother grunt, but she remained calm. She had seen her share of rodents in the settlement house cellars so the mouse didn't disturb her in the least. "Where did you find it?"

"In the flowers." His face drooped. "Lucy liked purple flowers." Bursting into tears, he ran to the back of the house.

"Why did you have to upset him?" Richard looked genuinely distressed. "He's like a child, don't you see?"

"I'm sorry," said Adele softly.

"I was referring to the sheriff, Miss Gossling, not you."

"I apologize, Mr. Tanning," said Hatfield. "We must ask our questions of everybody."

Richard glared at him and remained silent as they walked to the police station.

As the young man settled in the chair opposite Hatfield, Edison scurried into the file room and came back with a pair of boots. "Will you please examine these, Mr. Tanning?"

Richard inspected the boots. "What about them?"

"These are the boots you gave Edison when they came around to fetch the shoes you were wearing the night of the party?"

"They look like the boots," said the young man.

"Then they are yours?"

He examined them inside and on the soles. "Well, no."

"You just told us these are the boots you gave Deputy Assistant Edison," Jackson said.

"Yes, I gave them to him," he said. "I recognize the V shapes on the soles. But now that I look closely at them, I see they aren't the boots I wore that night."

"They're your size?" asked Hatfield.

"They're my size, but they aren't mine."

"Maybe Edison took the wrong ones," Jackson suggested. "I wouldn't put it past him." He shot the young man a wary look.

"What does it matter if they're my boots or not?" the young man asked.

"I must tell you, Mr. Tanning," said Hatfield. "The soles of these boots match plaster castings my specialist took from footsteps we found in the brush behind the Blackstone house."

"Well, surely, that's not surprising," said Richard. "I told you I went out to meet her."

Hatfield settled back in the large chair. "I'd like you to tell me everything you can remember about that meeting, sir."

Richard took out a handkerchief and wiped his face. It was then Adele noticed his eyes were damp. "I've told you already."

"Tell me again."

The man sighed. "Lucy sent the note asking to meet me at ten o'clock that night."

"How did she send the note?" asked Jackson.

"Her maid brought it, as she always does – did," said Richard.

"What were you doing before you went to meet her?"

"I don't quite remember." The young man looked annoyed. "Things get all muddled at a party, Mr. Gossling. You ought to know that."

"Where were you, then?" the sheriff asked.

The young man thought back. "In the kitchen. I remember now. I was playing checkers with Danny. My brother gets anxious at social gatherings, so I always try to spend a little time with him."

"You're very patient and devoted to him," said Adele.

"Kind of you to say so, Miss Gossling." He smiled.

"Until when did you play checkers?" asked Jackson.

"Just before ten. Then I went out the back door."

"To the spot crossing," the sheriff said.

"Yes."

"And she never came?"

He nodded. "I waited about twenty minutes. That's when I went home."

"How did you feel, sir?" Hatfield inquired. "About Lucy not showing up, that is?"

"Quite annoyed. Sometimes Lucy could be a little thoughtless. I wish to God I hadn't been now." He lips quivered. "I wish to God I had waited a little longer. I might have stopped her – her –"

"Killer," Jackson finished in a soft voice.

The sheriff looked straight at Richard. "You're holding something back from us, aren't you, Mr. Tanning?"

"I don't know what you expect me to say, Sheriff." The young man rose. "If you'll excuse me, I have work to do."

"I expect you to tell the truth." The sheriff's voice rose. "I expect an actual account of your and Miss Blackstone's relationship and not some whitewashed version." He placed his hand on Richard's shoulder. "Come, sir. Your father isn't here now."

The young man sat down again. "I'm sorry."

Jackson leaned forward. "We've heard some things, and we want to know if they're true."

"You've heard things," the young man repeated.

"We heard you and Lucy were something more than friends." Adele tried to sound as delicate as possible.

He looked at her. "I can't lie to you, Miss Gossling. And I didn't lie – not exactly."

"Explain yourself, sir," said the sheriff.

"I told you we'd been friends for a long time," he said. "We were still friends when I came back from the university. We saw one another quite often. In secret, of course."

"Hence the notes," said Adele.

He nodded. "But it became something more." He looked at the sheriff. "We did nothing to be ashamed of. It just –"

"Blossomed." Hatfield nodded. "An old-fashioned way of putting it but apt nonetheless."

"We fell in love." His eyes spotted with tears. "I know we should have resisted it for the sake of our fathers, if nothing else."

"One cannot direct whom one loves," Jackson said. Adele tried to catch his eye but he refused to look at her.

"You say you fell in love only after you came back to town," said Hatfield. "We heard a slightly different story."

The young man looked up sharply.

"You were corresponding with Vanessa Faderman while you were away, is that right?" asked Jackson.

Richard stared at him. "How the devil did you know that?"

"Mrs. Faderman told me," Adele said.

"The post office near your university confirmed it, Mr. Blackstone," said Hatfield.

"There's nothing suspicious about my writing to a childhood friend, is there?" the young man grumbled.

"You demanded to know about Lucy's conquests in those letters," said Hatfield.

Richard stared at him, then threw his head back and burst out laughing. It was not a happy laughter but one laced with nervousness.

"I'm sorry, Sheriff," he said. "But if Mrs. Faderman told you that, she's more imaginative than I thought."

"Then it isn't true?" asked Jackson.

"I suppose it is in a way," Richard admitted. "I said we fell in love when I got back, but what I really should have said was Lucy fell in love with me."

"You, on the other hand, fell in love with her quite some time ago," Hatfield said.

Richard nodded. "I suppose I did ask a lot of questions about Lucy in those letters, but I doubt I was 'demanding,' and I don't recall asking specifically about her conquests. Not that I wasn't aware she had them."

"Quite so, sir," Hatfield said. "I'd like you to tell us the truth this time about why she wanted to meet with you that night."

"I believe." Richard stopped, unsure of what to say next. "I believe she intended to give me an answer."

"An answer to what?" asked Adele.

"My proposal," he said. "I'd asked Lucy to marry me a week before."

"Why didn't you tell us this before?" asked Jackson.

"Isn't it obvious?" Richard asked. "Our fathers had no idea what was going on. Lucy said she wanted some time to think it over. We decided it was best not to say anything until it was settled."

"You gave her a lilac diamond for an engagement ring," said Adele.

He blinked at her. "You know about that."

"It was on her bracelet the night of the party."

"Was it?" He closed his eyes. "I didn't notice. I hardly saw what she was wearing that night. I hardly saw anything. I was so anxious, you see."

"Any young man would be." There was deep sympathy in Hatfield's voice. "Was there anything in the note she sent you to indicate whether she decided to accept or not?"

"I explained what was in the note already, Sheriff." Richard's lip was tight.

"Yes, well, it would help if we could see it."

"I told you, I burned all of Lucy's notes!" The young man's voice rose above the squall of birds somewhere beyond the reaches of the study windows.

"And the ring?" asked Hatfield. "Do you have it now?"

The young man looked ready to bang his fist on the desk, but he steadied himself. "If I gave it to Lucy, why would *I* have it?"

"Surely it's on the bracelet," said Adele.

"Which we still haven't found," Hatfield added. "You wouldn't know where it was, would you, sir?"

Richard stared at him. "No. Why would I?"

There was a flurry of loud voices at the door, and Edison came flying in with Mr. and Mrs. Tanning at his heels.

"Sheriff, you can't do this!" Mr. Tanning's face was distraught. His wife sobbed into her handkerchief.

"Sir?" Hatfield looked genuinely confused.

"You can't arrest my son!"

"No one is arresting your son, Mr. Tanning," Jackson said.

"It's all right, Mother." Richard sat his mother down in a chair. Adele took a place beside her, murmuring kind words in her ear.

"May I ask how you knew Richard was here?"

"Danny told us he saw his brother leaving with the sheriff," said Mr. Tanning. "Naturally we thought —"

"Naturally, you jumped to conclusions," Jackson finished.

"The police are always the enemy, eh?" Hatfield sat down slowly behind his desk.

"I know you're only doing your duty, sir." Mr. Tanning was completely calm now, wiping his damp brow.

"We just needed to speak with your son, sir," the sheriff assured him.

"In the future, I would appreciate it if you would question my son in my presence."

"Papa, I'm not a child," snapped Richard.

The sheriff gave him a keen look. "What are you afraid he will say, Mr. Tanning?"

"Of all the —" But the growl was immediately replaced with regret. "I suppose I can see how it would sound that way. I only mean Richard is so tormented, he might not realize what he's saying."

"Papa!"

"I'm trying to protect you."

"Mr. Tanning," said Jackson, "your son can speak for himself."

"Consider it overzealousness, then," said the father with a smile.

The sheriff rose. "We're finished for now, Mr. Tanning. I see we've taken up too much of your time already."

"I'm sorry if I sounded defensive," said the young man. "I just want this damn business to be over with."

"Richard has his own life to live," Mrs. Tanning said, sniffing.

"I'm afraid I'll have to ask you not to leave town just yet." The sheriff glanced at Richard.

Richard's hands pressed hard on the desk. "Then you intend to arrest me some time in the future?"

"I didn't say that, sir."

"Don't evade the question, Sheriff." Richard's voice was hard. "I know the law, after all. I'm clearly the most obvious suspect, and unless there is no one else, I'll be arrested."

"As you know the law." The sheriff was equally hard, "I'm sure I don't need to remind you this is a murder investigation, and everyone who might have been intimately involved with Lucy in one way or another needs to stay close at hand."

"But he's made plans!" Mr. Tanning insisted.

"Nevertheless, I must ask you delay your departure for the time being."

Jackson touched the young man's arm. "It's standard procedure, Richard, nothing personal."

"It's a little hard to believe –" His father's voice rose, but a cry came from Mrs. Tanning.

"What does it matter?" Richard sighed. "I've no immediate position waiting for me in the city."

"I'm sure my father's partners could do something for you," Adele started, but a glare from her brother made her stop.

Jackson slipped him a card. "Friends of mine," he said. "I'm sure they can help you."

"Anspaches?" Adele raised her eyebrows.

"Not everyone considered us little better than cads, Del," said her brother with a small smile. "At least *they* deal with highly respectable clients."

She bit her lip and didn't answer.

# CHAPTER 19

*A*dele didn't see Hatfield the rest of the day and Jackson only that evening. She stayed late at her shop to arrange the window display with Nin, who, despite her attraction to flowing dress, had an eye for elegant colors and patterns.

She came home at around eight o'clock. The men in the house did not hide their annoyance at the late hour. Tomas, a knife in his hand, pointed it at her like an accusing finger. Even Marco, the Cordobas' only son, frowned with three-year-old disapproval as his father threw him over his shoulder and carried him down the stairs.

Jackson, having waited dinner on her, sat in the parlor with the evening papers. The way he straightened the pages with a snap when she greeted him reminded her of the evenings when he and her father had fought. Adele knew better than to try and speak to him. She went upstairs and changed into a comfortable muslin dress and washed her face. When she came down, he was sitting at the dining room table with his linen napkin in his lap.

"All right, if I deserve a reprimand, you may as well give it to me now." She took her place at the table.

"You really ought to send word when you'll be late, Del."

Jackson did not look up from his paper. "At least Ruth could serve a hot dinner then."

"Is that why you're so furious with me?" She couldn't help but feel amused. "Because your soup is cold?"

"I don't like the idea of you traipsing around at night in that shop of yours," he growled.

"No one thought twice about it when Papa walked came home after midnight," she grumbled.

"Father had clients who made their own rules," Jackson said.

"What makes you think I don't have my own demanding clients?"

"I can hardly believe you would in a place like this."

"And if my shop were in San Francisco?" she challenged. "I could come home as late as I liked?"

He broke off the heel of a loaf of bread. "Since you insisted on having a telephone in the house, you might at least use it!"

"I would, if Tomas weren't so frightened of it," she said. "I do believe if it ever rang, he would throw knives at it."

His annoyance broke as he tried to hide a smile. She poked him in the stomach until he was laughing, a game they had played since they were children.

After dinner, they retired to the parlor. Jackson played poker against himself while she pricked her fingers over her needlepoint. It occurred to Adele how absurd they both looked. Jackson had given up poker years ago and she was as attracted to needlepoint as she was to marriage. But ever since their father died, they had searched for an evening ritual of domesticity they never really had.

She was sure there was something on Jackson's mind beyond her lateness. He was slow in laying the cards, as if he were contemplating something other than the game. Finally, he abandoned the cards and sat back, reaching for his pipe.

"I think you ought to know, Del," he began. "Hatfield arrested Richard tonight."

The needle she had been trying to thread dropped onto the rug. She bent down to retrieve it. "He promised the Tannings he wouldn't."

"He never made such a promise," Jackson insisted. "He felt he needed to make a move." In a more defiant tone, he added, "He has the authority."

"All the more reason I expected him to use it wisely!" Adele tossed the needlework back in the basket.

"He has been," Jackson insisted. "You don't think he would have arrested Richard if he didn't have the evidence to do so."

"What evidence?" Her throat was tight.

"The kind of evidence one finds with a search warrant," said Jackson. "Hatfield thought Richard wasn't telling him the truth about burning Lucy's note."

"Why would he think he was lying?" She tried to keep her voice calm, as she knew any kind of agitation would send Tomas and Ruth running to them with alarm. They seemed to take exception to any hint of harsh words between her and Jackson.

"It stands to reason, Del. A man waiting for an answer to a proposal wouldn't burn a note like that."

She sat with her hands in her lap. "So you searched Richard's house and found the note."

"We found it along with Lucy's bracelet hidden in the Tanning's cellar," he said.

"And what about the ring?"

"It wasn't on the bracelet."

Adele settled into a rocking chair. "If they were hidden, he probably forgot about them."

Her brother glared at her. "You don't believe that for a moment."

"All right, I don't," she challenged. "And the missing ring?"

"Someone wanted it to disappear," he said.

She glanced at him. "What are you implying?"

He puffed on the pipe.

"A tramp could have taken it," she said. "How do we know a tramp didn't stumble upon Lucy's body, and, knowing the ring was valuable, stole it?"

"And left Lucy's bracelet behind?"

"Maybe he was partial to diamonds!" she exploded.

Ruth peered through the parlor door, holding a tray with coffee.

"Just leave it here, Ruth," said Jackson. "I think we could use it."

Adele lowered her voice. "So you broke into the Tanning house and turned it inside out to search it?"

He snapped the pipe from his lips. "We did not break in, Del. Search warrants give us legal authority to search for evidence."

"Call it what you like." She walked around the room. "What else did you find, other than the note and bracelet?"

"All of the notes."

"What do you mean, 'all'?"

"All of Lucy's notes to Richard," said Jackson. "He didn't burn them as he said."

"Well, what of it? Wouldn't you keep notes from the woman that you loved?"

"I would." His voice softened. "If I ever loved a woman that much."

"If Richard kept the notes, he would have kept the ring he gave her too," Adele pointed out.

He shook his head. "We searched all over the house, Del. Hatfield thinks it's the key to the motive."

"Motive?"

"He thinks Richard met Lucy that night, and she refused his proposal," said Jackson. "She gave him back the ring and he killed her for it."

"Then why not keep it?" she asked. "A memento of his getting even with the woman who rejected him."

"You talk like a melodrama," he snapped. "Naturally Richard wouldn't risk its being found."

"Jack." She sat down on the couch beside him. "You can't seriously believe all this."

He smoked the pipe in silence for a few moments. "If you ask me, do I want to believe it? The answer is no. But I've seen men — brilliant, kind, well-respected men — kill the woman they love. And for less reason than a rejected proposal."

"Is Richard in jail now?" She clutched a lace pillow.

"Hatfield agreed release him on bail," said Jackson.

"How long will he remain under arrest?"

"Until the trial, of course," he said.

"When will that be?"

Her brother shrugged. "Who can tell with the sheriff? He certainly does things informally here."

She jumped up. "Then there's not a moment to lose, Jack." She snatched a closed bottle of brandy from the cabinet. "I think the Tannings could use a good brandy, don't you?"

"What nonsense is this, Del?" Her brother rose.

"Very simple, dear brother." She was already at the door. "You and I are going to pay the Tannings a visit."

She expected him to protest, but, to her surprise, he unhooked his coat and hat from the stand in the hallway.

The maid let them in, her earlier smiles now subdued under a veil of tears. They found the Tannings in the parlor with only one gaslight illuminating the room, as if they were trying to hide their sad faces from one another.

Mr. Tanning approached Jackson, his face carved in ice. "I don't know if I should admit you, sir."

"Papa, for God's sake!" Richard grasped an empty glass in his hand.

"Perhaps this will help." Adele handed him the bottle.

"You needn't waste such precious liquor on us." Mr. Tanning's voice was chilly. "Absolve my son from these ridiculous accusations, and I'll give *you* a bottle of good brandy."

"We will if we can, sir," said Jackson. "But your son did lie to us." He sat down next to Richard. "You told us you burned Lucy's notes."

"I was embarrassed to say I kept them," the young man admitted. "Sentiment is for chickens, Papa always says." His father lowered his head.

"You told us you didn't have the bracelet either."

He peered at Jackson. "I don't know how it got in the cellar. I remember seeing it at the party for a fleeting moment but not since then."

"And what about the boots?"

"They're not mine!" He slammed down the brandy glass, breaking the stem. "Good God, will no one listen to me?"

A cry escaped from his mother. He instantly was at her side with his arms around her. "Mother, please don't worry."

"We'll find out everything we can," Adele promised.

"I believe *you* will, Miss Gossling," said Mr. Tanning. "But your brother is part of the police force now."

"I'm merely helping with the investigation at Sheriff Hatfield's request," Jackson said stiffly. "I'm just as anxious to find the real killer as he is. Whether it's your son or someone else."

"I think you'd better leave now," said Mr. Tanning.

Adele rose, smiling at Richard and taking Mrs. Tanning's hand before they retreated to the hallway. "Don't be hurt, Jack."

He brushed aside a bending rose as they headed toward the gate. "I should have expected it."

She heard a high-pitched whistle. "Good evening, Daniel," she said without turning around. Jackson pulled her arm but she ignored him.

"Good evening," said the young man in a slow, unsure way.

"How are you feeling this evening?" she asked.

"Rick's gone bad!" He burst into tears.

She took his hand. "You don't think your brother would do anything bad, do you?"

He shook his head, and the scarf hanging around his neck fell to the ground. Adele snatched it up, shook the dirt and leaves from it, and tied it properly around the young man's neck.

"We must be getting on, Del," Jackson growled.

"Daniel, would you like to help us prove your brother hasn't gone bad?" The man nodded, shaking with excitement. "Tell us about the night of Lucy's party."

"Del!" her brother hissed, but she gave him a little kick.

The man peered at her. "Will you be my sister?"

She was touched by his anxious eyes. "I already have a brother, Danny. But I'll be like a sister to you."

"I always wanted a sister," he said.

"Danny, you were in the kitchen the night of the party with your brother and Mickey. Do you remember that?"

He nodded. "We drank hot chocolate and played jacks."

"What time were you there?"

"Del, really!"

The man shut his eyes. "Bong! Bong! Bong! Bong! Bong!"

"We get the idea," Jackson mumbled.

"Bong! Bong! Bong! Bong!"

"Nine bongs," she said. "Nine o'clock. Is that what you mean, Danny?" He nodded. "And how long was Richard there?"

He shrugged. "A long, long time."

Adele gave him a peck on the cheek. "Thank you, Danny."

"The best worms come out at night," he said. "I go digging for them."

"Good night, Danny," she said.

"A kiss, please?"

She allowed him to give her a peck on her cheek as she had given him. He disappeared inside the house with a whoop.

"You shouldn't have allowed that, Del," her brother growled as they left the house.

"Don't you see, Jack?" she insisted. "He's part of Richard's alibi."

"A feeble-minded brother?" Jackson snorted. "No jury would take his word for anything."

"Then they would be idiots," she snapped. "If women served on juries, it would be different. Women know reliable information can come from seemingly unreliable sources." She pressed his arm. "Jack, we must go to the Blackstone house again."

He stared at her. "Are you playing policewoman now?"

"Why not?" she continued, more to herself than him. "The butler knows us by now. He'll let us in if you say it's official business."

"This is preposterous!" he growled. "I've no official business of any kind."

"But you do," she insisted. "You're working privately for the Blackstones, remember?"

"I'm no longer working for anyone." He fidgeted with the end of his walking stick.

Adele took his arm. "We must speak to the servants again and without Mr. Blackstone at home."

"You're being very mysterious, Del."

"He intimidates people," Adele insisted. "Especially his own household. Don't tell me you haven't noticed."

"Of course I've noticed." He sniffed. "I don't see why it's so urgent for us to speak with the servants."

"We have some pieces to fit together," Adele said.

"What pieces?"

"I'll tell you all about it tomorrow," she said. "What time does Mr. Blackstone leave?"

"Nine o'clock, nine-thirty," he said.

"We'll go then." She stared straight ahead.

She felt her brother's eyes on her. "You're determined to go, aren't you?"

"I am," she said. "With or without you."

He sighed. "I suppose the sheriff would prefer if I went with you rather than let you go alone." He slid aside a pinecone with the tip of his shoe, careful not to disturb the polished leather. "I still think we ought to tell him, Del."

"He'll want to be present," she said. "You know as well as I do how servants are very guarded with police. They'll tell us more without him."

"What is it you expect them to say?" He eyed her.

She was silent, staring down the dusty road.

# CHAPTER 20

When they saw the Blackstone carriage pull away from the house the next morning, they came through the field, careful not to go near the crime scene Hatfield had sectioned off. James answered the door. "I'm afraid Mrs. Blackstone isn't well," he said. "She will see no one."

"We only wish to ask permission to speak with you and the servants again," Adele said. "Upon the sheriff's request."

Her brother stood erect, authority written all over his face. "We would like to ask the kitchen staff just a few more questions."

James bowed and took Adele's card to Mrs. Blackstone and, obtaining her permission, led them to the servants hall.

Betty was finishing the breakfast dishes while Mrs. Brown sat with the day's menu. Rawlings had the silver sprawled out before him, lazily polishing.

"Come help me with this, Bet!" he called without looking back.

"You keep to your job, my boy, and she'll keep to hers." Mrs. Brown snapped. Her tone changed "Why, Mr. and Miss Gossling, this is a pleasure."

"We've come for your excellent tea, Mrs. Brown," Adele said, smiling. "Please say you'll make some for us."

"Certainly," said the woman, rising. "Be glad to."

Once they were sitting in the dining hall with a feast of cakes and tea, Jackson nodded at Adele.

"Mrs. Brown," she said. "I'm sure you've heard Richard Tanning has been arrested."

She pulled her handkerchief out of her apron pocket. "I'm sure he couldn't have done it, miss. He and Lucy were friends when they were just so high."

"We wanted to go over a few things with you again," she said. "You told us on the night of the party, Richard came down to the kitchen and played with Daniel and Mickey. Daniel thinks it was about nine o'clock. Is that right?"

"I can't be sure, miss," she said. "As I said before, I was busy with the food."

"But you did say Mickey usually goes to bed at nine o'clock, and he stayed up until quite a bit later that night."

"I said he was allowed to stay up later." She pressed her lips.

"They were playing jacks?"

"Build-a-picture," the cook corrected.

"Yes, of course," said Adele. "Richard told us he left a little before ten o'clock. Does that sound about right to you?"

"It *sounds* about right," Mrs. Brown said. "I couldn't say for sure." A vacant look suddenly appeared in her eyes.

"You remember something?" Jackson leaned forward.

"I was just going to say I do remember I had to watch the time for the cream."

Jackson leaned back. "I see."

"I finished whipping it at a quarter before ten," she continued. "I did look at the clock then. You have to, you know, when you've got cream. Even a minute longer and it curdles."

"Was Richard still there when you took it out?"

"Yes, miss. Of that I'm sure."

Adele gave Jackson a triumphant look. "So Richard was here at least forty-five minutes."

"I don't follow you, miss," said the cook.

She patted the woman's hand. "You've been a great help, Mrs. Brown. May I take some of your honey cake home? I simply can't resist it."

The woman's grin showed gold tooth fillings as she sent them away with a basket.

"Hello!"

The boyish voice rang out as they crossed the parlor. Mickey sat on the couch with the ball in his hands.

"Young man, you say 'good morning' at this time of day," said Jackson.

The boy peered up at him, unimpressed. "What's wrong with hello?"

Adele sat next to him. "You're not sad anymore, are you, Mickey?"

"A little sad," said the boy. "Mama is sad. She sleeps all the time now."

"I'm sorry to hear that," said Adele. "Mickey, dear, the night of the party, you played with Daniel and Richard Tanning, right? Jacks and build-a-picture?"

"*They* played build-a-picture," said Mickey. "I'm not interested in pictures."

"Del," Jackson whispered to her, "he's just a boy."

"And boys can't tell time?" she whispered back.

"I can tell time!" Mickey declared. "You needn't speak of me as if I weren't here."

Jackson retreated to the doorway with his walking stick.

"Of course you can tell time," said Adele. "But you have to look at the clock to know the time."

"I look at clocks," said the boy. "Sometimes I think I'm the only one who does."

Adele put her arm around the boy's shoulders. "That's the

only way to learn how to tell time."

"I was telling time when I was seven," he boasted. "Especially at night. I don't like to go to bed."

"So you were looking at the clock the night of the party because you were hoping to stay up later?"

"Oh, yes!" He skipped around the room, throwing the ball up and catching it. Adele couldn't hide her smile as Jackson's anxious eyes followed him.

"Can you tell us when Richard came down to play with you?"

"It was nine oh three," he said. "Exactly. I think the clock in the servants' hall is off by two minutes. I've told Papa, but he says it's good for servants to think they have two minutes less to do their work."

She heard Jackson snort in the background.

"When did Richard leave?"

"Nine fifty-eight," he said. "Exactly."

"When did you go to bed, young man?" Jackson asked.

The boy was clearly annoyed. "Ten twenty-six. Papa came and rushed me up. He's always doing that, rushing me up to my room. I try not to make too much noise, but he's always rushing me up."

"I'm sure you're a good boy, Mickey." Adele kissed the top of his head.

"Will they hang Richard?" he asked.

"I hardly think a boy your age should be thinking about such things." Jackson held out his arm, signaling he'd had enough of the boy's antics.

Adele rose. "Not now, dear. At least, we hope not now." She left the boy staring back at them with wondrous eyes.

*I*t was early afternoon before Adele got to her shop. Her mind was preoccupied with the Blackstone servants and Daniel. Although she knew Jackson was still apprehensive, and she anticipated the sheriff would feel the same, she had faith in the young man's accuracy and Mickey's childish observant eye.

Business was slow, but she was thankful for the quiet. She stayed mostly in the back of her shop to do some cleaning she had neglected in the rush of her grand opening, including leaving mouse traps for critters she had seen lingering in the tall weeds in the back of the building. When she came back up front and looked out the window, an extraordinary sight greeted her.

Parading up and down Bridge Street were Mrs. Faderman, Mrs. Lynn, and the rest of the hens. They were dressed with adornments that made their hats tip and their dresses sparkle in the sunlight. They walked slowly, avoiding the mud and horses. Each woman had a tea cup in her hand while one maid carried a tray with a teapot, sugar bowl, and cream pitcher, and another a tray with cakes.

Nin leaned against the doorway of her shop, regarding the clan with amusement. "Now you've seen the moveable tea party."

"I beg your pardon?"

"No one told you?" She grimaced. "I suppose they didn't expect to have one so soon, but with the arrest and all –"

"You mean they have a tea party while walking around like that?" Adele asked.

"Nothing like airing gossip out in the street," said Nin. "Why not have tea while doing it?"

With her pince-nez swinging back and forth, Mrs. Faderman approached them. "Won't you join us, Miss Gossling?"

She slipped her arm in Nin's. "Miss Branch and I would be delighted to join your party."

Mrs. Faderman's eyebrows rose with annoyance but she

nodded at the maid to fill two more cups. They joined the knot of women outside the vacant lot a few stores away.

"Such a shame to hear about Richard Tanning," Mrs. Leighton's daughter Cora sighed with a flutter of her eyelashes.

"Oh, dear, do be quiet," said her mother.

"I knew there would be some serious falling out between the Blackstones and Tannings," said Mrs. Faderman in a knowing voice. "I anticipated it would come from the fathers, not the children."

"What do you mean?" Adele leaned against the empty wall on one side of the lot.

"Dear, don't dirty yourself." Mrs. Faderman patted the dust off her with a handkerchief, talking all the while. "Michael Blackstone and Lowell Tanning, of course. I expected them to come to blows by this time."

"Over the swamp, you mean?" Adele asked.

"That and — other things," said the woman with sly eyes. "It's been brewing for some time. Since the grandfathers, in fact." She inspected Adele, satisfied with her work, and deposited the dirty handkerchief on the tray as the maid passed by.

"A family feud from a long time ago," Nin agreed.

The woman picked up her pince-nez and gazed at her. "You ought to know, Miss Branch. Your family dates back almost as far as theirs."

Nin peered at her with a glass eye. "I'm sure you haven't forgotten my family has fallen from grace in these parts, Mrs. Faderman."

Adele was curious about this statement but did not pursue it.

"Albert Blackstone and Owen Tanning were like brothers growing up." Mrs. Lynn said. "My own grandfather was a boyhood friend of theirs."

"So were many of our grandfathers," Mrs. Abberton declared.

"They built this town as young men, really built it," Mrs. Lynn continued. "It was little more than marshland when they came."

"Let's not be prejudiced, Caroline," said Mrs. Faderman. "The entire area was underdeveloped. Ours was the first town with running water and horse troughs. Why, I remember –"

"If Mr. Blackstone and Mr. Tanning's grandfathers were boyhood friends," Nin interrupted, "what made them fall out?"

"A woman, I think," said Mrs. Lynn.

"You think?" Mrs. Faderman gave her a knowing look. "It was a woman."

"Oh, they did come to blows over her!"

"Can't think why," muttered Mrs. Faderman. "Lydia Gaines was never worthy of any man coming to blows with another."

"Who won Lydia's hand?" asked Adele.

"Neither of them," said Mrs. Lynn. "She went East and married a banker."

"They had their flighty girls even then," Mrs. Faderman remarked.

"And the land?"

"I don't know the particulars," said Mrs. Lynn. "I only remember my father telling me there was a dispute over some valuable property north of Arrojo."

"Who won that?" asked Nin.

"Albert, of course." Mrs. Faderman sniffed. "Oh, that Blackstone man was a devil!"

"They never patched things up for the sake of their sons?" Adele sighed. "Pity."

"Pity indeed," said Mrs. Faderman. "If they had, perhaps the good name of this town wouldn't be tarnished by murder." She peered into the distance and, raising her hand, flocked to a woman with a violet dress and peacock feathers in her hat.

"You must excuse her." Mrs. Lynn was not a little embarrassed. "She has so much to do when she's hosting one of our little parties."

"For Michael Blackstone and Lowell Tanning to have

continued the feud of generations past seems – well, unreasonable."

"Oh, they didn't exactly," said the woman. "I can't say there was any love lost between them, mind you, but they nodded at one another on Sundays at church or at the annual community picnic. There was certainly no hatred between them."

"They fought over land too," Nin guessed.

Mrs. Lynn's eyes grew cloudy. "Yes. Yes, undoubtedly." She leaned in. "About six months ago, the town council called a town's meeting to decide about the pond."

"The pond Mr. Tanning owns?" Adele asked.

"The land was in his family for generations," she said. "There was some concession made in his grandfather's will to give it to the town which is why there was a meeting about it. Mr. Blackstone wanted the pond to be drained."

"And Mr. Tanning was opposed." Adele sipped her cold tea.

"He insisted it was clean." She lowered her voice. "He said there were fish in it and could yield a tidy profit."

"I take it the vote was for draining the pond," said Adele.

"I daresay Mr. Tanning didn't have much of a choice," Nin said.

"Mr. Blackstone is very influential," said Mrs. Lynn. "He contributed quite a lot of money to the building of the city hall and police station."

"Say no more, Mrs. Lynn." Adele smiled. "What did Mr. Tanning say?"

"There are rumors he threatened Mr. Blackstone."

Adele grasped her cup. "With violence, you mean?"

"Oh, but he couldn't have." Mrs. Lynn was clearly distressed. "He's far too nice a man."

Adele took the woman's hand. "Mrs. Lynn, you said before it wasn't just the land they were fighting over."

The woman glanced at Mrs. Faderman a few feet away. "As it was with the grandfathers, so it was with the sons."

Adele suddenly realized what she was saying. "You mean a woman."

"What woman?" Nin asked.

"I'm sure I don't know, Miss Branch." Mrs. Lynn set her empty teacup down on the table. "I really *must* be getting back to my errands."

When the woman was gone, Nin whispered, "She's just gossiping, Adele."

"Gossip usually begins with the truth," said Adele. "A woman is enough for two men to hold a grudge against one another for generations. But is it enough to provoke a murder?" She reached for the key to her shop, turning it around in her hands.

Mrs. Faderman's voice boomed. "A healthy woman's mind doesn't ask such sordid questions, Miss Gossling."

"Life is sometimes sordid, Mrs. Faderman," Adele said. "Even for the well-protected."

"Too true," the woman sighed. "It's a good thing there will no longer be any more sordidness about the Blackstones."

"You mean the murder?" Nin asked.

"Miss Branch, please refrain from using that ugly word." The woman shuddered. "Yes, that is what I meant. The culprit has been apprehended, hasn't he?"

"Maybe he's not the culprit," Nin said. "Maybe it was someone else."

"I trust our police know what they're doing," said the woman.

"It may have been the father," Nin pointed out. "Mr. Tanning Senior had as much of a motive as Mr. Tanning Junior. More so, in fact."

Adele turned to her friend. "Why do you say that, dear?"

"Mr. Tanning held the grudge, not his son," Nin reminded her.

"Yes, we must consider that," Adele admitted. "Jack told me once, every crime is like a ball of yarn one must unravel to get to the end."

"I hardly expected such a refined gentleman as Mr. Gossling

to discuss such matters with his sister." Mrs. Faderman was truly appalled.

"He could hardly help it, Mrs. Faderman," said Adele. "I plied him with questions."

"How morbid of you," the woman murmured. Then, she gave one of her hostess smiles. "Well, we can now all put it all behind us, can't we?"

"I'd like to know more about this Blackstone-Tanning feud," Adele said. "From the beginning."

"You sound like Missy Grace," Mrs. Faderman remarked. "'Follow the drain pipe to the river, and you'll find the source of the water,' she once said to me. I think it was her father who said it, really. I do wish fathers would be more discreet with what they tell their daughters. I would never allow Mr. Faderman —"

As the woman rattled on, Adele's mind wandered. Her eyes fell across the street to the flapping sign *Arrojo Courier*. "Nin, dear, will you watch my shop for a few minutes?" She handed her the key. "I've an important errand."

Nin's fox gaze fell on her. "Your wandering mind has found a place to rest?"

"In a manner of speaking." She opened her parasol against the overanxious sun.

As she started across the street, Mrs. Faderman called to her," Miss Gossling, where are you going?"

Adele glanced back, smiling. "I'm following the drain pipe back to the river, Mrs. Faderman." She couldn't help but feel a little self-satisfied as the woman stared at her through the pince-nez.

*S*he found the office of the *Arrojo Courier* not much bigger than the police station. The mimeograph machine danced above the street noises. Dust flew and papers were sprawled all over the floor. Adele had to be careful to step aside of ink stains. Missy Grace looked frazzled in her untamed red curls and limp lace trim.

"Goodness, you've caught me at a bad time!" The woman dropped the machine handle and tucked a strand of runaway hair under her bun. "I'm to go to press in half an hour."

"You're here all alone?" Adele looked around.

Miss Grace grinned. "This isn't the *San Francisco Examiner,* Miss Gossling."

"I won't take up much of your time, then," Adele promised. "And call me Adele, please."

"Then call me Missy." She gasped. "Oh, the interview! Lord, I never did get to that, did I?"

"No, you didn't," Adele said gently.

The young woman sank into a hard wooden chair. "I do apologize, Miss Gossling. Running a paper alone can be very overwhelming."

"I can well understand."

"I've been at it for only a year, but my brothers still laugh at me because only people in town buy my paper." Her tone became fierce. "But I will make a go of it. You'll see, they'll be reading the *Courier* from here to San Francisco."

"I have no doubt about it," said Adele. "You dealt very tactfully with the story of Lucy's murder."

"It's distressing enough," Missy sighed. "Lucy was a friend of mine and so is Richard. I don't believe he did it, do you?" She shot her a look and crossed her legs.

"Jack says even the most respectable men do foolish things for the woman they love," said Adele.

"So that's what the police think, is it?" Her hand crept to the pad and pencil on the desk. "They think it was a crime of passion?"

"I didn't say that," Adele insisted.

"I won't print it, then," the woman said. "I wouldn't print anything I couldn't quote." She glanced back at the calendar on the wall. "I'd be delighted to interview you for our next edition."

"I haven't come for the interview," said Adele. "I need some information."

"Local information, I take it." Missy began to gather the papers on the floor.

"Yes, as a matter of fact," she said. "I just heard about the rivalry between the Blackstones and Tannings from Mrs. Lynn and some of the other ladies."

"Yes, I can imagine." Missy glanced outside. "I saw them parading with their teacups."

"I'd like to know more about it," said Adele. "Do you keep copies of past newspapers?"

"I do, but I'm not sure my father would have written about it," she said. "He grew up in Arrojo, you know. He had a loathing for idle gossip."

"In a town like this, much of the news is made up of local

gossip," Adele said delicately. "Your father, I'm sure, was as good a newspaper man as you are a newspaper woman."

Missy smiled and led her to a room below the office. "I'm afraid I can't help you much, but feel free to look for yourself. These are copies of all the newspapers Papa published since he opened the paper. Thank goodness he had enough of an orderly mind to arrange them by date." She paused. "Do you know what year you're looking for?"

"I've no idea," Adele admitted.

"Well, good luck, then." She climbed back up the narrow staircase, leaving the door open.

Adele began looking at the dailies from fifty years ago, estimating the grandfathers would have been young men around that time. Despite the dim light, she found what she was looking for. There was ample reporting about a piece of land called Cattle Ridge, named so because it was ideal for grazing. The newspaper accounts confirmed the gossip: The elder Blackstone and Tanning had fought tooth and nail over it, and Blackstone had won, according to the insinuations of the press, not by entirely honorable means.

She looked for mention in the society column for Lydia Gaines. At first, she found little more than a bit about Miss Gaines. She was the daughter of former Arrojo councilman Horace Gaines, who had gone to Philadelphia without so much as a by-your-leave to Owen Tanning and Albert Blackstone. A year or so later, the newspaper reported she married the son of the prominent Philadelphia banker Wallace P. Tucker (Adele marveled at Mrs. Lynn's sharp memory), and they were happily installed in the Tucker mansion with a baby boy named William.

A story dated only two days afterward mentioned the feud between Owen Tanning and Albert Blackstone. The story spoke of a "gross misunderstanding" between the two men, Owen having been badly bruised in the face and Albert treated for a broken arm.

She did not find any mention of either family until some twenty years later, when the names of Missy's brothers graced the newspaper letterhead. Glancing through these pages, she noticed the sons had less finesse than their father. In fact, their style resembled the yellow journalism so popular in city papers.

One story caught her attention about a ball where Lowell Tanning gave away many of his dances (perhaps too many) to one Marissa Blackstone. The article further implied it was not the first time Mr. Tanning had paid compliments to Mrs. Blackstone. There were even insinuations they had been seen together in a teashop in San Francisco.

Adele left the newspaper office with her mind spinning. It was already nearly dark, and street lamps burned through the gray sky. Most shops were beginning to close up for the day.

Jackson was standing in the doorway of her shop when she approached. "You might tell your friend not to shut me out," he grumbled. "She wouldn't let me in the door until you arrived."

Adele peeked through the window. Nin was showing a customer a stylish fountain pen just arrived from the city. The dark-haired woman caught her eye and winked. Adele couldn't hold back a smile.

"Jack, dear, you must resign yourself to the idea there is one woman in this world who refuses to fall for your charms." She took his arm.

"I don't think my charms are better or worse than any other man's," he said stiffly. "But I do expect a little consideration from your friends. I am your brother, and we're not exactly enemies."

"Perish the thought!" She kissed his cheek.

"You will close now, won't you?" He slipped out the pocket watch their father had left him and peered at it.

"With a customer in the shop?"

"It's almost seven," he growled. "She can come back tomorrow, can't she?"

Her anger rose. "Jack, a businesswoman who turns customers

away because it's seven o'clock is very soon no longer in business."

"I thought you want to help us clear Richard."

She looked at him. "What has that to do with it?"

"I told Hatfield about our little chat with the Blackstone servants," he said. "He wants to verify a few things, and he thinks you ought to be there, especially if Mrs. Blackstone is up and about."

"Say no more." She smiled.

She made him wait until Nin finished with the customer. Hatfield was waiting on the Blackstone veranda with a glass of lemonade.

"You're late." He gave Jackson a sharp look. "Police business won't wait."

"It can when the sale of an expensive fountain pen is at stake," said Adele in a brisk voice.

He took his hat off. "Far be it for me to interfere with anybody else's business, Adele."

Mr. Blackstone strolled out, the lines of his face deep under the strong light. "Mr. Gossling, I want a word with you!"

Jackson shot his sister a look of "I told you so" as they entered the house, quietly handing his coat and hat to James. "It might be better if we spoke in private, sir."

"Perhaps you would prefer to speak in the servants' hall," the man sneered. "I heard about your little visit this morning."

Adele stepped forward. "That wasn't Jack's doing, Mr. Blackstone. It was mine."

The man's eyebrows arched. "I might have known a woman was behind it."

"The lady of the house gave us permission to speak with the servants," Adele said. "We went through the proper channels."

"You took advantage of my wife's fragile state of nerves," the man thundered.

Hatfield said in his calm tone, "I'm sorry you're upset, sir. I sent the Gosslings on police business this morning."

Adele felt a wave of gratitude.

"I don't object to police business, Sheriff," said Mr. Blackstone. "It's police tactics I can't abide by."

"I suggest a brandy for ourselves and a sherry for Miss Gossling," Hatfield said. "So that we may all calm down."

The brandy did indeed seem to make the bull in Mr. Blackstone retreat. "I always thought Richard was a fine young man in spite of his father." He swirled the liquor in the glass. "Had I dreamed for a moment he was capable of –" His face grew vicious.

Jackson crossed his legs. "We're not entirely sure Richard Tanning is guilty."

The man glared. "I thought you had all the evidence. Sheriff."

"I told you nothing is ever conclusive until it's conclusive," said Hatfield. "We now find there may be a few inconclusive points. That's why we need your help again."

"You sound as if you want him to be guilty, Mr. Blackstone," Adele remarked.

"Del, I don't think Mr. Blackstone implied any such thing," Jackson insisted. "We all want to catch the killer, whoever he may be."

"I'm sorry," she said. But the thought of what she had read in the *Arrojo Courier* could not leave her mind.

"We are verifying Richard's whereabouts at the time of the crime," said Hatfield. "Your son has been of great help to us."

"Mickey?" The man's face grew pale. He glared at Jackson. "I understood you spoke with my servants this morning. No one said a word about you speaking to my son."

"They were probably too terrified, Mr. Blackstone," Adele said.

Mr. Blackstone put down the brandy glass with a thump. "I

don't tolerate impertinent remarks like that, Miss Gossling, not even from a woman."

"You mean especially from a woman," she snapped.

"I assure you we were very discreet, sir." The color rose on Jackson's face.

Mr. Blackstone grabbed the decanter. "He's only a child!"

"Is that why you see him as just another part of your property, Mr. Blackstone?" Adele shot out.

The man scowled. "I thought you were occupied enough with that shop of yours, Miss Gossling. But I see you're determined to become a lady detective too."

"Mr. Blackstone, I've asked Adele to help us." The sheriff's booming voice matched Mr. Blackstone's anger. "I don't propose to have you or anyone else tell me how to run my investigations."

This had an effect on the man. He leaned back and drained the rest of the brandy in his glass.

"Mickey's a very clever boy who's been telling time since he was seven," Adele declared. "He told us how he stayed up so late the night of the party."

"What are you getting at, Miss Gossling?" The man eyed her.

"I remember how my father let Jack stay up past his bedtime when there was a party. He even allowed you to watch from the top of the stairs, didn't he, Jack?"

"As long as I remained unseen and unheard," her brother answered.

"Mickey told us he stayed up until ten twenty-six," Adele continued.

"Preposterous," Mr. Blackstone growled. "I would never allow him to go to bed at such an hour."

"It's what he told us," said Adele. "He said you came down to the kitchen at about ten-thirty and rushed him up to bed."

Mr. Blackstone smiled calmly. "Mickey sometimes has trouble telling the time when the hands are in the last half of the clock. I'm not sure why."

"Then you didn't send him up to bed at ten-thirty?" asked Hatfield. "When is Mickey's usual bedtime?"

"Mickey goes to bed at nine. I let him stay until nine-thirty that night," said the man. "It was nine-thirty when I went down to the kitchen to 'rush him' to bed. I don't think a half hour did him much harm."

"Are you sure about that, sir?" Jackson asked.

"Of course I'm sure," he said. "Marissa and I agreed to allow him a half hour past his bedtime because of the festivities, so I know exactly what time it was when I came down." He leaned his elbows on his knees. "Sheriff, exactly what does this have to do with Richard's arrest?"

"As I said before, Mr. Blackstone," explained Hatfield, "we're simply trying to check some things."

"Well, you might have done it without involving my son's bedtime," he remarked.

Adele caught a flash of gray going up the stairs. It was Alice Cummings, Mickey's nurse, with a glass of milk balanced on a tray.

She quickly excused herself and caught the nanny halfway up the stairs. "Can I help you with that, Miss Cummings?"

The woman's hands were a little shaky as she graciously handed her the tray.

"I get nervous about these stairs," she whispered, "Marble stone, you know. I always have to watch so Mickey doesn't slip."

When they reached the top, Adele set the tray down on the hall table. "Miss Cummings, I'd like you to settle an argument for us."

"Argument?"

"About Mickey's bedtime the night of the party," she said. "Mickey tells us he went to bed at ten-thirty, but the servants insist it was nine-thirty."

Miss Cummings leaned against the hall table, nearly disturbing the glass of milk. "Mickey's bedtime is nine o'clock."

"Yes, Mr. Blackstone told us," said Adele. "But he also said he allowed Mickey to stay up later that night because of the party."

The woman regarded her with curiosity. "Why you want to know?"

"We're trying to find the man who murdered Lucy, as you know," said Adele. "This could be important."

Miss Cummings rubbed her hands, and they were again shaking again. She realized the woman was not as young as she appeared. "I can't tell you the exact time, I'm afraid."

"Well, can you tell me if it was closer to nine-thirty or ten-thirty?"

"Oh, not nine-thirty!" She lowered her voice as a stir came from inside the room at the end of the hall. "If it had been, I shouldn't have objected so strongly. Mr. Blackstone — he was terribly annoyed at me."

Adele patted her shoulder. "You would be well within your rights to object if Mickey was sent to bed long past his usual bedtime, even for a special occasion."

"Perhaps because it's a late child," she mused.

"I beg your pardon?"

"Parents tend to be more permissive with a young child later in life." She quickly added, "Oh, not that the Blackstones are old. But there is – was – quite an age difference between Lucy and her brother."

"I know what you mean." Adele lowered her voice. "Miss Cummings, do you think the Blackstones were less permissive with Lucy than with Mickey?"

"Mr. Blackstone is quite strict," she said.

"But more so with Lucy than with her brother?"

"I think so, yes."

"How do you know?" Adele asked. "You told me you were never Lucy's nanny."

The woman smiled. "One can tell. I mean someone who

knows children." Her confidence grew. "I practically raised seven brothers and sisters, you see. I *know* children."

"I can hardly imagine Lucy would take that lying down," Adele mused. "I didn't know her for long, but I gathered she was rather headstrong."

"She was, to be sure," the nanny agreed. "It's been my experience the more headstrong an adult is, the more restricted he or she was as a child. Especially a woman."

"You don't consider Mickey to be headstrong?"

The woman shook her head with a laugh. "Mischievous perhaps. But he readily gives way to what people ask of him."

She heard her brother calling. "I mustn't keep you from your bedtime, Miss Cummings," Adele apologized.

"It was nearly eleven when I put Mickey to bed that night." She picked up the tray. "I remember thinking it was the third night in a row Mickey went to bed past his bedtime, and I intended to speak to Mr. Blackstone about it. He is, after all, a reasonable man."

"Yes, he is a reasonable man." Adele stepped down the stairs. They were indeed a little slippery.

# CHAPTER 22

Adele had little difficulty coaxing Hatfield into joining them for dinner, as the scent of Ruth's turkey and coconut macaroons decided him well before Adele's pleadings.

After dinner, they retired to the parlor. Jackson settled into the big damask chair he had already claimed as his favorite. "Would you mind telling us why you accosted Mickey's nanny while we were trying to get Mr. Blackstone to cooperate?"

"I was making my own inquiries." She smiled. "Miss Cummings confirms Mickey went to bed closer to eleven. That means the boy was telling the truth when he said he was sent upstairs at ten-thirty."

"Michael Blackstone was lying?" Hatfield moved his head aside as Tomas placed the coffee on the table.

"I don't know that he was," Jackson said. "He likely remembered nine-thirty instead of ten-thirty. He's been very distressed since that night, and people are apt to forget small details when in distress."

Adele poured the coffee. "Have you enough now to let Richard go, Sheriff?"

"I'm afraid not, Adele," said the man.

She stared at him, her hand poised midair over the macaroons. "You have two witnesses who saw Richard in the kitchen at the time of Lucy's murder!"

"Two unreliable witnesses," Jackson reminded her. "A feeble-minded young man and a boy."

"Oh, nonsense!" Adele snapped. "There are the servants too."

"Also unreliable to a jury," Hatfield said quietly. "No, I'm afraid we're still short on evidence."

Adele fiddled with the silver spoon. "Sheriff, you know that boy didn't kill his beloved just as much as I do."

"Women's intuition?" Jackson eyed her with a sour smile.

She threw the spoon at him. "Don't condescend, Jack!"

"Women's intuition isn't always nonsense." She was surprised to hear Hatfield come to her defense.

"Why, Richard's father had more reason to kill Lucy than Richard!" she insisted.

Her brother glanced at her. "I thought you liked Mr. Tanning."

"I do," she said. "But murderers can still be likable, can't they?"

"Why do you think Mr. Tanning had more of a motive?" Hatfield leaned back.

"Deep-rooted family feeling," said Adele. "And a broken heart, perhaps. Sheriff, did you know Mr. Blackstone and Mr. Tanning may have had a falling out over a woman?"

"I can't say I did."

"I went to the *Arrojo Courier* office today," she said. "I wanted to know more about the Blackstone-Tanning feud."

"I think I know why." Jackson raised his eyebrow. "I saw the hens gathering on the street today."

"Idle ladies often pick up more than they realize." Hatfield nodded. "Go on, Adele."

"If the newspaper stories are right, that woman was Mrs. Blackstone," said Adele. "She was quite friendly with Mr. Tanning. I saw that at the party." She held the macaroons out to Hatfield.

"I didn't notice anything unusual," Jackson said.

"You never do, Jack," she said. "They didn't say a word to one another. That in itself is odd."

"I don't think so," said the sheriff. "If her husband isn't on friendly terms with Tanning, it would hardly follow Mrs. Blackstone would be."

"It was a feeling between them," Adele said. "An exchange of looks."

"You sound like your clairvoyant friend," Jackson said. His sister regarded him with a vicious glare.

"Well, Mrs. Blackstone is a beautiful woman," Hatfield admitted. "Less now, perhaps, than twenty or so years ago, but the death of a child can take its toll on a parent."

"A man might kill for land or a lady," Adele remarked. "I vote for the lady."

"Del, you're really going the limit," Jackson snarled.

Hatfield's fingers intertwined. "I don't know how many fights I stopped at port between sailors over a woman. And the woman was much less worthy than Marissa Blackstone."

"But to suggest –"

"It would give Lowell Tanning an additional motive, wouldn't it?" the sheriff said. "A man spurred by love, and now his love's daughter wishes to marry his son, perhaps to spur him too eventually."

Jackson snorted and lit his pipe. "You ought to write for the theater, Del."

Adele glanced at Sheriff Hatfield. "You don't seriously believe that, do you?"

"What do *you* believe, Adele?" he asked.

She sighed. "I don't know what I believe anymore."

"All this is pure conjecture," Jackson pointed out.

"We've no proof any of it is true," Hatfield agreed. He rose and circled the room with his hands in back of him, lingering at the window to admire the lace curtains Ruth had sewn.

"How do we get proof?" Jackson asked. "We can't very well ask them, can we?"

Without turning around, Hatfield said, "We might get the chance."

The bell rang several times in a row. Tomas came flying into the room with Lowell and Richard Tanning at his heels.

"Sheriff!" Mr. Tanning's voice rang through the parlor. "You must drop these charges against my son."

"Why is that, sir?"

The man sank into a chair. "Because I did it."

"Papa!"

"I killed Lucy," he said.

The moment the words spilled out of his mouth, Adele reprimanded herself for ever considering this man, who had been so kind to her when she first came to town and had shown nothing but love and concern for those around him could do anything as reprehensible as murder a young woman, family feud or no family feud. Her eyes filled with tears, and she wiped them away with her handkerchief.

"You had better tell us everything, Mr. Tanning." Jackson pulled his chair nearer to the man. "Tomas, bring us more coffee. And the brandy."

"I won't allow this, Papa." Richard's hands clenched as if trying to keep back emotion. "Sheriff, can't you see what he's trying to do?"

"Perhaps you ought to let your father speak." Hatfield gently led the young man to the couch. "I think a brandy will do us all some good."

Adele brought the decanter along with the glasses to the coffee table. She brought one for herself as well even though she never drank it.

They all had a round while Tomas set a fresh pot of coffee on the table.

The brandy seemed to calm both men, and when Mr. Tanning spoke, his voice was clear. "I did what any father would do."

"What do you mean, sir?" Hatfield asked.

"I knew, you see, I knew Richard had asked Lucy to marry him," said Mr. Tanning. "And I couldn't have it. I just couldn't have it."

"Why?" Jackson glanced at him. The man looked confused. "You told us earlier you liked the girl."

"The families, of course." The man became impatient. "I knew Blackstone would never let them marry. I was afraid he would banish Lucy away, and if he did, Richard would go with her. I couldn't lose him."

"How did you know about the meeting?" asked Hatfield

"I saw Lucy's maid leave the envelope with the footman, and I read it before it got to Richard."

"Papa, that's bosh and you know it!" Richard insisted. "Lucy's maid gave me the envelope herself."

His father braced himself. "I'm quite prepared to take my punishment."

"Very noble of you," Hatfield mumbled. "Go on."

"I knew Richard was going to meet Lucy that night at ten o'clock and I knew where."

"How did you know?"

"I beg your pardon?"

"The note said to meet at the spot crossing," said the sheriff. "According to Richard, this was a secret meeting place of theirs since childhood. So how did you know where it was?"

"Well." Mr. Tanning seemed thrown for a moment. "Well, Richard told us. When you questioned him earlier, he told us."

"But that was *after* the murder," said Adele.

"He must have told me a long time ago." The man wiped his face with his handkerchief.

"We never told anyone!" Richard was nearly shaking. Jackson poured another glass of brandy and pushed it into his hands.

"Oh, what does it matter?" cried Mr. Tanning. "I knew where they were meeting and that's all."

"I think we'd better let you tell us the rest of it." Hatfield crossed his hands on his knees.

"I left the party just before ten." He turned to Adele. "You saw me. You said as much."

"A quarter to." She nodded.

"I got there before Richard did and I strangled her," the man continued. "I hid the body. I knew Richard would come in a few minutes, and I didn't want him to see." He hid his face in his handkerchief.

"Where did you hide the body?" Asked the sheriff in a quiet voice.

The man blinked. "In Miss Gossling's gazebo, of course. I carried her in my arms and hid her where no one would see her until morning or perhaps even a few days. I — I didn't know how often Miss Gossling went there."

Jackson's eyes met his sister's.

"You carried the body into the gazebo," the sheriff repeated. "You're sure of this?"

"Why of course. I ought to know!" He turned to Adele. "I'm terribly sorry, but it was the first thing I thought of."

"How did you know my sister's house has a gazebo?" Jackson asked.

"All the houses around here have them," the man insisted. "I thought — I assumed — oh, what does it matter?"

"Mr. Tanning." Hatfield rose. "You've told us a plausible story for admirable reasons. Many fathers have done less for their children."

"You don't believe a word of it, do you?" Richard's face relaxed. "Oh, thank God!"

"The police often withhold details of a murder investigation from the press," said Jackson. "We told them Lucy's body was discovered in Del's gazebo. But we left out how it got there."

Both men stared.

"Lucy's body was dragged part of the way in the brush," Adele said. "Whoever did it left marks in the dirt."

"Well, naturally, I forgot about that." Mr. Tanning's face was pale.

"You forgot you dragged the body of a girl you just killed in the dirt?" Jackson eyed him.

"One can't remember everything, Mr. Gossling!"

"You're a gentleman, Mr. Tanning," Adele said softly. "No gentleman would leave such a horrid sight where the eyes of a woman would discover it. Am I right?"

The man broke down, burying his face in his handkerchief again. Richard put his arms around his father's shoulders.

# CHAPTER 23

She and Jackson had a restless night. Neither had much of an appetite at breakfast, enduring Tomas shaking his head behind veils of steam from the coffee and pancakes for Adele and the big bowl of oatmeal Jackson insisted upon eating every morning. The youngest Cordoba daughter, Ana, had taken a liking to him and peeked from behind the doorway. He usually whistled to her and she would come, giving him a marvelous smile and accepting a muffin or a sweet. But this morning Jackson stayed buried in his paper. Adele noticed he did not turn the page the entire time they were at the table.

"I want to go with you to the police station," she announced as they started walking toward Bridge Street. "There's something I must see."

"What must you see?"

"That letter," she said. "The one Lucy wrote Richard. It's been needling me all night."

"Del, you've done all you could for Richard."

"No, there's something not quite right."

"About what?"

"The timing." Adele avoided a small pile of mud in the road. "The night was too bright."

"What on earth are you talking about?"

She remained silent as the click of horse hoofs rose behind them.

A rather flustered Edison told them Hatfield was out. As he spoke, Adele realized he was trying not to look at her and not succeeding very well. She had long ago realized the young man was a little infatuated with her.

"What is your first name, Deputy Assistant Edison?" she asked. "You don't mind my asking, do you?"

"I don't mind, miss," he said in a shaky voice. "Only, it's rather old-fashioned."

"I like old-fashioned names." Adele gave him her sweetest smile.

"Seymour, miss."

She was just in time to kick Jackson in the ankle to keep him from laughing. "That's a lovely name." The young man ducked his head and Jackson snorted as he sat down at one of the desks.

"My brother has been telling me how helpful you've been throughout this terrible business." She sat at the edge of the desk Jackson had taken, feeling his questioning eyes on her.

"I'm happy to do anything I can, Miss Gossling."

She leaned closer so as to block Jackson's disapproving glaze. "I'd like to see some of the evidence from the Lucy Blackstone case."

"Oh, well, miss, I'm not sure –"

"It's very important or I wouldn't ask," she said. "You wouldn't want an innocent man to hang for a crime he didn't commit, would you?"

"Oh, but I thought it was all cut and dried."

"Nothing is ever cut and dried, Edison," Jackson said in a brittle voice.

"I didn't mean to imply, sir –"

"Of course you didn't," said Adele. "But you wouldn't mind bringing out the box from the Blackstone case, would you?"

The young man glanced out the window, as if expecting the sheriff to burst in at any moment .

"You heard my sister, Edison," said Jackson. "Give her what she asks. I'll take the responsibility."

The young man brought out the box with the evidence from the Blackstone case, depositing it on the desk with nervous hands.

"Jack," Adele hissed as Edison retreated to his corner of the office, "you needn't be so severe with the poor boy. He's only trying to help."

"He ought to know when to mind his betters, then." He watched Adele take out the items until she found the note Lucy had written to Richard.

"It says exactly what Richard said it did," said Jackson.

She shook her head. "That isn't what bothers me." She took out a magnifying glass that had belonged to her father and held it up to her eye.

"You really ought to get a chain for that, Del," he said. "It's far too delicate to bury in your bag with all the rest of the jumble."

"Jack, look at this." She pointed to the latter half of the note. "Lucy writes, 'Meet me at the spot crossing at 10 o'clock tonight.'"

"We've already established that was their meeting place," her brother pointed out.

"I told you there was something off about the time," she mused. "If you were writing a note to a woman asking for a rendezvous, would you write the time as a number, or would you spell it out?"

"Does that really matter?" He regarded her with wary eyes.

"It might," she said. "The number is written in a clumsy way compared to the rest of the note, don't you agree?"

"People often write crudely when they're in a hurry," he said.

"If the note was secret, Lucy might have wanted to get it to Richard as quickly as possible before her father or anyone else found it."

"You don't understand, Jack," she said. "Lucy wrote in a very careful and clear style."

"How do you know?" He eyed her.

"The party invitation," she reminded him. "Lucy's personal message was on it."

"I forgot about that," he said.

"Most girls write in a fancy style and take their time about it," she continued, examining the page.

"I've never known you to do so," he said dryly. "The note seems straightforward enough."

"Exactly," she said. "It's a rather innocuous message for a rendezvous with a lover and possible future husband."

"Lucy may have been more practical than anyone realized," Jackson remarked.

"The zero seems the only ornate thing Lucy wrote," Adele observed. "It has a nice little loop inside of the 'o.'"

"I never knew you took so much interest in other people's letters," he said. "You wanted me to burn Mama's old letters, remember?"

She glared at him. "Only because they were love letters she wrote to Papa. I didn't think it was right."

"Why is the zero bothering you, Del?" he asked. "It hardly seems important."

She gave the note back to him. "Perhaps it isn't."

As she walked slowly toward her shop, Lucy's image floated like a ghost above her head, trying to send her a message.

~

*T*he ghost knocked at her head all through the quiet morning. At lunchtime, she could bear it no longer. She closed her shop and went to Nin's.

Her friend had met with two women from the city who looked as scraggly as scarecrows hung in a field. They had come to consult her, as she followed in her mother's footsteps in her knowledge of healing herbs. "Mama had a reputation as a healer," she had told Adele with pride. "She never accepted money. She said it let her turn away whomever she felt unworthy of her gifts."

The women were just leaving as Adele entered. One of them let her fingers trail the lining of Adele's skirt as if she were part of the power Nin possessed. The other one clutched a packet to her chest.

"Poor woman," Nin sighed as she watched them leave. "Her niece is getting married next week, and she has terrible stomach pains."

"I'm surprised you didn't tell her it was the sign of a troublesome future," Adele said dryly.

The woman looked at her. "Whatever I think of the married state, I would never interfere with vibrations to the contrary if they came from the Generous Ones."

Adele pressed her hand. "I'm sorry. My humor gets prickly when I'm disturbed by something."

"Yes, I can feel it." Nin closed the shutters of the window. "Mama used to say only good can ease a distressed mind."

"Then let's both do our good deed for the day," Adele said. "Let's bring Frances Tanning lunch. The woman must be in very low spirits with her son's arrest."

They went to Dora's Tea Shop and picked up some dainty roast chicken sandwiches and cherry tarts and took them to the Tanning house.

The housekeeper was relieved to see them. "Mrs. Tanning will be happy you've come." She lowered her voice, "You're just the ladies to cheer her up."

They found the woman in the garden staring at the roses folding under the sun, looking ready to fold herself. They moved her chair under a large shady tree and sent the maid into the kitchen for some water.

"You mustn't make yourself ill, Mrs. Tanning." Adele handed her a fan.

"Why not?" She sprang to life. "For whom have I to make an effort if Richard —" She burst into tears. "Forgive me."

Adele arranged the sandwiches in a china plate. "Your son won't be under suspicion much longer."

"We should have never moved back here," the woman lamented. "I wanted to stay in Sacramento but Lowell wouldn't hear of it. Here he was born and here he would die, he insisted. And so would his children. But not with the noose, God help me, not with the noose!"

"He won't die with the noose, Mrs. Tanning," said Nin in a kind voice.

The woman grabbed her arms. "I know you're some sort of clairvoyant."

"The vibrations don't lie," Nin said. "Your son will be set free and very soon."

Richard came out of the house. He looked a mess with his hair and clothes disheveled. Adele's heart went out to the gray, haggard face.

"You're just in time, Richard." She took his arm. "We've brought the most delightful refreshment from the tea shop."

"I'm not hungry." His voice was as dim and disheveled as his appearance.

"Come now." She seated him under the tree next to his mother. "When a woman invites a gentleman to lunch, he must accept or else cease to be a gentleman."

"Do gentleman kill the innocent women they love?" He looked at her with a glassy eye.

She returned it with a determined stare. "You know they don't. And neither did you."

"Miss Gossling, I know what you're trying to do," he said. "But there isn't much use, is there? Not with all the evidence the police have."

"That evidence might not be as conclusive as you or they think," she said.

"Richard, dear." His mother looked at him anxiously. "Miss Branch says –"

"Yes?" He turned the glass eye on Nin.

"She says no harm will come to us," said Mrs. Tanning.

He held a glass of water in one hand and a sandwich in the other, looking at each as if it were going to bite him.

Adele sat down in front of him. "Richard, I must ask you something." He turned his gaze on her. "When Lucy wrote you those notes, how did she write the meeting times?"

He blinked. "I don't know what you mean."

She took a pencil and notepad from her bag. "If she wanted to meet you for lunch at one o'clock, say, did she write out the word or the number?" She then proceeded to write *1 o'clock* and *one o'clock*.

It took him some time to understand. "Lucy always wrote the number. She hated wasting good letter space on drab details, she said." His smile was faint. "She preferred to write pretty words."

"Yes, she did." Adele patted his hand. "I want you to do something for me. I want you to finish your lunch and go back into the house and bring me all the notes Lucy wrote you."

"What possible use can they be now that the police have gone through them?"

"The police were looking for something else," she said. "I have my own ideas."

He complied and she and Nin spread them on the grass, placing rocks on top to keep the wind from blowing them away.

Having taken Jackson's advice, Adele removed the magnifying glass from the chain around her neck and examined these letters even more carefully than the one at the police station. When she found what she was looking for, she called out to Richard. She handed him a note written on July tenth. "Did Lucy always make her zeros that way?"

He squinted at the blurred ink. "How are zeros made?" he asked in a vague tone. "I seem to have forgotten."

"Did she always make her zeros in one solid circle like that?"

"I suppose so," he said. "Don't the other notes have them too?"

"There isn't a zero in any of the others," she said. "That's why I wanted to see if you remembered."

"Yes, yes!" He sat back on his heels, his face slowly lighting up. "We had a teacher at school who was most peculiar about the girls' penmanship. She used to say a woman's message had to be clear, or she could lose her a potentially good match." He seemed embarrassed. "She didn't have your progressive ideas, Miss Gossling."

"Looking over these letters, it's clear she gave her message in a simple and clean way."

There was a shadow of a smile on his face. "Lucy believed a man ought to take the time to discover a woman's charms without her having to push them on him. She always received low marks on penmanship from that teacher."

"Now take a look at this." She pulled the note from the police station out of her bag.

He peered at it, his face clearly confused.

"Look at the ten o'clock." She handed him her magnifying glass.

His entire figure was rigid. "The zero isn't the same!"

"And this is the note you received, just as it is?"

"It must be," he said. "I came at ten, after all." He looked at her. "But what does it mean?"

She folded the note back in her bag. "It might mean somebody tampered with the note before it even reached you."

"Tampered?" He brushed his forehead with his hand.

Mrs. Tanning put her arms around his shoulders. "Dear, I think you ought to go inside. The sun is far too hot this afternoon."

"May I keep these for a little while?" Adele nodded at the notes lying on the grass.

He almost smiled. "I'd sooner have you take possession of them than the police. Only for a brief time, of course. "The roughness came back to his voice. "You can't imagine how precious they are to me now."

As his mother led him into the house, he glanced back at Adele. Some of the grayness had disappeared from his face.

"Come, Nin." She handed her friend the packet tied with a ribbon she had found in her bag. "We've a theory to propose to the police."

But Hatfield seemed less than pleased to see her.

"I hear you've been scheming your way into a certain ignorant assistant deputy's affections and taking evidence," he said. "Edison!" The young man nearly stumbled across the room. "Isn't that what you told me?"

"Sir?"

"Taking evidence." Hatfield eyed him.

"Not taking," Adele insisted. "Borrowing." She nudged Jackson but her brother seemed quite content to let her get out of the situation all by herself.

"You have the letter you took with you, I hope." Hatfield held out his hand. His usual good-natured face was immobile. "We have an arraignment next week to prepare for."

"Arraignment?" She set her things down on a chair. "I thought you were going to look into releasing Richard."

"There is still evidence against him, Del," said her brother. "We wouldn't be doing our duty if we ignored that."

"What if it was eleven and not ten?"

"Del, we haven't the patience for your riddles."

"Oh, stop being a nuisance!" Nin snapped. She sat on the floor, even though Edison had put a chair out for her. This made the assistant deputy draw back into his corner.

"Please be clear, Adele." Hatfield sat at the edge of his desk.

She laid out the note from the evidence file along with one she had taken from Richard. "The zeros are different."

"Well, for heaven's sake!" Jackson growled.

"They're wildly different, in fact." She shoved them toward Hatfield.

The sheriff reached for his magnifying glass and examined them. "All right, they're different. What are you proposing?"

"She just told you," Nin said.

He glanced at her.

"I think someone changed the time on this note from eleven o'clock to ten o'clock," Adele explained. "You could easily make a zero out of a one." She took an envelope lying on the desk and drew a one, then made it into a zero.

"Why would someone do that?" asked Nin, looking over her shoulder.

"To buy time," she said. "To misguide the police, maybe. If someone changed the eleven to a ten before the note reached Richard, it means Richard went to meet Lucy an hour early."

"It was a risk," Hatfield remarked. "What if Richard had decided to wait all night for her?"

"It's hardly likely, sir, even for a man in love," Jackson said.

"Or," Adele suggested, "he may have known both of them well enough to know Richard sometimes lost patience when he thought Lucy was playing games with him."

"What reason might someone have to buy time, Del?" Jackson asked. "You're not making an sense."

"It would be perfect, wouldn't it?" said Adele. "Richard comes at ten, but no Lucy. He leaves. Lucy comes at eleven, just as she intends, meets the murderer instead of Richard. The murderer kills her and makes it look as if Richard did it. The timing would be inscrutable."

"We don't know anybody changed anything," Hatfield reminded her. "Isn't it plausible Lucy changed it herself? Perhaps she put eleven when she meant ten, then wrote over it herself."

"But wouldn't she have crossed out the eleven and written ten?" Jackson asked.

"Not Lucy," Nin sneered. "She didn't give two cents for decorum."

"Your views on the virtues of womanhood are all too familiar, Miss Branch," Jackson said. "Perhaps you'll spare us your venom for the present."

"It's true, Jack," said Adele. "Richard told us Lucy never wasted time or space. She would never cross out a word in her correspondences when she could save space and write over it." She snatched up the notes. "Sheriff, will you let me keep the last note for a few more days?"

"You're asking a very big favor, Del," said Jackson.

"May I know what for?" asked Hatfield.

"I have a good friend in the city whose father is a document expert," she said. "He works mostly with historical papers, but I'm sure he could help us. I'd like to ask him to take a look at it along with those Richard gave us. He might be able to tell us if the time of the meeting was changed and even whether Lucy or someone else changed it."

"You're thinking of Elsie Blessings father, no doubt," Jackson said. "The man's a bit off, sir."

"He's a recognized expert," Adele insisted. "Perhaps you would be kinder to the Blessings family if Elsie had chosen to marry your boorish friend rather than lead a suffragist's life."

This made Nin burst out laughing, and Hatfield himself smiled.

"You're not a whimsical young woman, Adele." The sheriff put on his hat. "If you assure me you'll take good care of it and return it in a few days, I'll trust you."

"Thank you, Sheriff. You're as decent a man as they come."

"Decent," he winked, "for a man of any kind."

Adele's face grew heated. "I may be a suffragist, Sheriff, but I have no loathing for the male sex."

He waved his hand as he fled out the door before Edison had a chance to zip across the room and open it for him.

CHAPTER 24

*D*espite having accepted his sister's independence long ago, Jackson put his foot down when she suggested taking the Beaton Roundabout to San Francisco.

"It's bad enough I need to worry about you roaming the city streets with rogues and scalawags," he said. "It's sheer cruelty to make me fret over whether you'll survive the rocky roads and bypasses in that infernal contraption."

"That infernal contraption, dear brother, will one day outrun a horse," she said as she laced up her shoes. "You know quite well the Blessings live in one of the most respectable neighborhoods of San Francisco."

"Where the rogues and scalawags roam also," he insisted.

To reduce his anxiety, she agreed to take the train and a chaperone with her. He was less pleased when she chose Nin, especially when Sheriff Hatfield volunteered to allow Edison to go with her.

"I'd sooner trust Nin against a scalawag than that blushing young man." She winked as she put her short jacket over her shoulders and picked up her parasol. She dressed as plainly as possible because Elsie abhorred it when women took too much of an interest in their appearance.

"Perhaps, but two women traveling alone is two women traveling alone," he insisted.

"We won't be alone," she reminded him. "We'll have a train full of people, including gentlemen, Jack."

He grumbled but remained silent.

From the moment they stepped into the passenger car, Adele realized Nin was afraid. The woman's eyes became as wide as a raccoon's, and she kept clawing at the walls between the narrow hallway on their way to their compartment as if she wanted to push them down. Her breath was unsteady and only when they were able to open a window did she relax a bit.

"You don't like trains, dear?" Adele took her hand and squeezed it.

"I don't like closed spaces," she said. "You've never been to my flat but it's one very large room with no doors." She leaned her cheek against the window, her face reflecting like a fairy. "I love sitting in the middle of that room looking at all that space around me."

"Just keep your eyes on the window and you'll feel better."

As they settled in, a pleasant breeze entered their little car. This seemed to ease her friend's nerves. They both fell into a deep sleep even through the rumblings and scrapes, not awakening until the porter informed them they had reached the city.

Elsie was the tallest and most athletic New Woman Adele had ever known. Her arms and legs were muscular and she boasted of being able to lift a chair with two dogs sitting on it with one hand. Her convictions about human rights, and especially women's rights, were just as strong. Her father complained between the settlement houses, the workers' clubs, and the suffragist meetings, he rarely saw her more than to say goodnight.

"You look so parochial, Del." Her voice was as loud as

Hatfield's in the crowd. "How charming to bring a country waif with you." She linked her other arm with Nin's and pulled her along while Nin kept up in hurried small steps.

"Parochial dust is cleaner than city dust, Elsie," Adele remarked.

"You've come at the right time." She threaded them between clumps of people, ignoring their stares. "We're setting out at eleven tomorrow night."

"Setting out?"

"The Lilith Crusade." Elsie hailed a hansom. "You know I don't like to splurge, but this is a special occasion. I can't very well let you and the country waif spoil your wretchedly shiny shoes." She grinned at Nin who glared back.

"Setting out where, Elsie?"

"Saint Augustine's Church." She lowered her voice and slapped shut the top of the hansom, blocking the sound of the driver's whip. "Can't risk some old dog hearing about it."

Adele stiffened. "You promised me no more military tactics."

"This isn't a raid, dear," she said. "We're merely going to smash the look of righteous indignation off the faces of some of those saints painted on the windows."

"Not a mere trifle for the congregation that must pay to replace them," Nin said.

Elsie regarded her with contempt. "I'm sure you've no match for our crusade in the country so you could hardly understand what we're fighting for."

"Your crusade, Elsie, has become unfit for decent politics," Adele snapped.

"Decent politics don't exist." Elsie's voice rose. "The sooner you dainty ladies with your banners and parades and letters to the governor realize it, the better off women will be."

Adele took a few deep breaths. She had one experience of smashing windows that landed her in jail for a few hours where she had been marked as a traitor for encouraging the ill girl in the cell with her to eat while the others refused. It taught her there were other ways to gain the freedom for women they all wanted so desperately.

"I didn't come to talk politics, Elsie," she said. "Jack and I need your father's help."

"How is your brother?" Elsie asked. "Not trying to push one of his chums on some poor unsuspecting lady, I hope?"

Nin grinned as she looked out the window.

"That's all in the past," said Adele. "He's helping the local police with a murder investigation of a young woman."

"One of her gentleman friends did it, I've no doubt." Elsie knocked on the roof of the hansom as it pulled over. "Not that I would call a man who murders a gentleman."

"That's exactly what I'm trying to prove didn't happen," said Adele. They stepped out to the street, wider and dirtier than those in Arrojo. Adele could see even Nin, who was usually not fussy about her skirt dragging in the mud, pick up the hem to her ankles.

"Living in the country has melted your convictions." Elsie grabbed her arm. "Del, tell me it hasn't."

"Not every man, gentleman or not, is evil." Adele gently loosened her grip.

"No, not every man," Elsie admitted. "But even one is too many."

Adele smiled. "I'll come down to the city one weekend soon, and I promise we'll talk about politics as much as you like. I might even agree with you on one or two points."

Elsie pressed her shoulders. "See that you do. And bring the country waif with you." She glanced at Nin. "It might prove quite educational for her."

The slow and subtle Arrojo pace made the crackling wheels and Elsie's vigorous steps too much for her, and she took Nin's arm.

Dr. Blessings was much more benign than his daughter. He

was as tall as Elsie and the box chin and nose showed the clear family resemblance. His manner and tone were restrained. Unlike the proverbial professor, his mind and eyes were as sharp as a wolf's.

"I can tell by your flushed cheeks Elsie's been at you, my dear." He greeted Adele with a quick peck on the cheek.

"I've only been reminding Del where her heart is, Papa." His daughter undid her jacket and flung it across the room, along with her buckled boots. She folded back the sleeves of her blouse, exposing her somewhat blotchy skin up to the elbows in a fashion that made the man servant standing over her father turn away in disgust.

"I'm quite tranquil, I promise you." As Adele leaned forward to return the greeting, she whispered, "You know what she's planning tonight, don't you?"

He shrugged, looking helpless. She knew he had given up trying to convince Elsie to take less drastic measures for her cause a long time ago.

She introduced him to Nin. "Miss Branch has been the friendliest person to me in Arrojo. I'm a puzzle to some of the people there, to put it mildly."

"I don't doubt it." Elsie rang for coffee.

"They're none too pleased with my helping Jack with this case." She sat down beside Nin on the couch. "They don't believe a lady ought to be involved with such sordid matters as murder."

"Anything true to life is too sordid for a *lady*," Elsie mocked. "Perhaps you should have reminded them the most sordid task of a lady's life is childbirth. I've yet to see a man capable of tolerating it."

Her father flinched. "Your brother is on the police force now, Del?"

"He's only helping the local sheriff," said Adele. "He'll be going back to the city after it's all over." She could not keep the melancholy out of her voice.

Dr. Blessings patted her knee. "Don't worry, my dear, we'll make him change his mind. He could hardly have reason to stay if you're not here. It's only you and him now, after all."

The clang of a trolley bell crept through the frosted windows, lending a vibrant call to the smothering air. "Yes, only he and I."

"We'll say no more about it," Elsie insisted, handing Adele the coffee. "Papa, Adele says she's come to see you, not me."

"Indeed?" He blinked. "I'm honored."

Adele leaned forward. "Dr. Blessings, you once said you could tell from one handwritten letter to another if a man be true to his character." The man nodded. She took Lucy's notes from her handbag. "Then you can help us a great deal."

"Adele is convinced Lucy's fiancé is innocent," Nin chimed in. "If indeed he even was her fiancé. That's a question in itself."

Dr. Blessings looked confused. Adele explained about Lucy and her own feeling regarding the notes.

"It sounds as if you're a better hunter than your brother, Del," said Elsie. "As far as predators go." She picked up a magazine and propping her legs over the arm of her chair, began reading it.

Dr. Blessings examined the note Lucy wrote the day of the murder along with the others sent to Richard. "You realize people aren't always consistent with their handwriting, my dear," he said. "I'm sure two letters of yours would produce slightly different *n*'s and *t*'s and the like."

"But no one has accused me of murder, Dr. Blessings," she pointed out.

"Not yet at least," Nin said with a sly smile.

"I cannot commit myself to anything definite." He put the eyeglass he had used, much more powerful than Adele's, back in its case.

"Oh, Papa, stop being so stuffy." Elsie sat up. "Was that loopy zero written by the girl or wasn't it?"

"I cannot commit –"

"Well, you can *guess*, can't you?" his daughter demanded. For once, Adele was grateful for Elise's bulldog style.

"I am *guessing*," he said slowly, "it is entirely possible the zero may not be the same one as in the other notes."

Adele gave Nin a satisfied look.

"I can even make another guess," Dr. Blessings continued. "One black ink pen isn't the same as another."

"No one knows that better than I." Adele smiled. "I sell ink and pens now, remember?"

"I don't understand, Papa," Elsie said.

"Someone might have used a different pen," Nin supplied.

"How very clever of you," the woman murmured.

"You can tell that just by looking at it through that glass?" Nin was clearly impressed.

"I cannot commit myself," he insisted. "I would need to make further examinations in my laboratory to know more."

"Then by all means, do so, Dr. Blessings." Adele rose. "We would need the letters back in a day or two."

"Adele!" Nin's voice was shrill.

"My friend is afraid because we persuaded the sheriff to let us borrow the last note Lucy wrote." Adele put on her gloves. "It's part of the evidence against Richard."

"I promise I'll be very gentle," said Dr. Blessings dryly. "Provided the police are through with it."

"They are." Adele nodded.

"Then I daresay your sheriff will get it back in more pristine condition than he found it."

"Papa is nothing if not pristine," Elise added.

"As I said, we can only leave it with you for a day or two," Adele said. "The arraignment is next week and the sheriff will need it back by then."

"I shall go down to the university now and conduct my examination," he promised. "You'll have my results tomorrow evening at the latest. I'll bring them myself, as I'll be down that way."

"That's very kind of you." She gave him a kiss on his cheek.

"Well, if it's a question of a young man's innocence, it's the least I can do. The official report might take a few more days, though." He rose as well, and Adele suddenly noticed a stick lying beside him.

"Were you injured, Dr. Blessings?"

"Heavens, no." He gave her a wan smile. "I carry this for professional dignity. You've no idea how students become more attentive when they see a professor with a walking stick." As he took it, Adele stole a glance at Elsie, who gave a devastated look. Adele guessed the cane was more than just professional dignity.

"You and Miss Branch ought to stay the night," said Elsie. "It'll give us an opportunity to chat about old times."

"I'm afraid we can't." Adele glanced at Nin, who nodded.

"At least stay for lunch," the woman insisted. "Shall we go to that tea shop on Union Street you're so fond of?"

Adele exchanged a look with her friend, who nodded again. "I think we can manage that."

"I'll leave you to our guests, dear." Dr. Blessings took Adele's hand and then Nin's. "Such color in your cheeks, both of you! Elsie, darling, we must visit the country sometime soon. It would do us both good."

Elsie snorted. "Don't forget dinner, Papa. I ordered grilled salmon especially." She sighed. "It's a shame you're not staying a few days. Both you and your friend could have come with us to St. Augustine's." She glanced at Nin. "You've no friends in the city, Miss Branch?"

"My mother considered the city no better than a pocket of dead air." Nin pulled her cape around her. "This is only the second time I've been here."

"You must tell me at lunch about the first." Elsie trudged down the stairs. "I'm sure it's bound to be fascinating."

They spent a pleasant afternoon with Elsie as her father buried himself in his laboratory. The woman was, if nothing else, a perfect hostess, having played that role as a young woman when her mother died. She could be very entertaining with her talent for mimic. She had them laughing over her interpretations of certain people she and Adele knew well, including figures in the city such as politicians and newspaper men.

They left in the early evening. Out on the street, Adele felt alive again. She could not deny the city streets always had a certain invigorating feeling.

"That was quite naughty of you, you know." Nin took her arm.

"What was?"

"Leaving those letters with Dr. Blessings," said her friend. "Neither the sheriff or your brother will be thrilled to discover a part of their evidence against Richard is being scrutinized by a man with one great glass eye."

Adele laughed and lowered her veil over her face. Though she usually rejected hat trimmings, the city chaos made her conscious of unsolicited stares from men. "They'll understand it was necessary once we explain. Jack is as anxious to prove Richard's innocence as we are."

"And the sheriff?" Nin asked as they began walking. "I've read few detective stories, but I believe the police are always anxious to close a case."

"Precisely," said Adele. "This case is a little too closed, don't you think?"

Before Nin could answer, Adele whirled around, her hand grabbing what she thought were a man's probing fingers, ready to snarl her retribution. The fingers belonged to John Bellows.

"Adele!" He kissed the palm of her hand. "I haven't seen you for ages."

"I moved to the country a month ago, John. Remember?"

"Only too well, my dear, only too well." He looked at Nin expectedly.

"Miss Branch, this is John Bellows, a friend from the city.

John, this is Miss Branch, a dear friend from the country." Her friend promptly hid her hands behind her back.

"Quite a courageous experiment, this sudden retreat to the backcountry," John remarked. "I'm surprised your brother allowed it."

"That shouldn't surprise you," she snapped. "You always believed Jack was too permissive with me." She could hardly keep the anger out of her voice, though she knew John wouldn't take much notice. He was a lawyer and believed everyone was as objective as he was.

"Indulgent, perhaps, but never permissive to a fault," he protested. "None of us understood why you were in such a rush."

"No, none of you would," she said softly.

"How are you getting along in – where is it you live now? I don't recall you told us that."

"The town's name is Arrojo." Adele raised her parasol. "It means 'spunk' in Spanish."

"That certainly suits you," he said, not without a little self-satisfaction.

"You may also tell everyone I bought a house and a business which is doing quite well, considering."

"Considering what?" John peered at her.

"That's none of your business," Nin snapped.

He took Adele's hand. "Dear, you wouldn't have to work so hard if you would just be a little less —"

"Permissive with myself?" she challenged.

"I was going to say stubborn." He chuckled. "But I suppose permissive with yourself will do just as well."

She took Nin's arm again. "I'm sorry, John, but we've a train to catch."

"Oh, please come and have lunch with me," he insisted.

"We've had lunch," Nin growled.

"I told you, I have a business to run, and Miss Branch does

too," said Adele. "You wouldn't expect us to keep you away from the law firm, would you?"

"Ah, but that's different."

"Is it?" She glared at him.

As if realizing his mistake, he cleared his throat and raised his hand. "You'll at least let me hail you a cab." A hansom instantly appeared.

"You seem to have great powers of persuasion, Mr. Bellows," Nin remarked. "At last as far as horses are concerned."

Adele held back a grin.

"My powers of persuasion don't seem to extend to your stubborn friend." He held the door open for them. "I've been trying to get engaged to her since we were fifteen."

"You don't approve of the New Woman, Mr. Bellows?" Nin ignored the hand he held out to her.

"Do you?" he challenged, glancing at her soot-stained skirt.

"Wholeheartedly," she shot back.

"I don't know that I do," he admitted. "I suppose I'll get used to her in time. I may even come to like her." He gave Adele a long look, then closed the cab door, directing the driver to the train station. "I'm sure I shall come to like whatever Adele decides for herself."

"You'll be waiting for her to decide, no doubt," said Nin.

"I'll be waiting for a telegram when you decide to come back to us." John looked at Adele. "I hope you'll call me when you do."

Adele remained silent. Only when the hansom pulled away did John allow his hand to slip out of hers.

"He'll be waiting an awfully long time." Nin leaned back in the seat.

"An awfully long time," Adele agreed.

*I*t was a relief to reach the station and see the locomotive blocking the green hills behind it. Nin waited while Adele selected a generous pile of city newspapers to take back with her for Jackson. Just as they reached the platform, she felt a tug on her collar.

"So you crept into town, and you're about to creep out again?" The voice was deep and reassuring.

She greeted Valda, a Polish woman who had come to San Francisco when she was a child. Other than her name, nothing of her Slavic disposition remained. Her voice was smooth and her hands adept at doing the work of three people. It was she who found Adele handing out loaves of bread on the street in the Tenderloin, and realized she was as aimless as an arrow. Valda provided the bow necessary to make Adele's progressive intentions hit their mark.

"I believe I passed through Arrojo once on my way to Sacramento," said Valda, shaking Nin's hand. "A bit dusty for my taste, but rather charming."

"Perhaps you ought to tell Elsie Blessings," said Adele. "She seems to think it's the drollest spot in the country."

"She would." Valda laughed. "At heart Elsie is just as much a snob as any of her Pacific Heights friends." She doused her wrists with rose water, then offered it to the women. "The smell of the train always makes me dizzy." She put the bottle back in her bag. "You've been to see Elsie?"

"Her father," said Adele. "We had some business there."

"Ah, the epistolary business." The woman smiled. "How's it going?"

"Not that sort of business," said Nin. "We were on the business of murder."

Valda took this into stride. "Maybe the town of Arrojo isn't so charming, then."

"I'm more worried about the sticks and stones business at the moment." Adele huddled closer to Valda. "The Lilith Crusade is up to their old tricks."

"Heaven help us," sighed the woman. "I've been hearing things the last few days but I was hoping they weren't true. When and where?"

"St. Augustine's at eleven tomorrow night," said Adele. "You'll stop them, won't you?"

"I'll do my best." A train pulled in and they all stepped back. "It's a shame empires weren't made up of women. Elsie would have made a fascinating Nero."

"I would rather see her avoid his fate," said Adele with a laugh.

"My train." Valda squeezed Nin's hand. "You must pay me a visit the next time. You know what marvelous highballs I make." She winked at Adele as she mounted her train.

Their own came about ten minutes later and they both spent the trip looking out their separate windows in silence. When they stepped onto the Arrojo platform, Adele caught sight of her brother waiting on the platform. The look on his face registered gravity and her hands dampened inside her gloves. She yanked them off as she hurried toward him.

"I took a chance you caught the three o'clock." Jackson took her hands.

"We've lots to tell you and the sheriff."

"I wouldn't mention anything about your visit just yet, Del."

"What's wrong?"

"There's been another murder." Before she could speak, he said, "It's Eddie Goodwin, Michael Blackstone's valet."

This time Hatfield was ahead of the game. When they arrived at the Blackstone house, the entire street was roped off, and twice as many men scrounged around the brush. The family stood on the veranda, Mr. Blackstone with his arm around his wife and Mickey playing with a rubber ball a few feet away.

"One of the volunteer deputies discovered him an hour ago." Hatfield lifted a hanging weed from the ground so the women could pass through.

Gas lamps helped to illuminate the slight figure of Eddie Goodwin who, Adele was thankful, was lying face down, his arms raised above his head. A man in an overbearing suit with a scruffy beard snapped his head up when he heard the scraping in the brush and regarded the sheriff with an irritated look.

He rose. "If I don't have to repeat what I have to say to half a dozen people at half a dozen different times, I might make dinner while it's still warm."

"You'll appreciate yours is not the only dinner spoiled, Doctor," Sheriff Hatfield said with tried patience. He introduced them to Dr. Anvil Rhodes, the official Arrojo county medical examiner. "Pity you didn't send that nice lad Mr. Sanders."

"Yes, well, we don't want to spoil two dinners, do we?" the doctor grumbled. "The man was strangled."

"That's rather obvious," Nin remarked.

He glared at her. "I see no reason for the ladies to be present."

"Maybe you don't, sir, but I do," said the sheriff.

"How was Mr. Goodwin strangled, Doctor?" Jackson asked.

Dr. Rhodes gave him a fishy look. "And who might you be?"

"Mr. Gossling is helping me with the investigation." Hatfield had clearly lost his patience. "I would appreciate it if you would concentrate on your job and not my people."

The man sniffed. "Strangled is strangled."

"In your line of work, perhaps strangled is strangled." Jackson was unamused. "But in ours such insignificant details matter."

"My brother has experience with police work," Adele chimed in.

"From behind, judging from the position of his arms," said the doctor. "He probably grabbed the rope to loosen its grip, then fell with his hands willy-nilly that way."

"You're sure it was a rope?" the sheriff asked.

"Of course I'm sure," said the man. "You can't see the burns very well in this dim light, but you will under the morgue lamp. Come take a closer look if you've a strong stomach tomorrow morning." The last was said with a meaningful look.

"Anything else you can tell us?" Jackson asked.

Dr Rhodes shook his head, taking out his pocket watch. "The roast should have cooled down by now."

"You haven't yet told us the time of death," said the sheriff.

"Ten to twelve hours, I'd say," said the man. "That would make it early this morning."

Jackson stared. "You mean the body has been lying here all day and no one reported it?"

"I can hardly help that, can I?" The doctor snorted as he

passed the women. He stopped and examine Adele. "You're Miss Gossling, aren't you? New in town?"

"I've been here a month or so," she said.

"And you haven't been to see me?" He dug into his coat pocket and pulled out a card. "All the ladies in this county come to see me. I'll expect you to make an appointment very soon."

"Expect!" Adele barked after he was gone. "He has about as much bedside manner as a flea."

"He wasn't very helpful," Hatfield agreed.

Nin knelt down and closed her eyes. In a soft voice, she said, "This man's death is connected to Lucy Blackstone's."

"How?" Adele knelt beside her.

"Very close."

"How close?"

Her friend only shook her head.

"Perhaps a few moments of star gazing will make it clearer," Jackson grumbled. "If you'd care to climb Del's roof, I would be happy to accompany you."

Adele was about to reprimand him for teasing her friend, but the sheriff intervened. "This is no joking matter, Jackson. Miss Branch's predictions have proven very helpful so far."

Jackson bowed and took off his hat. "Please accept my apologizes, Miss Branch."

"It's your doubt I don't accept, Mr. Gossling." The woman rose without brushing the dirt from her dress. "Your apologies do me and my kind precious little good." She took Adele's arm with her usual warmth.

"I think we can assume Goodwin's death so near the Blackstone house is no coincidence," Jackson said.

"The man seemed shady to me," Adele said. "Still, I can't imagine him killing Lucy unless he overstepped his duties as a valet and made advances toward her."

"One of the question marks we must answer," said Hatfield, looking toward the Blackstone house.

Mr. Blackstone admitted them. "My wife went to bed with a sedative powder, Sheriff," he said. "But she could hardly add much insight about Goodwin. You'll appreciate he had very little to do with the women in the house."

"Including your daughter?" Jackson eyed him.

The man glared. "What are you implying, Mr. Gossling?"

"We have to look at every possibility, Mr. Blackstone," he said. "We believe the death of your valet and your daughter are in some way connected."

"Preposterous." The man clasped his hands together.

"Mr. Goodwin was somewhat of an unsavory character, wasn't he?" Sheriff Hatfield's voice was more delicate than Jackson's.

"No more than I would expect," said Mr. Blackstone.

"Why do you say that?"

"Well, he was a servant," said the man. "Every servant has a somewhat dubious character, wouldn't you say?"

"I can't say, Mr. Blackstone," said the sheriff dryly. "I've never had the pleasure of employing one."

"It seems more than mere chance Mr. Goodwin was murdered only a week after your daughter," said Jackson.

"Only a week." Mr. Blackstone's face grew haggard. "Yes, the police would think of it that way."

"How do you think of it, Mr. Blackstone?" asked Adele.

"I think of it as nine days since I lost my precious child, Miss Gossling."

"Yes, it would be that way for you, sir," said Hatfield with kindness. "Do you happen to know if Mr. Goodwin was involved in something that could have been considered, well, unsavory?"

"I don't pry into the private lives of my servants, Sheriff," said the man. "You may question them if you wish. They might know more about Eddie than I did."

"I didn't get the impression Mr. Goodwin associated much with the household," said Jackson.

"You must appreciate a valet stands on different ground than a kitchen maid," said Mr. Blackstone. "Surely, with your background, *you* must know that."

"Indeed I do, sir," said Jackson without further comment.

Hatfield rose. "We'd like to look over Mr. Goodwin's room before we speak to the others, if you don't mind."

Mr. Blackstone rang for the butler. "James, show these people to Eddie's room. I expect you and the servants to be at the sheriff's disposal."

"Yes, sir," said the man.

Mr. Blackstone leaned against the arm of the couch. "You might consider another possibility, Sheriff." Hatfield looked interested. "I have friends in Rosa Gris who have been telling me about a madman running around loose there the past few months."

Adele stared at her brother. By the startled look in his eyes, she realized he was hearing about this for the first time.

Sheriff Hatfield was unalarmed. "We know about him, sir."

"Don't you think it's worth pursuing?" The man peered at him. "It might just as well have been a maniac who killed Eddie as anyone else."

"The madman, as your friends call him, is going after game, not people," said the sheriff. "In fact, it may not be a madman at all. We have evidence the perpetrators are several young men with nothing better to do than amuse themselves by taking shots at ducks and chickens on private land."

"You're not taking it very seriously," Mr. Blackstone chose a cigar from a box lying on the table without offering one to either of his male guests.

"I take two murders very seriously," said Hatfield.

"I suppose I can't complain since you caught the killer of my daughter." The man sighed. "I expect you'll catch Eddie's killer eventually."

As they followed James out of the room, Jackson said in a low voice, "You don't think it possible these young men graduated from game to people?"

"Not in the least," said Hatfield.

Eddie Goodwin's room was half a flight above the other servants' rooms, avoiding the perpetual cooking smells the rest of the downstairs shared. This slight elevation was clearly something the man cherished. His furnishings looked more expensive than his fellow servants', and the room was tidy and bright.

"Goodwin was certainly a fussy lad," remarked Hatfield, moving aside a chair.

"Perhaps he had help," said Nin. "He may have persuaded a kitchen maid to run a dust mop over his belongings on her day off."

"Is that clairvoyance or experience speaking?" Adele asked.

The woman grinned. "Neither. It's an educated guess." Adele laughed.

"I don't doubt you're right, Miss Branch," said Jackson. "I've seen his kind before." He wandered to the small table under the window. "He even had his own desk. Fancy."

"Pardon me, sir." James stood at the doorway. "Mrs. Blackstone redecorated the house a few years back and intended to give it to charity when Mr. Goodwin asked if he could have it. I believe he has – had – three sisters in the East to whom he was very fond of writing. He also helped some of the other servants write letters home. He was very keen one should never neglect one's relatives."

"Probably the only endearing thing about the man," Hatfield mumbled.

Adele examined the butler's masked gaze. "James, how do you feel about Mr. Goodwin's death?"

"I don't know what you mean, miss."

"Are you sorry about what happened to him?"

"Anyone would be, miss." His frozen countenance made it clear he was neither sorry nor surprised at what had happened.

"Do you think the rest of the servants feel as you do?" she persisted.

"I'm sure they're all very sorry, miss." He then stepped back into the hall.

Nin leaned close to her. "Don't waste your time, Adele. He's about as revealing as a stone wall." She turned to the sheriff. "You should try contacting Mr. Goodwin's sisters, Sheriff. They might know something."

"A very good idea, Miss Branch." He nodded with approval. "We might make a policewoman out of you yet." Nin gave him a look before she turned away.

"I doubt they would have much to say," said Adele. "Brothers can be quite opaque about themselves when they write their sisters." She gave her own a meaningful look.

"Only when they're trying to protect them," Jackson snapped. "Well, well."

"You've found something?" Hatfield asked.

"Del may be right about Mr. Goodwin being shady." He handed him a sheet of paper. "Read that."

The sheriff glanced at it.

"May I?" Adele held out her hand.

The page was a note scrawled in thick ink: *The big tree in the yard. Three o'clock. Money will do.*

"Money will do," Adele repeated. "That sounds like someone asking for money, doesn't it?"

"And getting it," Nin chimed in.

"Blackmail," Jackson said. "A Fine motive for a murder. We have only to find out if it was Eddie or someone else who wrote it."

Hatfield motioned to James. "We'd like to use the dining hall again. We'll be as brief as possible."

A second interview with the staff proved most of them had hardly seen Eddie beyond mealtimes. Rawlings, the footman, mentioned he had seen Goodwin at the Bright Lights Saloon on

Quarry Lane a few times with another man with whom he looked to be "on intimate terms."

"Good or bad terms?" asked Jackson.

"Oh, good, sir, definitely good." The young man grinned. "They bought beers for one another."

"You wouldn't know his name, of course."

"No, sir," said the young man. "But he's there often playing cards and pinching the barmaids, if you'll excuse me." His face turned red as he glanced at Adele and Nin. "He wears a very big hat and spurs, sir."

"A cowboy," Jackson said warily. "I thought we were rid of them thirty years ago."

"We might be thankful we weren't, since ten-gallon hats are easy to spot," said the sheriff.

It was with no surprise the name of Quarry Lane came up in connection with Eddie Goodwin. Adele had heard about the Bridge Street turn-off where a trickling stream spilled into the river and led to a side street called Quarry Lane. She had heard words exchanged here and there in her shop from people and had come to realize Quarry Lane was the place where the brash, harmful, and explosive elements of town people did not want to see or hear congregated.

Jackson did his best to persuade her and Nin not to accompany them in the search for the cowboy. Adele pulled her jacket closer to her shoulders, ground her heels, and refused to be deterred. "What harm could possibly come to us with two policemen at our side?"

"I've always wanted to see it," Nin admitted.

"Del." Jackson took her hand. "Think of your reputation."

"My reputation, as you call it, is already precarious," Adele pointed out. "One more uncertainty won't matter."

"You sound more afraid than she is, Mr. Gossling." Nin eyed him.

"I know what to expect from a place like that," he said.

"And I don't?" Adele glared at him. "My work led me into the bowels of the city, Jack."

"Perhaps we ought to let the sheriff decide." Jackson looked at the man. "It's his investigation, after all."

Hatfield gave him a wary look. "I'm happy to see you remember that, Jackson."

Her brother buried his hands in his pockets and looked down.

"I admire your pluck, Adele," the sheriff turned to her, "but do consider the consequences. It might mean the cold shoulder from Mrs. Faderman and her followers for a few days."

"I can stand it," Adele insisted.

"So can I," Nin said. "She's been cold-shouldering me since Mama died."

"I can't see any harm in either of you coming with us, then," said the sheriff. "It might even be beneficial."

"How so, sir?" Jackson asked.

"Men in such places are apt to be more amenable to speak with women," Hatfield said. "And never disrespectfully if the woman is respectable."

"I don't think I like that." Jackson sniffed.

"Nobody asked you, Mr. Gossling," Nin said with a triumphant grin.

Jackson acquiesced but insisted he and Hatfield walk in front of the women, since they could act first should any trouble occur.

Shops on Bridge Street were beginning to close for the evening. Many people nodded or tipped their hats at them. A few men shook the sheriff and Jackson's hand, asking how the investigation into Lucy's death was progressing. Adele realized her brother was becoming as well known and well liked in Arrojo as the sheriff.

"We must hurry, Jackson," the sheriff mumbled. With a blush, he added, "I don't like to leave Ma alone past my working hours."

They ran right into Mrs. Faderman standing near Chapp's Livery with a few packages in her arms. "Miss Gossling!" the woman's voice crowed above the neighing horses inside the stable. "A lady does not run on the street."

"I beg your pardon, ma'am." She slowed down.

"And where are you going in such a hurry?"

"I'm sure you wouldn't be the least bit interested, Mrs. Faderman," said Nin. "We're going to a saloon."

Her friend's candor made Adele burst out laughing. Jackson caught up with them.

"Good evening, Mrs. Faderman." He bowed. "Lovely evening for a walk, isn't it?" He took firm hold of both their arms.

"If you're going for a walk, Mr. Gossling," Mrs. Faderman said, "you're going in the wrong direction."

A carriage pulled up and Mrs. Faderman's daughter Vanessa's head popped through the window. As Jackson pulled them along, Adele felt Mrs. Faderman's eyes glowing like a torch.

"I told you!" her brother hissed.

They reached Quarry Lane. People of all shades regarded them with interest as they passed. Adele could smell cooked rice and meat from the low buildings. She caught sight of a group of boys playing jacks in front of a closed shop. Their dusty caps, torn pants and wayward look made her suddenly think of Mickey. The boy was about their age, and, she was sure, had never torn any of his clothes in his life.

The crowd thickened as they neared the street's commercial area. The grate of broken pianos came out of swinging doorways and a man's broken song flooded into the street, dulled by too much beer. Squealing women, screaming curses patterned the night air, surprisingly clean for such a place.

Their entrance caused a stir because she and Nin had not come through the back door reserved for women. Jackson took her arm. Standing dignified, he looked ready to arrest every man in the place.

Hatfield approached the bartender and showed his badge. He described the man they were looking for.

"Rainer, most likely." The bartender tightened the strings of his apron around him. "You're in luck. He's in the corner."

Mr. Rainer looked just as Rawlings had described him, wearing a large hat, spurs, and a vest made of cowhide. The man's head was bent over a plate of ham and eggs but when the sheriff called out his name, he showed a face so grizzled the only thing Adele could see clearly were the sun-drenched blue eyes.

"Well, I do declare, what a pleasant little lady." He gave her a wide smile. "One that ain't painted up like a China doll for a change. I'd like to buy you a beer, if you're so inclined."

"She isn't." Jackson slid in the booth beside him.

"On the contrary." Adele smiled. "I'd be delighted."

"Del!"

"Don't pay him no mind, Miss —"

"Gossling."

"Miss Gossling." The man signaled the bartender. "I'm sure you'll find my company to your liking."

"You speak like an educated man, sir," said Hatfield.

"And you, sir, hold your head like a policeman."

"You're quite right." The sheriff found a chair for Nin. "I regret to inform you that your friend Eddie Goodwin is dead."

"You mean murdered." The man shook his head. "Heard about that. Too bad."

"But you're not surprised," Adele guessed.

"He was an ornery character, Miss Gossling." Mr. Rainer smiled again. "Not one to worry your pretty little head about."

"You will refrain from addressing my sister in such an insolent manner, sir," Jackson ordered. "Or I will make you regret it."

"Jack, please."

Mr. Rainer burst out laughing and held out a good-natured hand. "I meant no disrespect, sir. If I'd known I was speaking to the lady's kin, I never would have been so forward."

"You never should have been so forward regardless," Nin growled.

"Maybe that's true, Miss —" When she didn't answer, he continued, "Maybe that's true, but I ain't one to look a gift horse in the mouth and a pretty lady is indeed a gift." He held up his beer glass in salute.

Adele took a drink even though it was clearly inferior stuff. But she knew the more she drank, the more he would chatter. "That's very kind of you, Mr. Rainer."

"I assume you have some questions for me about Eddie?" The man turned to the sheriff.

"What kind of a man was he?" Hatfield leaned forward.

"The kind you don't speak about in front of ladies." Mr. Rainer winked. "Not that I blamed him much. He came from as ornery a life as he lived."

"He took airs for a servant," said Jackson.

"Oh, airs, sure," he said. "Eddie was proud of working for one of the richest men in this town. Now, me, personally, I would have stayed with the ranchers. The wages might not be as steady, but who wants to spend their lives shining boots for an uppity man?" He grinned.

"Surely that's not all he did," said Adele.

"Just about, miss." He drained the rest of his beer. "And don't think he didn't resent it neither." He cocked his head. "I saw Mr. Blackstone once. He came looking for Eddie ranting about a missing stickpin. Stickpins! Eddie had bigger fish to fry, as the saying goes. He always had bigger fish to fry."

Hatfield leaned forward. "What do you mean?"

"Eddie used to tell me stories about causing trouble for his employers," he said.

"Trouble?"

"I suspect Mr. Rainer means he discovered something about them they didn't want others to know and got them to pay him to keep it quiet," Jackson said. "I know the pattern."

Mr. Rainer regarded him with an amused eye. "You look as if you would, sir."

Jackson glared back. "From what you say, this would be a blackmail letter, then, wouldn't it?" He handed the man the letter fragment they had found.

Rainer read it slowly. "Yep, that sounds like Eddie's style all right. Meet and hand over the cash and that's all there is to it. Nice and clean."

"Do you know who he was blackmailing?"

The man leaned back with a deep laugh. "We weren't that good friends, Sheriff."

"Do you think it was his employer?" asked Adele.

"Could have been," said Mr. Rainer. "Eddie said he wasn't going to try that again for a while, though. I guess once a man succeeds with one trick, he's bound to get tired of it and find another."

"Did he tell you anything at all?" asked Jackson.

"He did say something once that struck me as funny." The man looked down at a pouch of tobacco lying on the table.

"You may smoke, Mr. Rainer." Adele pushed it toward him.

He smiled and rolled a cigarette. "We were sharing a whiskey bottle one night, and he said he was going to get even with someone who'd done wrong by him."

"When was this?" asked the sheriff.

"Days, weeks ago. I don't keep a watch."

"And you have no idea who he meant?"

"Could have been any number of ornery gentlemen." Mr. Rainer's head was bobbing a little, and Adele wondered how many beers he had already had before they arrived.

Jackson pushed his notepad and pencil at him. "We'd be much obliged if you could write down the names of these ornery gentlemen."

He scrawled some names, then leaned with his elbows on the table and regarded Adele with a hungry look. "I don't suppose you would oblige by having dinner with me, Miss Gossling?"

"You haven't finished this dinner, Mr. Rainer." She pushed the cold plate of ham and eggs under his chin and rose.

"Thank you for your time, sir," said Hatfield. "You've been most helpful."

"Hope you find the killer, Sheriff," said Mr. Rainer. "Eddie was a bad egg but nobody deserves to go before his time. Nobody."

When they left the saloon and were safely back on Bridge Street, Jackson remarked, "Quite a humanitarian, this Rainer."

"He gave us a start, at least," said Hatfield. "I'll get Edison and the lads working on this list tomorrow first thing."

"One who treated him badly for years," Adele echoed. "Do you suppose he meant Michael Blackstone?"

"I expect Goodwin felt everyone who sneezed on him treated him badly," Jackson snorted. "I wouldn't take too much stock in that."

"It might be one of the family," Nin suggested. "I don't suppose the Blackstones would see their servants as anything but cattle."

Jackson glanced at her. "A fine observation, Miss Branch."

Adele stopped walking. "The funeral!"

"What about it?" Hatfield asked.

"Mr. Blackstone was arguing with Mr. Goodwin on the back porch when I went out into the hall for some fresh air. Mr. Blackstone told me it was about his pay, but I wonder."

They stopped by the gate of Hatfield's house. "Goodwin's death may not have had anything to do with Lucy's," he said. "For a man like Goodwin, his crimes catch up with him sooner or later."

Jackson nodded. "I think it hardly likely the man would have been involved in murder. One thing I learned from the Anspatches is a criminal usually finds his game and sticks to it."

"I should think it hardly means one man's criminal acts cannot coincide with another's," Adele said.

The light of the full moon seemed to dance in agreement.

# CHAPTER 26

The morning brought a flock of birds cawing in the wind as Adele and her brother sat on the porch for breakfast. Ruth and the children had done an admirable job clearing the dust and debris so the back yard looked respectable and clean. Tomas swore on the Virgin Mary he would put his skills as a gardener to work and build Adele a Garden of Eden, though she promised him her expectations would be far more modest. She couldn't help but remember the horrors of only a few weeks before every time her eyes fell on the gazebo.

As Jackson put sugar into the large bowl of oatmeal in front of him, Ruth came out with the sheriff.

"Join us." Adele motioned for Maria to bring another chair.

He eyed the lumpy bowl in front of Jackson. "Not if your idea of breakfast is that mush."

"It's Jack's idea of breakfast." Adele couldn't hold back her smile. "I have different ideas." Ruth brought out a plate heaping with scrambled eggs, slices of ham and tomatoes.

"Isn't it usually the ladies who avoid the heavy foods?" Hatfield sat down.

"My sister insists on being everything but a lady, Sheriff," said Jackson. "Any word from Edison yet?"

"He and the lads were at it early this morning." Hatfield speared a slice of ham. "Nothing so far."

"You don't sound as if you expect anything," said Adele.

"Chances are Goodwin's associates were as fickle with their ideas of justice as he was," said the sheriff in a rough voice. "They covered their tracks."

"One of them may be lying," Jackson suggested.

"Goodwin was small prey to them. I doubt they would dirty their hands to kill him, even for blackmail."

"They likely wouldn't have given him much beyond a few whippings anyway."

"Nevertheless, all loose ends must be tied up," said the sheriff. "That's one more loose end we're tying up."

"What do you intend to do now, Sheriff?" Adele handed him another cup of coffee.

"I'd like to question the Blackstones again," he said. "Mr. Blackstone for certain, but also Mrs. Blackstone."

"What would she know about her husband's manservant?" Jackson asked.

"She's proved to be observant," Adele pointed out. "Consider what she had to tell us about the man in Lucy's room."

"Mr. Blackstone, unlike Goodwin's other associates, would be in a position to offer more than a few whippings," said Hatfield. He glanced up as Ruth set a plate of English muffins in front of him. "Speaking of ladies, Adele, I received an earful yesterday from your precious Mrs. Faderman."

"I knew it!" Jackson's spoon dropped with a clang.

"You shouldn't have said that in front of my brother, Sheriff." Adele gave him a steel look. "Any breath of impropriety sends his heart aflutter."

"And yours?" He eyed her.

"I'm made of much stronger stuff."

"I told you –" Jackson began.

"Yes, yes, dear Jack, you're always telling me and you're always right," Adele sighed. "Now I'd like to hear what the good woman had to say."

"The good woman went on about how I ought to have questioned the wisdom of allowing young women to become involved in something as abhorrent as police work."

"Good Lord!" Jackson held his hand to his forehead.

"And, further, what could I have been thinking in allowing not one but two young ladies to venture past the point of the railway station, be they progressive or not," he continued, somewhat amused. "She seems convinced the station is where respectability ends and immorality begins in this town."

Jackson pushed away his plate. "Ruth, take this away, please. I've lost my appetite."

"Is there any more?" Adele asked.

"She proceeded to interrogate me about what we were all doing on the immoral side of town and what possible cause we had to make a full spectacle of ourselves in going there."

"What did you say?" Adele was beginning to feel amused too.

"I showed her my badge and reminded her what it was for." He pounded the silver star on his chest.

"And what else?" Adele asked.

"I told her you and Miss Branch were helping me and whatever police business brought us to the immoral side of town was confidential," said Hatfield. "I'll be damned if I'll allow some hen with little tact and even less regard for human equality dictate to me how I should run my investigation."

"Bravo!" Adele clapped her hands.

But her brother was less amused. "You must invite her and the other ladies for tea and explain, Del," he insisted. "Reassure them you don't intend on doing anything like that again."

"Maybe I will do it again," Adele said slyly. "You heard Mr. Rainer invite me to dinner."

"You wouldn't!"

Adele leaned back, laughing. "Not if it's going to distress you, dear brother."

"Jackson is right, Adele," Hatfield said. "She may be a pompous woman, but her opinion matters in Arrojo."

Adele was silent for a moment. "Did she come to the station to see you?"

"She would hardly soil her dress over the threshold," he snorted. "No, she paid me a visit at home."

"Then Lady Augusta was there."

"Indeed she was." Hatfield leaned back. "Ma heard the whole thing."

"And what did she do?"

"She ordered Rowena to bring in a plate of *petits fours* – apparently, they're Mrs. Faderman's favorites – and reprimanded me for acting unwisely."

"That was for Mrs. Faderman's benefit," Adele guessed.

"That's what I thought too," he said. "But then Ma left the room and came back with my father's 1848 Colt Dragoons – both of them – and waved them around, saying I ought to have brought them with me into a saloon in case of a showdown." He grinned. "Mrs. Faderman didn't stay very long after that."

Adele was laughing into her handkerchief, and even Jackson relaxed as if the picture of Mrs. Faderman's startled face at a woman in a moveable chair waving guns around made up for his sister's social inadequacies.

"We said no more about the subject." Hatfield finished his coffee.

Adele shook out her handkerchief. "Will you please convey my gratitude to your mother for being on my side?"

"Ma's a progressive woman herself in spite of her age," he said. "She didn't think your sojourn with Miss Branch to the city alone was anything to quiver over."

"I only wish more ladies in this town felt as she does," Adele sighed. "I'm sorry we haven't had a chance to tell you about that sojourn."

He held up his hand. "First the Blackstones."

Mr. Blackstone was waiting for them in the parlor. Mrs. Blackstone was again indisposed. "My wife is not used to such violence, and it's upset her terribly."

"But you said she barely had any contact with Mr. Goodwin," Jackson pointed out.

"He was a servant in our household, Mr. Gossling," the man said. "That meant something to both of us."

"My brother meant no offense, Mr. Blackstone," said Adele. "We regret to hear Mrs. Blackstone is still indisposed. I'll have Ruth bring over an angel food cake. I know how much Mrs. Blackstone likes them."

"That is kind of you, Miss Gossling," he said.

"We've discovered more about Mr. Goodwin, sir." Hatfield declined the offer of a cigar. "A note we found in his room suggested blackmail, and one of your servants led us to a friend of his named Rainer who confirmed this."

Mr. Blackstone leaned back and stretched his legs out. "He was an insipid man."

"You don't seem particularly distressed about it," Jackson said.

"I told you, it was expected of a man in his position."

"Rainer," the sheriff continued, "couldn't tell us exactly whom Mr. Goodwin was blackmailing. But he did say your valet had a policy with his employers."

"A policy?"

"He would make, shall we say, discoveries about them and ask for money to keep it quiet."

"The cad!" Mr. Blackstone's roar brought tumbling feet down the stairs. Mickey burst into the room, a rubber ball in his hand.

"Papa, did the ghosts come?" The boy leapt into his father's lap.

"Never mind, Mickey, go play with Miss Cummings." He lowered his son back to the floor with steady but decided hands.

Mickey spun around and came face to face with Jackson. "Want to play ball with me?"

"Not just now, son." Jackson smiled. "You ought to do as your father tells you. Go play with Miss Cummings."

"Miss Cummings is tedious!" he declared before he ran out of the room.

"A bright boy, that one," Hatfield remarked.

"Sheriff, had I known Eddie was in any way involved in criminal activity, I would have fired him and told you." Mr. Blackstone rose and pulled back the curtain on the French windows. He stared out into the sunshine.

"Then you were not the one he was blackmailing?"

"Why would I be?" asked the man.

"I suppose," said the sheriff in a slow voice, "it would depend on what it was he had to blackmail you with."

"This entire conversation is most insulting," Mr. Blackstone growled.

"I must inform you Adele saw you and Mr. Goodwin arguing the day of your daughter's funeral," Hatfield said. "Perhaps you'll tell us what that argument was about."

"I'm sure Miss Gossling already told you." He shot her a look. "Eddie came to me for his salary. Most inopportune moment."

"Nothing more?" asked Jackson.

"Nothing more."

Adele had been watching Mr. Blackstone at the window. She could see only the profile of his handsome, lined face, his heavy brow and well-adjusted nose. She rose and approached the window, looking out. In front of her was a view of the carnations Lucy had shown her. "They're blossoming, aren't they?"

He blinked without looking at her.

"I think Lucy would be pleased to find you're looking after her garden," she said softly.

"My father taught me about gardening." He turned to look at her for the first time. "You wouldn't think to look at me, but I do all right as my own gardener."

"I'm sure you do." She smiled. Then, with a touch more delicacy, "Mr. Blackstone, if you were being blackmailed, the police must know. You do see that, don't you?"

He gazed out in silence. Then, he shut the curtains and poured himself a tall whiskey and soda. "You're too sharp, Miss Gossling. All right. I believe Eddie intended to blackmail me."

"Intended?" Hatfield eyed him. "The note we found was quite clear."

"May I see it, Sheriff?"

He handed it to Mr. Blackstone. The man read it with obvious distaste on his lips.

"You wrote that note." Jackson watched him.

"I did not," said Mr. Blackstone. "My manager did."

"I don't understand, sir."

"I say Eddie *intended* to blackmail me because he went after my manager. He asked for a sum he knew the man could never pay."

"So the manager came to you?" asked Jackson. "Rather odd. Blackmailers usually prefer to work directly with their victim."

"I'm glad to hear you consider me a victim, Mr. Gossling." He poured himself another whiskey and soda and eased into a chair. "My manager didn't start out as a go-between. As I said, he has no ready money, not the kind Eddie was demanding. Eddie claimed he had some information. He knew how loyal my manager is to me."

"Why not come to you directly?" asked Jackson.

"I don't know, man!" Mr. Blackstone flared. "Who knows the twisted workings of the criminal mind?"

"What was the information Mr. Goodwin had that he thought was worth money, Mr. Blackstone?" The sheriff asked.

"Eddie discovered there were some problems with permits I

acquired for a new venture," said the man. "Nothing illegal. But I admit my finances aren't what they were, and I had to cut some costs."

"Cut costs where?" Hatfield asked.

Mr. Blackstone coughed. "Oh, building materials and such. Still good but not quite meeting Sacramento city ordinance requirements."

"So Goodwin was going to tell the authorities unless you paid up," Jackson guessed.

"This blackmail was business-related, then?" asked Hatfield.

The man regarded the sheriff with a steady look. "Why, of course. What did you think it was about?"

"There's still the matter of your daughter's death, sir."

"You needn't remind me!" Mr. Blackstone slammed the empty whiskey glass on the table. "I've told you what you wanted to know. Now kindly leave."

"The note said three o'clock by the big tree," said Hatfield. "Did you meet him?"

"My manager and I did," said Mr. Blackstone. "We brought Eddie the money and the letter of reference. After that, I never saw him until they found his body." He pressed his hands together. "That's the truth, Sheriff. I swear to that and so will my manager."

The sheriff rose. "We'll need to verify that with your manager, of course. If you would be so kind as to give us his name and address."

Jackson gave Mr. Blackstone a pad and pencil. Adele watched the steady hand scrawling the information.

Hatfield asked Adele to accompany them to the police station before she went on to her shop. "I'm ready to hear about your adventures in the city," he said. "I'm sorry this business kept us preoccupied." He herded her into the most comfortable chair in the office. "Edison! Coffee for my guest."

"You do your job very well, Sheriff," Adele said. "We're all very grateful."

The man blushed like a schoolboy. "I suppose you're going to tell me you're on your way to clearing Richard?"

"I may be." She told Hatfield about her visit with Dr. Blessings.

When she finished, the sheriff seemed more annoyed than enlightened. "You mean to tell me you left evidence in the hands of an unauthorized person without asking me?"

"I had your permission to show him the letter," she reminded him.

"But you didn't have my permission to leave it with him!" The man's entire face flared. "I didn't give you permission to allow someone to do experiments on it."

"Dr. Blessings is a fine scientist and a careful one," said Jackson in a soft voice.

Adele set down her coffee cup. "Sheriff Hatfield, you must do your duty, but I know you don't want to close your case just to close it. If there's a chance Richard isn't guilty, isn't it worth bypassing a few procedures?"

The sheriff looked bewildered. Jackson burst out laughing. "I should have warned you Del knows how to confuse the tail off a fox. It was how she used to get my candy money when we were children."

"Only to save your precious teeth, darling Jack." She turned to Hatfield again. "It'll only be a few days before we can prove the handwriting doesn't belong to Lucy."

"And how do we prove to whom it does belong?" Hatfield arched his brows. "That's what the district attorney will want to know."

"I've an idea, Sheriff," she said. "A test, really."

"A test of my endurance, no doubt," the man remarked and Jackson burst out laughing again.

"Of your indulgence." She bowed. "Invite Richard here and have him do a sum of numbers. Then we can see a sample of his writing and compare it to the last note Lucy wrote once Dr. Blessings returns it."

"*If* he returns it in the same condition so we can actually see the writing," growled Hatfield.

"Sheriff, while I don't sanction what Del did, I can vouch for the man," Jackson insisted. "I'll admit his daughter can be impossible." His sister rewarded him with a glare. "But Dr. Blessings is a most respected professor and handwriting expert and very responsible."

"Since you're so filled with regard for what is proper and responsible," the sheriff eyed him with amusement, "I consider that quite an endorsement."

Adele rose. "Will you invite Richard to the station and test my theory?"

"Not a very scientific way of finding a culprit," Sheriff Hatfield remarked. "But I've yet to see science be more useful than sheer creativity in a murder case."

"It's more than that, Sheriff." She raised her parasol as she opened the door, as the air was a little damp with sprinkles. "It might be the way to catch a murderer."

# CHAPTER 27

That evening a sprinkle of rain turned into a thunderstorm. Despite Adele's protests, Ruth sent out her two eldest, Maria and Consuela, to the veranda with brooms and mops.

"The rain, she cleans," said Ruth with her serene smile. "Sweep, sweep!" She waved her arms at her daughters.

"Jack, tell her it's dangerous," she said as they sat in the front parlor, she with her lace and he with his pipe. "What if they get struck by lightning?"

He chuckled. "Remember how Mama used to say rain is a blessing we have to embrace?"

Her voice was quiet. "I remember how she stood outside and let the rain wash over her."

He stared at her. "How can you remember that? You were only four when she died."

"Five," she corrected. "Five and three months, to be exact."

They were both silent for a time. Adele was engaged in memory of the mother everyone had praised with quotes from Patmore's poem on the angel in the house, a woman she had barely known but Jackson had loved intensely. Leonora Clagg

Gossling had taken the light out of her brother's eyes when she died of an illness too sordid for her father describe to her even as an adult.

Jackson cleared his throat. "I spoke with Mr. Hodges today."

"Mr. Hodges?"

"Mr. Blackstone's manager." He grasped his pipe. "Have you heard anything I've said, Adele?"

"Of course." She rang the bell. "More coffee, please, Tomas."

"The man is about as formidable as a fish," Jackson continued. "Kept telling me what an excellent employer Mr. Blackstone is."

"Maybe that's why Eddie Goodwin thought it prudent to go to him rather than Mr. Blackstone directly," Adele suggested. "A loyal employee would do anything to convince his employer a blackmailer is worth cooperating with to protect his reputation. What else did he say?"

"He confirmed what Mr. Blackstone told us. Goodwin contacted him and threatened to go to the authorities. They met Goodwin at three o'clock, paid him, and sent him on his way. Alive and kicking back the dust, as Mr. Hodges put it."

She watched as he stared with intent at the coffee pot as Tomas poured. "You're dissatisfied, Jack. I know that look."

He shook his head. "I believe Mr. Hodges wasn't altogether truthful."

"Why do you think that?"

"He was too calm, too insistent," said Jackson. "He reminded me of the outlaws I used to trail. I'd play a game of darts with them over beers while asking questions. Every time the outlaw spoke, he would hit the target."

"It's a shame Mr. Hodges wasn't playing darts with you." Adele smiled. "Do you think he was lying or hiding something?"

"Both, very likely. I had an earful about how Mr. Blackstone found him on a train bound for Los Angeles, dirty and desolate without a penny to his name and patiently taught him the business, working him up from a brick layer to a manager."

"It sounds as if he would do anything for Mr. Blackstone," said Adele in a quiet voice.

"That's what worries me."

Ruth came in with a small curtsy and announced Dr. Blessings had come to see them.

Adele gave him a warm embrace, feeling the matted beard against her cheek. Jackson shook his hand, giving the cane a glance. He insisted the man take his chair, the most comfortable one in the room.

"Have you had dinner?" Adele motioned to Ruth standing just outside the doorway.

"I've come from the train," he explained. "Those dining cars have certainly made their menus most attractive, though not very edible for a man my age." He chuckled.

"Coffee, then?" Ruth had already taken the pot in her hand.

"A rather late visit but always a pleasure." Jackson offered him a cigar.

"I'm on my way to a conference in Sacramento," said Dr. Blessings.

"Then you must stay the night," Adele insisted.

"I've a room at the Arrojo Inn, quite nice," he said.

"I won't hear of it." Before Dr. Blessings could utter a protest, she ordered Tomas to take the wagon and bring back Dr. Blessings' baggage from the inn and sent Ruth to arrange a room on the second floor.

"Heaven help those of us who have headstrong women." The professor winked at Jackson.

"Heaven help you if you hadn't," Adele said in earnest and her brother laughed. "Speaking of headstrong women –" She turned anxious eyes on Dr. Blessings.

He knew immediately what she was thinking. "Nothing happened, my dear. Some ladies of the invisible corset type talked the others out of it and she begrudgingly went along."

Adele smiled as she handed him a coffee and a slice of lemon pound cake, making a mental note to send Valda a thank-you note.

"You ought not to allow her to engage in such nonsense, Professor," said Jackson.

"My dear sir, if there's one thing I've learned in all my years of being the only gentleman in the house, it's never try to direct a determined woman," he said. "It worked little wonder for my wife, and it certainly doesn't work with Elsie." He patted Adele's hand. "You need have no fear of your sister, Jack. She's determined but sensible."

"If men continue to ignore our sensible ways, we might need to resort to chaos," Adele warned. She pulled her chair closer to the professor's. "Did you bring the note, Dr. Blessings?"

He reached into his pocket and came up with a small packet tied together with string like a package. "I preferred to have them on me rather than risk putting them in my baggage. I thought it would be most prudent, since they are, after all, evidence in a criminal investigation."

"Were you right about the ink?" asked Jackson.

"My examination shows," he said, resting the cigar on the ashtray, "the pen used to make the zero in the last letter was definitely different from the one used in the other letters."

Adele's eyes were shining. "That means someone tampered with it. Someone not Lucy and not Richard."

"Del, we can't know that for sure," said Jackson. "A different ink proves nothing."

"You forget, dear Jack," Adele insisted, "letter writing is my business. I've sold many inkwells and not once have I ever seen anyone buy more than one type. It might be a different color, but rarely a different type."

"I've found the same thing in my work," said Dr. Blessings. "People tend to get attached to certain writing tools until they're as unchangeable as their handwriting."

Adele realized he had eaten two slices of pound cake and was reaching for a third. She motioned to Ruth, and whispered in her ear and in a moment, the good woman came back with a plate of sandwiches, salad, and a bottle of wine. The professor tucked into them with a gracious smile.

"I suppose we could check every ink well in the Tanning house against the ink on the letter." Jackson pressed \his pipe against his temple.

"If Richard changed the time on the note himself, he would have known when Lucy wanted to meet, wouldn't he?" Adele argued. "We know he went out at ten, not eleven, to meet her. If he intended to kill her, why would he go to meet her at a time he knew she wouldn't be there?" Jackson could not deny this, so she went on. "What kind of ink was Lucy using and why was it so different, Dr. Blessings?"

"It would take too much scientific garble to describe." He wiped his mouth with a napkin. "If you show me that last note again, I can point out some of the details to you."

As they looked over his shoulder, he took out his magnifying glass. "As you can see, the zero is just a touch thicker here, as if someone wrote over part of it. It's also a shade darker there, though it's hard to see in this light. The ink is of higher quality than the rest of the note, almost, I'd say, an executive quality. Like what a businessman or a wealthy man would use for his correspondences."

"Like this one, Dr. Blessings?" Adele went to the desk and handed him the bottle of ink that she used for her correspondences.

"Not quite, my girl." He searched the desk and picked up a few sheets of paper. "More like this ink."

She studied them. One was a message from her lawyer, who helped her with the lease for her shop. Another was a sales slip from one of her suppliers. The third was a note written by the Blackstones thanking her and Jackson for attending the funeral.

"A man fresh out of law school like Richard might use such

ink." Jackson glanced at Adele. "His father might even have made him a present of it."

"We must compare the handwriting, Jack," she insisted. "I'm sure it will prove Richard couldn't have altered that letter."

"If it was altered," he said.

"I'm fairly certain it was," said Dr. Blessings. "Naturally, my tests aren't infallible, but they have stood up in court." He leaned into the cane. "And now, I must excuse myself. It's been a long train ride."

"Forgive my thoughtlessness, Dr. Blessing," said Adele.

Jackson took his arm, as the doctor was a little unsteady on his feet. "Thank you for all you've done, sir." He helped him toward the stairs one step at a time.

# CHAPTER 28

*E*arly the next morning, they fed Dr. Blessings a hearty breakfast and pushed a lunch basket at him before they saw him off. They entered the police station, quiet at that hour of the morning with only Edison yawning at his desk and Hatfield bending over the water basin with his safety razor. He was taken aback when he saw Adele.

"Ma insists I eat my breakfast piping hot," he said with some fluster as he half-turn away from her. "Some nonsense about better digestion. It doesn't leave me much time in the morning."

"Would it make you feel less self-conscious if I told you I used to watch my father shave when I was a little girl, and he always let me pat his face with cologne?" She could not help but be amused at the man's antiquated modesty.

"I shall dispense with your services there, Adele." He rolled his eyes.

"Dr. Blessings came to see us last night." Jackson threw the packet of notes on Hatfield's desk.

"We have our evidence back, at least." The sheriff wiped his face with a clean towel and slipped into his coat. "No worse for wear, I hope?" He inspected the notes with satisfaction.

"Why not invite Richard down to the station this morning?" Adele insisted.

Jackson raised his hand to silence her. She strolled back and forth with the point of her closed parasol touching her heel as she waited for him to explain what the professor had told them.

Sheriff Hatfield leaned back in his chair with his hands together. When Jackson finished, he turned to Adele. "You think we ought to get Richard down here and ask for a specimen of his writing."

"Several specimens," she said. "Five or six at least."

"Have you considered what will happen if the handwriting proves to belong to him?"

"Sheriff." Adele felt the anger rise in her chest. "Whatever you might think of me, I am not one of those swooning women who faints at the sight of a young man in handcuffs."

"I realize that," said the man. "But sometimes things may not be as we would wish them."

"Don't talk to me like I'm a child!"

Jackson took over soothing his sibling, seating her in the most comfortable chair and getting her a glass of water. Edison observed the exchange with interest, though he tried desperately to hide it among the stack of folders on his desk. Adele noticed this and raised her parasol at him with a menacing look. He hunched down and Hatfield burst out laughing.

"Edison, I think you ought put the coffee pot to good use, eh?" The sheriff waved him away and the young man was only too eager to disappear in the corner. "You know, you shouldn't take your anger out on the lad. I apologize for my tone."

"And I apologize," she said in a quiet voice. "I suppose you had the right to treat me like a child. I acted like one."

"A very charming child, I must say," Hatfield mumbled.

"It can't hurt to have Richard come down, sir," Jackson pointed out. "To test Del's theory, if nothing else."

"I'm always willing to test theories." The sheriff smiled. "Edison!" The young man came running, and he dispensed the order to fetch Richard Tanning.

Richard arrived with his father at the station a short time afterward. Adele hadn't seen them for several days and they looked worn but eager.

"We heard about Mr. Blackstone's valet," said the young man. "Do you suppose the same person who killed the valet also killed Lucy?"

Hatfield studied him. "Did you know of any impropriety between Mr. Goodwin and Lucy?"

Richard sprang at him with vicious eyes. "Lucy was a decent girl! She would never have allowed such a creature to give her so much as a bow."

"I'm inclined to believe you, sir." The sheriff seated him at Edison's now abandoned desk. "We must ask these questions."

"We understand, Sheriff." Mr. Tanning dropped into a chair beside his son.

"I want to give you back the notes Adele borrowed some days ago." Hatfield laid the packet on the desk. "All except for the last. We still need that for evidence."

Richard looked down at them as if they had come alive. Adele pressed the notes into his hands. "Take them. For the memories, if nothing else."

He nodded, putting them carefully in the inside pocket of his coat.

"I'd also like you to do me a favor." He found a piece of paper and a fountain pen and pushed them toward Richard. "I'd like you to write down the numbers one hundred to one thousand in multiples of one hundred in a column, please." Both men looked at him as if he were mad. "We're testing out a theory. In your favor, I assure you."

Richard took the pen. Hatfield and Jackson bent over the numbers alongside Lucy's last note. Adele sat stiffly in her chair, the small of her back tingling with agitation.

It was a long time before the sheriff raised his head. "What sort of ink do you use in the house when you write your correspondences?"

They glanced at each other, somewhat confused.

"I'm not quite sure," said Mr. Tanning. "We've several ink wells, of course."

"Not from my shop," Adele said softly.

"We were waiting to run out before we bought them from you." He looked embarrassed. "We bought the ink at Raleigh's though I don't recall he has much of a selection. He's rather tight with such things."

The ribbon around Adele's skirt went flying as she jumped up. "Sheriff, Raleigh only sells ink of very standard quality. I know because I went into his shop to see his stationery before I made my orders when I first came to Arrojo. I didn't want to stock what he was already offering."

"Are you sure?"

"Certainly," she insisted.

"If that's the case," said Jackson, "It's entirely possible Richard never touched that note."

She grasped his arm. "You mean his zeros aren't the same as in the note, Jack?"

"Look for yourself," he said.

She examined the numbers against the note and saw he was right. Richard made zeros with a clean sweep up top while the zero in the note had an extra loop folded inside. His zeros were more oblong while the zero in the note was rounder. "Oh, thank heaven!" She sank into her chair again.

"What does all this mean?" Mr. Tanning looked at Hatfield.

The sheriff gathered the pages. "We will still need Dr. Blessings' report, but for now, we're letting your son go."

"I said I was innocent all along!" Richard cried.

His father pressed his shoulder. "I suppose you can tell us the purpose of this strange experiment now."

"We've established that this note –" he waved it at them, "–was altered by someone whose handwriting is different than your son's and who likely used a very different ink than the one you use." He looked at Richard. "You told us you went out at ten to meet Lucy that night because of the note?"

"Yes, sir," said the young man.

"We have reason to believe Lucy wrote for you to meet her at eleven but someone got hold of this note before it came into your hands and altered the time."

"Dear God!" Mr. Tanning murmured.

"That's what you meant." Richard peered at Adele. "When you said they weren't the same."

"We think someone wrote over the second 'one' to make it a zero," she ventured. "That's why we asked you to write those numbers. We wanted to see if they matched the one on the note."

"It's also the reason you never saw Lucy," said Jackson. "You came to the meeting an hour too early."

"This is all madness!" Richard looked about ready to collapse. Hatfield nodded to Edison, and the assistant deputy brought a cup of strong coffee to the young man.

"Lucy's clothes were different than those she wore at the party because she changed before the meeting," Adele continued. "If she intended to meet you at ten, she would have gone up to change much earlier, wouldn't she?"

"It would seem so." The deep crease on her brother's forehead eased.

"Edison!" The young man jumped up. "Accompany the Tannings home and collect all the inkwells they have in the house, including those belonging to the servants. Mind you don't miss even one!"

Richard suddenly seized Adele's hand and gave it a warm kiss. She could see his eyes were moist.

Sheriff Hatfield continued with the business at hand, "Jackson, get to the telegraph office right away. Send Dr. Blessings a telegram and ask him to bring us his report as soon as he can. He'll be in Sacramento until tomorrow afternoon, won't he?" He glanced at Adele. She nodded. "Ask if he can stop by the station on his way back to San Francisco."

"Whatever for?" Jackson put on his hat and gloves.

"To take the Tanning inkwells back with him, naturally," said Adele.

"And the letters and Richard's numbers," Hatfield added. "The whole lot."

# CHAPTER 29

The next evening, in gratitude for what Adele had done, Frances Tanning sent around a feast of roast turkey, mushroom stuffing, salad, and a chocolate cake with roses and ribbons iced on top.

She coaxed Nin into joining them. Although Nin had told her she had an independent income, she discovered Nin's purse did not always bear out her high social origins. In fact, Adele suspected Nin had been slave to bread, potatoes, and coffee for dinner more than once.

The food added to their festive mood, and even Jackson did not say a word when he saw his sister pouring out more than one glass of the wine Mr. Tanning sent over as his contribution.

"Perhaps we ought to give you an honorary badge, Del." Jackson teased.

"Women have more of sense than men," said Nin. "We prefer to save one from the gallows rather than pull the rope."

"Very philosophical, Miss Branch." He set the plate of potatoes aside when Tomas pushed the candied peas in front of him. The man was sniffy because he saw their feast as an insult to Ruth's excellent cooking. "But perhaps you're elevating women too high on a pedestal."

"Only because some men insist on bringing them down in the mud." The sharp corners of Nin's face sharpened.

"I should think the vibrations you feel tonight are light as bird feathers." Adele smiled at her friend.

"They're never light, Adele," she said in a grave voice. "But I'm happy Richard is free."

"I never believed he was involved," Adele insisted. "I don't think you did either, Jack."

"It's a lucky thing we went to see Dr. Blessings," Nin agreed as they retreated to the parlor. Tomas followed them, coffee tray in hand.

"Hatfield wants to put in a request to hire him in future." Jackson adjusted his tall frame in his favorite chair. "If he does, you'll get to see him more often, Del."

"And you with him?" Adele peered at her brother.

"Perhaps." He smiled.

Nin put her chin in her hand. "Now explain to me about the inks."

"It's very simple," said Adele. "The workman writing to his family in Ireland wouldn't use the same ink as the doctor writing a letter to a specialist for his highest-paying client."

Nin gave a coarse smile. "Yet another way to show up the rich man to the poor one."

"It's a matter of purpose as well," Jackson added. "I have acquaintances who use a bleeding ink to write their fathers just to annoy them."

"Did you, Mr. Gossling?" Nin gave him a sly look.

He bit down on the pipe he had yet to light without responding.

"The ink the murderer used –" Adele continued.

"*If* it was the murderer," Jackson said.

"– was much finer than that used in the rest of Lucy's note," said Adele. "Dr. Blessings is almost sure it was an executive ink."

"Executive ink? Praise be, the pomp of a man with deep pockets," Nin grumbled. She glanced at Jackson leaning toward the match Tomas held up to his pipe. Her distaste was clear in her eyes.

"It's an ink of higher quality. It's darker and bleeds less." Adele went to her desk and drew out four pages, laying them side by side on the coffee table. "It's not so uncommon."

The first page was a shopping list she intended to give Ruth tomorrow morning. "This is a more common ink I use for household purposes," she said. "These three are notes written by my lawyer, a wholesaler, and the Blackstones."

As Nin studied them, she became unable to contain herself any longer. "Mr. Gossling, I would appreciate it if you could take your pipe outside. The scent of tobacco interferes with the messages of the Generous Ones."

He jumped up, clearly ruffled. "You ought to have said so before I lit it, Miss Branch." He strolled outside.

As Adele gathered the notes from the table, her eyes caught the Blackstone note. Something about the jagged handwriting made her stomach tighten.

"Your brother can be most impertinent," Nin growled.

"He's right, though," Adele said. "If you had said something before, he would have put it away. Jack's a gentleman, whatever you may think of him."

"A gentleman senses when a woman is uncomfortable." Nin sniffed.

"Not every gentleman is that observant." Adele's voice was distant.

Nin eyed her. "You're not talking about your brother now, are you?"

"I was thinking of Michael Blackstone." She leaned forward. "I don't think he was telling us the truth."

"About what?"

"I'm not sure." She played with the velvet tassels on a pillow. "That's the trouble."

"Well, that's a fine place to start," Nin remarked.

"He seems a rather attentive father, wouldn't you say?"

"I wouldn't know." Nin took up the coffee pot. Tomas jumped from his corner and tried to grab it from her but she managed to pour herself a cup before he could do so. Dejected, he retreated back to the corner with a frown. "My own didn't see fit to pay much attention to Mama or me. He ran off when I was two."

Adele pressed her hand. "I didn't know."

Nin stiffened. "Mama and I got along without him perfectly well. Why is it important Mr. Blackstone be an attentive father?"

"Perhaps he knew more about Lucy's involvement with Richard than he's telling us. A father like that would at least suspect his daughter of having warm affections for a young man even if he didn't know who the young man was."

"Perhaps he wasn't as attentive as you think," Nin pointed out. "With all that bowing and treating women like paper dolls."

"His wife is rather fragile," Adele reminded her.

"I meant the young women."

"You mean us?"

"Us, and Lucy's friends." Nin pressed the rim of the cup against her chin. "I went to school with them, when I went to school, that is. They're younger than I am but I would always see them, ribbons bobbing against their backsides as they fluttered and chattered."

"What were they chattering about?" asked Adele.

"Nothing," Nin snorted. "They were just giggling."

Adele laughed and motioned to Tomas to remove the tray. "I'll get Jack to take you home."

Nin rose. "I prefer to walk alone in the fresh air after that pipe. I don't know how you stand it."

Adele lingered for a moment in the front hall as Nin gathered her things. "I don't recall seeing Lucy's friends at the funeral."

"They're not the kind to attend such a solemn occasion," said Nin. "They were all at the party, though. Still with the same bows bobbing on their backsides and the same giggling."

Adele smiled. "I wonder if they feel about the girls at the Wrigley school as Mrs. Faderman and her bunch do."

Nin snorted. "Everyone around here thinks they're little angels."

"Then they may help me give the little angels a party."

Her friend looked at her squarely. "Just what do you have in mind?"

"Lucy may have confided in them about Richard." Adele's eyes sparkled

Nin shrugged. "I've no expertise when it comes to women friends." Her voice was dim under the porch light. "I had none until you came along."

Adele took both her hands. "And I've had none so precious as you."

"Thank you," said Nin. For a moment, with her long curls and flowing cape, she looked like a princess caught in the darkness.

# CHAPTER 30

The next morning, Adele found herself at the Wrigley School for Girls. The girls were out in the courtyard playing when she entered the office but Mary, Beatrice, and Rachel saw her through the oblong windows. They waved wildly even as one girl smacked Beatrice's shoulder. Adele nodded at them but did not venture out the back door.

Clara Wrigley's manner was frosty as she led her into the office where pictures of past graduates at their weddings stared down at her looking more mournful than joyous. "Miss Gossling," she started, "you have been dishonest with me."

"Dishonest?"

"The women in town informed me that while you do have a brother, he is unmarried at present." Her voice was as stiff as her posture. "They also told me you have no niece named Anita."

"I'm sorry about that," said Adele.

"I teach my girls to be honest and virtuous," she said. "I don't approve of, if you don't mind my saying so, progressive young women with silly ideas of independence."

"That's your privilege, Mrs. Wrigley," she said.

The woman seemed satisfied. "I'm glad you're being reason-able about it. Now, what can I do for you?"

"I've a proposition to make."

"A donation would be better," the woman mumbled.

"This is a donation," said Adele. "I donate my garden and refreshments to your pupils for a party."

"To raise money for the girls?" Mrs. Wrigley's tone immediately changed. "I'm most obliged, Miss Gossling. You can imagine even with the good people of Arrojo we haven't had much support."

"I was thinking more along the lines of an outing for the girls." Adele set her heels firmly against the wooden floor. "You'll agree the tragedies of the past few weeks have been grisly, especially for impressionable young minds."

"Tragedies?"

"The murders!" Adele could not help but marvel at the complete isolation of the place. "Lucy Blackstone and the Black-stone valet."

The woman's face wrinkled. "We heard about them, of course. I've had a time keeping the girls away from the *Courier*, though they manage to get hold of it somehow. Do you suppose Miss Grace has been giving them a copy?"

Adele tried to hold back a smile. "I shouldn't think so."

"You never know what kind of corrupt stories these newspapers will tell," said Mrs. Wrigley. "They believe they're doing a world of good, droning on about workers' rights and suffragism, but I believe –"

"I'm sure it's nothing like that, Mrs. Wrigley." Adele tried to keep the agitation out of her voice. "But I thought it would be a nice gesture to give the girls a little leisure in light of recent events. A party with cake and ice cream might be just the thing to take the burden off their impressionable minds."

"Oh, I see." Adele thought she was disappointed, but the

woman smiled. "That's most kind of you, Miss Gossling, most kind. And at your expense too. We're most grateful."

"Shall we say three o'clock Saturday afternoon at my house on Caliber Lane?"

"I'm afraid I don't –"

"The old Rosemont house," she reminded her.

"Of course," said the woman. "I remember the ladies telling me you bought it. Rather a big place for a young woman alone." She eyed her.

"I'll expect the girls to dress in their Sunday best." Adele rose. "We're anxious to make the party as festive as possible."

"We?"

"I'm asking some of the young ladies in town to help me," said Adele. "Vanessa Faderman and Mary Lynn and some of the others. We want the girls to have the right kind of influence." She emphasized this last point.

"That's very wise of you, Miss Gossling."

The woman led Adele to the front gate. There was clearly something else bothering her, something that made her thin lip press down.

Adele peered at her. "If you're concerned we'll overindulge the girls, I promise you we'll be very careful."

"It wasn't that," she said. "I don't want you to think I deprive my girls of little joys in life. I was thinking of something else."

"Yes?"

"Your brother, Miss Gossling." The woman faced her squarely.

"Jackson? He loves children," she lied.

"The ladies said he's most gentlemanly," said the woman. "But, well, some of them are practically young ladies."

Adele closed the gate. "I don't follow you."

"I've never seen him, of course," the woman continued. "But I've heard whispers among the older girls, though I don't see how they could have seen him."

"Whispers?"

The woman's cheeks turned red. "They called him a dashing young man."

Adele could not hold back her smile. "I think I understand."

"You know how young girls are." Mrs. Wrigley grasped the iron gate. "They needn't much encouragement to concoct unwholesome fantasies."

"I believe Jackson will be taking tea with Sheriff Hatfield and his mother on Saturday," Adele assured her. "He won't be back until after the girls have gone. They won't even see him." Her brother had never been invited to the Hatfields' for tea, but she resolved to make sure he was.

Mrs. Wrigley clasped her hands. "You are most understanding, Miss Gossling. I didn't know how to tell you. You never know how someone feels about his or her kin. I certainly didn't want to offend you."

Adele smiled. "Jackson and I are very close, but I've witnessed several young ladies make fools of themselves over him, and I don't wish to add to the list." She left before Mrs. Wrigley had a chance to respond.

Getting Lucy's friends to agree to help her with the party turned out to be a much easier task than she anticipated. She chose to ally herself with the only person in town capable of managing the most delicate social situations. She went to see Lady Augusta Hatfield. It was already mid-morning and the regal woman answered the door herself.

"I sent Rowena on her errands." She pressed Adele's hands. "Rowena always has iced tea and sugar cookies on hand in case of visitors. Would you get them for us, dear?"

"I'd be delighted," Adele smiled.

"If it weren't for this confining chair, I would be rushing about like a banshee," she mused. "Once it was nothing to me to have callers all morning." There was a touch of sadness to her voice. "Now, to what do I owe this charming visit?"

"I've come to thank you," Adele said. "Your son told me how you defended Nin and me to Mrs. Faderman."

"I only wish I could have accompanied you," said the woman. "I would have rolled into that saloon with guns blasting, as the saying goes."

Adele laughed. She cleared her throat. "I've come to ask for your assistance again with the ladies. Or rather, their daughters."

"Oh?" Lady Augusta produced a pair of glasses from her dress pocket and propped them on her nose.

"I want to give a party for those poor girls at The Wrigley School," she said. "I promised Mrs. Wrigley Vanessa Faderman and Mary Lynn and a few others would help me."

"I can hardly imagine you would need help handing around sweets to those girls," The woman threaded her hands in her lap.

"They're quite spirited," Adele pointed out. "Even incorrigible."

Lady Augusta eyed her. "You talk as if you've dealt with them before."

"Well, in a way I have." Adele began to scrape large grains of sugar from top of the cookie.

"Don't do that, dear," the woman said. "It makes them look quite undressed."

Adele laughed. "Girls can get to places and hear things adults can't. They can ask questions and no one will think twice about it."

"I see." Lady Augusta slid her chair nearer to the table. "You've an entire net of spies."

"I told the sheriff, but I don't think he quite approves," said Adele.

"Yes, Horatio can be quite sanctimonious with the opposite sex, especially the young opposite sex," the woman chuckled.

"Do you think he'll tell Mrs. Wrigley?"

"I rather doubt it," said Lady Augusta. "I once remarked how

Mrs. Wrigley reminded one of a bee and Horatio agreed with me."

Adele giggled behind her napkin.

The woman took out a handkerchief and dabbed at her face. "You have some purpose in mind for this party?"

"I'd like to reward them for their help," she said.

"I meant another purpose."

Adele finished the lemonade. "Well, yes, as a matter of fact. I heard Vanessa and Mary and their friends were school chums of Lucy's."

"And you believe they might know something about her death?" The woman cupped her chin in her hand. "Horatio gave them a thorough going-over, in the nicest way, of course, the day after it happened."

"I realize that, Lady Augusta," she said. "But sometimes a police officer doesn't know the right questions to ask or the right way to get young ladies to talk. Another young lady does."

The woman gave her a glowing smile. "Horatio never was very artful with the ladies."

Adele reached for her gloves, hoping the woman wouldn't see the redness in her cheeks. "Some of us prefer plain-speaking men, Lady Augusta."

"Indeed," said the woman. "When is the party?"

"Saturday at three o'clock."

"Rest assured the entire entourage of young ladies shall be there."

"Do you mind if I ask how you propose to do that?"

"Very simple, my dear. I will speak to Mrs. Faderman and emphasize your cause and remark upon how unfair it would be to leave one charitable young woman to deal with all those girls on her own."

Adele grinned. "And no one can refuse Mrs. Faderman."

"No one dare refuse Mrs. Faderman," the woman corrected,

leading her to the front door. "Yes, that woman has set things up for herself in Arrojo quite nicely."

"Lady Augusta," Adele ventured. "You'll forgive my indulgence in asking one more favor of you?"

"Anything I can do."

"Will you invite my brother to tea on Saturday at two-thirty and keep him here until well past five?" she asked.

"He doesn't want to be at your party?" The woman's eyes arched.

"Mrs. Wrigley doesn't want him there," she said. "Some of the girls have taken a fancy to him."

"Well, that's no surprise," she said. "If I were a young girl, I might do the same."

"Mrs. Wrigley is afraid they might develop unwholesome fantasies if they get even a glimpse of him," Adele mumbled.

Lady Augusta threw her head back and laughed. "They probably would. They always struck me as the sort of girls to hide French novels among their linens."

Adele laughed. "I had to promise he wouldn't be in the house when they came."

Lady Augusta patted her hand. "I shall suggest to Horatio that he invite Jackson for tea and a game of poker. Once my son gets a game of cards going, he can play until daybreak."

"Not for money, I hope." Adele raised her parasol against the blinding lunchtime sun.

"Not at all, not at all," the woman assured her. "When he was a child, we had a chestnut tree in our yard and he and his father would play for chestnuts. The winnings were roasted over a fire."

Adele laughed and a wave of sentiment not unlike a granddaughter to her grandmother washed over her.

# CHAPTER 31

Saturday began with fog, and Ruth hurried her eldest daughters outside before breakfast to take the washing down so the clothes would not dampen. Adele kept peering through the window at breakfast looking for the sun. Jackson teased her about shaking her fist at the sky so it could see she meant to have a bright day for her party. Toward lunchtime, the sun rose, drying out specks of morning dew, giving the flowers Tomas had proudly tilled a pleasant hue. Even the gazebo lost its morbid luster and shone bright green from all the hanging vines.

Jackson helped with setting the table she had borrowed from Mrs. Faderman, who had thrown herself into the function with enthusiasm and a surprising organization. When the clock struck two, Adele hurried him away to the Hatfields' before Lucy's friends arrived.

Vanessa and Mary and two others arrived first. Cora Leighton carried her head unsteadily under a hat piled high with paper flowers and birds. Bertha Golde, the daughter of Arrojo's Presbyterian minister, joined them and helped to arrange the party favors, the cake, and the lemonade between hushed whispers and giggles. Watching them, Adele could see why Nin referred to them as giggling geese.

"Mother is so happy you've taken on some civic responsibilities, Miss Gossling." Vanessa's voice was as authoritative as her mother's. She lost her initial timidity, as had many of the other girls, within the first week of Adele's arrival.

"We must do what we can for the poor things," Bertha agreed.

"It's a girls' school, Bertha, not an orphanage," a voice rose behind them. Tomas led a young woman dressed in a black suit and hat out to the garden. She held out her hand to Adele. "I'm Susan Grate."

"I don't think we've met before," Adele said, shaking her hand.

The girl smiled. "I was Lucy's friend since childhood."

"Well, we're all that," said Mary, a little annoyed.

"But you weren't at her funeral like I was," said Susan. The shadow of her friend's death was still clearly upon her, as all of her movements seemed weighed down.

Vanessa sniffed. "Mama thinks a young lady should avoid such morbid occasions."

"And my mother does whatever her mother does," Mary said in a mechanical voice.

"Will there be any more coming?" Adele asked.

"Oh, just two," said Vanessa. "Sybil Pringle you know, of course."

Adele nodded. She had often seen the girl sitting at the head of Pringle's Restaurant with her mother, surveying the place in between courses.

"And Missy Grace," Mary added.

Adele held a tablecloth in her hands. "I had no idea she was part of your circle."

"Missy was a year ahead of us in school." Mary studied the spoons she had just placed around a table. "She can't help it if her brothers ran away to the city and left the *Courier* in her hands."

"I rather thought she enjoyed the challenge," said Adele.

"It was all just a front." Vanessa leaned toward her, the artificial cherries on her hat bobbing. "She had no choice, really. Arrojo must have a paper, Mother says."

"She ought to have sold it to Phillip Crain. That's what I say!" This came from Cora's rather throaty voice.

Adele eyed her. "You don't approve of businesswomen, Miss Leighton?"

"In the city, perhaps, where ladies can do as they wish, even if they step out of the bounds of respectability." The girl yanked a plate of cookies from Ruth's hands. "But not here."

"Cora, you're just being mean-spirited," Vanessa said. She added in a loud whisper, "You know Miss Gossling owns a stationery shop in town."

Cora's lips grew white and she turned away.

"Nowadays ladies of all classes are working." Adele tried to hide her smile. "They may even step out of the bounds in other ways, like dancing the waltz or even riding a bicycle in bloomers."

"I repeat what I said before, Miss Gossling." Cora's tone was icy.. "Those things might be fine in the city but not here in Arrojo."

There was no time for Adele to argue, as Mrs. Wrigley arrived with her girls. Missy trailed after them with her pad and pencil and a Brownie camera. The girls pulled her in all directions, excited to be photographed for the *Courier*.

It was clear the young ladies weren't used to such high-spirited youngsters, as their attention went every which way, their hats tilting too far off their heads and their gloves smearing with cake frosting. It was almost impossible to get much conversation with them. Adele did learn they endured probing inquiries from Mr. and Mrs. Blackstone about where they were going and what they intended to do whenever they went out with Lucy.

"I suppose you can't really be surprised." Sybil scraped at the hard ice cream in the barrel. "Most fathers want to know where their girls are these days and what they're doing."

"You speak from experience," Adele guessed.

The girl shook her head. "My father is a dear. He trusts me to be sensible and I've never betrayed that trust." There was sharpness to her eyes as she pushed a dish of ice cream at one of the girls.

"How did Lucy feel about her parents' questions?"

"She was always going off about how her father had become a tyrant since she turned fifteen," said Sybil. "She thought he ought to have been a lawyer, he was so good at answering questions with questions."

"Lucy wasn't much for giving answers, was she?" Vanessa chimed in as she placed another cake on the table. The girls rewarded her with more loud squeals.

"So she never really answered the questions?"

"Oh, she answered well enough to suit him," said Vanessa. "They never quarreled, if that's what you mean. He's a civil man, Mr. Blackstone. Always polite and decent."

"Always polite and decent," Adele repeated.

Tomas's gesticulations pulled her away from the young ladies for a moment as she calmed down his ravings about the girls crushing his prize rose bush. When she returned to the garden, the young ladies were preoccupied with the girls. Only Susan was free, having retreated to the gazebo, which Jackson insisted they block so the girls wouldn't enter.

Adele moved the crates her brother had put in front of the entrance and sat down beside her.

"She was found here, wasn't she?" Even under the wide brim of her hat Adele could see her eyes were red.

"I'm sorry," she said. "I should have asked Jackson to hide it."

"No, I want to be here," Susan insisted. "This is what I came for, you see. I feel – I feel her closeness here."

"You were very good friends." Adele's voice was gentle and low.

"Miss Gossling," the young lady turned to her, "Lucy wasn't silly like *they* are." She glared into the garden.

"I know she wasn't."

"She knew her own mind." Susan reached inside her purse for a handkerchief. "She knew what she wanted, and she wouldn't stand for anyone telling her she couldn't have it. I don't mean in a spoiled way – well, perhaps she was spoiled a little. But she had more sense than anybody ever gave her credit for. She had dreams no one but me knew about."

Adele stared at the wall of ivy. "I remember Lucy saying something to me about wanting to go to San Francisco."

Susan looked at her with wide eyes. "Fancy her telling you that. I don't mean any disrespect, Miss Gossling, but —"

"You thought she told only you," Adele finished.

The girl fidgeted with the lace on her dress. "She had very definite plans, you see. She wanted to go there someday and open up her own flower shop specializing in carnations." The girl's eyes filled with tears. "You know how fond of them she was."

"Yes, I know," Adele said, taking the girl's hand. "What was her relationship like with her father?"

The girl's hands clutched at the now damp handkerchief. "Has it anything to do with the investigation into Lucy's death?"

"Why do you ask that?" Adele glanced at her.

"It's all over town you're helping the police just as if you were a policewoman yourself."

Adele bit her lip. "My brother was a private detective at one time, and such things have always interested me. Since Lucy was found on my property, I feel responsible for helping to find who killed her."

"Why would Mr. Blackstone have anything to do with it?"

"I never said he did," said Adele briskly. "But my brother once told me it helps to know about the victim's relationships. Some daughters are close to their fathers and some aren't. I was very close to mine."

"Lucy was close to her father in some ways."

"But not in others?" Adele guessed.

"No, not in others." Susan settled back.

"I heard Mr. Blackstone asked a lot of questions and Lucy didn't always answer them."

"Oh, that," said Susan. "He could be nosy at times. But most fathers are concerned with their girls, aren't they?"

"But Lucy wasn't a girl," said Adele. "She was twenty."

The girl began to cry. "She had her whole life ahead of her!"

Adele comforted her until the tears subsided. "Susan, this is very important, so you must tell me the truth. Do you think Lucy's father knew about her engagement to Richard Tanning?"

The young lady took a long time to answer. "He knew all of Lucy's friends."

"Richard was more than just a friend."

"But how was he to know that?" The voice came out jagged and loud.

Vanessa noticed them and started toward the gazebo. But Adele held up her hand and the young lady, clearly an excellent study of social cues, retreated back to the party.

"Did he know about the engagement?" Her voice was stronger.

The handkerchief fell to the ground. Susan snapped it up and put it back in her sleeve. "Now that you know about it, I suppose I can tell you. I think he did."

"What makes you so sure?"

"Lucy told me she caught him asking her maid all kinds of questions."

"When?" Adele felt the small of her back straining from stiffness.

"I don't know," said Susan. "But a few weeks before that party she gave you, Lucy said she was looking for Gerda one night to help her choose a dress and she saw Gerda coming out of the library in tears. Her father came out a few moments later looking very grave."

"What did Lucy think was going on?"

"Oh, she joked about some senseless reprimand, but I think she was worried. She didn't want to get Gerda in trouble, you know. She always liked that girl." Susan rose. "We should to get back to the party, shouldn't we?"

"Yes, of course." Adele put her arm around her shoulders as they made their way back to the table. Nin had been right to say Lucy's friends regarded the girls as "little cherubs" and hovered over them, plying them with cake and ice cream until the girls' faces turned red and damp. Mrs. Wrigley, she guessed, was one of those school mistresses who confined her strictness to school grounds. She paraded around making sure none were being left out of the fun.

At four o'clock, Adele, who was speaking to Missy Grace, heard Mrs. Wrigley's cackling voice. "Miss Gossling! Miss Gossling!" It was clear the day had proven too much for her. "We ought to be getting along now. The girls must prepare for their evening activities."

Adele gave her a hostess's smile, partly because she caught sight of the relief on Tomas's face.

The young ladies happily abandoned their duties, though Vanessa and Mary insisted on staying to help clean up. They ran right into Jackson on their way out and their giggles at his tipping hat and bow echoed through the house as they left.

"I see you managed quite well." Her brother smiled. "And did your fishing expedition go well?"

"I wasn't fishing, Jack. I was inquiring," said Adele with a shade of annoyance. "I need you to locate someone."

"My specialty," said Jackson. He was not exaggerating, as during his days with the Anspaches he gained a reputation of unearthing the most elusive characters.

"Gerda Jennings," she said. "Lucy's maid. She's now working for another family, I know that much. But we must find out where. I must talk to her."

"Oh?"

"An experiment, my dear Jack, nothing more," Adele assured him.

He accused her of playing games as she did when they were children. Nonetheless, the next morning, he produced the address of Gerda Jennings new employers. They were a prominent family living in Rosa Gris.

She drove there in the Beaton, stopping several times to wind the motor after it had given out, and arrived at the Stewart house by mid-morning. She had hesitated to send a note to Gerda beforehand, afraid she might refuse the interview. Instead, she told Mrs. Stewart she wanted to see Gerda in connection with her former employment. She had put on her fanciest day dress and hat and kept her manner haughty like some of their Nob Hill acquaintances in the city. She realized right away Mrs. Stewart was a snob. The woman responded with easy acquiesce to Adele's request.

Gerda looked less pale than the last time Adele had seen her. She indicated she was subdued in her new position if not content. "How is Mr. Richard?" she asked, her eyes anxious.

"He's no longer a suspect, Gerda."

The woman burst out in tears, covering her face with her hands. "Oh, Miss Lucy would have been so happy! So happy!"

"It's about Miss Lucy I need to speak with you," said Adele. "You realize we haven't yet found her murderer?" She nodded. "Gerda, Mr. Blackstone asked you to give him information about Lucy, didn't he?"

The girl stared at her. She nodded again. "He was strict, miss, always making sure his family was behaving properly. Little Mickey got into a tussle once with one of his mates and, oh, you should have seen the talking-to his father gave him."

"What exactly did he want to know about Lucy?"

"Everything, miss. Where she'd gone, who she'd seen, even what she was planning on wearing."

"And you never told Lucy?"

"I couldn't!" The girl shrank back. "I'd have lost my job."

"Of course." Adele pressed her hand. "You did the only thing you could, Gerda."

"I suppose a father has a right to inquire after his daughter," said the girl. "But not in that way, oh, not in that way."

"What way?' Adele leaned forward.

"Like he couldn't bear not to know every little detail. If I told him Lucy went walking by the river, he would give me a map and ask me to mark the path she'd taken."

Adele felt the fury rise in her chest. "Did you ever tell him she was meeting Richard?"

"Oh, no, miss! Nor when she was meeting anyone, for Miss Lucy was a popular young lady. We always worked out beforehand what I was to say in case anyone asked. I would never have betrayed her."

"Oh, I know that, dear," said Adele. "Do you think Mr. Blackstone knew she was meeting Richard?"

The girl sighed. "I expect so. But," her head went up, "not in the way that you think."

"You mean he didn't know they were courting?"

Gerda nodded. "To Mr. Blackstone, he was a friend just like any other."

"But you knew they were courting?"

The girl picked at the handkerchief Adele had given her, unrolling the embroidered edge of it, back and forth, back and forth.

She watched the nimble fingers. "Gerda, if you have something more to say, say it."

"Just this, miss." Her bright eyes were almost bold. "I heard them one night."

"Heard whom?"

"Lucy and her father. They were talking in her room. He knew Mr. Richard asked Miss Lucy to marry him."

Adele bolted from her chair and circled the table before she sat down again. "You're sure of that? You're absolutely certain?"

"Yes, miss. I couldn't hear all the words, but there were plenty of them to make me sure of that."

"They were arguing?"

"I suppose you could say so."

"This is very important, dear." Adele said. "Tell me everything you heard them say."

"Miss Lucy said she was in love with Mr. Richard and he asked her to marry him," Gerda began. "Mr. Blackstone said something, and Miss Lucy answered with something like 'That's none of your concern, Father.' He made her promise something because I heard her say, 'Oh, very well, I promise.' That's all I heard."

"Why didn't you tell this to the police?" Adele asked.

"Oh, I couldn't, miss! I knew Miss Lucy wouldn't have wanted it, and when Mr. Richard was arrested –"

"You didn't want to add fuel to the fire." Adele rose. "You've been most helpful, Gerda. More than you know."

"But what's Mr. Blackstone's knowing about the engagement have to do with anything?"

"Maybe nothing." Adele opened her parasol, as a little rain started to fall as she came out of the servants' entrance. "Maybe everything." She said the last to herself as she walked back to her car.

# CHAPTER 32

That night, she only half listened to Jackson's talk during dinner until the name Blessings caught her attention. "What? What did you say?"

"I said Dr. Blessings sent back Lucy's notes and his report by special delivery to the station today."

"And?" She sat up in the chair.

"His tests confirm our suspicions," he said. "The handwriting used for the zero couldn't be Richard's, and the ink used didn't match any we got from the Tanning household." He fingered his pipe, but since Nin's visit he seemed more reluctant to light it. "That clears Richard, but it doesn't do us much good at all. We're back where we started."

"Perhaps not." She told him about her conversation with Gerda Jennings.

"I don't see why you're so excited about Michael Blackstone wanting to know everything his daughter did," said Jackson when she had finished. "Fathers are naturally protective of their daughters."

"To the point of wanting to know the exact footpath their daughter took on a stroll by the river?" Adele gave him a sharp look. "Any girl would balk as such intrusion, even from a protective father."

"I know you would," said her brother with a little glint in his eye. "You used to throw tantrums when Papa wanted to know what book you were reading."

"That's not true and you know it," she insisted over his deep laugh. "A man interrogating his daughter's maid alone in the parlor is a little more invasive than a father asking his daughter what book she's reading."

"Lucy wasn't as independent as you," Jackson reminded her. "She was probably used to it."

"She may have been used to it, but it irked her nonetheless," said Adele. "Lucy's friends confirm that."

Ruth announced Nin's arrival. The moment Adele saw her, she knew the woman was nearly torn inside. Her hair and dress looked frayed and dark creases appeared under her eyes.

"You look a sight, dear." She sat her down, instructing Ruth to bring her a hot cup of water. When it arrived, she took the chamomile leaves Nin had given her from her bag and made tea.

"You use my gifts well." Her friend's smile waned as she drank.

"Shall I call Dr. Rhodes, Miss Branch?" Jackson asked. "You do look ill."

"I would sooner be treated by a lion than that wretch." Her snarling voice alerted Tomas, who, approaching with a plate of cookies, backed away.

"I suppose women like you heal themselves." As if he suddenly recalled Nin's aversion to the pipe, Jackson quickly put it out.

"Is there anything wrong?" Adele took her hand.

"Vibrations are like unwanted voices." Nin stared at the picture on the wall of butterflies caught in a net. "They simply won't stop until they're heard."

"Perhaps we can make them go away," Jackson suggested.

She glared at him. "Mr. Gossling, they're not like mosquitoes one repels with a little kerosene."

"He was trying to help you, Nin," said Adele.

Nin leaned her head back and closed her eyes. "I'm sorry I disturbed your conversation."

"We were talking about Gerda Jennings, Lucy's former maid." Adele rose, suddenly feeling agitated, and wandered around the room.

"We know now Mrs. Blackstone hearing Lucy speaking with a man in her room was not a figment of her imagination," said Jackson. "Gerda heard it too."

"And we know Mr. Blackstone knew about Richard's proposal." Adele straightened the row of china dolls on the mantel, making a mental note to instruct Ruth on the order of the dolls the next time she dusted. "What was it he made her promise, I wonder?"

"Fathers extract the most unreasonable promises at times." Nin spoke as if she knew.

"Perhaps he asked her not to rush into anything," Jackson suggested. "She was, after all, only twenty. I'm sure, Miss Branch, even you would agree it's not an unreasonable request to ask a young lady to wait a little before marrying." The dark-haired woman shrugged.

"Twenty is of age," Adele reminded him. "She could do whatever she liked, with or without his consent." She wandered to the desk, playing with the feather fountain pen Jackson had given her as a going away present.

"She just wasn't the type to do it," Nin said.

"On the contrary," Adele said, swishing the feather around. "She was exactly the type to do what she pleased without asking anybody's permission, least of all her father's."

Her brother raised his eyebrows. "If you play with that feather like that you'll spill ink all over the desk. I don't think Ruth would appreciate that."

Adele abandoned the pen and folded and unfolded the corners of a page sitting on the blotter.

Revived by the chamomile, Nin peered at her friend. "If she promised him not to marry, he would hardly have a reason to kill her. That's what you're thinking, isn't it?"

"I don't think that's what my sister was implying, Miss Branch," Jackson said.

"You don't think a father could kill his own daughter?" Nin glared at him. "A father can be very cruel to his children."

"Yes, I know." Jackson stared into the fire.

Adele absently lined up the edges of a small stack of pages on the desk. Her eyes fell on the Blackstones' note. Her blood turned cold. "Did Dr. Blessings send the notes to the station?"

Jackson nodded. "They're part of the evidence now. He sent his best wishes to you from Elsie, by the way. To you and 'the country waif.'" He eyed Nin. "You must have made quite an impression on her, Miss Branch."

"I suppose I made as much an impression on her as you did, Mr. Gossling," Nin answered.

Adele was not listening. She hurried to the hall and slipped into her coat. "We must go there right away, then."

"Where?" Jackson asked.

"The police station." She pulled Nin to her feet. "I assume Edison is there."

"What now?" Jackson sighed.

"I have to see. I have to know," she murmured.

"Edison's on duty," he confirmed. "Can't this wait until morning?"

"No, now," she said. She clutched the Blackstone note. "You'd better come with us, Jack."

"You're being mighty cryptic, Del." But he rose and slipped his jacket on.

"She has to see and know," said Nin. "She made that quite clear."

"See and know what?" Jackson was clearly exasperated.

"I'd rather not say until I'm sure, Jack," she said. "But if I'm right — dear God, what could it mean?"

"You're behaving as if this is a matter of life or death, Del."

"I hope it won't be."

They hurried to the station. She banged on the door. Before Jackson could get the key, Edison swung it open, a cup of coffee in his hand.

"Is there an emergency?" He was clearly half asleep.

"It's all right, Edison," said Jackson as they stepped in. "We've come to view some of the evidence on the Blackstone case."

"Anything I can do to help?"

"The notes, Edison," said Adele.

"Notes, miss?"

"She means Lucy Blackstone's notes," said Jackson. "The ones we received from Dr. Blessings this afternoon." He sifted through the papers and found the pile tied with a red ribbon.

She found the last note Lucy had sent and laid it out carefully next to the thank-you note Mr. Blackstone had written. "Take a look at this, Jack."

The date on the note Mr. Blackstone had written was April 16, 1902. She pointed to the zero in the year. He was very quiet for a moment. "Just like the one in Lucy's note," he murmured.

"The ink, Jack, the ink," she said.

Edison peered between their shoulders. Her brother whirled around. "Back to your duties, man!" The young assistant deputy scurried back to his desk. "What about the ink?"

"It's the same executive ink as on Lucy's note."

"You can't know that, Del."

"Not without Dr. Blessings," Adele agreed. "But just look at it."

"I agree it looks like it could be the same type of ink," Jackson said. "Mr. Blackstone is one of the largest property owners in this area. Naturally he uses the same kind of executive ink."

"Yes, he is an executive, isn't he?" Adele sank into a chair. "He's used to getting what he wants."

"Del –"

"Even when it's his daughter." The space in front of her had turned into a painting of a garden crowded with pink carnations smelling sickly sweet. "If the daughter says, 'No, Father, I'm going to marry him because I love him' – well, he wouldn't accept that, would he? But what would he do to stop it? What would he do? Who would pay the price? The footprints. The blackmail."

The painting disappeared and she saw only the dusty floor of the police station. Nin was holding a glass of water to her lips. Behind her, Edison peered at her with his hands behind his back.

"It's time to go home and go to bed, Del." Jackson's voice was soft and gentle.

"Don't condescend, Mr. Gossling," Nin began. But as if something caught her attention, she reached into the evidence box Edison had left sitting on the desk. She took the violet carnation, wilted and browed at the edges. She closed her eyes and Adele almost held her breath.

"I would appreciate it if you wouldn't touch evidence, Miss Branch," Jackson said.

"This was not Lucy's," she said.

Adele rose, feeling completely composed. "I want to hear what Nin has to say, Jack." She turned to her friend. "Whose was it, dear?"

"I don't know." She looked at Adele, her eyes almost terrified.

"It's not your worry any longer, Del, or yours, Miss Branch," said Jackson. "I'll tell Hatfield we have to verify the note again."

"No!" Adele's voice echoed in the chamber-like room.

"I think you've had enough excitement for one night." Jackson held out his arm.

"You're not to say one word about what we found tonight to the sheriff," she hissed. "Not yet."

"You're being absurd," he growled.

"In your stringent mind perhaps," she shot back. "But in mine, it's all perfectly logical."

He rolled his eyes. "Heaven help me with the logic of women." Both his sister and her friend glared at him.

"For that, you're going to keep quiet to the sheriff," she said. "And you too, Assistant Deputy." She gave the young man a fierce look that almost made him whither.

"He won't lie, Del, and neither will I," Jackson insisted.

"I'm not asking you to." She was calm now. "Tell him just what you told Mr. Edison — that I wanted to take another look at the evidence. You needn't tell him we discovered anything."

Jackson studied her for a moment, then picked up his hat. "Shall I see you home, Miss Branch?"

"You shall not, Mr. Gossling," said Nin promptly.

"Oh, come now," he insisted. "You don't want to go about alone at this time of night."

"I'll see Nin home." Adele took her friend's arm.

"And how are *you* going to get home safely?" He eyed her.

"Don't be a fool, Jack!" His sister was halfway out the door. "This is Arrojo, not San Francisco."

"She's right, sir," Edison prompted. "The boogeyman doesn't linger on our streets."

"But murders still happen, or need I remind you?" he called out, but she and Nin were already on the street. He didn't try to follow them.

Adele spoke in a low voice. "I must speak with Mr. Blackstone alone."

Her friend looked frightened. "It could be dangerous."

"I'm practically a friend of the family, remember?"

"And what do you expect him to tell you?" Nin asked.

"I don't know." Adele looked into the gray air. "I only feel he will tell me something. Something important."

They reached Nin's shop and her friend stood erect. "I'm a friend of the family too. I shall go with you."

"Dear, it isn't necessary."

"I tell you it is!" Nin's sweet voice sounded ragged on the empty street. "There's evil in that man, I know it!"

"I want to see him alone," Adele protested.

"I'll come to see Mrs. Blackstone," said Nin. "She's been kind to me. She likes me." Her tone resembled a wishful child. "I won't let you go alone, Adele."

Adele pressed her hands to her friend's cheek, feeling its warmth.

# CHAPTER 33

She hardly slept that night. She was relieved to see Nin waiting for her in the dining room when she and Jackson went down to breakfast. Tomas was clearly put out when Nin insisted on standing and rejected breakfast, as his face displayed a stiff agitation.

"It will do my sister good to have your company today, Miss Branch," Jackson said.

"We shall be company to one another," said her friend.

"Nin and I are going to the Blackstones to inquire after Mrs. Blackstone's health," she said in a light tone.

She guessed her brother wouldn't entirely believe the story but he took it in stride. "That's good of you."

"They would expect a visit from me after all this time," Adele continued.

"And Miss Branch?" He eyed her.

"Mrs. Blackstone is fond of me," her friend insisted. "There are some people who don't regard me as a pariah even in Arrojo, Mr. Gossling."

To this, her brother sniffed and poured himself another cup of coffee.

The Blackstone butler didn't bat an eyelash when they asked to see Mrs. Backstone. As he led them to the parlor, Adele asked kindly, "How are the servants doing, James?"

"Very well, miss," he said. "Mr. Blackstone engaged another valet and he seems perfectly satisfactory."

Adele wanted to tell him she was not asking about domestic matters but about the general state of mind but, realizing the man's wax-like countenance would never admit any show of feeling, she only nodded.

Mrs. Blackstone was as usual stretched out on the chaise with a lace handkerchief in her hand while Mickey played with his nanny on the other side of the room.

"You're just in time for coffee, Miss Gossling." She held out her hands with a smile. Although still frail, she looked more serene. "I'm glad you brought Miss Branch with you."

Adele took hold of her hands. They were warm and bony, and she suddenly felt the burden they had already endured and might still endure before the day was out.

Nin sat on the floor in front of the woman. "We thought you would want us to come after so long."

"Michael has been very protective." Her eyes trailed to Mickey turning a small train around on a figure-eight track. "He wanted me to stay in bed a few more weeks but it isn't fair to Mickey. After all, I have him to take care of." She dabbed at her eyes.

"I think you're wise," said Adele. "The morning sun is so beautiful in this room." She gazed out the French windows at the swinging vines of the garden. "I wanted to thank you for the note you sent us."

"Note?"

"After the funeral," she said, lowering her voice.

"It was a lovely sentiment," Nin echoed. Adele realized for the first time her friend had received one as well.

"Oh, that would be Michael," Mrs. Blackstone said with a

faded smile. "I never did have patience for correspondences, and at the time – well, it wasn't exactly the right time for me."

Adele's pulse quickened. "I'd like to thank Mr. Blackstone personally. Is he here?"

"He went up to the Mulligan farm but he should be back shortly," said Mrs. Blackstone. "I had to beg him to go. He didn't want to leave me alone, poor darling. He's been so attentive."

"He seems to love his family very much." Adele sat with her hands in her lap.

"Oh, he's always looking after people," she said. "His workers too. He likes to know what they're doing when they're not working. He takes an uncommon interest in them."

"Uncommon," Adele muttered.

"Do you know," the woman leaned forward, "he remembers every one of their birthdays? He always had Edward take a bottle of wine to them on their birthday."

"Edward? Oh, Eddie Goodwin," said Adele.

"Before the poor man died, of course." She blinked.

"That was very thoughtful of your husband."

"Michael has always been thoughtful," she said with a sigh. "We spoke of sending Mickey away to school next year but now he wants to keep him here so I won't be alone."

"I suppose Lucy was a sort of companion to you," said Adele.

"She had many interests like all young ladies do." Mrs. Blackstone said.

Adele leaned forward. "Mrs. Blackstone, did Lucy ever confide in you?"

"Oh, girls don't do that nowadays," she said with a laugh. "Michael said it was just the way of young ladies." Her voice became somber. "Perhaps if I had known some of her secrets, she wouldn't have been killed."

"No, no!" Nin insisted.

The woman looked first at Nin and Adele with wide eyes.

"How could Richard think of doing such a horrid thing? We trusted him!"

"Mrs. Blackstone, Richard has been exonerated." The woman blinked. "Didn't your husband tell you?"

"What do you mean?"

"It's been proven Richard didn't kill Lucy."

"But how?"

"Good morning, Miss Gossling, Miss Branch," an almost harsh voice sounded behind her and she rose to greet Michael Blackstone. "You've come to pay my wife a visit?"

"Adele wanted to see you too, dear," said Mrs. Blackstone. "She says Richard is innocent."

"Yes, I met Sheriff Hatfield in town and he told me," Mr. Blackstone said.

"But that's good news!" Her skin suddenly looked less pale. "It *is* good news, isn't it?"

"I said I had nothing against the boy." He wandered to the corner where Mickey was still playing and touched the edge of the caboose with the heel of his shoe. "It's not good news to the police, I imagine."

"No, it isn't," Adele agreed.

"It means they have to start all over again," Nin added.

He gave her a condescending smile. "That's generally the way of country police, Miss Branch. They chase after the wrong people more than they do the right ones."

"But even country police generally find their man at the end," Adele said, watching him.

Mr. Blackstone continued in his polite manner, "It's kind of you to visit Marissa now that she's feeling better."

"I came to see you as well," said Adele. The tightness in her stomach returned.

"Oh?"

"There are a few things I thought you might clear up," she said.

"Still playing lady detective?" He smiled, though he looked less than pleased.

"Not in the least," she said. "Miss Grace wants to put some things into her paper and she asked me questions I can't answer about Lucy." She ignored the sharp gaze from her friend. "I'd love to see how you've kept up the garden."

"If you wish." He turned to his wife, looking a little worried.

"I'll be happy to keep Mrs. Blackstone company," Nin said.

"I should like that, Miss Branch." The woman took her hand. "Bring me a flower from the garden, will you, Michael? A carnation." The word breathed heavy in the air.

"Of course, dear." He bowed. "I saw a bush in bloom on the south side just this morning."

The moment he closed the French doors behind them, she said, "Mr. Blackstone, please believe this isn't easy for me."

"It hasn't been easy for us all," he sighed.

"I didn't mean that." Her hands felt damp inside her gloves. "I think you ought to know I spoke with Gerda Jennings."

"Who?" He flicked a bee away from one of the blooms. "Oh, Lucy's former maid. Yes, how is the girl?"

"Quite well, although I did get the sense she enjoys her new position considerably less than she did her old one."

"Lucy was quite indulgent with her," he agreed. He motioned her to a bench. "Not that I don't know the Stewarts can be a little trying. Both of them." There was a moment's glint in his eye.

"She told me you took an interest in your daughter's activities," said Adele. "An uncommon interest, I believe is how your wife puts it."

"Uncommon?" He let out a laugh. "I suppose a progressive woman such as yourself might call a father's interest in his daughter's whereabouts uncommon."

"I call interrogating one's maid in private uncommon. Intrusive, even." She looked him in the face. "Most people would."

He swept up a few dry leaves. "Not if they saw the father had good reason for doing so."

"What reason could there be?"

"You said it yourself," he said. "Lucy could be flighty. Wild, even."

Adele held tight to the parasol in her lap. "I don't believe I ever said Lucy was wild."

"Perhaps you didn't use that word," he said with creases in his forehead. "I'm well aware of what people in town thought about her."

"I don't think Lucy was any wilder than most young ladies her age."

"Ah, but you didn't know her for very long." He circled the bench where she sat.

"Girls only get wild when they feel their family is holding the reins on their lives too tightly," said Adele. "If you don't mind my saying so." Her voice was softer.

"I do mind, Miss Gossling," he glared at her. "I prefer not to tarnish my daughter's name now that she's not here to defend herself."

"It's not her name that is under scrutiny."

He stared at her. "What the devil do you mean?"

"Gerda also told me she heard you talking one night with your daughter. You knew about Lucy's relationship with Richard. You knew he asked her to marry him."

He stepped away from his path to a plot of carnations just behind Adele. He carefully chose a flower. Then, he sat down on the bench. "The girl is very much mistaken."

"Is she?"

"I knew of no such thing."

"But you knew she and Richard had become closer than just friends?"

He examined the flower. "I suspected she was becoming serious about him. I was concerned. Do you blame me?"

"I know you and Lowell Tanning haven't been on the best of terms for years and I know why," said Adele. "Did you have a conversation with her about Richard that night? Mr. Blackstone," she pressed her knees together, "Gerda heard your voices. She's quite certain about it. Don't forget your wife can confirm this as well."

The lines returned to his face. "I did speak with Lucy about Richard. I wanted to warn her."

"Warn her?"

"The Tannings are a bad lot, always have been," said Mr. Blackstone. "I didn't want her making a mistake."

"She was in love," Adele said in a soft voice.

"Even girls in love can make mistakes," he snapped. "Especially girls in love."

"What was it you made her promise?"

He stared at her.

"Gerda said she heard Lucy promise but she didn't hear what the promise was," said Adele. "I don't want to be harsh, Mr. Blackstone, but the police will want to know."

"Aren't you playing lady detective now?" He glared at her, the carnation still in his hand.

"I'm trying to find out the truth," said Adele. "As unpleasant as it usually is."

"I asked Lucy to break things off with Richard and she promised she would."

"So you believe Lucy's intention in meeting Richard the night of the party was to break off her relations with him?" Adele sat up.

"You see why I didn't mention it to the police," he said. "It would have been quite incriminating toward Richard. Since the police were so sure he did it, I didn't feel it necessary."

He examined the carnation, a perfect cream color with a fresh, sharp scent. He began to open the flower, one thin petal at a time.

"The garden reminds me so much of that night," Adele mused. "I still see Lucy dressed in violet wearing a striped carnation and lilac pearls."

"I remember how we planted these flowers," he said. "Lucy was only ten. I bought her mother a bouquet of carnations, and Lucy fell in love with them. They were the special kind with the white and violet stripes. You see how the petals are perfectly aligned with one another like a crown?" He showed her. "When you try to open other flowers, the petals fall to pieces, but not this one."

The flower's open face gazed up at her, its spikes looking like tears.

"We spent a whole day planting them together," he said in a distant voice. "We would go out after breakfast every day to see how they were growing." He chuckled. "Lucy was impatient as all children are. They don't understand the way things grow slowly."

Violet surrounded her, a different shade than the sweeping purple flowers around her. She saw lilac organdy and a broken string of pearls, an open carnation lying smashed on the ground.

Adele slowly rose to her feet. "Lucy liked her flowers closed."

"I never quite understood that," he lamented. "The point of a flower is to see the bloom." He slid the carnation in the buttonhole of his riding jacket.

"And you, Mr. Blackstone." She could not look at him. "You like your flowers in bloom. You were wearing an open carnation that night, weren't you?" Her chest rose and fell. "Nin was right. She was right."

He headed down the path but stopped a small distance away. "I suppose you're going to tell the police about the conversation I had with Lucy. It's only right, I suppose. Since Richard has now been cleared, it can't do him any harm."

Adele grabbed her parasol. "Mr. Blackstone, how much did Eddie Goodwin know about Lucy and her relationship with Richard?"

He eyed her. "What a silly question. He was my manservant."

"Yes," Adele said. "He was your manservant, so I imagine he knew too much."

The perfumed air suddenly turned as salty as the sea. A shadow of the sun hiding in the clouds lent a foreboding hue to the garden. When Mr. Blackstone spoke, his voice was tight. "What are you trying to insinuate, Miss Gossling?"

"I've no call to make insinuations," she said. "I'm not the police, Mr. Blackstone."

His thundering voice rang through the quiet garden, "Women ought to stay in their place!"

"Mr. Blackstone —"

"The violet, yes, yes! Capriciousness, that I could accept. But the stripes — how dare she?" He gathered steam like a train lurching forward, his fists clenched and his face distorted with rage. "How dare she do that to me?"

"To you?" When he didn't answer, she asked quietly, "what did the stripes mean?"

"Refusal!"

Adele backed away, fearing she would faint. She felt the brush of leaves and she grabbed at the shrub behind her. She remembered Lucy's words that day in the garden: *Striped is a gentle 'no' but a 'no' just the same. One may take a 'no' any way one wishes, whether it's lightly or violently.*

Nin hurried down the dirt path, her skirt dragging against the dark mud. "We must fly." She grabbed hold of her friend's hand. "Business is business, you know, Mr. Blackstone."

Mr. Blackstone bowed. "Thank you both for your visit. My wife enjoys your company." He leaned toward the violet carnations. "Take a bouquet before you go, won't you?"

"No, no!" Nin pulled her friend away. Adele could still feel the dull purple burn inside of her as they fled the house.

$\mathcal{A}$dele was so shaken, she sank against a tree once they were on the street. Nin held firm to her arm. There was something lovingly savage about Nin, small and bottle-like as she was like a cavewoman with a solid foundation.

"Thank you," was all Adele could manage.

"The vibrations were so harsh I thought I would faint," said her friend. "I had to do something."

Nin insisted they stop at the Gossling house and shooed Tomas away with his grave face and mumbling Spanish. She poured a glass of brandy and made Adele drink it. The liquor steadied her nerves.

"Nin," she said, "I know who killed Lucy and Eddie Goodwin. I'm sure of it now. It's horrible!" She buried her face in her hands.

Her friend took hold of her shoulders. "For Lucy's sake, you must tell the sheriff. A life taken isn't worth much if there is no justice."

"I know that but —"

"There's no peace for the dead if there's no justice." Her tone was fierce. "You fight for justice for living women. Why not the dead ones?"

The soothing voice calmed Adele and she wiped her face with her handkerchief. "Yes. We must fight for the dead as well as the living." She rose, steadier on her feet.

Sheriff Hatfield sprang up when they walked into the station. Jackson looked up from a corner where he was examining some papers.

"I heard you gave Edison here quite a fright last night," he said. "You shouldn't do things like that, Adele. He's a very sensitive lad." He glanced at the young man, whose face was somewhat perturbed behind his typewriter.

Adele sank into a chair. "I think I know who killed Lucy and Eddie Goodwin. And I know why."

The stack of papers her brother had been looking at slid to the floor. Both Hatfield and her brother stared at her.

"Del!" Jackson took her hand. "You didn't get yourself in trouble, did you?"

Her voice rang through the dense room. "Michael Blackstone killed Eddie Goodwin. And he killed his daughter. God help him."

The sheriff was his usual lackadaisical self but his mustache twitched a little. "Have you evidence to prove this?"

"I think I do," she said. "An open flower, a lilac diamond ring, a changed hour, a muddy pair of boots, and a broken promise."

"Riddles," Jackson muttered.

"I just left Mr. Blackstone in a state," she said. "For the first time, I felt as if I were facing a bull."

"If you made accusations against him, I shouldn't wonder," her brother remarked.

"She made no accusations," Nin insisted.

"If you bring him down here, I think he'll confess," said Adele. "Especially if he has to face Richard Tanning. The young man was his nemesis in many ways."

"I see," said the sheriff quietly.

"He deserves to know the truth," said Adele. "Mr. Blackstone tried to make him the scapegoat for his crime."

The sheriff stared at her. "Your brother told me you had some strange ideas about this case."

"Perhaps you should do as she says and rather than push it off as women's strange ideas," Nin snapped.

"I always do, Miss Branch," said Hatfield. "But you must appreciate I can't bring a man down for questioning about murdering his daughter and his valet if I have nothing to go on."

Adele relayed to him all she knew and suspected. When she came to the conversation she had had in the garden with Mr. Blackstone, the sheriff's face became like granite. "Jackson, would you be so good as to fetch Mr. Blackstone? He must be in his office by now."

"You really think —" her brother ventured.

"Edison!" The young man was all attention. "Bring Richard Tanning to the station. And no dawdling!"

When Jackson entered with Mr. Blackstone a little later, the station was filled with the intoxicating scent of coffee. Richard Tanning and his father were already there, shifting their weight from one foot to the other. Mr. Blackstone was his usual reserved self, looking less than impressed with the ceremonious state of the room. "This is quite a gathering, Sheriff."

"One always needs to have all the pieces on hand when one is solving a puzzle, Mr. Blackstone." Hatfield indicated a chair.

Mr. Blackstone sat down slowly. "If this is about my conversation with Miss Gossling, I imagine she's made more of it than is necessary."

"Did she indeed?" Hatfield raised an eyebrow.

"Eddie Goodwin was blackmailing me for the reason I told you," he insisted. "Not for any other reason."

The sheriff propped his legs on a chair, which clearly annoyed Mr. Blackstone. "Why do you think Adele thought you killed him for any other reason?"

"I didn't kill anybody!" The man lost his temper for a moment but regained his composure, clearing this throat.

"You admit you knew about Lucy's intimate relationship with Richard Tanning and his marriage proposal."

"What?" Richard's voice exploded in the room. Then, he dropped into one of the chairs. "Perhaps it's just as well."

"We know a great deal more than that," said Jackson.

"Indeed?" The man leaned back. "I'm anxious to hear what you know, sir."

"You wore a violet carnation the night of the party, sir?" Hatfield asked. "An open violet carnation?"

"A carnation in bloom, yes," said Mr. Blackstone. "Adele asked me about that as well. Is that so important?"

"Such a flower was found near your daughter's body."

This clearly astounded the man, as his face froze for just a moment. He blinked and said, "Lucy was giving away her flowers that night. She always did at a party."

"No, she wasn't, Mr. Blackstone," Nin spoke up, making all heads turn.

He glared at her. "And how would you know that, Miss Branch?"

"I asked her if she would give me one," said Nin. "She declined with an apology and said they were the exclusive domain of two people – you and she." Her voice shook with rage.

"I did circle the grounds a bit during the party, just to make sure there were no vagabonds anxious to sneak into the house," Mr. Blackstone said. "It must have dropped from my lapel."

"The body, if you recall, sir, wasn't found on the grounds of your estate, but in my sister's gazebo." Jackson folded his hands. "You can't tell us your circling took you that far out of your way."

The man looked annoyed. "Then the wind must have blown it away. I don't know, man!"

"It was quite crushed." Hatfield reached inside a box and pulled out a paper packet, which he unfolded to reveal the violet carnation. "Consistent with some heavy movement and activity."

"What does all this mean?" cried Mr. Tanning.

"It means Mr. Blackstone was with the dead body," said Hatfield. "The flower could have belonged to no one else."

"I said the wind swept it away." Mr. Blackstone rose. "This is all preposterous. I don't like what you're trying to do. I shall call Mayor Willett –"

"Sit down, Mr. Blackstone." Jackson said.

The men's eyes met with equal fervor. In a few silent moments, Mr. Blackstone resumed his seat.

Adele turned to Richard. "Mr. Blackstone told me Lucy promised him a few days before the party she would reject your proposal."

Richard was startled. "She never breathed a word!"

"No," said Adele. "Because she had quite the opposite intention. She intended to accept your proposal."

Mr. Blackstone's clutched the handles of the chair so tight, the knuckles were white. "You can't know that!"

"Yes, sir, she can," said Hatfield. "You knew it as well."

"I knew of no such thing," he growled. "Lucy told me she would break it off, and I had no reason to doubt her."

"True, sir," said Jackson. "You had no reason to doubt her until the night of the party when you saw the engagement ring on Lucy's bracelet." He pulled the bracelet out of the box. "Richard, this is the ring you gave Lucy, isn't it?"

Both the Tannings leaned forward, and Richard's eyes filled with tears as he nodded. "I never noticed it on her bracelet."

"That was the idea," said Adele. "Lucy didn't want anyone to see it, least of all her father. So she created that story about not being able to wear rings on her fingers."

"But how did you know?"

"The look on Lucy's face when she told me it was a family heirloom," said Adele. "I knew it wasn't the truth."

"Not hers anyway," Nin corrected as she glanced at Richard. "But it's an heirloom of your family, isn't it, Mr. Tanning?"

The man nodded. "It belonged to a great aunt of mine." He put his arm around his son's shoulders.

Adele turned to Mr. Blackstone. "You knew too, didn't you, Mr. Blackstone? I saw your face when she was showing it to us. You knew it wasn't from your family. And you must have known who it was from."

The man's lips trembled. "What you're suggesting –"

"Seems to me she hasn't suggested anything, Blackstone," Mr. Tanning growled. "You've been doing the suggesting."

The sheriff sat down at the edge of the desk. "I shall do some suggesting now. I suggest you killed your daughter because she intended to marry a young man you couldn't accept."

"I tell you, she promised she would break it off!"

"But she didn't keep her promise," said Adele. "Isn't that the real reason you killed her, Mr. Blackstone? You're a very exacting man. Your wife said you took an uncommon interest in the people who worked and lived with you. And you expect obedience in return. When a man wants obedience and doesn't get it, it can drive him to the depths of hell, if you pardon the rather dramatic expression."

"You devil!" Almost as soon as he spoke, Richard collapsed into a heaving sob.

By this time, a stony gaze had appeared on Mr. Blackstone's face. In a cold voice, he said, "I don't tolerate broken promises. Not from my tenants, not from my workers. And most certainly not from my family."

"Oh my God," said Mr. Tanning in a low voice. But Hatfield held up his hand to quiet the man.

In an almost dizzy voice, he told the story of the murder of Lucy Blackstone. He admitted to changing the time on the note to Richard after he found it in Lucy's room the morning of the party. "I didn't have any intention of killing her." On this point, he was emphatic. "I only wanted to avoid a rendezvous between them that night."

Hatfield nodded. "Go on."

"I knew Lucy would be there at eleven. I slipped out after I put Mickey to bed. She was surprised to see me and a little angry. Lucy never liked being on the receiving end of an unexpected visit." He grimaced.

"What did you say to her?" Jackson asked.

"I asked her about the ring, and she admitted she decided to accept Richard's engagement after all. When I confronted her about her promise —"

"What was the promise?" Adele interrupted.

He looked at her. "She promised she would hear what Richard had to say to her that night and consult me before she did anything."

"The violet of capriciousness," Adele murmured.

This shook the man for a moment, but he went on. "She insisted she was tired of my prying and probing into her life. She knew about my meetings with her maid and she never liked me questioning her friends."

"I loved her," Richard whispered.

Mr. Blackstone's head reeled and he glared at the young man as if not really seeing him but something gray and heavy passing through him. He continued in an almost thoughtful tone, "Love never entered into it. She was going to run away with you, did you know that?" His face was stone once more. "She told me she intended your meeting that night to be a plan of escape. Can you imagine anything so preposterous?" He began to laugh, his body shaking.

Richard struggled to rise, but his father calmed him down.

"I couldn't let that happen, of course. Losing my daughter to a Tanning would have been bad enough, but to defy me in such a way?"

"So you killed her." Jackson's voice was soft.

"I had her necklace in my hand before I knew what was happening. I could feel the soft skin against it. And I just kept twisting and twisting –" His control gave way to morbid grief.

"Why did you move the body?" Hatfield asked.

"So it wouldn't be discovered until morning," said the man. "I wasn't lying about the patrolling. I only lied about who did it. I sent James to do it before we went to bed that night."

"And you tried to put the blame on Richard," said Jackson. "Tell us about that."

"I suppose it was a moment of opportunity," said Mr. Blackstone. "I knew the note had to be discovered along with the bracelet. And the boots. I got the idea when you told me you were collecting them. All it took was to exchange Richard's boots for mine and planting the note and the bracelet. I was lucky to get at them before your men did." He smirked at the sheriff.

Hatfield pressed his lips together. "And Eddie Goodwin saw you."

"He was the one I sent to exchange the boots and put the note and the bracelet where I knew the police would eventually find them," said Mr. Blackstone. "He was a sharp fellow, Eddie. He laughed about how his act as a tradesman was so appealing to the maid, he had no trouble leaving a window unlocked when she let him in so he could come back later and get into the house." Mr. Tanning glared. "I never imagined he would take advantage of the situation."

"He put two and two together and knew you murdered Lucy," Jackson suggested.

"He wanted a thousand dollars and a boat ticket to Paris," said Mr. Blackstone. "I've no qualms about what I did. The hangman's noose would have gotten him eventually if I hadn't."

"And your daughter?" Adele asked. "Have you qualms about that?"

Mr. Blackstone looked at her with dead eyes. "A father is

within his rights to do something about a daughter's disobedience."

"But murder?" Nin growled.

"Yes, even murder, Miss Branch, even murder!" the man thundered.

Hatfield studied him with a disgusted look. Then, with a nod toward Edison, he said, "Take this man away, lad."

When Mr. Blackstone was gone, Adele approached Richard. He looked worn, staring down at his open hands while his father pressed his shoulders. "I'm so sorry, Richard."

He looked up. "Can we bury the ring next to her? I want everyone to know she would have been my wife."

The next morning, they all went to the gravesite and buried the ring next to Lucy's grave.

# CHAPTER 35

As promised, Lady Augusta Hatfield gave them a lavish dinner a few weeks later. They sat in the long dining room with all the china and crystal gleaming under the gaslights and the beauteous chandelier hanging above them.

"There is a special place down below for men who do such things to their daughters. Depend upon it." Lady Augusta handed Jackson the wine.

"It's frightening to think he really thought he had the right." Nin shuddered.

"How is Mrs. Blackstone doing?" Lady Augusta glanced at Adele, who had been to see her that morning.

"As well as can be expected," she said. "She has Mickey to think of. I believe that's the only thing keeping her head up. She intends to go to San Diego next week and start a new life. She has a cousin down there."

"I think that's a wise decision." The woman nodded.

"She's a wise woman," Adele said. "Wiser than anyone gave her credit for."

"And you, Jack?" Hatfield turned to Jackson. "What do you intend to do now the case is done? Go back to San Francisco?"

Adele looked down into her wine glass, suddenly feeling melancholy.

"I've really nowhere else to go," Jackson said.

"That's a poor reason to return," said Nin sharply.

"Perhaps it is, Miss Branch," he said. "But as my sister will tell you, I've been in too many places for too many years. San Francisco might not be much in your estimation, but it's home to me."

Adele grasped his hand. "Home is where one finds others to care for, Jack."

"I think your sister is trying to say she'll miss you," Hatfield said quietly.

"I'm sure others won't, Sheriff." Jackson glanced at Nin. The woman looked away.

"And what will you do?" asked the sheriff. "I hardly picture you as a club man, even if your father did have money."

"I'm not sure yet, sir."

Lady Augusta gave her son a sharp glance. "Horatio! You heard the man say he was looking for a position. Offer him one!"

Hatfield cleared his throat. "I had every intention of doing so, Ma. I was waiting for the right moment."

"Bosh!" His mother scoffed. "One doesn't wait for the right moment. One creates it."

"Indeed you're right, Lady Augusta." Adele smiled.

"As you've seen, the police here is quite lacking," Hatfield began. "The lads are willing, but they lack experience and guidance. I try to give them as much guidance as I can, but they all seem afraid of me."

"Is it any wonder when you go around yelling out their names like you do?" his mother growled. Adele hid a smile.

"I need a proper deputy sheriff by my side," Hatfield said. "Someone with brains and know-how."

"Even if those brains and know-how come from the Anspaches?" Jackson asked in a wry tone.

"You recall we talked about a gentleman and his unfinished business some time ago?"

Her brother peeled the orange in his hands carefully and didn't answer.

"I expect you have unfinished business."

"I've unfinished business elsewhere," said Jackson in a soft tone.

"I don't think so, sir," said Hatfield. "You'll allow my powers of observation aren't perhaps as strong as your sister's, but they have merit nonetheless?"

"Horatio was always a nosy fellow," Lady Augusta put in. "I had a time pulling him away from listening in on the most intimate conversations."

"You were a very patient woman, Ma," said her son with a grin. He turned to Jackson. "One's unfinished business begins with oneself. It's easier to do that in a quiet place than a busy one like San Francisco. And you could do worse than Arrojo."

"You're right," said Jackson. "I could do worse. And have."

"Then you'll accept the position?" Adele clutched her napkin.

He gave her an amused look. "I can't make snap decisions like you, Del. Not on a house or a job or a life."

Lady Augusta pulled back her chair. "Well, in any case, think about it, won't you?" Her head flicked back. "We shall retire to the parlor for coffee. I've the most wonderful cherry cake." Her voice faded as her son pushed her through the hallway.

Adele held on to her brother's arm. "Jack, perhaps our life is over in San Francisco."

"But to retire to the backwoods?" he snorted.

"Oh, it's not so bad," she said. "I intend to change the minds of some of the fossils around here."

"If they don't change yours first!"

When she gave him a look of defiance he burst out laughing. Hatfield glanced back over his shoulder at them and grinned.

~~~~~

## Author's Note

Hi there! I'm so glad you reached the end of *The Carnation Murder*. I hope you liked the book.

*The Carnation Murder* started out as an experiment for me back in 2013. At the time, I was writing contemporary literary women's fiction and it just wasn't working for me (I got over that by turning contemporary into historical women's fiction). Then National Novel Writing Month came up in November. This is a challenge to write a 50,000 word novel in 30 days which draws hundreds of thousands of writers every year who cheer each other on and share a community online. NaNoWriMo (as it's affectionately called) has always been a time for me to experiment and go outside of my creative comfort zone. I've always loved classic traditional mysteries (think: Agatha Christie, Dorothy L. Sayers, and Katharine Anne Green) so I decided to go for it and make my NaNo project a traditional whodunit set in the past.

Thus, Adele Gossling was born and so was the town of Arrojo, California. I fell in love with Adele right away and had a blast making up the mystery puzzle and exploring the other characters in the book you've just read. But I learned quickly a well-told mystery needs planning!

Did I finish the book or even reach the 50K word mark that November? Sadly not. But I did finish the book eventually and the result is what you just read.

I believe justice has to be done in every mystery and Adele, as a turn-of-the-century New Woman, believes in justice for women, both the living and the dead. So it's no surprise she's willing to fight for all women, even those who might be be... well... all that pleasant to deal with.

What am I talking about? I'm talking about Millie Gibb in *A*
~~~~~

*Wordless Death*, Book 2 of the Adele Gossling Mysteries. To get a taste of what I mean, turn the page to read more about the book and get an excerpt.

*H*appy reading!
Tam

*Is the death of a schoolteacher suicide or something more sinister?*

Adele Gossling is adjusting well to small-town life after the hustle and bustle of San Francisco. Despite her progressive ideas about women and her unladylike business acumen, even Arrojo's most prominent citizens are beginning to accept her. Provided she sticks with the business of fountain pens and letter paper and stays out of crime investigation, that is…

But that's just what she can't do when Millie Gibb, the new teacher at the local girl's school, is found dead and everybody in town assumes the homely, unmarried spinster committed suicide. After all, what enemies could a harmless, middle-aged woman have?

Adele and her clairvoyant friend Nin intend to find out. But can they prove Millie's death was foul play based on a cigar stub, a letter fragment, and a cigarette lighter before the case is closed for good?

Read on for an excerpt from this book!

After the men had left, both her brother and the sheriff rose, brushing coal dust from their clothes.

"No glass, I take it," said Adele.

"No, but something much more interest," said her brother. "Something in your line of work, Del."

He showed her what looked like a fragment of a written document. The edges were crisp and charred and written on it was small dark print she could barely read.

"That explains why there was a fire burning last night even though it's been rather mild these past few days except for the wind," he remarked.

"A discouraging lover, you think?" Hatfield raised an eye.

"It wouldn't be uncommon," said Jackson. "Though perhaps a little surprising."

Adele did not fail to catch his meaning. "Miss Gibb might not have been a beauty, Jack, but many men appreciate intelligence and education more than giggles and curls."

She was rewarded by Hatfield's deep chuckle of approval.

"Love doesn't usually go with money, though, does it?"

Jackson said. "Whatever this letter contained, it had to do with a lot of money." He showed the sheriff what he meant.

Here, the croak sounded from Mrs. Taylor and they all looked at her.

"Begging your pardon, sir," said the woman. "I don't get into the business of my guests unless —"

"Unless?" Hatfield head went up.

"It's necessary, of course," was her resolute answer.

"You know something about this?" he asked.

"Well, no, sir, not that in particular," said Mrs. Taylor. "But more than once Millie had to ask to delay her payment here. Had a cousin who was rather in a bad way financially." She looked embarrassed. "I don't like to go 'round telling the private business of my guests but —"

"That's all right, ma'am," said Jackson. "We're police, not gossips."

"Well, now that I see everything is all right —" But she still hesitated and Adele understood the woman' concern. Her sense of decorum had gotten a jolt at the idea a room she only rented to women boarders was now being trampled over my male footsteps.

"I'll make sure everything is all right, Mrs. Taylor," she said in a low voice.

The woman rewarded her with one of her gummy smiles and departed without ceremony.

"Could be this cousin was asking for money again," Jackson said.

"Why throw the letter in the fire, then?" asked Hatfield. "I've had more than one of Ma's uncles write us for a few gold coins and even when I refused, I never threw the letter out."

"Perhaps she didn't want other people in the house to know she had a mercenary cousin," Adele said.

"A relative that keeps asking for money is not a favorite relative," Jackson agreed.

"The question is, could he be a relative that kills?" Adele murmured.

**Did this mercenary cousin kill schoolteacher Millie Gibb? Or did someone else do it? Pick up a copy of *A Wordless Death* to find out here:** https://tammayauthor.com/books-2/the-adele-gossling-mysteries/a-wordless-death-book-2.

**How about a little more of the Adele Gossling Mysteries, right here, right now? Read on for how to get hold of my free novella, *The Missing Ruby Necklace*.**

*When a jewel and a girl go missing on New Year's Eve...*

Eleanor McCarthy, a lovely though somewhat flighty debutante, has graced the tiny town of Arrojo, California, with her presence. One of Arrojo's prominent ladies throws a New Year's Eve shindig to introduce her to Arrojo's high society — whatever little of it there is. Naturally, the daughter and son of one of San

Francisco's influential lawyers, Adele and Jackson Gossling, are invited.

But screams replace popping champagne corks when Eleanor's priceless ruby necklace is discovered missing. And soon, so is Eleanor!

In this historical cozy mystery set in the early 20th century, follow Adele Gossling, stationary store owner and amateur sleuth, and her clairvoyant sidekick Nin Branch as they search for a ruby necklace that may or may not have been stolen and a young woman who may or may not have run away.

Want to read an excerpt from this book? I got you covered!
    Turn the page.

"Coffee!" Miss McCarthy laughed. "Heavens, no! I haven't had my first taste of champagne yet." She flung her hand out to her brother. "Bring me a bottle of champagne, my good man."

"I don't mind," he said.

Before he could saunter out the door, Mrs. Abberton jumped up. "I'll get it."

"I really think we ought to get coffee," Mr. Abberton mumbled.

"She wants champagne," Mrs. Abberton was almost stern. "It's a celebration, after all!" She practically fled from the room.

Adele followed her and caught her arm. She spoke in a soft tone. "Mrs. Abberton, why did Miss McCarthy faint?"

"She just told you, didn't she?" The woman gave a shrill laugh. "Albert said we ought to open some windows, but it was such a windy night, I —"

"It wasn't the windows," said Adele. "Or the corset."

"Of course it was!" The woman examined some bottles on the floor. "I never could read these labels."

"You were staring at Miss McCarthy as if something that wasn't there."

"What an imagination you have, dear." The woman said.

"Miss McCarthy had her hands on her throat when she fell," Adele continued. "You kept looking at her throat."

"Nonsense," the woman hissed.

"Miss McCarthy wasn't wearing her ruby necklace," Adele declared.

Mrs. Abberton tore through a row of bottles lying on a table. One rolled onto the floor with a crack and the bubbly drink spilled across the marble. She sunk into one of the chairs. "You're too observant, Miss Gossling."

"You saw it too."

"Just before the lights went out," she said. "But Eleanor is one of those girls who gets easily flustered with her jewelry. She says it weighs her down."

"If that's true, why were you so alarmed just now?" Adele said.

"I wasn't," the woman insisted. "She locks that necklace in a box. Albert tried to persuade her to put it in our safe at the finance company, but she refused."

"That's rather unusual," Adele said.

"Eleanor's a lovely girl, but rather flighty," The woman said in a harsh tone. "I expect Celestine spoils her."

"If the necklace is missing, there might be a theft involved," Adele suggested.

**Jewelry goes missing all the time. But does that mean theft? And why is Mrs. Abberton so nervous?**

**How can you get your hands on a copy of *The Missing Ruby Necklace*, not available in any bookstore? Simple. Go to this link: https://landing.mailerlite.com/webforms/landing/12u0c3. What else will you get when you get this novella? How about fun facts about women in history and true crime classic mysteries, which are just as fascinating, if not more so, as contemporary true crimes?**

As soon as Tam May started her first novel at the age of fourteen, writing became her voice. She writes engaging, fun-to-solve historical cozy mysteries featuring sassy suffragist Adele Gossling. Her mysteries empower readers with a sense of "justice is done" for women, both dead and alive. Her fiction is set in the San Francisco Bay Area because she adores sourdough bread, Ghirardelli chocolate, and San Francisco history.

Tam is the author of the Adele Gossling Mysteries which take place in the early 20th century and feature amateur sleuth and epistolary expert Adele Gossling, a forward-thinking young woman whose talent for solving crimes doesn't sit well with her town's Victorian ideas about women's place in society.

Tam has also written historical women's fiction. Her post-World War II short story collection, *Lessons From My Mother's Life*, debuted at #1 in its category on Amazon, and the first book of her Gilded Age family saga, the Waxwood Series, *The Specter*, remains in the top 10 in its category.

Although Tam left her heart in San Francisco, she lives in Texas because it's cheaper. When she's not writing, she's devouring everything classic (books, films, art, music) and concocting vegetarian dishes in her kitchen.

**Tam May can be reached at:**
WEBSITE: http://tammayauthor.com/
EMAIL: tammay70@tammayauthor.com
FACEBOOK: https://www.facebook.com/tammayauthor
INSTAGRAM: https://www.instagram.com/tammayauthor/